John Addington Symonds, Carlo Gozzi

The Memoirs of Count Carlo Gozzi

Vol. I

John Addington Symonds, Carlo Gozzi

The Memoirs of Count Carlo Gozzi
Vol. I

ISBN/EAN: 9783337060510

Printed in Europe, USA, Canada, Australia, Japan

Cover: Foto ©Raphael Reischuk / pixelio.de

More available books at **www.hansebooks.com**

THE MEMOIRS OF
COUNT CARLO GOZZI

TRANSLATED INTO ENGLISH

BY

JOHN ADDINGTON SYMONDS

With Essays on Italian Impromptu Comedy, Gozzi's Life,
The Dramatic Fables, and Pietro Longhi
By the TRANSLATOR

WITH PORTRAIT AND SIX ORIGINAL ETCHINGS
By ADOLPHE LALAUZE

ALSO ELEVEN SUBJECTS ILLUSTRATING ITALIAN COMEDY BY MAURICE SAND
ENGRAVED ON COPPER BY A. MANCEAU, AND COLOURED BY HAND

IN TWO VOLUMES
VOLUME THE FIRST

LONDON
JOHN C. NIMMO
14, KING WILLIAM STREET, STRAND
MDCCCXC

LIST OF ILLUSTRATIONS.

VOLUME THE FIRST.

- ·· —·

The Etchings designed and etched by AD. LALAUZE. The Masks, illustrating the Italian Commedia dell' Arte, by MAURICE SAND, engraved by A. MANCEAU, and coloured by hand.

PREFACE.

AFTER the appearance of my work on Benvenuto Cellini, Mr. J. C. Nimmo proposed that I should undertake a translation of Count Carlo Gozzi's *Memorie Inutili.*

The suggestion that such a book might be of interest to the English public emanated originally, I believe, from Mr. E. Hutchings of Manchester, in a letter addressed to the *Academy.*[1]

To this gentleman my warmest thanks are due, not only for starting the idea, which I have carried out, but also for the interest he has shown in my work during its progress, and for the assistance he has liberally rendered by the loan of rare books.

I entertained the proposal with some doubt.   What

---

[1] Under date August 31, 1885, with the assumed signature of E. H. Westbourne.   See *Academy*, No. 696, Sept. 5, 1885.

b

I already knew about Carlo Gozzi amounted to little ; and it seemed to me improbable that the world would willingly have left his Memoirs in oblivion if they possessed solid qualities.

At the same time, the little that I did know of Gozzi roused my curiosity. The picturesque aspects of Venetian decadence allured my fancy. I foresaw that I should have to handle the attractive subject of Italian impromptu comedy. Finally, it so happens that autobiographies have always exerted a peculiar fascination for my mind. I rate them highly as historical and psychological documents. The smallest fragment of a genuine autobiography seems to me valuable for the student of past epochs.

I had strong inducements, therefore, to undertake the proposed task.

The first thing to do was to procure a copy of the Memoirs, which exist only in one edition of three volumes. Mr. Hutchings placed the first two volumes of the book at my disposal; but the third was missing. It had been purloined while its owner was stationed in one of the South American cities. Mr. Nimmo and I waited through four months, making continued applications to the best European dealers in old books, before a complete copy was at last disinterred from a Venetian library.

The extraordinary rarity of the *Memorie* stimulated my growing interest. After making a preliminary study of the text, I perceived that this was no common specimen of self-portraiture. In some respects it seemed to me to be a masterpiece. I felt no doubt that it possessed both psychological and historical value. A man of a very marked type stood forth from those pages. He was, moreover, the Venetian representative of a well-defined social and literary period. This period corresponded pretty closely with that of our own Samuel Johnson, Fielding, Goldsmith, Reynolds, David Hume. It was the period which ended with the earthquake of the French Revolution, the signs of which catastrophe were felt more ominously in Italy than in our own land. At the same time I recognised salient qualities of healthy moral sense, of analytical acumen, of vigorous intelligence, and of caustic humour in the author, mingled with literary merit of no ordinary kind, vivid transcripts from contemporary life, dramatic narration, incisive sketches of character, original reflections on society.

According to my own standard in such matters, Gozzi's Memoirs ranked as an important document for the study of Italy in the last century.

But was the book worth translating? Would it

not suffice to leave the few existing copies in their
obscurity, and to indicate their value for historians
by composing a critical treatise on the author and
his times ?

My own predilection for autobiographies, and my
sense of their utility, caused me to reject this alternative. I decided to translate, and to illustrate my
translation by tolerably copious original essays.

While engaged upon the work, I have not, however, felt always quite at ease. It has recurred to
my mind that many readers of these volumes will
exclaim : " An English version of Gozzi's self-styled
' useless memoirs ' cannot fail to be twice as useless
as the original ! " Not all people share that partiality for autobiographies which in me amounts
almost to a passion.

Besides, I had to face other difficulties. The
three chapters which contain the narratives of Gozzi's
love-adventures could not be omitted. They are too
valuable for the light they throw upon his age,
and too important in the man's estimate of his own
character. Their suppression would have been unfair to Gozzi, and would have shorn his Memoirs of
some brilliant bits of local colour. Nevertheless, I
knew that the frankness and the cynical humour of
these episodes are out of tune with modern taste.

Much is pardoned by the virtue of our age to classics
—to Plato or Cellini—which would not be excused
in a writer of inferior eminence. But Gozzi is no
classic. The fact of his neglect by his own nation
proves that overwhelmingly. Why drag him from
deserved oblivion if these love-stories are indispensable to the rehabilitating process?

My answer to this perplexing query was that the
debated passages are good in literature, true to
nature, sound in moral feeling. Their candour is
the candour of a cleanly heart, resolved to bare its
secret by an effort of self-portraiture. Gozzi describes passions common to that age, and ours, and
every age; but he also shows how a determined
character, upright and honourable, can free itself
from the entanglements of natural frailty. The
lesson may be somewhat harsh, but it is salutary.
Gozzi has written no single word unworthy of a man
of principle—nothing which is calculated to make
vice alluring. Only one—

> " Who winks, and shuts his apprehension up
> From common sense of what men were and are,
> Who would not know what men must be :"—

only such an one can take exception to the narratives
of Gozzi's love-adventures.

Reasoning thus, I determined to include the love-tales in my translation, having already decided that no translation could be given to the world without them, and that the book was worthy of resuscitation. But I felt myself justified in removing those passages and phrases which might have caused offence to some of my readers.

To translate Gozzi with the minute attention to his style which I bestowed upon Cellini would have been unpractical.   I should even have inflicted an injury upon my author.   It is in many respects an annoying style ; redundant, unequal, diffuse ; bearing the stamp of garrulous senility and imperfect (though copious) command of language.

To condense and manipulate the Memoirs at my own free will, following the plan of Paul de Musset's abridgement, seemed to me unscrupulous, even if I abstained from that amusing writer's deliberate mysti-fications.

I resolved to convert the larger portion of the book into equivalent English, allowing myself the license of curtailing certain passages, and rearranging the order of some chapters.   All cases of important con-densation or omission have been indicated in my notes.   My account of the Memoirs and the causes which led to their publication (Introduction, Part i.)

sufficiently explains my right to transpose material from one place to another. Readers of the Introduction will perceive how carelessly and accidentally, to serve occasion, the original and unique edition was put together. It is due in part, I think, to Gozzi's indifference and haste of compilation that so curious a specimen of autobiography fell into almost absolute oblivion.

We have only one edition of the *Memorie*, that of Palese, under the date Venezia, 1797. Therefore nothing need be said upon the topic of bibliography. I may, however, mention that the few copies of this rare book which have fallen under my inspection present some features of difference, indicating the random way in which the sheets were made up for publication.

Among English critics of distinction, one only, so far as I am aware, has mentioned Gozzi's Memoirs. That is Vernon Lee, in her *Studies of the Eighteenth Century in Italy*. But Vernon Lee knew the book only through Paul de Musset's "perversion." Accordingly, what she has to say about the man is less valuable than the vivid, if not always accurate, account she gives of his *Fiabe*.

The volumes I am now presenting to the public claim at least one merit—that of dealing with a hitherto almost untouched document of historical and literary importance.

I flatter myself that readers will be found to appreciate the brilliant, though prolix and desultory, portraiture of life in Venice during the last century which these " useless memoirs " offer to their imagination.

Finally, I wish here to record my mature opinion about Carlo Gozzi's character for veracity and general uprightness. I think that I have been hardly just, and certainly not generous, to Gozzi in the Introduction and the notes appended to my version. Wishing to avoid the *lues biographica*, I assumed a somewhat too purely critical attitude while writing. Careful perusal of the proofs makes me feel that the truth would not have suffered had I entirely suppressed some suspicions and concealed some personal want of sympathy with the man. Allowing for his peculiar and occasionally repellent character —the character of an " original " and a confirmed old bachelor—Gozzi seems to me now to have been as honest and open-hearted as a gentleman should be.

JOHN ADDINGTON SYMONDS.

AM HOF, DAVOS PLATZ,
March 25, 1889.

BOOKS USED AND REFERRED TO IN
THIS WORK.

1. CARLO GOZZI. "Memorie Inutili." 3 vols. Venice. 1797.
2. CARLO GOZZI. "Opere." 10 vols. Venice. Colombani and other publishers. 1772-1791.
3. ERNESTO MASI. "Le Fiabe di Carlo Gozzi." 2 vols. Bologna. Zanichelli. 1885.
4. PIER ANTONIO GRATAROL. "Narrazione Apologetica." 2 vols. Venezia. Gatti. 1797.
5. PAUL DE MUSSET. "Mémoires de Charles Gozzi." Paris. Charpentier. 1848.
6. GIOV. BATT. MAGRINI. "Carlo Gozzi e le Fiabe." Cremona. Feraboli. 1876. The same work, second edition : " I Tempi la Vita e gli Scritti di Carlo Gozzi." Benevento. De Gennaro. 1883.
7. MICHELE SCHERILLO. "La Commedia dell' Arte in Italia." Torino. Loescher. 1884.
8. ADOLFO BARTOLI. "Scenari Inediti della Commedia dell' Arte." Firenze. Sansone. 1880.
9. ALFONSE ROYER. "Carlo Gozzi, Théatre Fiabesque." Paris. Michel Lévy. 1865.
10. CARLO GOLDONI. "Mémoires." 3 vols. Paris. Veuve Duchesne. 1787.
11. FERDINANDO GALANTI. "Carlo Goldoni e Venezia nel Secolo xviii." Padova. Sarnin. 1882.
12. P. G. MOLMENTI. "Carlo Goldoni." Venezia. Ongania. 1880.
13. VERNON LEE. "Studies of the Eighteenth Century in Italy." London. Satchell. 1880.

14. MAURICE SAND. "Masques et Bouffons." 2 vols. Paris. A. Lévy 1862.

15. S. ROMANIN. "Storia Documentata di Venezia." Vols. vii.-ix. Venezia. Naratovitch. 1860.

16. GIUSEPPE BOERIO. "Dizionario del Dialetto Veneziano." Venezia. Cocchini. 1856.

17. PHILARÈTE CHASLES. "Études sur l'Espagne, etc." ("D'un Théatre Espagnol-Véuitien au xviiime Siècle et de Charles Gozzi"). Paris. Amyot. 1847.

18. N. TOMMASÈO. "Storia Civile nella Letteraria." Roma, Torino, Firenze. E. Loescher. 1872.

19. EUGENIO CAMERINI. "I Precursori del Goldoni." Milano. Sonzogno. 1872.

20. "Mémoires de Jacques Casanova de Seingalt, écrites par lui-même. Bruxelles. Rozet. 1876.

THE MEMOIRS

OF

COUNT CARLO GOZZI

———

INTRODUCTION

INTRODUCTION.

Part I.

CARLO GOZZI AND PIERO ANTONIO GRATAROL.

1. The ancestry and social standing of Count Carlo Gozzi—His collision with Piero Antonio Gratarol, Secretary to the Venetian Collegio—How this quarrel led to the composition of Gozzi's Memoirs—Their importance as a document for the social history of Venice in the eighteenth century.—2. The interweaving of this episode in Gozzi's Life with his literary warfare against Goldoni, which culminated in the production of his ten dramatic fables.—3. Sketch of Gratarol's life, and his relation to Andrea and Caterina Tron—Gozzi's *liaison* with the actress Teodora Ricci—Gozzi's comedy, *Le Droghe d'Amore* —Turned by Mme. Tron into a satire upon Gratarol—Gratarol flies from Venice to Stockholm, is proscribed by the Republic, and loses all his fortune—His *Narrazione Apologetica*—Gozzi takes up the pen in self-defence—The Inquisitors of State forbid the publication of his autobiographical polemic—Gratarol's death in Madagascar—Circumstances which induced Gozzi in 1797, after the fall of the Republic of St. Mark, to complete and publish his Memoirs.—4. Gozzi's literary style and personal character—The false conception of the man and his work which has been diffused by Paul de Musset.

I.

IN the year 1797 there appeared at Venice a book entitled *Memorie inutili della vita di Carlo Gozzi, scritte da lui medesimo e pubblicate per umiltà,* " Useless Memoirs of the Life of Carlo Gozzi, written by himself and published from motives of humility." Its author, though he bore the title of Count, and

A

belonged to an honourable family in Venice, was not of patrician descent. That is to say, none of his lineal ancestors had acquired the right of voting in the Grand Council or of holding the highest offices of state. They ranked with the citizens of the Republic, who took no direct part in the government, but who were permitted to discharge important functions as secretaries of several departments and as ambassadors of the second class. By his mother he drew half of his blood from one of the oldest and proudest of Venetian noble families, the Tiepolos. Thus, socially, if not politically, birth placed him almost on a level with the best Venetian aristocracy.

In the year 1797 he was seventy-seven; and although he had been a man of some mark in his early days, the public had lost sight of him for the last seventeen years. His reputation depended upon a large number of dramatic pieces, satirical poems, and prose compositions, mostly of a controversial kind. Two main episodes in his literary life conferred a slightly dubious notoriety upon his name. The first of these was the long and bitter war he waged against the two playwrights, Chiari and Goldoni, between the years 1756 and 1762. The other was an unfortunate series of events which brought him into collision with a certain Pier Antonio Gratarol in 1777. Gratarol, like his adversary, was a Venetian citizen, allied by descent to the great patrician family of Contarini. Unlike Gozzi, he early embarked on a political career, was one of the secretaries of the Collegio, and looked forward to the highest appointments which were open to a man of his rank. The collision with Count Gozzi, which I shall have to describe with some minuteness, ended in Gratarol's voluntary exile from Venice, the confiscation of his property by the State, and a public scandal of sufficient importance to attract the attention of serious historians.[1] Had it not been for this tragi-comic episode in his past life, Gozzi would never have written his Memoirs; and had the memory of the scandal not been revived some years after Gratarol's death, when the old Republic of S. Mark had fallen in the crash of the French Revolution, he would never have published them.

This autobiography is distinctly an apologetical work, a portrait drawn by Gozzi in self-defence, and intended to vindicate himself from the aspersions cast by Gratarol upon his character. Its main object is to set forth in the fairest light his own conduct during the unlucky collision to which I have alluded. Yet though so limited in aim, the interest which it possesses for us at the present time, is far wider than belongs to that unhappy squabble, long since buried in oblivion. Gozzi's conception of an *Apologia pro vita sua* was a comprehensive one. He resolved to reveal his character under all its aspects,

---

[1] See Romanin, *Storia Documentata di Venezia*, vol. viii. ch. 7.

from his childhood until the date 1777, dealing now
with matters of general importance, now with the
private affairs of his home, touching upon the literature of his age, discussing fashions, criticising philosophy, entering into minute particulars regarding
theatres and actors, describing his love-affairs with
a frankness worthy of Rousseau, and painting a series
of lively portraits in which a large variety of individuals from all classes are presented to our notice.
The result is that his autobiography, although in the
strictest sense of that term an occasional production,
forms one of the most valuable documents we possess
for a study of Venetian society during the decadence
of the Republic. Gozzi was gifted with a penetrative and observant mind, strong sense of humour, and
a power of brilliant description. On the faults of
his style and the defects of his character, I shall speak
hereafter. At present it is enough to indicate the
importance of the Memoirs as furnishing a vivid
picture of Venetian life in the eighteenth century.
Venice, at that period, was fortunate in autobio-
graphers. She possessed Goldoni and Casanova as
well as Gozzi, not to mention smaller folk like Da
Ponte, the poet of Mozart's *Don Giovanni*. But
when we compare the three life-records of Goldoni,
Casanova, and Gozzi, by far the deepest historical
interest, in my opinion, belongs to the last. Casanova's Memoirs are almost excluded from general
use by the nature of their predominant pre-occupa-

tion. Moreover, they deal but partially with Venice, and only with limited aspects of its social life. Goldoni's, though more humane, and in all that concerns tone impeccable, turn too exclusively upon the history of his dramatic works to be of great importance as an historical document. Moreover, the scene is laid in several provinces of Italy and transferred before its close to France. Gozzi, on the contrary, never quits the soil of Venice. Except when he served as a soldier for three years in the Venetian province of Dalmatia, he does not appear to have travelled further than to Pordenone on one side and to Padua on the other. Of strong aristocratic instincts, but condemned to comparative poverty by the reckless expenditure of his parents and grandparents, Gozzi enjoyed opportunities of studying the society of Venice from several points of view. His enthusiasm for literature and partiality for professional actors brought him acquainted with the scholars and the Bohemians of that epoch. His management of the encumbered estates of his family introduced him to advocates, solicitors, brokers, Jews, tenants, and all manner of strange people. His birth made him the companion of patricians. His military service involved him in the wild pleasures and perils of scapegrace lads upon a foreign soil. Consequently, the records of a life so varied in experience, while strictly confined within the narrow circuit of Venetian society, could not fail to be rich in details for the

student. It may be regretted that Gozzi chose to
write in a didactic spirit. We could willingly have
exchanged his long-winded excursions into the sphere
of moral philosophy for a few more graphic sketches
in the style of his Dalmatian adventures.

II.

This biographical and historical interest, far more
than Gozzi's quarrel with Goldoni or his collision
with Gratarol, is the reason why I thought it worth
while to translate a book which has become excessively rare in the original. Nothing can be duller
or more contemptible, to my mind, than the chronicle
of literary quarrels. The Goldoni-Gozzi episode
would be devoid of permanent attraction were it
not for the curious light thrown by it upon the
obscure subject of impromptu comedy, and for the
ten extraordinary *Fiabe Teatrali* from Gozzi's pen
to which it gave rise. Again, the Gratarol-Gozzi
episode, as we shall presently see, is almost humiliating in the pettiness of its details, and painful
through its tragic termination.

The Memoirs contain a full and tolerably accurate
account of the Gratarol incident. Yet I cannot dispense with a summary of this affair, based upon a
comparison of Gozzi's story with that of Gratarol in
his *Narrazione Apologetica.* The extreme import-

ance of the event in the lives of both men, and the fact that it constitutes the subject of Gozzi's autobiography in quite as serious a sense as that in which the Persian war forms the subject of Herodotus' history, render this unavoidable.

III.

Pier Antonio Gratarol was a young man between thirty and forty in the year 1776. He had grown up with an ample fortune and without a father's control; had imbibed French ways of thinking and French customs; had married, and after marriage had separated from his wife.[1] He represented that class of intellectual and political Liberals whom Gozzi, with his Conservative prejudices, regarded as dangerous to the well-being of the State. He was an open libertine in his relations with women, and

---

[1] Gratarol was not formally divorced from his wife. This appears from several passages of his *Narrazione Apologetica*. It may, however, be here observed that scandalous irregularities with regard to matrimony formed one of the main signs of Venetian decadence. Between 1782 and 1796 the Council of Ten received no fewer than 264 petitions for divorce, and the Patriarch is said to have had 900 applications at one time before him, requiring his decision in matters relating to a dissolution of the marriage tie. See Magrini, *op. cit.*, p. 23; and Macchi, *Storia del Concilio dei Dieci*, vol. ii. p. 355. It seems that the most shameless reasons were collusively alleged by the parties in these cases for breaking a tie which the Church regarded as indissoluble. In 1782 the Ten passed a law requiring a divorced woman to enter a convent.

did not strive to conceal those principles of personal
liberty which the *philosophes* were spreading throughout Europe. At the same time he represented a
family which had served the Republic in distinguished offices for many generations ; he possessed
excellent abilities, and had every reason to expect
a brilliant future. There was nothing in his conduct or in his domestic circumstances to distinguish
him unfavourably from a multitude of gay livers and
free-thinkers in the corrupt Venice of that epoch.
He had recently become eligible for the post of
ambassador at a foreign Court; and was already
nominated as Resident in Naples. This nomination
required, however, to be confirmed by the Grand
Council ; and circumstances, which need not be
enlarged upon, rendered the grant of money for his
embassy a matter of debate.[1] Unfortunately, Gratarol was a person of vain, imperious temper, puffed
up with the sense of his own merits, and incapable
of correcting his antipathies. His French tendencies — political, moral, social, literary — fashionable
for the most part — prejudiced the minds of influential
people in the highest departments of the government
against him. Finally, he had made an implacable

---

[1] A short while before, he had been appointed Resident at Turin,
and had received the usual equipment for that service. Circumstances
independent of his own will in the matter prevented him from assuming the office. His political ill-wishers were able to point to the un-
used grant which he had pocketed.

enemy of a great lady, who at that time exercised almost dictatorial control over the councils of the State. This was Caterina Dolfin Tron, the wife of Andrea Tron, Procuratore di San Marco, whose immense influence in the Council of Ten, the Consulta, and the Senate enabled him to do what he liked with the Grand Council.[1] Caterina's husband was popularly known as *Il Padrone*, or the Master of Venice, and he doted on her with a blind affection. She was a woman of brilliant parts, imbued, like Gratarol, with advanced French notions, meddlesome in public matters, aspiring to manage the politics of Venice and to dictate laws to society from her own reception-rooms. Gratarol began by paying her wise attentions; but for some reason unknown to us, he had lately dropped his courtship and indulged in satirical comments upon Caterina's private conduct. She vowed to effect his ruin, and circumstances enabled her to do so.

Gozzi, meanwhile, had for the last five years or so assumed the position of titular protector to a married actress called Teodora Ricci. He does his best to persuade us that the *liaison* was one of friendship; but it is clear that, upon whatever footing he stood toward the Ricci, he felt a real affection for

---

[1] Caterina was the daughter of the ancient and noble, but impoverished house of Dolfin. She contracted her first marriage with a member of the Tiepolo family, obtained a divorce from him, and married her lover, Andrea Tron.

this woman. For her he composed the dramatic
works of his second or Spanish manner. He attended her in public, introduced her to the houses
of his friends, and stood godfather to her second
child. We are, in fact, met here by an obscurity not
unlike that which involves the more famous connection of Congreve with Mrs. Bracegirdle. Gratarol,
pursuing the usual course of his amours, made the
Ricci's acquaintance, became her lover, compromised
her reputation, and wounded Gozzi so deeply in his
sense of honour, that he broke off familiar relations
with the actress.

Such was the position of affairs when Gozzi, who
wrote assiduously for the theatre, produced a drama
modelled on a Spanish piece by Tirso da Molina.
It was called *Le Droghe d'Amore*, and contained a
minor part, which might well have passed either
for a sketch of manners or for a personal satire on
Gratarol. Gozzi vehemently and persistently denied
that he had any intention of caricaturing his rival on
the stage ; and if we trust what he relates about the
composition of the play in question, it is hardly possible that he can have had Gratarol in view when he
designed it. At the same time, we are bound to
concede that the offensive part of Don Adone fitted
nicely on to Gratarol. Mme. Ricci, smarting under
Gozzi's withdrawal from her intimacy, took for granted
that a satire was intended. This woman's hysterical
imagination turned a mere *jeu d'esprit* of her old

friend into a formidable weapon of attack against
her new lover. Through her dangerous interference
it became an instrument, in the hands of other parties,
to annoy Gozzi and to overwhelm Gratarol. She began
by poisoning the latter's mind with gossiping insinuations. Gratarol's fretful vanity and sense of self-
importance made him boil with fury at the thought
of being put upon the stage. He moved heaven
and earth to get the play suspended; imprudently,
as it turned out, because this step brought him
face to face with his real enemy, Mme. Tron. The
manager of the theatre, to whom Gozzi had given
his comedy, took the manuscript at once to that
lady. This unscrupulous person now saw her opportunity for inflicting vengeance upon Gratarol. She
induced the manager to redistribute the parts so
that the *rôle* of Don Adone should be assigned to
an actor who resembled Gratarol. She taught this
man how to imitate Gratarol's dress and gestures,
and turned what may in fact have been an innocent
production of Gozzi's pen into a satire of the most
insulting pungency. At that point the *Droghe
d'Amore* passed out of the control of those whom it
privately concerned.

After this, Gratarol, driven mad by wounded self-
conceit, floundered from one imprudence into another
He applied to the highest tribunal of the State, and
laid an information against Gozzi. Whether the Inquisitors did not choose to cancel the license already

granted for the *Droghe d'Amore*, or whether they were influenced by Mme. Tron, does not greatly signify. At any rate, the comedy continued to be acted. Gratarol grew more and more irritated, uttered indignant invectives against the tyrants of the State, and displayed a spirit of insubordination which was perilous in Venice. Mme. Tron followed up her advantage, and caused his appointment to the embassy at Naples to be suspended. Thereupon Gratarol made up his mind to quit Venice. He knew that this act would expose himself to outlawry and his family to ruin. A civil servant of the Republic had no legal right to sever himself from his engagements without permission. The mere fact of doing so caused him to be treated as a contumacious rebel. But instead of assuming an indifferent attitude, instead of biding his time in patience and letting the storm blow over—which it certainly would have done, since a popular reaction had already begun to operate in his favour—he departed for Padua on the 11th of September 1777, proceeded to Ceneda, crossed the frontier on the 25th, travelled to Munich, thence to Brunswick, and finally to Stockholm, where he arrived in March. Meanwhile a proclamation was issued against him at Venice. This curious document is a relic from the savage days of the Middle Ages.[1] It set a price upon his head, offered rewards to any

---

[1] It may be read in Gratarol's *Narrazione Apologetica*, vol. ii. p. 78, &c.

one who should bring him alive to Venice or should prove his assassination, cancelled all contracts made by him during twelve months before the date of December 22, 1777, confiscated his property during his lifetime, and ordered the whole of it to be sold by public auction. The latter portions of the ban were carried into effect. Everything which belonged to Gratarol was sold by the Avogadori;[1] and what seems really scandalous in this transaction is that his furniture and jewels passed into the possession of an Avogadore, Zorzi Angaran, while his landed estates fell to the share of the Avvocato fiscale dell' Avogaderia, Galante, at the ridiculously low sum of 2000 ducats.[2] Even his wife, who possessed a dowry of 25,000 ducats, had to institute long and costly lawsuits for the recovery of what belonged to her and formed no part of the outlaw's estate.

Caterina Dolfin Tron, aided by her victim's rashness and impatience, had succeeded in her plan to ruin him. But a retribution awaited this lady in the form of an eloquent invective hurled by Gratarol

---

[1] These magistrates acted for the Fisco or Treasury of the Republic.

[2] It has been suggested that Gratarol so heavily mortgaged his lands before leaving Venice that they were not worth more than this sum, after allowing for rent charges on them and *fidei commissa*. See the observations of a self-styled impartial writer printed at the end of the *Narrazione Apologetica*, ed. 1797. I must, however, observe that this writer is by no means impartial. The essay in question is a piece of skilful special pleading in defence of Mme. Tron, her husband, the oligarchs of Venice, and the officers who executed the *bando* against Gratarol.

against his enemies from Stockholm. The so-called
Narrazione Apologetica was printed there in 1779,
and soon found its way to Venice. It contained a
detailed account of the events which had induced
him to take flight, arraigned his powerful enemies in
terms of the bitterest sarcasm, exposed their private
foibles, and flashed a sharp light upon the political
corruption of the decadent Republic. Gozzi, of
course, came in for his share of abuse;[1] but Gratarol's most telling shafts were directed against Mme.
Tron and the patrician ring which tyrannised over
Venice. It is believed that the scandal of this pamphlet was one reason why Andrea Tron failed to be
elected Doge in 1779.

On perusing Gratarol's *Narrazione Apologetica*,
Count Carlo Gozzi determined to clear his own
character and to lay his version of the story before
the public. With this view he composed a lengthy
Epistola Confutatoria, taking up each of Gratarol's
points in detail, and discussing his arguments with a
strange mixture of acuteness, fury, and contemptuous
severity. He also conceived the notion of writing
his Memoirs, in order that the whole tenor of his life
might be clearly understood.[2] The Confutation and

---

[1] Gratarol pays high tribute to Gozzi's genius. But he sticks to the
conviction that the *Droghe d'Amore* was meant to turn him into ridicule,
and that its author could, if he had chosen, have withdrawn it from the
stage.

[2] He tells us that he began the Memoirs on April 30, 1780. *Memorie,*
vol. i. p. 3. The passage occurs in Gozzi's manifesto, of which more

the larger part of the Memoirs were finished in 1780. But the Government decided that Gratarol's scandalous pamphlet should be left unanswered. No Venetian pen was allowed to notice it ;[1] and Gozzi received information that the Inquisitors of State would take the matter up if he attempted to show further fight. The authorities acted with prudence in this matter. Nobody but Gozzi had anything to gain by his refutation of Gratarol. With regard to the corruption of Venice, the despotism of a few leading patricians, and the back-stairs influence of Mme. Tron, Gratarol had only told the truth. He had told it indeed emphatically, bitterly, and probably with some exaggeration. Yet, unhappily, it was the truth. No amount of apologetical rhetoric could have broken down his arguments. A public discussion would have disturbed the public mind, and many dark secrets and dirty jobs must certainly have come to light.

Gozzi had to choose between the *piombi* or the sacrifice of his already finished manuscripts. Of course he did not hesitate. Both Confutation and Memoirs were thrown at once aside ; and they might

---

anon. I may add that the manifesto is not included in all copies of the Memoirs.

[1] An anonymous answer, entitled *Riflessioni d'un Imparziale,* appeared at Lugano. This was ascribed to Carlo Gozzi's pen ; but he repudiated the pamphlet, and it does not bear the mark of his style. It may be found at the end of vol. ii, of Gratarol's *Narr. Apol.,* ed. 1797, Venice, Silvestro Gatti.

even now have been lying in some neglected corner
of his ancient mansion had it not been for the events
which have to be related.

Gratarol never returned to Venice.   From Sweden
he passed to England, where he was hospitably received and befriended by members of our aristocracy.
Failing, however, to get any appointment in London,
he crossed to North America, travelled southwards
to Brazil, and again left that country in the train of
some political adventurers.   The party were betrayed
and robbed by the captain of their vessel, and cast
ashore upon the coast of Madagascar.   Here Gratarol
perished miserably in October 1785.   His English
friends sent information of this event to the Venetian
Government; but the evidence was judged insufficient, and the restitution of his estates to two female
cousins, who were his only heirs, was refused until
the fall of the Republic.   When that took place,
Gratarol's friends immediately republished the
Narrazione Apologetica at Venice, and appealed to
General Bonaparte for justice.   This was in 1797.

Gozzi, who had now nothing to fear from Inquisitors of State, and whose reputation was again exposed
to calumny, took his manuscripts from their drawer,
dusted them, and placed them in the hands of a
publisher.   In the month of July 1797 he issued
a manifesto to the Venetian public, proclaiming his
intention.[1]   "Availing myself of the beneficent free-

---

[1] *Memorie*, vol. i. pp. 3–15.

dom now permitted to the press, I have drawn my manuscript from the tomb in which it has lain during the past seventeen years." He refers to the recent republication of Gratarol's *Narrazione*, and declares that this alone has forced him to resuscitate the memory of bygone quarrels and offences. At the same time he pays a high tribute to Gratarol's work. "This book, which appeared at Stockholm in 1779, and which I had forgotten, without however forgetting the unjust tricks and jobs by which its truly pitiable author was overwhelmed with ruin, contains a great number of indubitable truths, and it is only to be regretted that he dictated it under the influence of blind anger and venomous resentment, instead of philosophic calm."

It appears that at this time Gozzi did not intend to publish his *Epistola Confutatoria*, written in 1780, and certainly dictated under the influence of anger as hot, hatred as fierce, and resentment as venomous as any which inspired his adversary. Indeed, it may here be observed that Gratarol, though he calls Gozzi a hypocrite, a huckster, an impostor, and so forth, is more measured in his language than the latter. Yet, while Gozzi was passing the sheets of his Memoirs through the press,[1] Gratarol's friends issued another book entitled *Last Notices regarding Pietro Antonio*

---

[1] This is evident from the appearance of the *Ragionamento del Citta-dino Carlo Gozzi a' Cittadini amici della Memoria di P. A. Gratarol* at the beginning of the *Memorie*, vol. ii.

Gratarol, with documents relating to his death.   In this they expressed a hope that Gozzi would not proceed with the publication announced by his manifesto, and incautiously printed a document alluding to Gozzi in the following by no means flattering terms : " the infernal hypocrisy of a satirical liar." [1]   Furthermore, upon the 29th of August, having obtained a decree for the restitution of Gratarol's property to his cousins, they published this edict together with a preface, signed Widiman,[2] in which they had the folly to rake up the whole tedious story of Gratarol's wrongs again.   Once more Gozzi was annoyed with well-worn phrases like the following : "'The persecuting furies of a haughty woman, the talent and the passion of a very famous author, made him (Gratarol), to the horror of all right-minded people, become the object of scorn and ridicule upon a public theatre prostituted to the uses of a vile and infamous buffoon."   This was more than Gozzi could stand.   Firmly holding to the opinion that it was only Gratarol's folly and Mme. Tron's vindictiveness which had caused the scandal of *Le Droghe d'Amore*, he now resolved to publish everything which could establish the truth of his own story.   Therefore he incorporated the *Epistola Confutatoria* in the third volume of the Memoirs, and printed the notorious comedy for the first time at the end of the book.

---

[1] *Memorie Ultime,* p. 39 ; Gozzi's *Memorie,* vol. ii. p. x.

[2] The family of Widiman or Widman was of patrician rank in Venice.

Meantime he invited Gratarol's friends to inspect the MS. of this play, which he declared to be the sole and original autograph, in order that they might convince themselves that his statements regarding its composition were accurate. Having now made up his mind to supplement the two parts of his book with a third, he carried down his Memoirs to the date of March 1798, when they came to a sudden termination. All three volumes bear the date 1797; but their pagination and some other trifling matters lead me to believe that the first two were printed in that year, the third in the following spring.

IV.

The circumstances under which Gozzi's *Memorie* were produced sufficiently account for their peculiar form, or rather formlessness. He wrote hurriedly, with a polemical object in view, and paid no attention to style. This he confesses in the manifesto.[1] "I have not striven to express myself with the exactitude, the raciness, and the elegances of our language." As a literary performance, this autobiography is remarkably unequal, a thing of rags and patches, some of which are of fine silk or velvet, others of rough sackcloth. Their main defect as

---

[1] Vol. i. p. 4.

regards composition is prolixity. Gozzi does not
know when to stop, and he uses three phrases where
one would have sufficed. He is also very incoherent,
spinning interminable periodic sentences, which sometimes do not hang together grammatically or logically.
While insisting so magisterially upon the purity of
Italian diction, he indulges in uncouth Lombardisms,
and slips at times into Venetian dialect. We must
remember that he grew up practically without education. He acquired his knowledge, cultivated his
taste, and formed his style by reading without dis-
crimination and by writing without fixed purpose.
This accounts for the digressive, irregular, improvisatory manner of his prose. It has its own merits,
however, of vehemence, a copious vocabulary, dramatic vigour in narration, and occasionally graphic
descriptions.

It may be asked why he called his Memoirs " useless." Partly no doubt out of an ironical self-con-
sciousness, which marked his peculiar species of
humour ; but partly also as a slap in the face to his
readers. He tells them candidly in one of his prefaces that he considers the moral reflections with
which the book is filled to be both sound and valuable, but that the false science of the age is certain
to render them of no effect.[1] In like manner, when
he asserts that the Memoirs were published out of
humility, this is partly true and partly false. Gozzi

---

[1] Vol. ii. p. xvi.

piqued himself on being what I may call a Stoic-
Democritean philosopher. It was his pride to bear
everything with endurance and to laugh at everything, himself and his own concerns included, with
contemptuous indulgence. Yet he deserved the
stinging epigram which Goldoni uttered on his character: " A smile upon his lips and venom in his
heart." His light-heartedness and risibility were often
assumed to hide bitter resentment or boiling indignation. No man had less of genuine humility than
Gozzi, or more of the " pride which apes humility."
Umiltà upon his title-page has much the same effect
as *Umiltà* in huge Gothic letters beneath the coro-
nets and crests of the Borromeo family above their
haughty palace-portals. As a single instance, I might
select the supercilious condescension with which he
invariably treats his friends the actors. They are
canaille, to be consorted with by a gentleman merely
for amusement. His repeated boast that he gave his
literary work away, and his sneers at his brother
Gasparo for making money, do not savour of a really
humble spirit. At the bottom of all he says about
his foolhardiness in Dalmatia there lurks a proud
self-satisfaction.

To what extent was he truthful? That is a difficult question to answer. I believe that in the main
he tried to be, and was, veracious throughout the
Memoirs; but that he considered a certain economy
of statement, a certain evasion of direct facts, and a

certain forensic chicanery to be permissible in openly
controversial composition.   This renders his account
of the Gratarol episode somewhat suspicious, particularly when we remember that he was writing with
the *Narrazione Apologetica* before his eyes.   It is clear
that he wished to conceal his real age, that he falsi-
fied the date of his departure for Dalmatia, and that
he somewhat misstated the nature of his intimacy with
Mme. Tron.   In each of these cases it was his object
to put himself in as favourable a light as possible
face to face with Gratarol, first by making it appear
that he was ten years or so younger than his actual
age when he began the liaison with Mme. Ricci, and
secondly by slurring over the fact of a partial collusion with Gratarol's deadly enemy.   It would take
up too much space to expand the arguments by which
I have arrived at these conclusions; but the notes
to my translation will make each point clear in its
proper place.

On the whole, Gozzi strikes me as rather inclined
to the vices of too open speech and cynicism than to
those of dissimulation and hypocrisy.   He can hardly
have been a lovable man.   His language about his
mother proves that.   She treated him ill, it is true,
and gave him but a scanty share of her maternal
kindness.   Yet this does not justify the freezing
sarcasms with which he refers to her.   They are
no doubt humorous, but their humour is of a
savage kind.   Toward the rest of his family he

behaved with fairness, candour, and uprightness.
He devoted himself to the task of repairing their
ruined fortunes, and discharged the duties of soli-
citor and estate-agent for all of them through a long
series of years.   He bore their bad tempers and
frivolities with good-humoured contempt, and did
not even resent being satirised by Gasparo in a
comedy upon the public stage of Venice.   Gasparo,
his weak but genial elder brother, he truly loved,
although, with characteristic acidity, he always lets
us understand what a poor creature he was.   Women
had not the privilege of being highly appreciated
by Gozzi.   He treats them in all his writings as
inferior creatures, and exposes their frailties with
ruthless severity.   Either he only knew the worst
side of the fair sex, or was incapable of seeing the
best.   To men he shows himself more just and
sympathetic.   Though he made but few intimate
friends, these remained firmly attached to him till
death.

We must divest our minds of the false conception
of Gozzi's character with which Paul de Musset
hoaxed the French critics and Vernon Lee.   He
was no dramatic dreamer and abstract visionary,
but a keen hard-headed man of business, caustic in
speech and stubborn in act, adhering tenaciously to
his opinions and his rights, acidly and sardonically
humorous, eccentric, but fully aware of his eccentricities, and apt to use them as the material of

burlesque humour. Nobody would have laughed more loudly at De Musset's fancy picture of his fairy-haunted palace than Gozzi would have done, or have more keenly relished the joke of turning his practical self into a sprite-tormented idealist.[1]

The Memoirs lie now before English readers, and Carlo Gozzi will be known to them for the first time—certainly for the first time as he really was. It is not necessary, therefore, to spin out this introduction. Otherwise, it would have been interesting to compare the portraits painted of themselves by those four eminent Italian contemporaries—Goldoni, Gozzi, Casanova, and Alfieri. Four characters more diverse in quality, and more admirably placed upon the literary canvas, could hardly, I think, be found in any other nation or in any other century.

---

[1] De Musset, in order to support his view of Gozzi as the precursor of Romanticism and of Hoffmann, strains to the utmost the chapter on *Contrattempi* in the Memoirs. He furthermore professes to have extracted a very bizarre account of the reasons why Gozzi abandoned his *Fiabe*—in plain words, because the elves and spirits he brought upon the stage were resolved to be revenged on him—from a letter addressed to Gasparo by Carlo Gozzi (*Mémoires de Charles Gozzi*, pp. 184–188). De Musset adds no reference to the source of this alleged letter, which is mentioned by neither Magrini nor Masi. Indeed, Signor Ernesto Masi informs me that he knows nothing about it. I too have failed to discover it. In his Memoirs, and in the prefaces to several plays, Gozzi gives a very different account of the reasons why he stopped producing *Fiabe*. I am loth to draw the conclusion that the letter in question was a deliberate forgery of Paul de Musset's. Further researches may bring it still to light, but at present it has to be regarded with the greatest possible suspicion.

THE

ITALIAN COMMEDIA DELL' ARTE, OR IMPROMPTU COMEDY

Part II.

THE ITALIAN COMMEDIA DELL' ARTE OR IMPROMPTU COMEDY.

1. A brief sketch of the origins of written comedy during the Italian Renaissance—Its dependence upon Latin models.—2. Further description of the so-called *Commedia Erudita.* — 3. Emergence of dialectical literature in Italy during the period of the Catholic reaction — Improvised comedy begins to supersede the written drama of the Renaissance.—4. Farces at Naples and Florence— The Sienese company of I Rozzi—The Paduan Beolco—The four principal masks—Pantalone, Il Dottore, Arlecchino, Brighella.—5. Relation of modern impromptu comedy to the old Latin comedy of mimes and exodia—the Osci Ludi, Fescennini Verses, Satura, &c.—In what sense the modern masks are descended from those antique elements—Infusion of fixed characters adopted from the plays of Plautus and Terence.—6. Lombard, Neapolitan, Florentine ingredients in the *Commedia dell' Arte*—Lasca's carnival song of the Zanni and Magnifichi about the year 1550.—7. A review of the principal masks and their subordinate species, as these were finally developed—Modifications introduced into the masks, or fixed parts, of the *Commedia dell' Arte*, by men of genius who supported them.—8. The plots and subjects of improvised comedies— Buffoonery and indecency.—9. Description of the *scenari* or plays in outline which were acted impromptu by the comic companies— Method of concerting a comedy and distributing its parts—The function of the Capo Comico.—10. Qualifications of a good impromptu comedian—Stock repertories, commonplaces, speeches to be introduced on set occasions, soliloquies, &c.—The *Lazzi* or sallies of buffoonery and byeplay—Tendency to degeneration in this improvisatory art of comedy.—11. European celebrity of the Italian comedians—In Paris, Spain, Portugal, London—References to

I.

THE history of the Italian theatre is closely connected
with the history of the Classical Revival.[1]   The
literary drama—as distinguished from performances
by tumblers, mimes, and masquers, from sacred plays
and from plebeian farces—began with the representation of Latin tragedies and comedies.   At the close
of the fifteenth century it was usual to crown courtly
festivals with scenic recitations of favourite pieces
by Terence and Plautus.   Rome vied with Florence,
Venice with Naples, Ferrara with Urbino, in the
magnificence of these spectacles.   At a time when
humanistic erudition formed the main preoccupation
of society, and when to be illiterate was unfashion-
able, princes and great prelates afforded their guests
the refined amusement of seeing the *Menæchmi* or
Amphitryon, the *Eunuchus* or *Miles Gloriosus*, on
their private stages.   At the same time, obeying the
decorative instinct of the Renaissance, they set these
jewels of classical antiquity in arabesques of the
richest and most fantastic workmanship.   Allegorical
masques, dances with musical accompaniment and

---

[1] I have treated the subject of the Italian drama elsewhere : *Renaissance in Italy*, vol. v. ch. 11.

pantomimic interludes, were interposed between each of the five acts, enhancing the simplicity of the Roman plays and gratifying the vulgar by an appeal to their senses. These hybrid spectacles, eminently characteristic of Italian taste in the age which produced them, contained the germs of several dramatic species, afterwards known as the *Commedia Erudita*, the pastoral play, the ballet, and the opera. Meanwhile Italian literature, stimulated and powerfully influenced by humanism, acquired independence; and the comedies of Plautus and Terence were translated and performed in the vernacular. During the last years of the fifteenth century these translations began to take the place of the originals upon the temporary stages of princely patrons. As yet there were no public theatres.

Such, briefly sketched, was the origin of Italian comedy; and the specific character of the *Commedia Erudita*, or written comedy of the sixteenth century, may be ascribed to the peculiar conditions out of which it grew. The genius of men like Ariosto, Machiavelli, and Aretino never wholly freed the form they handled from subservience to Latin models. It remained, in spite of their close imitation of contemporary life and their audacious realism, a sub-species of that dramatic art which the Romans adapted to their uses from the new comedy of the Attic stage.

II.

The first attempts at national Italian comedy were
the *Calandra* of Bibbiena and Ariosto's *Cassaria*.
The former appeared at Urbino between 1503 and
1508 ; the latter, in its earlier prose form, at Ferrara
in 1508. During the next fifty years a large number of comedies were produced by a great variety of
authors. Men of letters like Machiavelli, Cecchi,
Dolce, and Il Lasca, men of fashion like Lorenzino
de' Medici, philosophers like Bruno, free lances of
the pen like Aretino and Doni, artisans like Gelli,
devoted themselves to this species of composition.
The type remained fixed, although some notable
exceptions, especially in the case of Aretino's plays,
arrest attention. Taking the intrigue of Latin
comedy for their ground material, these playwrights
adapted it to conditions of Italian society. The ava-
ricious father, the cunning courtesan, the parasite,
the slave merchant, the swaggering soldier, the young
spendthrift in love with a virgin of unknown parentage, the astute serving-man, the faithless wife,
the pedant, the cynical priest or friar, the vicious old
man in his dotage, the reckless adventurer, the pirate,
the country-girl exposed to the corruptions of the
town ; such are the stock characters of this dramatic
hybrid. Everywhere we find the plots of Terence or

of Plautus interwoven with a Novella in the style
of Boccaccio. As in Latin comedy, the knot is frequently loosed by unexpected discoveries of lost
relatives; and the magnificent realism with which
contemporary manners are depicted, clashes too often
with the stiff and antiquated *ossatura*, or dramatic
mechanism, to which the authors felt themselves
obliged by fashion to adhere. From hints in pro-
logues and prefaces we are able to discern that playwrights chafed against these traditional limitations
of the *Commedia Erudita*.

Aretino, as I have just observed, broke the fetters
of convention, and presented scenes of pure Italian
life; but his plays were too hastily composed or ill-
constructed to start a new style. The originality of
Machiavelli in his *Mandragora* was not of the sort
to encourage a departure from the beaten track.
Like many other masterpieces of Italian art, the
Mandragora stands forth by itself, a sole inimitable
monument of genius; peculiar and personal; accomplished by one single act of vigorous expression.
Before a really national species of written comedy
emerged into distinctness from the *Commedia Erudita*, the literary impulse of the Renaissance began
to decline, and the Italians in the middle of the
sixteenth century entered upon that new phase of
intellectual evolution which is marked by the Tri-
dentine Council and the subsequent metamorphosis
of Catholicism.

III.

One prominent feature of this transitional epoch was the reappearance of popular forms of art and literature in Italy. The Italian provinces had retained their local characteristics with undiminished vitality through centuries of civic conflict and the dominance of humanistic culture. Now that this culture was decaying, each district and each city contributed some novelty of its own local vintage. Things which had been overgrown and screened by scholarship put forth their native vigour. A rich jungle of dialectical poetry sprouted from long-hidden roots. Men of birth and breeding began to pique themselves upon the use of their provincial language. A polite public, tired perhaps of too much polish, yielded to the charm of realism. The habits of the peasantry and artisans were transmitted to writing by educated pens. Scenic representations of a simple character, which had formed the delight of villagers from time immemorial, claimed the attention of learned coteries. Farces and morris-dances became fashionable. The buffoons and mimes and masquers, against whom the Church had fulminated in the Middle Ages, and whom the scholars of the Revival looked down upon with condescending indulgence, now lifted up their heads. Suddenly, by an imperceptible process of development, which it is impossible to trace in all its stages, Italy found herself in possession of what looked like a novel type of comedy. This improvised comedy, or *Commedia dell' Arte*, as we must henceforth call it, was not really new.[1]   On the contrary, the elements out of which it sprang were among the oldest, most vital, most national possessions of the race. Yet it was due to the peculiar conditions of the last years of the Renaissance, to the reaction against exhausted forms of artificial literature, and to the fresh interest in dialects, that this hitherto neglected plaything of the proletariate assumed a rare and bizarre shape of beauty. The Italians, still capable of exquisite artistic creation, had just now lost their liking for the *Commedia Erudita*. Public theatres were beginning to be built. These naturally introduced a more popular tone into the drama. Spectacles were adapted to the taste of a mixed audience. Improvised comedy succeeded to the heritage of written comedy. This younger daughter of Thalia invested the motley characters and masks of her invention with the cast-off mantle of her elder sister. She entered the sphere of the fine arts by continuing the tradition of Italian comedy upon an altered system, and with novel elements of humour.

---

[1] The full title would be *Commedia dell' Arte all' Improviso.* It is also called *Commedia a soggetto, Commedia non scritta, Commedia improvisa.* The written comedy, beside *Commedia Erudita*, was also called *Commedia sostenuta, scritta,* or *letteraria.*

To talk of younger and elder with reference to
these two types of comedy involves some confusion
of ideas.   Nothing is more significant of Italy than
the antiquity and complexity of all the forms of art
which flourished there.   The *Commedia Erudita*, as
we have seen, was derived from Latin, and through
Latin from Athenian sources.   The *Commedia dell'
Arte* had an even longer pedigree than this.   In a
powerfully mimetic race like the Italians, the rudiments out of which it was constructed were, as we
shall see, indigenous.   Before Rome rose upon the
Tiber, the comedy of masks and improvisation had,
in some shape or other, amused the people.   The
fall of the Empire, the formation of the Christian
polity, the centuries of the Middle Ages, the culture
of the Renaissance, did not extirpate it.   Though
we know but little of its history during that long
period, there is every reason to believe that the
elements which gave it individuality survived all
changes.   To this topic I shall have to return.   For
the present, it is enough to point out that the blending of the vulgar improvised comedy of vintage
festivals and market-places with what remained of
polite written comedy after the middle of the sixteenth century, determined the *Commedia dell' Arte*,
considered as a specific and strongly marked type of
dramatic art.   In this sense, and in this sense only,
it may be denominated the younger sister of the
Commedia Erudita.

IV.

Farces formed a popular species of entertainment all through the years of the Renaissance. At Naples they had the name of *Coviole*, at Florence of *Farse*. The playwright Cecchi has left us several specimens of the written *Farsa*, together with a general description of the type, which proves it to have been. not unlike the earliest of our own romantic plays.[1] A company formed itself at Siena, called I Rozzi, for the representation of rustic farces. Composed of artisans and mechanics, this company acquired such celebrity that Leo X. invited them in 1517 to the Vatican; and their influence must be reckoned in the evolution of the new Italian drama. A Paduan actor and playwright also deserves mention here. Angelo Beolco, born in 1502, made himself known upon the stage as Il Ruzzante, or the Frolic. He wrote rustic comedies with simple plots, distinguished by their realistic humour and their strong incisive pathos; and created the ideal character of the peasant or Il Villano. Beolco formed a school in the Venetian provinces, and died in 1542.[2]

---

[1] See what I have said at length upon this point in my *Shakspere's Predecessors*, p. 259, and *Renaissance in Italy*, vol. v. p. 188.

[2] To Maurice Sand, in his *Masques et Bouffons*, vol. ii. p. 77 *et seq.*, is due the merit of having resuscitated the fame of this great local dramatist, yet I think M. Sand exaggerates Beolco's influence in the creation of impromptu comedy.

Such are some of the traces we possess of a dramatic type in growth, which, after the middle of the sixteenth century, obtained predominance in Italy. It is not possible, however, for the critical historian to explain the several steps whereby the *Commedia dell' Arte* arrived at maturity. Like Harlequin, bounding from the sides and capering before the footlights, this new species makes a sudden apparition. We find it in full energy, possessing the public theatres and claiming the attention of all classes, at the close of the cinque cento. Described briefly, this comedy trusted to the improvisatory talent of trained actors and made use of masks. Companies were formed under the direction of a *Capocomico*, who took his name from one of the masks. Their stock in trade was a collection of plays in outline, *scenari* or *plats* (to use an old English phrase),[1] which the troupe studied under the direction of their leader. The development of the intrigue by dialogue and action was left to the native wit of the several players, and the performance varied according to the personal qualities of the members who composed the company. The masks or fixed characters were derived from all provinces of Italy, and represented types peculiar to each district.[2] Venice contributed Pantalone ; Bol-

---

[1] See Collier's *English Dramatic Poetry* (ed. 1879), vol. iii. p. 197.

[2] It is impossible to avoid the awkwardness of using the word *mask* in a double sense,—both to indicate the fixed character assumed by a certain species of actor, and also the vizard which concealed his features.

ogna lent the Dottore; Bergamo supplied the two
Zanni—Arlecchino and Brighella; Naples gave Pulcinella, Tartaglia, and the Captain. Tuscany made up
the characters of the comedy with the soubrette and
lovers. These Tuscan personages were unmasked
and spoke Florentine Italian.[1] The masks reproduced their native dialects.[2] Like Harlequin in his
coat of many colours, the *Commedia dell' Arte* wore
motley. Displacing the literary drama, which reduced contemporary life in Italy to the conventional
standard of classical Rome or Athens, this new
drama brought into salience local oddities and notes
of provincial eccentricity. The masks were permanent; yet they admitted of genial handling, since
these parts in the comedy were rarely written, and
every fresh sustainer of a mask had the opportunity
of impressing his own individuality upon the type he
represented.[3] In this way, as will soon appear, each

---

[1] It may here be mentioned that in English we still retain the names
of some of these masks, as Zany, Harlequin, Pantaloon, and Punch.
Our Columbine is the Neapolitan form of the *Servetta* or soubrette.
Our Scaramouch is one of the numerous forms of the Captain, which
obtained great popularity at Paris. Whether the Clown of our panto-
mimes has to be classed with the *Villano*, or rather with one of the
Zanni, I am uncertain. His traditional connection with the part of
Pantaloon seems to indicate the latter alternative.

[2] In a comedy by Virgilio Verucci (*Li Diversi Linguaggi*, Venezia,
1609), French, Venetian, Bergamasque, Roman, Sicilian, Bolognese,
Neapolitan, Matriccian, Perugian, and Florentine dialects were spoken.
See Bartoli, *op. cit.*, p. lxxix.

[3] Conversely, masks were sometimes created out of persons. Thus
the plebeian poet of Naples, Francesco Cerlone, moulded the mask of

mask multiplied and made a hundred. Plasticity
and adaptability were the essential qualities of a
dramatic species which relied on improvisation, and
had only the unwritten code of immemorial tradition.

V.

At this point it is necessary to inquire into the
relation between the modern Italian *Commedia dell'
Arte* and the old Italian comedy of mimes and
exodia. Much has been written, with meagre and
dubious results, about the origins of the Latin drama
One thing, however, appears certain, after shaking
the dust from ponderous tomes of erudition. The
Romans, like the modern Italians, had their *Commedia Erudita* and *Commedia dell' Arte*. Of the
two species, in classical times as afterwards, the *Commedia dell' Arte* was indigenous and popular, the
Commedia Erudita derived and literary. The latter,
whether it affected Greek manners, as in the so-

Don Fastidio upon a barber of his acquaintance, Francesco Massaro.
Here the man became a type ; and after he had made it famous, it was
continued by other players, who adapted themselves to his humours.
(See Scherillo's *Commedia dell' Arte*, chap. iii., for the history of Don
Fastidio). This mask was very popular for a time in Southern Italy.
When Casanova wanted to engage a troop at Otranto for performance at
Corfu, he had to choose between the rival companies of Neapolitan
Don Fastidio and Sicilian Battipaglia (*Mémoires*, vol. i. ch. xv.). The
Capocomici, as I have previously mentioned, were known by the names
of their masks.

called *Fabula palliata,* or Roman manners, as in
the so-called *Fabula togata,* remained in the hands
of scholarly authors and serious actors (*histriones*).
The former had its natural origin in popular habits,
and only at a comparatively late period submitted to
regular artistic treatment.   It was represented by
masked buffoons, *Sanniones, Planipedes, Stupidi,* and
so forth.   We hear of *Osci ludi* and *Fescennini versus,*
the former pointing to Campania and the vintage, the
latter to Etruria and village sports.[1]   The *Satura,*
which seems to have been an offshoot from the *Fes-
cennina,* corresponded pretty closely to what we now
call farce, and eventually developed into the *exodia*
or *hors d'œuvre* of the later Roman theatre.[2]   Out of
these indigenous elements, but with special relation
to the *Osci ludi,* grew a literary form of comedy
which obtained the name of *Atellana.*   It is supposed to have originated in the Oscan city of Atella,
close to Acerra, Pulcinella's birthplace.   In all these
native forms of drama, dialects were spoken and
masks were used; and this is a main·point of connection between them and the modern Italian *Commedia dell' Arte.*   Another feature in common is the
rank realism and open obscenity which marked the
humours of both species.

---

[1] *Fescenninus* is variously derived from the town Fescennia in South
Etruria, or from *fascinum,* the Latin form of *phallus.*

[2] The common meaning of *satura* and *farsa,* both of which have
reference to stuffing, is somewhat singular.

Among the ancient Roman masks four types are known to us by name—*Maccus*, a Protean fool or Harlequin ; *Bucco*, a garrulous clown or blockhead ; *Pappus*, a miserly, amorous, befooled old man ; *Dossenus*, a moralising charlatan.   We also hear of the *Stupidus* and *Morio*, *Manducus*, a notable glutton, and the *Sanniones*, so called possibly from their grin.

Further familiarity with the modern *Commedia dell' Arte* will make it clear how tempting it is to conjecture a direct transmission of these Roman masks from ancient to modern times.   Maccus and Bucco bear a strong resemblance to the two Zanni. The very word Zanni seems to suggest Sanniones ; although it is probably derived from the Bergamasque name for a varlet—Jack ; Zanni being a contraction of Giovanni.   Pappus looks uncommonly like Pantalone, and Dossenus like the Dottore.   The *Stupidus* has an air of our clown or Mezzettino or Il Villano. Manducus might be any glutton with a huge pair of champing jaws.   Yet nothing could be more uncritical than to assume that the Italian masks of the sixteenth century A.D. boasted an uninterrupted descent from the Roman masks of the fifth century B.C.   That assumption closes our eyes to a far more interesting aspect of the phenomenon.   The fact seems to be that ancient and modern Italy possessed the same mimetic faculty and used it in the same fashion. The peasants of modern Tuscany indulged in their Fescennine jibes, stained themselves with wine-lees, and jumped through bonfires, like their most remote ancestors.[1] The grape-gatherers of modern Nola and Capua ridiculed their neighbours with obscene jests, and pranked themselves in travesty, like the earliest Oscans or the first colonists from Hellas.[2] Out of the same persistent habits emerged the same kind of native drama ; and just as the Atellanæ of ancient Rome eventually brought the comedy of the proletariate upon the public stage in cities, so at the close of the sixteenth century the *Commedia dell' Arte* worked up the rudiments of popular farce and satire into a new form which delighted Europe for two hundred years.

Many details derived from the *Commedia Erudita* rendered the resemblance between the modern improvised drama and the vernacular comedy of ancient Rome superficially striking. The conventional characters of Plautus and Terence, the *senex*, the *servus*, the *meretrix*, the *mango*, the *ancilla*, the *miles gloriosus*, and the *parasitus* reappeared. In truth, this peculiar and highly complex hybrid combined strains of manifold varieties. Upon the wild and native briar, which in former times produced the *Osci ludi, Fescennini*

---

[1] I have seen them doing this with reticence and decorum at Montepulciano.

[2] A curious passage in the Life of Don Pietro di Toledo (*Arch. Stor.*, vol. ix. p. 23) shows what a startling impression these Dionysiac revels made upon a Spanish Viceroy in the early seventeenth century. Pontano's Latin poems are full of matter bearing on the vitality of antique rustic habits in the neighbourhood of Naples.

versus, and *Satura,* and which went on living its
own natural life beneath the drums and tramplings
of so many conquests, was now grafted the cultivated
rose of the *Commedia Erudita.* This, in its turn,
contained elements of the *Fabula palliata* and *togata.*
The result was a species eminently characteristic of
sixteenth-century Italy, and similar to the Atellan
farces of the Romans.

VI.

The *Commedia dell'Arte* yields, upon analysis, three
chief component factors. The four leading masks,
Arlecchino and Brighella, Pantalone and Il Dottore,
came respectively from Bergamo, Venice, and Bologna.
These were the contribution of Northern Italy. Pulcinella, Tartaglia, Coviello, and the Captain came from
Naples. They were subsidiary characters of great
importance, contributed by the South. The lovers,
primo amoroso and *prima amorosa,* upon whose
adventures the intrigue turned, and the *Servetta,*
came from Tuscany, or rather from the tradition of
written comedy, which adhered to the literary Italian
tongue. If priority in time is to be sought for any
of these factors, we must look to Lombardy. The
four masks which were indispensable to this dramatic
species, and which survived all its vicissitudes, had an
undoubted Lombardo-Venetian origin. The Neapoli-

tan masks were superadded, and the Tuscan intrigue formed little more than a conventional framework for the humours of the fixed characters. Scarcity of documents makes it impossible to speak with absolute authority on any of these points ; yet we have good reason to credit the tradition which connects the origin of the *Commedia dell' Arte* with Northern Italy.

A carnival song, composed by Anton-Francesco Grazzini, called Il Lasca, at Florence some time before the year 1559, throws light upon the subject.[1] It is entitled " Canto di Zanni e Magnifichi." The Magnifico corresponded to Pantalone ; and I need not repeat that the Zanni were best known as Arlecchino and Brighella. Lasca makes it clear in this poem that the Lombard masks were strangers to Tuscany, and that they performed comedies upon a public stage :[2]

> " Facendo il Bergamasco e il Veneziano,
>   N' andiamo in ogni parte,
>   E 'l recitar commedie è la nostra arte. "

---

[1] It was included in the first edition of the *Canti Carnascialeschi*, 1559, and is reprinted in Verzone's edition of Grazzini's *Rime Burlesche*, Firenze, Sansone, 1882.

[2] " Acting the Bergamasque and the Venetian, we roam the whole world over, and the recitation of comedies is our trade. . . . We are all of us Zanni, excellent and perfect players ; the other choice actors of our troupe, lovers, ladies, hermits, and soldiers, have stayed behind to guard our booth. . . . We have a stock of new comedies, so fine, so mirthful, and so witty, that when you hear them you will die of laughing. Afterwards you will see a dance upon our stage, all full of new

He also shows how the buffoon parts in these plays were interwoven with the intrigue of the regular drama :

"E Zanni tutti siamo,
    Recitatori eccellenti e perfetti ;
    Gli altri strioni eletti,
    Amanti, Donne, Romiti e Soldati,
    Alla stanza per guardia son restati."

Furthermore, he lets us know that acting was combined with dancing and mountebank performances, and drops the information that women in Florence were not allowed to attend the theatres where Zanni played :

"Commedie nuove abbiam composte in guisa
    Che quando recitar le sentirete,
    Morrete delle risa,
    Tanto son belle, giocose, e facete ;
    E dopo ancor vedrete
    Una danza ballar sopra la scena,
    Di varj e nuovi giuochi tutta piena."

It is therefore obvious that, at the middle of the sixteenth century, the *Commedia dell' Arte* had already taken shape and earned popularity. The companies who introduced it into Tuscany were recognised as hailing from Bergamo and Venice. Before another fifty years had passed away, this species absorbed the attention of Italy, adopted elements

---

and varied sports. . . . But since there is a certain custom in this country, ladies, which prevents your coming to our public show, if you will open your house-doors to us, we will let you taste in part the sweetness and the pleasure of our sports."

from every district, and settled down into a definite form of comedy, which lasted until the period of Goldoni's reform of the stage. It culminated about the middle of the seventeenth century, and maintained a high degree of excellence during the first half of the eighteenth. But when Goldoni attacked it, and Gozzi rose in its defence, the type was already on the wane. Depending, as any kind of improvised drama must necessarily do, upon the personal talents of successive actors, the *Commedia dell' Arte* died of inanition when theatrical genius was diverted into other channels.[1] Originality of humour then yielded to conventional buffoonery. The masks became more and more stereotyped, more and more insipid. Were it not for Gozzi's *Fiabe*, we should hardly be able to form a conception of the part they actually played for two centuries in Europe.

VII.

Let us watch the carnival procession of the masks defile before us. We may imagine that they are crossing the stage of a theatre, while we sit idle in our stalls. First comes Pantalone, the worthy Venetian merchant, good-hearted, shrewd, and canny, yet preserving a certain child-like simplicity, which

---

[1] The other channels were French plays, modifications of English plays, adaptations of Spanish plays, and musical melodramas.

long acquaintance with the world has not contaminated. His full title is Pantalone de' Bisognosi.
Sometimes he is called Il Magnifico, sometimes Babi-
lonio ; and old tradition gives a singular derivation
for his name of Pantalone.   Instead of having anything to do with the Saint called Pantaleone, he ought
really to be known as Piantaleone, or Plant-the-
lion.   In fact, he is one of those patriotic *cittadini*
who, partly out of zeal for S. Mark and partly with
a view to commerce, were reputed to hoist flags with
the Venetian lion waving to the breeze on every rock
and barren headland of Levantine waters.[1]   Pantalone wears a black mantle, woollen cap, short trousers, socks and slippers of bright red.   A black
domino conceals half of his face.   He is sometimes
a bachelor, but more frequently a widower with one
daughter, who engrosses all his time and care.   Easy-
going indulgence for the foibles of his neighbours,
combined with homely mother-wit, is the funda-
mental note of his character.   But as time goes on,
he degenerates, dotes, yields to senile vices.   At last
he becomes the shuffling slippered Pantaloon of our
Christmas pantomimes.[2]

---

[1] I do not vouch for this etymology, which Boerio, the compiler of the
Venetian Glossary, has adopted.   For myself, I should be well contented with the derivation from San Pantaleone, and would willingly
make him the patron saint of pantaloons and professed trousers-
makers.

[2] It is singular that Shakespeare, who uses Pantalone as the symbol
of old age in *As You Like It*, knew him already in decrepitude.

After Pantaloon walks the Doctor in his Bologna gown; a hideous black mask covers his whole face, smudged with red patches, like skin-disease or wine-stains, on the cheeks. He is Graziano, Baloardo Graziano, or Prudentio, and has a kind of bastard brother called the Dottor Balanzon Lombardo. Boasting his D.C.L. or M.D. or LL.D. degree from the august University, Graziano makes a vast parade of learning. *Bononia docet* is always on his lips or in his thoughts; yet he cannot open his mouth without letting fall some palpable absurdity. Law jargon, quibbles, quiddities, preposterous syllogisms, fragments of distorted Latin, misapplied quotations from the Pandects, mingle with metaphysics, astrology, and physical chimæras about the spheres and elements and humours, in his talk. He is a walking caricature of learning, and the low stupid cunning of his nature contrasts with the vain pomp he makes of erudition. To sustain this mask with spirit taxed the genius of a comedian. He had to keep a voluminous repertory of pedantic lumber always ready, to blunder with wit and pun in paradoxes, seasoning the whole with broad Bolognese dialect and plebeian phrases.

Pantalone and the Doctor were only half-masks; that is to say, they held something in common with the stationary characters of written comedy, and took a decided part in the action of the play. As the *Commedia dell' Arte* coalesced with the *Commedia*

L'rudita, they approached more and more nearly to the type of the *senes* in Latin comedy. The present generation has seen them both in Rossini's *Barbiere di Siviglia.*

Next come the two Zanni. These are thorough-going masks ; twin-brothers from the country-side of Bergamo, strongly contrasted in their characters, yet holding certain points in common.[1] First comes Arlecchino, the eldest and most typical of Italian masks, and the one who has preserved its outlines to the present day. His party-coloured, tight-fitting suit reproduces the rags and patches of a rustic servant. On his head is a little round cap, with a tuft made out of a hare's or rabbit's scut. He is always on the move, light-headed, gluttonous, gay, pliable, credulous, ingenuously naive and silly. The glittering ubiquitous Harlequin of our pantomimes transforms him into a mute ballet-dancer ; but when the type was created, Arlecchino spoke and amused the audience as much by his absurdities and uncouth jokes as by his perpetual mobility.

Time would fail to tell of the infinite modifications which this type assumed under the hands of successive able actors. Truffaldino, the delight of Venice,

---

[1] It was my good fortune, while writing these pages at Davos in the summer of 1888, to become acquainted with two brothers from Bergamo, who were living representatives of the Zanni. They had come to help at the hay-harvest, leaving their own farm in the Bergamasque hills. Brighella's wit and knavery amused me. I marvelled at Arlecchino's simplicity and suppleness.

Zaccagnino, Trivellino, Mestolino, Bagattino, Guaz-
zetto, Stoppino, Burattino, and the idiotic Mezzettino,
were all descended from this parent stock.

Side by side with Arlecchino goes his more astute
and knavish brother Brighella. He is also Bergamasque of the purest breed. But he holds something from the Davus and Geta of Latin comedy.
He is the roguish, clever, cowardly, pimping servant
of the young spendthrift, who helps his master to
deceive his father and seduce his neighbour's wife
or daughter. Brighella wears a loose white shirt
trimmed with green, and wide white trousers. On
his head is a conical hat, plumed with red feathers,
which yields place in course of time to the white cap
of our clowns. His mask is brown, cut off above the
upper lip, over which a pair of short moustachios
bristle. Like Arlecchino, Brighella gave birth to a
great variety of assimilated types. Unscrupulous
Pedrolino, Beltramo, Bagolino, Frontino, Sganarello,
Mascarillo, Figaro, Finocchio, Fantino, Gradellino,
Traccagnino are his more or less legitimate offspring.
He enters French comedy under the names of Scapin,
Sganarelle, and Frontin. He creates a character of
opera with Figaró. Unlike Arlecchino, who becomes
at last a silent ballet-dancer, Brighella grows more
vocal and distinct as time advances, until, in the plays
of Molière and Beaumarchais, he is hardly distin-
guishable from a *servus* of Latin comedy modernised.
Indeed, just as Pantalone and Il Dottore approximate

to the *senes*, so Arlecchino and Brighella shade off
into the *servi;* and all their countless progeny are
variations on the theme of stupid or roguish varlets.

The four main masks, with their attendant groups
of subordinates, have passed before us; but a multitude whom no man can number and no words can
describe press on from behind. Perhaps the first
place should be given to the *Servetta.* Her names
are legion. Colombina, the sweetheart of Arlecchino and Pulcinella, Rosetta, Florentine Pasquella,
Argentina, Diamantina, Venetian Smeraldina, Sapo-
rita, Carmosina; under all her titles, and with every
shade of character ascribed to her by the free handling of successive actresses, she remains the sprightly,
witty, shifty pendant to the Zanni.[1] Not a true
mask, however; for the Servetta wears her own face
and form, only assuming the costume and dialect of
the region she prefers to hail from. Like her lover
Arlecchino, Colombina underwent a long series of
transformations before she became the fairy-like
being who flits behind the footlights of our theatres
on winter evenings. And, like Brighella, written
comedy blended her with the fixed characters of
drama under the name of the soubrette. Susanna
in the *Nozze di Figaro* is a familiar example of
Colombina in her latest dramatic development.

The *Servette* in their many-coloured *Contadina*

---

[1] Carlo Gozzi at Zara in his youth created a new type of the Servetta,
adapted to Dalmatian circumstances, under the name of Luce.

COLOMBINA (1683)

Illustrating the Italian Commedia dell' Arte, or Impromptu Comedy

dresses have passed by. Close upon their heels
press forward a chattering grimacing group from
Naples. Pulcinella leads the way, for he must still
keep Colombina in sight. In him, far more than
in Arlecchino, the genius of a nation lives incarnate ;
and this he partly owes to a poor artisan of Naples,
Francesco Cerlone, who fixed the type with inimitable
humour in the last century.[1] Pulcinella has had
whole volumes written on his pedigree. Some authors
find him depicted on the walls of Pompeii ; others
trace him in statuettes and masks of antiquity. The
one point which seems to be certain is, that he made
his appearance on the public stage toward the end
of the sixteenth century, wearing the white shirt and
breeches of a rustic from Acerra. His black mask,
long nose, humpback, protruding stomach, dagger
and truncheon, were later additions. Whatever
connection there may be between Pulcinella and the
masks of classical antiquity — and I have already
attempted to show how I think that connection ought
to be conceived [2] — he was, at his debut, regarded
as the type of a Campanian villager, established at
Naples in the quality of servant. Pulcinella is thus
the Southern analogue of Bergamasque Brighella and
Arlecchino. Gradually he absorbed the humours of
the Neapolitan proletariate, and became the burlesque

---

[1] Scherillo, in his *Commedia dell' Arte*, has resuscitated Cerlone's
fame, as Maurice Sand made us acquainted with Beolco.

[2] See above, p. 38.

mirror of their manners and ways of thinking. Time's whirligig has made him the hero of our puppet-shows, and he enjoys cosmopolitan celebrity under the name of Punch.

Coviello goes along with him, a Calabrian mask, which was sustained with applause by Salvator Rosa at Rome. He belongs to the buffoon class, and is distinguished by his mandoline and ballad-singing. After him walks Tartaglia, afflicted with an incurable stammer, which renders his magisterial airs and graces ludicrous. Tartaglia has something in him of the Doctor; but this part lent itself to great varieties of treatment. We shall see what play Gozzi made with it.

But now our ears are deafened with a clash of arms, rumbling of drums, pistol-shots, and shouted execrations. A fantastic extravagant troop of soldiers march upon the stage. At their head goes the swaggering Capitano. He is a Spaniard, armed to the teeth, loaded with outlandish weapons, twirling huge moustachios, frowning, swearing, boasting, quarrelling, thieving, wenching, and shrinking into corners when he meets a man of courage. Sometimes he affects the melancholy grandeur of Don Quixote. Sometimes he leans to the garrulity of Bobadil. Sometimes he assumes the serious ferocity of a brigand chief or the haughty punctiliousness of a hidalgo. Still he remains at bottom the caricature of professional soldiers, as they plagued and infested

Italy under the Spanish domination. His language soars into the wildest hyperboles and euphuisms. He cannot speak without new-coined oaths and frothy metaphors and vaunts that shake heaven, earth, and sea. But the slightest trial of his valour breaks the bubble, and he cringes like a whipped hound.

The Capitano talked a mixture of Neapolitan and Spanish. His part, which required to be sustained at a high pitch of burlesque upon a single note of bragging insolence, was not unfrequently written, and none of these fixed characters assumed more stereotyped outlines. The *Miles Gloriosus* of Latin comedy reappeared in him, and helped to mould the modern type. The ramifications of this character were innumerable. A celebrated actor, Francesco Andreini (born at Pistoja in 1548), helped to create its form. He called himself " Capitan Spavento da Valle Inferna." Then followed Ariararche, Diacatolicon, Leucopigo and Melampigo (white and black buttocks), Coccodrillo, Matamoros, Scaramuccia (created by Tiberio Fiorelli of Naples), Fracassa, Rinoceronte, Giangiurgolo, Bombardon, Meo Squaquara, Spezzaferro, Terremoto. The list might be prolonged until the page was filled. Every variety of the burlesque son of Mars, from a delicate Adonis to a fire-eater, obtained impersonation from one or other able sustainer of the part. And a host of minor bastard braggarts, like the Trasteverine Meo Patacco, per-

petuated the fun long after the great Capitano had
quitted the public stage. Some of these types survive in literature. Scaramouche is known to us, and
Gautier has immortalised Fracasse.

In the rabble which follows this noisy band of war-
riors we discern several buffoons of the long-robed
tribe—Neapolitan Pancrazio, Biscegliese, and Cucuz-
zietto, Sienese Cassandro and Roman Cassandrino—
who have more or less affinity with the Dottore. Il
Pedante walks apart, and attracts attention by his
Maccaronic Latin and eccentric morals. He has the
poems of Fidenzio Glottogrysio in his hands, which he
presses on the attention of a smooth-chinned pupil.[1]
Don Fastidio distinguishes himself from the vulgar
herd by his enormous nose, and lantern jaws, and
long lean figure, and preposterous citations from the
law reports of Naples. Cavicchio tells silly tales and
sings his Norcian songs. Il Desávedo burlesques
the "dude" of Parma, and Narcisino plays the
"masher" of Bologna to the life. Burattino comes
upon the stage in a score of disguises, now gardener,
now shopkeeper, now valet, always the fool and knave
combined, impostor and imposed on.[2] The Notajo,

---

[1] For a short notice of these curious Maccaronic poems, *I Cantici di
Fidentio Glottogrysio Ludimagistro*, see my *Renaissance in Italy*, vol.
v. p. 328. The obscurity of their jargon veiled considerable indecency.
It is noticeable that this book, now exceedingly rare, should have become the text-book of the Pedante. But see Bartoli, *op. cit.*, pp. lii., lvii.

[2] Burattino is so kaleidoscopic that at last he becomes the patronymic
hero of marionettes in Italy. *I Burattini* are the acting dolls.

with huge spectacles upon his nose and swan's quill
stuck behind his spreading ears, murmuring a nasal
drawl, and tripping himself up at every step in his
long skirts, leads up the rear. Rope-dancers, ballerini,
Pasquarielli, Pierrots, conclude the show, dancing and
pirouetting after their more vocal comrades.

It is impossible, in a sketch like this, to do justice
to the manifold and motley crowd of the Italian
masks.   Even Callot, whose burin has bequeathed
to us so many salient portraits of the types he saw
in action, leaves the imagination cold.   As I have
remarked above, the *Commedia dell' Arte* combined
fixity of outline in the masks with illimitable plasticity in the details communicated by the genius and
personality of their sustainers.   The mask, the traditional character, was something which a comedian assumed ; but he dealt with it as he found it suited to his
physical and mental qualities.   Each distinguished
actor re-created the part he represented.   The improvised extempore rule of the game allowed him
boundless license.   Therefore, while the masks persisted, they varied with the men who wore them.
Arlecchino became Truffaldino in the hands of Antonio Sacchi.   The Capitano appeared as Scaramuccia
in the person of Tiberio Fiorelli.   Parts crossed
and intercrossed.   Pulcinella borrowed something
from Arlecchino ; Brighella patched himself with
rags from Coviello's wardrobe.   The dialect and local
humours of South Italy were engrafted on types

conventionalised in Lombard provinces. Tuscany took them up, and added her own biting wit. As in a kaleidoscope, the constituent fragments of the changeful whole assumed shapes and forms of infinite variety by clever shifting of each particle. Each company established for the performance of this comedy gave a fresh nuance to the combinations which the show permitted. In each district it adopted a new local colour. The mask was recognised; the man who wore it was expected to remodel it upon himself. Folk came to the theatres, less to see the masks, than to see how an Andreini or a D'Arbes or a Costantini or a Riccoboni would sustain them. We who have lost the men, and lost well-nigh the memory of their performance, cannot hope to reconstruct the comedy in its entirety. Histrionic art always and everywhere suffers from the ephemeral conditions under which it has to be externalised. But this disadvantage is crushing in the case of an art which was left to the spontaneous creativeness of its great representatives.

VIII.

Intrigue of a simple kind formed the staple of these improvised comedies. Anything like refined studies of character or the development of calculated motives was rendered impossible by the conditions

under which they were presented to the public.   An
artist pleased or displeased by the exhibition of his
personality in masquerade, and his creation of a
shade of difference for some known type.   The plot,
whether borrowed from the written drama, from
Latin plays, or from the gossip of the market-place,
was always of an amorous complexion.   Fathers,
lovers, guardians, varlets, priests, and panders played
their parts in it.   The action proceeded by means
of disguises, sleeping-potions, changelings, pirates,
sudden recognitions of lost relatives, phantoms, demo-
niacal possessions, burlesque exorcisms, shipwrecks,
sacks of cities, bandits, kidnapped children.   It is
singular in what a narrow circle the machinery re-
volves.   Unlike our own Romantic drama, the *Commedia dell' Arte* made but few excursions into the
regions of history, fable, mythology, and fancy.   Its
scene was an Italian piazza; and though we hear of
thrilling adventures by land and sea, in forest and
on fell, these are only used to loose a knot or to
elucidate the transformation of some personage.   We
ought not to marvel at the limitations of this drama.
They are explained by that close connection, on which
I have already insisted, between the *Commedia dell'
Arte* and the *Commedia Erudita*.   The new comedy
supplied little but its masks; and these masks, as we
have seen, were types of bourgeois and rustic characters, capable of infinite modification within prescribed
boundaries.   The end in view was not the delectation

of the audience by a scenic drama, but the caricature
and travesty of life as it appeared to every one.
That caricature, executed with inexhaustible finesse
and piquant sallies of fresh personality, accommo-
dated itself to the antiquated framework of plots as
old as Plautus.

If the *Commedia dell' Arte* lacked fancy and invention in its ground-themes, this defect was compen-
sated by audacious realism and Gargantuan humour.
The indecency of these plays cannot be described.
Men and women appeared naked on the stage.   Un-
mentionable vices were boldly paraded.   Buffoonery
of the vilest description enhanced the finest strokes
of burlesque sarcasm.   Actors who created types
which made the spirit of a nation live in effigy, condescended to tricks unworthy of a Yahoo.   We have
to accept the species, not as a branch of the legitimate drama, but as a carnival masquerade, in which
humanity ran riot, jeering at its own indignities and
foibles.

IX.

The stock in trade of an acting company consisted
of some scores of plots in outline.   Gozzi, writing in
the eighteenth century, calculates that there may
have been from three hundred to four hundred
dramatic situations.[1]   We possess a certain number

---

[1] In the *Ragionamento Ingenuo* and *Appendice*, Op., 1772, vols i. and iv.

of these *scenari*, as they were technically called
Flaminio Scala published a collection of fifty in his
Teatro delle Favole Rappresentative (Venetia, 1611).
The titles of about one hundred others survive from
the archives of Basilio Locatelli and Domenico Bian-
colelli, incorporated in eighteenth-century histories
of the Italian stage.   The records of the theatres
where Italians played at Paris supply titles of another
set, and a few have been disinterred from miscel-
laneous sources.   Quite recently a complete collection of well-formed *scenari* was given to the press by
Signor Adolfo Bartoli from a Magliabecchian MS. of
the last century.[1]   It contains twenty-two pieces.

Comparative study of these *scenari* shows that the
whole comedy was planned out, divided into acts and
scenes, the parts of the several personages described
in prose, their entrances and exits indicated, and
what they had to do laid down in detail.   The execution was left to the actors ; and it is difficult to form
a correct conception of the acted play from the dry
bones of its *ossatura.*   " Only one thing afflicts me,"
said our Marston in the preface to his *Malcontent :*
" to think that scenes invented merely to be spoken,
should be inforcively published to be read."   And
again, in his preface to the *Fawne*, " Comedies are
writ to be spoken, not read ; remember the life of
these things consists in action."   If that was true of
pieces composed in dialogue by an English play-

---

[1] *Scenari Inediti*, Firenze, Sansoni, 1880.

wright of the Elizabethan age, how far more true is
it of the skeletons of comedies, which avowedly owed
their force and spirit to extemporaneous talent!
Reading them, we feel that we are viewing the
machine of stakes and irons which a sculptor sets
up before he begins to mould the figure of an athlete
or a goddess in plastic clay.[1]

The *scenario*, like the *plat* described for us by
Malone and Collier, was hung up behind the stage.
Every actor referred to it while the play went forward, refreshing his memory with what he had to
represent, and attending to his entrances. But before the curtain lifted a previous process had been
gone through. This was called *Concertare il soggetto.*
The company met in their green-room. What followed may be told in the words of a seventeenth-century writer on the technique of the *Commedia dell'
Arte.*[2] "The Choregus, who rules and guides the
troupe by his ability and experience, has to plan the
subject, to show how the action shall be conducted,
the dialogues concluded, and new sallies of wit or
humour introduced. It is not merely his business
to read the plot aloud, but also to set forth the personages with their names and qualities, to explain

---

[1] It has to be mentioned that in plays of a more serious description,
the parts of character were frequently written out, and only the parts
of the masks left to improvisation. This was the method pursued by
Gozzi in his *Fiabe.*

[2] Andrea Perrucci, *Dell' Arte Rappresentativa premeditata ed all'
improvviso,* Napoli, 1699, quoted by Bartoli, *op. cit.,* p. lxxi.

the drama, describe localities, and suggest extemporaneous additions. For instance, he shall begin by saying: 'The comedy we have to represent is so-and-so; the personages such-and-such; the houses are on this side and on that.' Then he will unfold the argument. He will impress upon his comrades the necessity of bearing well in mind the place where they are supposed to be, the names of people and the business they are engaged in, so that they shall not confound Rome with Naples, or say that they have come from Spain when they are bound from Germany. A father must not forget his son's name, nor a lover his lady's. It is also most important that the houses in which the action has to take place should be accurately known. To knock at the wrong door, or to take refuge in the home of your enemy, would spoil all. Afterwards, the planner of the subject must indicate occasions suited to the sallies of the several characters. 'Here a piece of buffoonery is right. A metaphor, or sarcasm, or hyperbole, or innuendo, would make a good effect there.' In fact, he has to show each actor how to play his part to best advantage in the circumstances of the piece. Then he must look to preventing inconvenient entrances and exits, providing that the stage be not left empty, and indicating proper ways of bringing scenes to their conclusion. After the Choregus has read this lecture to the troupe, they will meet and sketch the comedy in outline. Then

they have the opportunity of bringing their own
talents forward, and combining new effects. Yet,
at such rehearsals, they must all be mindful to
maintain the outlines of the subject, not to exceed
their rôles, nor yet to trust their recollection of
similar plays performed under different conditions.
The piece has each time to be produced afresh by
the concerted action of the players who will bring
it on the boards."

The Choregus was usually the *Capocomico* or the
first actor and manager of the company. He impressed his comrades with a certain unity of tone,
brought out the talents of promising comedians,
enlarged one part, curtailed another, and squared
the piece to be performed with the capacities he
could control. "When a new play has to be given,"
says another writer on this subject,[1] "the first actor
calls the troupe together in the morning. He reads
them out the plot, and explains every detail of the
intrigue. In short, he acts the whole piece before
them, points out to each player what his special
business requires, indicates the customary sallies of
wit and traits of humour, and shows how the several
parts and talents of the actors can be best combined
into a striking work of scenic art."

---

[1] *Histoire Anecdotique du Théâtre Italien*, Paris, 1769, quoted by
Bartoli, *op. cit.*, p. lxxvi.

X.

More than natural cleverness and native humour went to the making of a good comedian. To begin with, he had to be a man of sense, tact, and obliging disposition. "When we speak of a good comedian in the Italian style," says Gherardi,[1] "we mean a man of solid parts, who depends on imagination more than memory in his performance, and composes everything he says upon the spot; he is one who knows how to play up to his companions on the stage, combining his words and gestures so well with theirs that he responds at a touch to their hints, and who is so ready with a repartee or move-ment that the audience believes the scene to have been concerted beforehand." In truth, fertility of fancy, quickness of intelligence, a brain well stocked with varied learning, facility of utterance, command of language, and imperturbable presence of mind, were required in a first-rate improvisatory actor. When he undertook to sustain one of the masks, he had first of all to live himself into the character. If, for instance, he chose the Dottore, nothing might escape his lips upon the stage out of harmony with that character, nothing which could remind the

---

[1] *Le Théâtre Italien*, quoted by Bartoli, *op. cit.*, p. lxx.

audience that anybody but a pedant from Bologna
was speaking. His every gesture had to contribute
to the same effect. The second nature of his part
had so to supersede his own instincts, that no
sudden accidents, the maladroitness of a comrade,
an unexpected turn in the dialogue, or any of the
inconveniences to which unpremeditated acting was
liable, should throw him off his guard.

It was further necessary that he should stock his
mind with what the actors called the *doti* of a play,
and with a repertory of what they called *generici*.[1]
The *doti* or dowry of a comedy consisted of soliloquies, narratives, dissertations, and studied passages
of rhetoric, which were not left to improvisation.
These existed in manuscript, or were composed for
the occasion. They had to be used at decisive points
of the action, and formed fixed pegs on which to
hang the dialogue. The *generici* or common-places
were sententious maxims, descriptions, outpourings
of emotion, humorous and fanciful diatribes, declarations of passion, love-laments, ravings, reproaches,
declamatory outbursts, which could be employed *ad
libitum* whenever the situation rendered them appropriate. Each mask had its own stock of common
topics, suited to the personage who used them. A
consummate artist displayed his ability by improving

---

[1] These phrases are used by Gozzi in his *Memorie Inutili*. Compare
what he says in his *Appendice al Ragionamento Ingenuo*, Op., 1772, vol.
iv. p. 40.

on these, introducing fresh points and features, and adapting them to his own conception of the part. They had to become incorporated with the ideal self he represented, and not to betray their origin in study. The tradition of the drama and the daily practice of rehearsing together made each member of a company know when such premeditated pieces were to be expected. They did not therefore break the general style of the performance. Habit enabled the actors to lead up to them and pass away from them upon the stream of impromptu dialogue.

Another highly important branch of the art was what were called the *lazzi*. "We give the name of *lazzi*," says Riccoboni in his history of the theatre, "to those sallies and bits of by-play with which Harlequin and the other masks interrupt a scene in progress—it may be by demonstrations of astonishment or fright, or by humorous extravagances alien to the matter in hand—after which, however, the action has to be renewed upon its previous lines." It was precisely in these *lazzi* that a comic actor displayed his personal originality to best advantage; but it required great tact and sense of the dramatic situation to render them natural, appropriate, and to keep them within bound and measure.

We have now seen what was expected of a first-rate artist, and understand to what extent the *Commedia dell' Arte* depended upon study and premeditation. Long familiarity with their own repertory undoubtedly reduced the improvisatory element to a minimum in the case of troupes who were accustomed to play together for years. Yet they strove to gain novelty by inventing fresh situations, giving unexpected turns to dialogue, and varying their action on successive nights. The best companies were those in whose hands a hackneyed comedy was always plastic, and who kept their improvisatory powers in exercise.

The defect of the art was that it tended to become stereotyped. The Zanni repeated their jokes. The Dottore used the same malapropisms over and over again. The *primo amoroso* served up the *crambe decies repetita* of his monologues. The *lazzi* degenerated into unmeaning horse-play and buffooneries, which had nothing to do with the action of the piece. Nature was forgotten. Every actor overplayed his part, ranted, raged, turned caricature into burlesque, spoke in and out of season, exaggerated his gestures, diction, gait, and declamation, until a pack of madmen seemed to have run wild upon the stage To control these tendencies towards a false and artificial style of presentation, which formed the inherent vice of improvisatory acting, was the duty of an able Capocomico. It could only be done by forcing the members of the troupe to study and reflect on what they had to represent, by compelling them to subordinate their several parts to the general effect, and by raising the tone of their intelligence.

Thus there was the greatest difference between a well-conducted company, intent on the perfection of their art, and a wandering rabble, satisfied with appealing to the lowest instincts of the proletariate. The value of these remarks will be apparent after reading what Gozzi has to say about Antonio Sacchi's company and the causes of its dissolution.

XI.

There is no doubt that during their flourishing period the companies of the *Commedia dell' Arte* afforded the rarest amusement, not only to the vulgar, but also to refined and cultivated audiences throughout Europe. They were especially appreciated at Paris. From the year 1572, when the *Confidenti* and *Gelosi* made their first appearance, to the close of the eighteenth century, Italian troupes at the Hôtel de Bourbon, the Hôtel de Bourgogne, the Palais Royal, and the Opera Comique, formed the delight of the French court and the Parisian public. Under various names, *Uniti, Fedeli, Barbieri's, Bianchi's,* and Cardinal Mazarin's men, actors who had learned their trade in Italy continued to seek larger profits and a wider audience in that capital. "The way in which Italian comedians compose, study, and represent their plays," says a French critic in the year

1716,[1] "is quite beyond the powers of language to describe. I might venture to call it inconceivable; with such a wealth of new and agreeable sallies and of unpremeditated dialogue do they adorn their scenes." Many anecdotes regarding these Italian players in their French homes have been transmitted to us, with detailed descriptions of their qualities. I will confine myself to two extracts.[2]   One is taken from Constantini's Life of Tiberio Fiorelli (1608–1694), the famous Scaramouche. "He was one of the most perfect mimes who have appeared in these last centuries. I call him mime advisedly, because he played his part by action more than speaking. Scaramouche was not satisfied with making what he represented intelligible by speech; he translated everything into movements of his face and body, adapting his gestures to his words and his words to his gestures with incomparable art. Everything became vocal in this man, his feet, his hands, his head; the slightest attitude he took had meaning and significance." Gherardi adds that "he could keep an audience in fits of laughter for a long quarter of an hour without uttering a word. A great prince, who saw him act at Rome, uttered these words, '*Scaramuccia does not talk, and yet he says everything*,' and at the end of the performance presented him with his coach and six horses." Of

---

[1] Quoted by Bartoli, *op. cit.*, p. lxxi.
[2] I am indebted to Maurice Sand, *Masques et Bouffons*.

Tommaso Vicentini, called Il Tommasino, who made
his début at Paris as Harlequin in 1716, we read :
" His suppleness, his natural gaiety, his graceful airs
of rustic simplicity, made him a first-rate Harlequin.
But nature had also made him an excellent actor
in the more extended sense of that phrase. True,
naïve, original, pathetic, amid the laughter he
excited by his buffooneries, a single trait, a single
reflection which became a sentiment by his manner
of expressing it, drew tears from the audience, and
surprised the author of the piece no less than the
public, and that too in spite of the mask, which
seemed intended to inspire as much fear as merriment. Often, when one had begun to laugh at his
way of simulating grief or pain, one finished by
being melted with the tenderness of the emotion
which came from the bottom of his heart."

Italian companies delighted the court of Spain
during the reign of Philip II., and were welcomed
in Portugal. We find them in Bavaria, at Dresden,
and in other parts of Germany. Nor were they
entirely unknown in England. Collier, in his " History of the English Drama," speaks of a certain
Drousiano, who played with his troupe in London
during the winter of 1577–78.[1] This was probably
Drusiano Martelli. The extempore plays of the
Italians are mentioned by Whetstone, Kyd, Jonson,
and Brome ; and it seems probable that the plat-

---

[1] Vol. iii. p. 201.

comedies, ascribed to the famous fools Tarleton and
Wilson, were modelled on Italian *Commedie a Soggetto.*   Kyd, in the *Spanish Tragedy,* shows that the
method of studying an improvised play was well
understood.   Hieronymo, who wishes to have a
certain subject mounted in a hurry, says to his
confidant—

> "The Italian tragedians were so sharp of wit,
> That in one hour's meditation
> They would perform anything in action."

Lorenzo replies—

> "I have seen the like
> In Paris, among the French tragedians."

The full history of Italian companies in foreign lands
still remains to be written ; but I have said enough
in this place to prove their wide popularity.

In its native country, the *Commedia dell' Arte*
was long regarded as the special glory and the unique
product of Italian dramatic genius.   Gozzi, though
he wrote as its apologist, only expressed common
opinion when he said :[1] "I reckon improvised
comedy among the particular distinctions of our
nation.   I look upon it as quite a different species
from the written and premeditated drama; nor have
I the shameless audacity to stigmatise with the title
of an ignorant rabble those noble and cultivated persons whom I see with my own eyes following and

---

[1] *Ragionamento Ingenuo,* Op., 1772, vol. i.

enjoying a play of this description. I esteem the
able comedians who sustain the masks, far higher
than those improvisatory poets, who, without uttering anything to the purpose, excite astonishment in
crowds of gaping listeners."

XII.

This essay would be incomplete if I failed to describe the decadence of the *Commedia dell' Arte*, and
the various inconveniences which attended its performance by incompetent or wilfully scurrilous actors.
Without such a sequel to the history of its development, Goldoni's reform of the theatre, and Gozzi's
energetic attempts to sustain the old style by works
of a peculiar and hybrid character, will not be intelligible.

In its higher manifestations, this comedy, as we
have seen, allied itself to fine art by singularly delicate links of connection. More than in other kinds
of drama, where actors make themselves the mouth-
pieces of poets whose creations they incarnate, the
performers of improvised comedy had to be complete
and finished works of living art in their own persons.
So long as they were conscious of their mission, and
earnestly aspired to the highest points within the
range and scope of their achievement, they supplied
a scenic travesty of actual life unequalled for its

freshness and its truth to nature—sparkling with
salient traits of character, seasoned with mirthful
sarcasm, and pungent by its satire of contemporary
manners.   But the roots of this unique and singular
species of the drama were grounded in a deep sub-
soil of vulgar instincts and dishonest proclivities.   It
clung to the tradition of mountebanks and mimes,
acrobats and jongleurs, circus-clowns and rope-dancers.
The rare flower of racy humour and refined parody,
which fascinated Paris in the age of Louis XIV.,
sprang from a stock discredited and outcast through
fifteen centuries of Christian teaching.   The Church in
council and in synod had anathematised the ancestors
of Andreini and Fiorelli, Sacchi and Darbes.   Burial
with the sanctities of religion was forbidden them,
as it is forbidden to suicides.   They were reckoned
among the enemies of social order and civil discipline.   The State, in its sumptuary laws, forbade
their entrance into decent houses, relegating them
to dark corners of the city, where they lurked with
thieves and prostitutes.   Saintly pastors of the flock,
like Carlo Borrommeo, carried on a crusade against
these corruptors of public morals.[1]   Even in Venice,
the city of their adoption—the sea-Sodom, as Byron
called it, of carnival licentiousness, the mart of
pleasure for all Europe, the modern Corinth—an
Inquisitor of State scourged them with these words

---

[1] Scherillo, in his book on *La Commedia dell' Arte*, ch. vi., has given
the history of San Carlo's efforts to suppress the theatre at Milan.

of stinging reprobation :[1] " Bear in mind, you actors,
that you are folk beneath the ban of blessed God's
almighty hatred, and that the prince allows you only
as pasture for the common people, who take pleasure
in your ribaldries." With such a record of contempt and disesteem and outlawry, the *Commedia
dell' Arte* was always sinking back into the slime
from which it rose. Unhappily, the same eyes
which delighted in its glory during the years when
genius shed brilliant lustre on its noblest representatives, had only to look on this side or on that, and a
crowd of shameless merry-andrews, the scum and
dregs of the histrionic profession, made the evidences
of its inherent immorality only too apparent.

I have already touched upon the scurrilities and
obscenities which were common in improvised
comedy. To enlarge upon the topic is not necessary. Everybody can perceive that a drama relying
in great part upon buffoonery, restrained by no
obligation to literary precedents, dependent on the
favour of mixed audiences, among whom women
scarcely showed their faces, and varying at each
performance with the whims and humours of masked
actors, who were *ex hypothesi* beyond the pale of
social decency, may have allowed itself licenses
which were well-nigh intolerable.

I have already described the tendencies toward

---

[1] Nicolò Maria Tiepolo, about 1778, quoted by Molmenti in his Essay
on Goldoni, Venezia, Ongania, 1880, p. 68.

exaggerative emphasis, stilted declamation, ill-con-
certed action, impertinent extravaganza, and weari-
some repetition of exhausted motives, to which the
species was peculiarly liable. There is no need to
expand those observations. They justify the severe
remarks of Goldoni in the preface to his theatrical
works, which, as these have a direct bearing upon
the subject of my next essay, I will summarise
here : [1]—" The comic theatre of Italy for more than
a century past had so degenerated that it became
a disgusting object for general abhorrence. You
saw nothing on public stages but indecent harlequinades, dirty and scandalous intrigue, foul jests,
immodest loves. Plots were badly constructed, and
worse carried out in action, without order, without
propriety of manners. If translations of French or
Spanish pieces were given, the improvisatory comedians mutilated and deformed them beyond recognition. The same fate befell the plays of Plautus and
Terence, and of our elder Italian dramatists. People
of culture, nay, the common folk, cried out against
these miserable travesties. Every one was wearied
with the insipidities and conventionalities of an
art upon the wane. You knew what Harlequin or
Pantaloon · was going to say before he opened his
lips."

Readers of Gozzi's Memoirs, to which these pages

---

[1] Pasquali's edition, 1761 ; also, *Teatro Comico*, act i. sc. 2.

serve as a prolusion, have means of judging, on the
testimony of a very partial critic and avowedly
Quixotical defender of the old *Commedia dell' Arte*,
to what extent the system of the theatre in Italy
was faulty. Students of Casanova's Memoirs will
remember the dark picture of the actress whom he
met at Ancona, with her epicene brood of children
and of changelings exposed to indiscriminate contamination.[1] The lighter pages of Goldoni's Memoirs
reveal a spectacle less revolting, but far from edify-
ing, of a comic troupe in its passage from one
Italian capital to another.[2] Leaving these accessible
sources of information regarding the social status of
the dramatic profession in Italy untouched, I will
close this chapter with some extracts from a well-
nigh forgotten book—Garzoni's *Piazza Universale*.
One of the most frequent charges brought against
the acting companies was that they dressed their
women up in men's clothes, and sent them about the
public squares of cities to attract the rabble. " No
sooner have they made their entrance," says Garzoni,
" than the drum beats to let all the world know that
the players are arrived. The first lady of the troupe,
decked out like a man, with a sword in her right
hand, goes round, inviting the folk to a comedy or
tragedy or pastoral in the precincts of the Pelle-

---

[1] *Memoires de Jacques Casanova*, Bruxelles, Rozez, vol. i. ch. 11.

[2] *Memoires de M. Goldoni*, Paris, Veuve Duchesne, 1787, vol. i.
ch. 5.

grino.[1] The populace, inquisitive by nature and
eager for any new thing, hurries to take places.
Paying their pennies down, they crowd into a hall,
where a temporary stage has been erected, the scenes
scrawled with charcoal as chance and want of sense
will have it. An orchestra of tongs and bones, like
the braying of asses or the caterwauling of cats in
February, performs the overture. Then comes a prologue in the manner of a quack-doctor's oration to
his gulls. The piece opens; you behold a Magnifico, who is not worth the quarter of a farthing; a
Zanni, who straddles like a goose; a Gratiano, who
squirts his words out from a clyster-pipe; a lover,
who acts like a narcotic on the senses of his neighbours; a Spanish captain, with nothing but a couple
of musty oaths in his whole repertory; a stupid and
foul-mouthed bawd; a pedant, who trips up in
Tuscan phrases at each turn; a Burattino, whose
whole humour consists in taking off and putting on
his greasy cap; a prima donna, who goes yawning,
drawling, twaddling through her mumbled part, with
eyes well open to the chance of selling her overblown
charms in quite another market than the theatre.
The show is seasoned with loathsome buffooneries
and interludes which ought to send their performers
to the galleys." Enlarging on this theme, Garzoni
proceeds as follows : " These profane comedians

---

[1] A common inn-sign. This reminds us of the earliest performances
of plays in the yards of London hostelries.

pervert the noble use of their ancient art by presenting nothing which is not openly disreputable and
scandalous. The filth which falls continually from
their lips infects themselves and their profession
with the foulest infamy. They are less civil than
donkeys in their action, no better than pimps and
ruffians in their gestures, equal to public prostitutes
in their immodesty of speech. Knavery and lewd-
ness inspire all their motions. In everything they
stink of impudicity and villany. When occasions
offer for veiling grossness under a cloak of decorum,
they do not take these, but pique themselves on bringing beastliness to sight by barefaced bawdry and un-
disguised indecency."

One of the degradations to which these comedians
willingly submitted was that of playing jackals to
quack-doctors on the squares of the Italian cities.
Goldoni in his Memoirs [1] speaks of a certain Buona-
fede Vitali who " maintained at his own cost a troupe
of actors. It was their business to collect the money
thrown to them in pocket-handkerchiefs, and to return
the handkerchiefs filled with pots of ointment and
boxes of pills to the purchasers, after which they performed plays in three acts with a certain kind of
pomp under the light of wax candles." In order to
form a conception of the scenes which were enacted
on an Italian piazza crowded with charlatans,
mountebanks and players, we must have recourse

---

[1] Ed. cit., vol. i. p. 228.

again to Garzoni. It is almost impossible to understand or to reproduce his language at the present day. Sarcastic sallies, which were doubtless piquant in their time, but to which the key has now been lost, abundance of ephemeral slang and racy innuendo, allusions to forgotten people and obsolete customs, topical jests, the coarsest Lombard patois seasoned with the salt of euphuistic rhetoric, all combine to render his motley descriptions untranslatable. Garzoni and writers of his class still lack the pains which Casaubon bestowed on Athenæus, and perhaps their matter is not worthy of such vast expenditure of industry. Yet the pith may be seized ; and following our garrulous cicerone, we stroll out on the piazza. "In one corner of it you will see our swaggering Fortunato and his boon companion Fritata spinning yarns, and keeping the whole populace agape into the night with stories, songs, improvisations, dialogues ; quarrelling, making-up, dying of laughter, coming to blows again, bustling about their stage, settling the dispute by fisticuffs and violent language, and lastly handing round the cap to reap the harvest of the pennies they have earned. In another corner, Burattino sets up his bray of brass. You would think that the hangman had got hold of you, to hear him yell into your ears. He carries a scavenger's bag and a common sailor's cap, and screams until the whole world gathers around him. The people crowd, the groundlings jostle, men of quality press

forward to the platform. When the burlesque prologue comes to a conclusion, Burattino's master puts
in his appearance. It is our old friend the Doctor,
with his Bolognese jargon, long-winded citations,
insipid tomfooleries, and absurd pretensions to omni-
science. The droning of this arrant humbug drives
as many of the audience away as the zany's merry
pranks and roguish whiskers and apish tricks have
drawn together. Meanwhile the curtains of the
booth open, and the Tuscan comes forth with his
tumbling girl. He begins some silly story in the
Florentine tongue, during which the girl draws her
circle and puts herself in position, straddling with
arms and legs abroad, flinging her body backwards
to pick up a piece of money with her mouth from
two crossed swords, and tickling the greasy varlets
of the market-place by the exhibition of her lascivious
graces. Not far away, you may see the Milanese
quack, dressed like a noble gentleman, velvet cap on
head and white Guelf feathers waving to the wind.
He is telling his man Gradello some story of his
hapless love. The groom cuts indecent jokes and
gibes in the background ; then swaggers forward,
twirls his moustachioes, vows to uphold his master's
cause against all rivals, and bristles like an enraged
bloodhound ; but, on a sudden, feigning to see foe-
men near, he drops his arms, knocks his knees together, befouls his breeches on the stage, and lets
himself be soundly drubbed. When that interlude

is over, Gradello acts another part.   He is a blind man
squalling out a ditty, and thrumming on a puppy in
his lap instead of a theorbo.   The climax of all
this buffoonery is a panegyric of some famous pills,
which lasts an hour or two, and leaves the charlatan
wrangling over cents and farthings with his swiftly
dwindling audience.   Toward evening the crowd of
quacks and blind musicians and acrobats thicken.
Here is Zan della Vigna with his performing monkey;
there Catullo and his guitar; in another corner
the Mantuan merry-andrew, dressed up like a zany,
Zottino singing an ode to the pox, and the pretty
Sicilian rope-dancer.   Tamburino spins eggs on
a stick; the Neapolitan capers about with brim-
ming bowls of water on his pate; and Maestro Paolo
da Arezzo makes his solemn entry with a waving
banner, on which you see St. Paul, holding a huge
falchion in one hand, while the rest of the field is
painted over with twining hissing serpents.   The
mountebank clears his throat and relates his fabulous pedigree.   St. Paul was his great ancestor, and
ever since that accident upon the island of Malta, all
the family have possessed miraculous powers over the
snaky tribe.   Hereupon boxes are opened, and horrid
vipers, water-snakes, and adders are drawn forth to
the terror of the bystanders.   'Do not be afraid,' con-
tinues Maestro Paolo; 'I have delivered your fields
and woods from these plagues and their poison.'
The trembling country-lads creep up and buy a box

of powders from the condescending hands of the
impostor. After the sight of all those asps and
crocodiles, stuffed basilisks, tarantulas, and Indian
armadilloes, there is not one of them would venture
out into the country lanes without a prophylactic.
Meanwhile, Settecervelli has laid his mantle on the
pavement, and is making his little bitch go through
her tricks, bark at the worst-dressed fellow in the
circle, howl at the name of the Grand Turk, dance
for joy in honour of her master's sweetheart, and
carry round the cap for pennies in her mouth. The
Parmesan is not to be outdone by these performances ;
he has his nanny-goat, whose antics are at least as
sight-worthy as the puppy's. The Turkish athlete
climbs the campanile, lets his brawny chest be ham-
mered like an anvil, dislodges a stout pillar by the
strength of his huge arms and shoulders, and wins a
bag of coppers heavy enough to pay his expenses to
the holy town of Mecca. The baptized Jew wails in a
lamentable tone of voice, *goi, goi, badanai, badanai,*
till he has attracted a crowd round him ; then he
tells the romance of his conversion to the true faith,
which leaves a strong impression on our mind that
if he has become a sincere Christian, which is more
than doubtful, he has certainly not lost the arts of
an accomplished cheat. Soon the whole piazza is
swarming with folk of this sort ; pills and powders,
for all the ills that flesh is heir to, are being hawked
about ; men are eating fire, and swallowing tow, and

pulling yards of twine from their throats, and washing their faces in molten lead, and finding cards in
the pockets of their unsuspecting neighbours ; every
conceivable article, which ingenuity can force on the
attention of simpletons, is flirted in one's face, and
vaunted with a deafening din by hoarse and squeak-
ing salesmen."

Garzoni has carried us somewhat astray from the
main subject of this essay. Yet it is not amiss to
have gained a full conception of the medium out
of which the *Commedia dell' Arte* emerged, and into
which it always tended to relapse, as well as of the
various low and ignoble branches of industry with
which the players were associated.

Part III.

GOZZI'S DRAMATIC FABLES, OR FIABE TEATRALI;
TOGETHER WITH A BRIEF HISTORY OF HIS
QUARREL WITH GOLDONI AND CHIARI.

1. Venice in the last century—The Liberals and Conservatives—Invasion of French theories in politics, philosophy, and social manners—Prevalence of French taste in literature—Conservative resistance to this revolutionary state of things.—2. Carlo Goldoni and Carlo Gozzi—Popularity of French sentimental dramas—The Academy of the Granelleschi founded in 1747 by literary Conservatives, to restore a taste for pure Italian style, and to promote the study of the Tuscan classics—Carlo Gozzi belongs to this Academy, and becomes one of its chief supporters—Goldoni, and the qualities of his genius—His perception that nature has to be closely followed in the drama.—3. A sketch of Goldoni's career, and of the steps whereby he became a professional playwright—Settles at Venice in 1747 as poet to Medebac's company—Goldoni's Venetian comedies, comedies in the French manner, melodramas—Goldoni's rivalry with the Abbé Chiari—Chiari's bombastic pseudo-Pindaric style—Martellian verses.—4. Indignation of the Granelleschi with both Goldoni and Chiari—Carlo Gozzi confounds them in one common hatred as corruptors of the language—His particular dislike for Goldoni, who had declared war against the *Commedia dell' Arte*, of which Gozzi professed himself the champion—Publication of Gozzi's satirical poem *La Tartana degli Influssi* in 1756—Return of Sacchi's company of impromptu comedians to Venice in that year—Vigorous warfare carried on by the Granelleschi against both Goldoni and Chiari during the next four years—Gozzi first shows his dramatic faculty in a severe Aristophanic satire upon Goldoni, entitled *Il Teatro Comico*—Chiari makes up his differences with Goldoni, and both playwrights now join forces against their conservative antagonists—Chiari defies the Granelleschi to produce a comedy—

Goldoni appeals from their criticisms to the public, who idolise him—
Gozzi determines to write a satirical play upon a nursery-tale, which
shall prove no less popular than Goldoni's comedies—The *Amore
delle Tre Melarancie* appears in January 1761—The true character
of Carlo Gozzi's dramatic fables—It is a mistake to suppose that
he was actuated by spontaneous Romantic genius—His affinity
with the elder Tuscan burlesque poets—His wish to rehabilitate
the Comedy of Masks—His conservative and didactic spirit.—
5. A translation of Gozzi's own account of *The Love of the Three
Oranges*, important in the history of the *Commedia dell' Arte*, and
illustrative of the way in which Gozzi handled his fabulous
material.—6. Success of *L'Amore delle Tre Melarancie*—Production and dates of the remaining nine dramatic *Fiabe.*—7. Gozzi's
method of writing, and employment of the Four Masks and the
Servetta—Interweaving of the comic element with the fairy-tale—
Gozzi does not rise to the height of imaginative poetry.—8. His
satire, humour, feeling for poetic situations—His conservative
philosophy of life.—9. Sources of the *Fiabe*—The artistic superi-
ority of *L'Amore delle Tre Melarancie.*—10. Analysis of *L'Augellino Belverde.*—11. Gozzi's temporary success—Goldoni retires to
Paris, and Chiari to Brescia—Posterity has reversed the verdict of
contemporary Venice—Fate of the *Fiabe*—Vicissitudes of Gozzi's
fame in Italy, Germany, France—Paul de Musset's condensed
abstract of the Memoirs, and their distorted picture of Carlo Gozzi.

I.

ABOUT the middle of the eighteenth century, Venetian society was divided into two main parties, re-
presenting what we should now call Liberal and
Conservative principles in politics and thought.
The Liberals were imbued with French philosophical ideas, French fashions, and French phrases.
The boldest of them, men like Angelo Querini,
Carlo Contarini, Giorgio Pisani, openly aimed at
remodelling the constitution. They aired new-

fangled theories of government, based upon the
Social Contract and the Rights of Man, within ear-
shot of the terrible Inquisition of State. · Some of
them went in consequence to end their days in
the dungeons of Cattaro or Verona. These patricians created a body of restless opposition in the
Grand Council, agitated the bourgeoisie and proletariate with the expectation of impending changes,
and succeeded in effecting some salutary but superficial reforms. Outside the sphere of politics, that
spirit of innovation which in France was silently but
surely working toward the Revolution, made itself
felt among the educated classes. The University of
Padua, while preserving external forms of mediæ-
valism in its discipline and teaching, fermented with
the physical hypotheses of modern science. The
deism of the Encyclopædists and Voltaire came into
vogue. Sentimentalism, thinly cloaking a desire
for liberty and license, ruled in morals. Rousseau's
speculations and the humanitarian utopias of the
philosophes disturbed the old foundations on which
social institutions rested. The word *prejudice* was
upon the lips of everybody, to indicate the restraining
influences of public order in the state and of ethics
in the family. These new ideas permeated society
and saturated literature. In the drawing-rooms
of great ladies, the clubs and coffee-houses of
the gentry, the theatres, concert-rooms, and little
houses, where men and women congregated, French

books were discussed, French fashions were affected, the French language was engrafted on the old Venetian dialect.   Frivolous butterflies of pleasure in that great mart of the world's amusement assumed fine airs of philosophy and science.   Wide-sweeping and far-reaching theories, which called in question the whole groundwork of man's previous beliefs, were freely ventilated by chatterers, who caught their jargon from flippant manuals of science and popular essays, poured forth by thousands from the press of Paris.   Unhealthy novels spread subversive moral doctrines flavoured with a spice of philanthropic sentiment.   It was considered *rococo* to admire the old Italian classics.   Staunch Liberals paraded their independence of precedent and prejudice by adopting a masquerade style which set the traditions of the language at defiance.

All this indicated a deep and irresistible fermentation in society.   The great catastrophe of the eighteenth century was preparing.   The stage of Europe was being made ready for that transformation-scene which opened a new era.   But few could foresee the inevitable future; few could distinguish what was wholesome progress from the delirious or somnambulistic ravings of the moment.   Therefore the Conservatives clung fast to their prejudices and precedents; to established forms of government, the national religion, the traditional customs of civil and domestic life.   To superficial observers it appeared that these

men held the strongest cards. Yet even rigid Conservatives were bound to admit that there was something ominously rotten in the state of Venice.   Her
commerce dwindled year by year.   Her provinces
were ill administered, and yielded less and less to
the exchequer.   Social demarcations disappeared in
the luxury and corruption which invaded all classes.
Pauperism assumed appalling dimensions.   In the
decay of industries and manufactures thousands of
workpeople were thrown famished upon public charity.
The ranks of the Barnabotti, or impoverished nobles,
who claimed state support, swelled, grew clamorous in
the Grand Council, gave signs of insubordination, and
contaminated the fountain-head of government by
their venality.   Meanwhile, the old machinery of the
constitution had fallen into the hands of a close oli-
garchy or commission of a few powerful patricians.
These corruptors of the State pulled wires, bought
votes, and manipulated the College and the Senate
to secure their own ends in the Consiglio Grande.
The more far-sighted among the Conservatives felt
the necessity of temporising.   Influenced by the all-
pervasive spirit of the age, but not prepared to join
the Liberal forces, they compromised, tampered with
institutions, and tried by stopping leaks to keep the
deep sea out.   This was the attitude of men like
Marco Foscarini, Alvise Emo, and Paolo Renier.

Apart from politics, the Conservatives stood on
firmer ground.   There is no doubt that the so-called

philosophy of the eighteenth century, both in its principles and in its consequences, offered points of patent
weakness to hostile criticism.   It was subversive
without being reconstructive.   Its foundations were
sentimental and fanciful rather than logical and
reasoned.   Hazy in the minds of its projectors, it
was almost universally misunderstood by the multitude which it illuded.   Immorality was encouraged ;
not that any speculative system is inherently immoral,
but that the confused postulates regarding personal
liberty, the right of private judgment in matters of
conduct, the light of Nature, and the tyranny of
custom and prejudice, from which this philosophy
started, enabled foolish or ill-minded people to hide
their vices and caprices beneath the specious mask
of systematic thinking.   Again, the literature which
sprang into existence under the predominance of
such theories, was in some respects pernicious, and
in many points of view ridiculous.   The Conservatives had a definite course before them when they
determined to vindicate the purity of Italian diction,
to maintain the traditions of a glorious past in art, and
to expose the foibles of the Liberal school of thinkers
and of writers.

II.

This brings me to the proper subject of the present
chapter, which is the conflict of Liberalism with

Conservatism in the theatre at Venice. The two protagonists are Carlo Goldoni and Carlo Gozzi, both Venetians, and both of nearly the same age. Goldoni was born in 1707, Gozzi in 1720. Gozzi entered the lists against Goldoni in 1756, when the latter had been working for the Venetian stage since 1748, and when he had already turned the heads of the public by his brilliant dramatic novelties.

The old *Commedia dell' Arte*, as we have seen, had sunk into decrepitude. It was not merely that the type itself was exhausted, though subsequent circumstances proved this to be the case. What was more important is, that the popular taste veered round against it. Under the prevailing dominance of French fashions, a style of drama, hitherto unknown to the Italians, came into vogue. The so-called *Comédie Larmoyante*, or pathetic comedy (of which Nivelle de la Chaussée, a now-forgotten archimage of middle-class sentimentalities and sensibilities, is the reputed inventor), caught the ear of Europe. The Père la Chaussée, to adopt an epigram of Piron's, preached every evening from his pulpit in a score of theatres through Europe. The titles of his most famous plays, *Mélanide, La Gouvernante, Préjugé à la Mode, L'École des Mères*, remind us of the revolution in the drama which converted the public stage from a place of amusement into a platform for the dissemination of political or social sentiments. Saurin's *Beverley*, Mercier's *Déserteur* and *L'Indigent*, De

Falbaire's *Honnête Criminel,* Voltaire's *Écossaise,*
Diderot's *Père de Famille,* carried on La Chaussée's
tradition.   Regarding their popularity at Venice,
enough is related in the verbose and bilious diatribes
prefixed by Gozzi to his dramatic works.   Among
plays of this description, an adaptation of our
George Barnwell—much in the style of Thackeray's
parody upon Lord Lytton's novels—attracted great
attention by the pathos with which a nephew murdering his uncle from the highest motives was
exalted to the rank of hero.   The Conservatives not
unjustly protested against the contamination of
public morals by the false sentiment of these tearful
dramas.   The perversion of taste by low domestic
arguments and clumsy realism, which had nothing
real but its vulgarity, seemed to them no less a sin.

They were particularly sensitive, moreover, upon
the point of language, diction, style.   Translations
and adaptations of French plays confirmed the growing
carelessness of authors.   Gallicisms were so fashionable that a stage-hack allowed himself all license in
that direction.   The jargon of science introduced
unheard-of phrases, which would have made the
fathers of the Della-Cruscan Academy shudder in
their tombs.   Moreover, the prevalent affectation of
independence and the fashionable revolt against
prejudice led ignorant scribblers to plume themselves upon their solecisms and plebeian lapses into
dialect.

. With the main object, therefore, of maintaining a standard of propriety in style, and with the secondary object of opposing theatrical innovations, the Venetian Conservatives (in literature) founded their Academy de' Granelleschi. It came into existence about 1747; and I need not enlarge upon its constitution, except to say that it was an academy of the good old Tory type, like the *Gelati*, *Sonnacchiosi*, *Storditi*, and so many scores of literary clubs with absurd names and trivial customs, whose members wasted their time over pedantic studies, and occasionally issued a piece of solid work among their otherwise ephemeral transactions. A sufficient account of this Academy is given in Gozzi's Memoirs. Its importance at the present moment is that out of this little camp Carlo Gozzi marched like David to attack the Goliath of Philistinism, Carlo Goldoni.

It is difficult to speak adequately and fairly of Goldoni. In making this man, Nature cast her glove down in the face of criticism, and defied analysis. He possessed indubitable genius; what is more, his genius obeyed generous enthusiasms, unselfish aims, pure-hearted sentiments. He perceived instinctively and correctly that a new age was dawning for the literature of Europe. He devoted his life to creating a comic drama adequate to the intellectual dignity of his nation. Goldoni was a good man, a modest man, a man complete in all the social virtues. But he was not a great man. And his genius, that

innovatory force of his, that infinite adaptability,
that inexhaustible scenic faculty which he possessed,
that intuition into the necessity of change, was, after
all, a genius of thin and threadbare quality. Can we
point to a single masterpiece produced by Goldoni?
After allowing the sediment to settle down of
his prolific works and various experiments, can we
select any one play which bears the stamp of the
supreme master? I think not. I shrink from placing
Goldoni, as a peer, in the company of Shakespeare,
Molière, Calderon, and Schiller. But, while saying
this, it is impossible to deny his actual achievement.
It is impossible not to recognise the honest motives
which prompted him to copy Nature's book. That
was his great discovery; and that keeps the memory
of Goldoni ever green among us. He saw that Nature
had to be loved and studied and followed by the
artist. He discerned this luminous point in a period
befogged by prejudice, tradition, pedantry, conven-
tionality, subservience to antiquated humours and
insurgent eccentricities. It was not Goldoni's fault
that birth and fortune denied him those higher capacities and favourable openings which might have
made his art-work monumental. His genial, shifty,
pliable, and yet persistent personality was forced to
humour obstacles and to fawn on circumstance. As an
inevitable consequence, his productions are mediocre
and unsatisfactory. Mediocrity of talent and of
character is stamped upon his plays, and self-revealed

in his good-humoured Memoirs. But what confounds criticism is that this mediocrity in the man and his equipment was combined with undeniable originality. His genius, though not of the purest water, was genuine. He had a correct perception of the requirements of his age, a clear intuition into the practical possibilities of the dramatic art he handled, and a vivid consciousness of the ground-principle that no artist can afford to lose sight of reality in practice. What would Goldoni not have been, we say, after summing up the survey of his qualities, had he been gifted with a finer fibre, a wider range of knowledge, a deeper philosophy, a more robust temper, a poetic talent equal to the task of externalising his just perceptions in forms of meditated art? As it is, he presents the curious spectacle of a man born to inaugurate a new epoch, but without the faculty to impose his own ideal successfully upon his contemporaries. The general public acclaimed him, and understood his aims. But the aristocrats of literature were able to inflict telling blows in their fight against him. We, who stand aloof, when all the dust of that conflict has subsided, see that Goldoni really won the day. It is only to be regretted that a champion of such small dimensions, soft heart, and feeble sinews, was commissioned to effect the revolution.

III.

Goldoni's instinct led him by an irresistible bias to the stage. He vainly attempted to form himself for the more lucrative profession of the law. During his youth he studied at a college in Pavia, but was expelled for giving free vent to his literary propensities in satire. He practised as an advocate at the Venetian bar, practised at Pisa in the same capacity, acted as Genoese Consul at Venice. Still though he courted Themis, his real predilections drew him toward Thalia. The first piece which revealed his leading talent was a comedy in outline ; *Il Gondoliere Veneziano*, represented at Milan in 1733. In the next year he produced a painfully bad tragedy at Verona entitled *Belisario*. Several pieces of a mixed character, between comedy and tragedy, followed. Yet he had not taken to the theatre as a profession ; and it was not until the year 1746, when he joined the comic company of Medebac, at Leghorn, in the capacity of their paid playwright, that he entered definitely upon the career of author for the stage.

During the years when Goldoni was thus wavering between law and literature, he attempted many kinds of dramatic composition—operettas for music, tragedies, tragi-comedies, farces, *scenari* for improvised

comedies, and comedies of which the dialogue was
partly written. His facile talent adapted itself to
every style in turn. All this while he recognised that
his strength lay neither in the direction of poetry nor
in that of serious drama. Nature had bestowed on
him a genius for comedy; and he felt born to edu-
cate Italian taste in that species. We have already
seen how deeply he deplored the degeneration of the
Commedia dell' Arte; and yet some of his pieces
had been performed by the best improvisatory actors
then alive, Sacchi the famous Truffaldino, and Darbes
the no less celebrated Pantalone.

While scribbling Harlequinades, Goldoni never
lost sight of the reform he had long meditated;
and this was to substitute written comedies of
character, in the style of Molière and the ancients,
for the old comedies *all' improvviso*. But he saw
the necessity of proceeding cautiously. On the
one hand, he had to consider the adherents of the
elder style. On the other hand, he was forced
to humour the comedians, who were jealous of
changes which increased their dependence upon
professional playwrights.[1] Accordingly, he advanced
with circumspection. In the *Momolo Cortesan*,
which he composed for the Pantalone of Sacchi's
company (a certain Golinetti), only the leading
part was written. The rest was left to improvisa-

---

[1] See his Mémoires, part i. ch. 40.

tion. Nevertheless, this piece was constructed on different principles from those which governed the *Commedia dell'Arte*. It aimed at being a comedy of character ; and thus Goldoni hoped by gradual steps to wean his actors from their bad old ways. Copying his mistress Nature, he saw that nothing could be done *per saltum*. It was necessary to prepare transitions, and to pass through the development of imperfect species to the exhibition of the type he had in view. This seems to have been the principle on which he acted. But Goldoni was so pliable and easy-going, so apt to take the cue from casual suggestions offered to his versatile ability, that he frequently lost sight of this leading principle. His Muse wore Harlequin's robe of many colours, and assumed the mask while waiting to effect the meditated revolution. This indecision at the commencement of his career exposed him to Gozzi's piratical attacks, and exercised, I think, a prejudicial influence over his subsequent career as playwright. But it was not in the character of the man to act otherwise. He could not divest himself of ready sympathy, fluency, and genial adaptability to the circumstances in which he was placed from time to time. Some natures are destined to achieve their ends by condescension. Goldoni's was essentially a nature of this kind. And the fact remains that, amid all his excursions into regions alien from his purpose, he kept one aim in view and finally achieved it. What survives of solid

in his work, is the select series of plays produced
upon the lines of the reform he calculated.

It was at Pisa in 1746 that the *Capocomico*
Medebac induced Goldoni to join his troupe. The
proposal was that a theatre at Venice should be hired
for five or six years, and that Goldoni should dedi-
cate his whole talents to the composition of plays.
Sufficiently good pecuniary offers were made; for it
seems that each comedy was paid at the rate of thirty
sequins, or about £12 sterling. Goldoni accepted.
Then travelling with his new partners by the road
through Modena, he reached Venice in July 1747.
His first venture, with a play called *Tognetto* or
Tonino bela grazia, was a failure. A couple of
pathetic pieces which followed, won more favour
with the public. Darbes, whom Goldoni learned to
appreciate and use with excellent effect, seconded
his efforts admirably; and in 1748 circumstances
seemed propitious for attempting the long-cherished
scheme of a revolution in the theatre. Accordingly
he wrote the *Vedova Scaltra*, which is distinctly a
comedy of character. It was performed during the
carnival season of 1749, and was received with intelligent sympathy by the Venetians. This induced
Goldoni to pursue the course he had begun. *La
Putta Onorata* obtained a similar success, and
met with emphatic approval from the gondolier
class, whose sentiments and manners had been
studied in its composition. Goldoni's novelties had

by this time roused the jealousy of rivals and the opposition of Conservatives.   A parody of the *Vedova
Scaltra* appeared at the theatre of S. Samuele.   This
was clever enough, and scurrilous enough, to attract
attention.   Goldoni received a check in mid-career,
which became serious when the Carnival of 1749
closed with the total failure of a new piece from his
pen, *L'Erede Fortunata*.   Upon this occasion, stung
to the quick, and piqued in his self-esteem, with the
sense of his own inexhaustible and facile forces
rendering the hazard light, Goldoni publicly declared his intention of producing sixteen new comedies within the next twelve calendar months.

He kept his promise, but at a considerable cost
both to his position as playwright and his health.
With the general public, the man's indomitable
pluck, his good-humour, and the variety of subjects
treated in his famous sixteen plays, created an indescribable enthusiasm.   The end of the Carnival,
1750, brought well-earned laurels to Goldoni, together with the good-will of the fickle multitude.
But unforgiving enemies, the supporters of the old
drama, the literary purists, and the Conservatives
who could not stomach sentimental comedies, were
watching him with Argus eyes.   In the heat of volcanic combustion, he had thrown up cinders and
rubbish along with several felicitous and brilliant
works of art.   The worst of his performances were
remembered and scored up against him by critics

TARTAGLIA (1620)

Illustrating the Italian Commedia dell' Arte, or Impromptu Comedy

like Carlo Gozzi.   The best were confounded in one plausible condemnation.

From this point forward for the next six years Goldoni met with no formidable opposition, except from a rival playwright. The man in question was the Abbé Chiari, a relic of the seventeenth century, pompous and bombastic in style, a blatant member of the Arcadian Academy, a bastard brother of Pindar in the matter of mixed metaphors and wild Icarian flights, a prolific scribbler of melodramatic pieces in rhymed Martellian verses,[1] and, after all his qualifications are summed up, a mere pretentious windbag. Chiari caught the public ear.   Venice divided itself into factions for Chiari and Goldoni.   On a smaller scale, the Bononcini and Handel conflicts of London, the Gluck and Piccini riots of Paris, were repeated. The most damaging feature of this contest for Goldoni,

---

[1] This is perhaps the proper place to explain the meaning of Martellian verses.   They owe their name to Pier Jacopo Martelli (1665–1725), who revived them, and used them for the drama.   Metrically speaking, Martellian verses are twelve-syllable lines of the Alexandrine type.   These long lines had been commonly employed in Italy during the thirteenth century, before the heroic verse of eleven syllables obtained ascendancy.   It is difficult to say why the Alexandrine, which Italy in the thirteenth century shared with France, died out in the former country and became the standard heroic line of the latter.   Possibly the reason may be found in the Italian tendency toward double rhymes ; the so-called *versi piani* of Dante being decasyllabic iambics with a redundant syllable rather than hendecasyllabics.   Anyhow, the Alexandrine has not flourished south of the Alps.   Martelli's revival did not prosper ; and Carducci, in his *Su' Campi di Marengo* (*Nuove Poesie*, p. 91), is the only recent poet who has attempted them with success.

was that Chiari, less gifted with originality, aped each
of his new inventions. Against Goldoni's *Pamela
Nubile* Chiari brought out a *Pamela Maritata*, against
his *Avventuriere Onorato* an *Avventuriere alla Moda*,
against his *Padre per Amore* an *Inganno Amoroso*,
against his *Molière* a *Molière marito geloso*, against
his *Terenzio* a *Plauto*, against his *Sposa Persiana* a
Schiava Chinese, against his *Filosofo Inglese* a *Filosofo Veneziano*, against his *Scozzese* a *Bella Pelle-
grina*. In spite of their mutual hostility, this game of
battledore and shuttlecock between Chiari and Goldoni enabled the literary Conservatives to regard both
playwrights as flying under one flag. But before the
Granelleschi opened fire in earnest, Venetian society
continued for five years to be pretty equally divided
in its sympathies. The best judges sided with Goldoni, while Chiari's glaring faults, which passed for
brilliant qualities with the vulgar, won him numerous
admirers. Carlo Gozzi has described this state of
contention : [1]

> " I partigiani ogni giorno crescevano,
> Chi vuole *Originale* et chi *Saccheggio ;*
> Tutto il paese a romore mettevano,
> Sicchè la cosa non è da motteggio.
> Nelle case i fratelli contendevano,
> Le mogli co' mariti facean peggio,
> In ogni loco acerba è la tenzone,
> Tutto è scompiglio, tutto è dissensione."

---

[1] *Opere*, ed. 1772, tom. viii. p. 27. " The partisans on both sides
gathered forces daily. One swears by *Original* (a name for Goldoni),
the other by *Plunder* (Chiari, because of his plagiarisms). The whole

IV.

The Granelleschi, in their zeal for sound literature, were justly enraged against the ranting, arrogant, bombastic Chiari. Although the more discreet Academicians, men like Gasparo Gozzi, recognised Goldoni's merits, they resented his slovenly and slipshod style. Carlo Gozzi, less tolerant and far more satirical than his elder brother, confounded both poets in a common loathing. This was obviously unfair to Goldoni, who, whatever his faults of diction may have been, ranked immeasurably higher than the Abbé. But Goldoni was guilty of an unpardonable sin in Gozzi's eyes. He had declared war against the *Commedia dell'Arte*, for which Gozzi entertained the partiality of one who was himself an excellent impromptu actor. The other reasons of this bitter hatred are sufficiently explained in those chapters of the Memoirs which describe the beginning of his career as playwright.

At last Gozzi thought the time had come for striking a decisive blow.[1] The Granelleschi professed

---

city was turned upside down, and indeed it is no laughing matter. Brothers fought with brothers, wives did worse with their husbands. Everywhere the wrangling was fierce ; nought but confusion, nought but discord."

[1] The details of the controversy between Gozzi and Goldoni are given at fuller length than I have attempted in Signor Ernesto Masi's masterly Introduction to his edition of the *Fiabe Teatrali*.

sincere admiration for an obscure burlesque Florentine
poet of the fifteenth century called Burchiello. Taking some of this man's enigmatical sentences for
prophecies, Gozzi compiled a sort of comic almanac,
in which the various woes impending over Venice
in the year 1756 were described. It was entitled *La
Tartana degl' Influssi per l'anno bisestile* 1756,[1] and
was modelled upon an almanac for country-folk, published at Treviso under the name of a certain Schieson.[2]
For each quarter of the year a *capitolo* in *terza rima*
was written, and a prophecy in octave stanzas was
dedicated to each month. Although the *Tartana* contained satires upon society in general, a considerable
part was directed specially against Chiari and
Goldoni. The introductory address to the readers
strikes the keynote. The month of February deals
with comedies, the month of November with Martellian verses, and the month of December invokes the
speedy return of Sacchi and his company of masks
from Portugal. Finally, in the sonnet addressed
to the bookseller at the end of the book, the two
poets are mentioned by name. Gozzi declared himself an implacable enemy of the plays in vogue, an

---

[1] *Opere*, vol. viii. *Tartana* is a large merchant vessel.
[2] The editor of this Venetian Zadkiel was originally Giovanni Pozzo-
bon. After his death it was continued by Giambattista Bada. Pozzo-
bon was nicknamed Schieson. The almanac was adorned with a
ridiculous portrait of a doctor in a huge wig. Owing to this fact,
Schieson came to signify any one with rumpled hair. See Boerio's
Dizionario del Dialetto Veneziano.

opponent of rhymed verses imitating the French
Alexandrine measure, and a zealous adherent of the
old *Commedia dell' Arte*. The prophecy with regard
to Sacchi's company was speedily fulfilled ; for the
earthquake of Lisbon happening in 1755, they were
obliged to quit the scene of that lugubrious disaster.
Soon after their return to Venice, Gozzi appears to
have courted their friendship. This we gather from
the *Canto Ditirambico de' Partigiani del Sacchi
Truffaldino* which he published in 1761.[1]

Irritated by the *Tartana degli Influssi*, Goldoni,
who usually kept silence under literary attacks, took
up the pen and wrote as follows :[2]—

> " Ho veduta stampata una Tartana
>   Piena di versi rancidi sciapiti,
>   Versi da spaventare una befana,
> Versi dal saggio imitator conditi
>   Con sale acuto della maladicenza,
>   Piena di falsi sentimenti arditi ;
> Ma conceder si può questa licenza
>   A chi in collera va colla fortuna,
>   Che per lui non ha molta compiacenza.
> Chi dice mal senza ragione alcuna,
>   Chi non prova gli assunti e gli argomenti,
>   Fa come il can che abbaia alla luna."

· [1] Opere, vol. viii. p. 164.

[2] The original exists in MS. at the Marcian Library. Goldoni wrote
the poem on the occasion of S. E. Bastian Venier's return from the
rectorship of Bergamo. When he reprinted it in the edition of his
poetical works (Pasquali, Venezia, 1764), he omitted the passage referring
to Gozzi's *Tartana*. The lines above are given in Magrini's and Masi's
essays. I add a translation. "I have seen a certain *Tartana* in print,
full of rancid and insipid verses, verses bad enough to terrify a goblin,
verses seasoned by the wise plagiary with acrid salt of evil-speaking, full

I have transcribed these verses for several reasons ; first, that my readers may judge for themselves of Goldoni's poetical style ; secondly, because the last six lines profoundly irritated Gozzi ; and thirdly, because they engaged him in the production of his first semi-dramatic pasquinade upon their author.

We need not describe the battle of sonnets, squibs, and pamphlets which raged after the appearance of Gozzi's *Tartana*. The Granelleschi were now committed to crush their antagonists ; and they spared no pains to do so. Men of birth and parts condescended to the filthiest ribaldry and the most savage personalities. On the whole, it must be allowed that the Granelleschi displayed superior wit and style. Gozzi, in particular, showed real powers for burlesque satire in his *Marfisa Bizzarra ;* and some of his occasional pieces are composed with a terseness and directness worthy of the classical age of Florentine literature. Goldoni replied from time to time, but feebly. In a poem entitled *La Tavola Rotonda,* he described his formidable antagonist as :[1]

> " Un Lombardo che affetta esser cruscante
> Col riso in bocca e col veleno in petto."

of false arrogant sentiments. One can, however, condone this licence in one who is out of temper with Fortune, she being not greatly well-affected toward him. He who speaks evil without any reason shown, he who does not prove his assumptions and his arguments, acts like the dog who barks against the moon."

[1] It was written for the marriage of Contarini Venier. "A Lombard who pretends to be a Della Cruscan, with a smile on his lips and venom in his heart."

This seems to me a fair, if somewhat pungent, description of Carlo Gozzi, who, in spite of his theoretical purism, rarely succeeded in writing with correctness or distinction, and who veiled a really caustic temper under the mask of Democritean philosophy. Touching upon the charges brought against himself of being neither a scholar nor a poet, Goldoni admits their truth with frankness: [1]

> " Pur troppo io so che buon scrittor non sono
> E che ai fonti miglior non ho bevuto ;
> Qual mi detta il mio stil scrivo e ragiono,
> E talor per fortuna ho anch' io piaciuto ;
> Ma guai a me se il fiorentin frullone
> A sceverare i scritti miei si pone."

Strong in the unwavering appreciation of the public, and confident in his own powers, Goldoni could afford to make this concession to his antagonist. But it argued a generous and modest mind, different in quality from Gozzi's.

Meanwhile Gozzi took up the glove of defiance thrown down by Goldoni in his *Tavola Rotonda*. A sonnet referring to that poem contains these lines: [2]

> " Ma acciò s'abbia a decidere
> S'io dissi il ver, sto facendo un comento,
> Che proverà l'assunto e l'argomento."

---

[1] "Only too well I know that I am not a good writer, and that I never drank at the best fountains. I write and reason as my style dictates, and sometimes by good chance I also have afforded pleasure. But woe to me if the Florentine sieve should be applied to sifting my productions."

[2] *Opere*, vol. viii. p. 183. "I am engaged in preparing a commentary which shall prove both the assumption and the argument."

This *Comento* led Gozzi eventually to the production
of his *Fiabe*. But a step or two remained to be
taken before Gozzi resolved to meet Goldoni on his
own ground, the theatre.

He began by circulating a satirical piece entitled
*Il Teatro Comico all' Osteria del Pellegrino tra le
mani degli Accademici Granelleschi*, or "The Comic
Theatre at the Inn of the Pilgrim, rough-handled by
the Granelleschi." Gozzi's Memoirs contain a sufficient description of this satire, which still exists in
MS. at the Marcian Library. They also explain why
he withdrew it from publication at the request of his
friend Farsetti and Goldoni's patron Count Widman.
Therefore it is not necessary to discuss it here in
detail : yet the meaning of the title may be pointed
out. Goldoni had already produced a comedy, called
Il Teatro Comico, setting forth his views regarding
the reform of the drama.[1] Gozzi, alluding to this
play, undertakes to expose the faults of Goldoni's own
theatrical writings. The satire is conceived in the
broad spirit of Aristophanic or Rabelaisian humour,
and is really a masterpiece in its kind. We feel for
the first time that Gozzi has found his proper sphere
by the breadth of handling, the free play of humour,
and the precision of touch, which reveal an inborn
dramatic faculty. The unmasking of the vociferous

---

[1] *Il Teatro Comico* was the first of the famous sixteen comedies of
1749-50. The list of the pieces to be expected was announced in it.
See Goldoni's *Memoirs*, part i. ch. 7.

four-faced monster which caricatured Goldoni, is eminently fit for scenical effect. While reading, we seem to be present at a new act in Jonson's *Poetaster*. The four mouths of the four-faced mask represent the four kinds of dramas written by Goldoni—his early harlequinades and *scenari*, his domestic comedy of the pathetic species, his heroic and Oriental melodramas, and his transcripts from Venetian life. A fifth mouth, the mouth in the belly, *la veridica bocca dell' epa*, as Gozzi terms it, utters Goldoni's personal aims and views, as Gozzi chose brutally to interpret them. This truthful witness confesses that all the four mouths of the masked head were subservient to its carnal needs. *Quis expedivit psittaco suum* χαῖρε? . . . *Magister artis ingeniquc largitor, Venter negatas artifex sequi voces.* "Who taught the parrot his word of welcome? That master of art and liberal dispenser of genius, the belly." That motto from the prologue to Persius' book of satires might be inscribed on the title-page of Gozzi's pasquinade. The blow inflicted, in a literal and metaphorical sense, below the belt, was unworthy of a gentleman. It betrayed Gozzi's critical insensibility to Goldoni's actual merits. It exhibited his aristocratic contempt for professional literature, combined with his comedian's readiness to take advantage of a powerful opponent. But it also revealed a literary athlete capable of striking home, and whose method of attack was certain to be formidable.

Goldoni bowed beneath the storm, and used his
influence to withhold the sanguinary satire from
further publicity. At this point Gozzi showed the
courtesy which might have been expected from a
man of his quality. He dropped the point of his
weapon at his antagonist's request, and prepared
himself to meet the playwright on his own ground.
In fairness to Gozzi, it is necessary to observe that
this resolution indicated no small amount of chivalry
and courage. Goldoni was the idol of the public.
He kept continually pointing to the concourse which
crowded the Venetian theatres when a new piece
from his pen was advertised. Gozzi was unpractised
in play-writing, a man in his fortieth year, and the
dramatic card on which he staked his luck might
well be considered hazardous. What that card was
we shall presently discover.

Chiari, involved in the same warfare with the
Granelleschi, had hitherto preserved a discreet
silence. Now he defied them to produce a play.
Gasparo Gozzi answered with a sonnet, which be-
trays his personal leaning toward Goldoni. Then
Chiari resolved to make common cause with his old
rival on the stage. This shows how the dropping
fire of the Academicians had told upon their oppo-
nents. The Abbé addressed Goldoni as *degnissimo
comico vate, poeta amico*, most worthy master of
comedy, my good poet friend. Goldoni reciprocated
the compliment with *vate sublime, vate immortale,*

sublime, immortal bard. Not without a touch of concealed irony, he compared himself to Chiari in this lyric flight :[1]

> "Si, tu sei l'aquila,
>   Io la formica ;
>   Tu voli all' apice
>   Senza fatica,
>   Mia Musa ai cardini
>   Salir non sa."

We trace in these verses Goldoni's perfect clarity of vision regarding his own powers, and his good-humoured indulgence of other people's foibles. He recognised the practical advantage of an alliance with Chiari. At the same time he disclaimed all honours for himself, and gently ridiculed his new ally's pretensions.

Chiari had defied the Granelleschi to produce a comedy. Goldoni had taken up his stand upon the popularity of his own plays. Carlo Gozzi conceived the bold idea of writing a fantastic drama upon the old lines of the *Commedia dell' Arte*, which should fill the theatre of his adoption and restore Sacchi's company to favour. If he succeeded, both Chiari and Goldoni would be hit with the same stone. This was the real origin of the celebrated *Fiabe Teatrali*. But before engaging in the attempt,

---

[1] "Yes, thou art the eagle, I am the ant. Thou soarest to the zenith without exertion ; my Muse cannot rise to the poles of the universe."

Gozzi looked about for a suitable subject. Nothing, he calculated, would floor his antagonists more thoroughly than the exhibition of a dramatised nursery tale by impromptu actors. Therefore, in the spirit of a burlesque duellist, in the true spirit of Don Quixote, he composed his *Amore delle Tre Melarancie*.

These facts about the genesis of Gozzi's *Fiabe* need to be insisted on, since French and German critics have distorted the truth. They regard Gozzi as a romantic playwright, gifted with innate genius for a peculiar species of dramatic art. According to this theory, the *Fiabe* were produced in order to manifest an ideal existing in their author's brain. Minute attention to Gozzi's Memoirs, his explanatory Essays (Opere, vols. i. and iv.), and the preface appended to each *Fiaba*, shows, on the contrary, that he began to write the *Fiabe* with the simple object of answering a certain challenge in the most humorous way he could devise. He continued them with a didactic purpose. His keen sagacity and profound knowledge of the Venetian public led him possibly to anticipate success. Yet he knew that the attempt was perilous ; and he made it, without obeying preconceived principles, without yielding to any imperative instinct, but solely with the view of giving Chiari and Goldoni a sound thrashing.

If it is worth while studying Gozzi and the *Fiabe* at all, this point has so much importance that

I may be permitted to resume the history of his literary conflict with the two poets.   Gozzi opened fire
with the *Tartana* in 1756.   Goldoni retorted that he
had only made himself ridiculous ; unless he proved
both his assumption and his argument, he was nothing better than a dog barking at the moon.   Gozzi
then declared that he was already engaged in the
production of a commentary.   This circulated in MS.
under the form of a satire called the *Teatro Comico*.
Meanwhile Goldoni parried all attacks by pointing to
his popularity, and Chiari openly defied the Granelleschi to write a comedy, instead of condemning the
plays in vogue.   Finally Gozzi, who had become
intimately acquainted with the actors in Sacchi's
company, resolved to write a *scenario*, which should
rehabilitate the *Commedia dell' Arte*, parody both
Chiari and Goldoni, attract the public in crowds, and
prove that a mere fairy tale, treated with romantic
gusto, was capable of arousing no less interest than
the works of professional playwrights following new-
fangled models.   The *Amore delle Tre Melarancie*,
produced at the end of January in 1761, rather more
than four years after the appearance of the *Tartana*,
was the result.

It is mistaken to suppose that Gozzi was animated
by the enthusiasm of a literary innovator.   The *Fiabe*,
in spite of their fantastic form, were the work of an
aristocratical Conservative, bent on striking a shrewd
blow for the *Commedia dell' Arte*, which he con-

sidered to be the special glory of the Italian race
In this respect, we might call Gozzi the Venetian
Aristophanes.[1] The *Fiabe* were his "Clouds," and
"Birds," and "Wasps." Goldoni and Chiari were
his Euripides and Agathon; perverters of the good
old comedy by vulgar realism, false pathos, and mere-
tricious rhetoric. Rousseau, Voltaire, Helvetius, the
French *philosophes*, were his Socrates and Sophists.
His art was the expression, not of creative instinct
evoking a new type of drama merely for its beauty
and romance, but of a militant, sarcastic mind, imbued with the ironical literature of the sixteenth century. Gozzi had little in common with Shakespeare.
Truffaldino is no twin-brother of King Lear's fool, nor
is Brighella cousin to the grave-digger in *Hamlet*.
These personages belong to the family of masks,
whose pedigree dates from immemorial antiquity in
Italy. The element of fable, as Gozzi repeatedly
informs us, was first adopted by him out of sheer
bravado to maintain a certain thesis, viz., that whole
nations could be made to laugh and cry over puerilities, when handled with the judgment of a master.
Gozzi's true ancestors in art were the Florentine
burlesque poets, notably Luigi Pulci. The blending
of magic, phantasy, broad comedy and serious tragic
interest in the *Fiabe* allies them to the *Morgante
Maggiore* far more closely than to Marlowe's *Doctor*

---

[1] Only in this respect, however; otherwise, as artist, Gozzi differs
widely from Aristophanes.

Faustus. In them, therefore, we observe the curious literary phenomenon of what at first sight appears to be spontaneous romantic art, but what is really the result of satirical and didactic intention. The preface to *L'Augellino Belverde*, in which Gozzi takes leave of the *Fiabe*, clearly explains the case.[1] "I addressed myself to the task of arousing great popular enthusiasm by a *tour de force* of fancy ; and at the same time I wished to cut short the series of my dramatic pieces, from which I derived no profit, and the burden of producing which was beginning to weigh heavily upon me. Besides, it seemed to me that I had fully achieved the end I had proposed to myself from the outset, in the indulgence of the purest capricious and poetical punctilio." *Punctilio* was the parent of the *Fiabe*.

At this point I shall introduce a translation of *L'Amore delle Tre Melarancie*. There are several reasons for doing so. First, although it only exists for us in the *compte rendu* of the author, and is therefore a description rather than a literal *scenario*, a very good idea can be gained from it of the directions given by a poet to extempore actors. Secondly, it shows the four Venetian masks, Pantalone, Tartaglia, Truffaldino, and Brighella, in action, together with the *servetta* Smeraldina. Thirdly, it is interesting for the light thrown upon Gozzi's controversy with the two poets in the critical observations he has inter-

---

[1] Opere, vol. iii. p. 9.

spersed.   These I shall enclose in brackets, so that
the *scenario* of the play may be distinguished from
extraneous matter.

V.

A REFLECTIVE ANALYSIS

OF THE FABLE ENTITLED

THE LOVE OF THE THREE ORANGES.

A Dramatic Representation divided into Three Acts.[1]

PROLOGUE.

(A boy comes forward and makes this announcement.)

Your faithful servants, the old company
Of players, feel sore shent and full of shame ;
Behind the scenes they stand with downcast eye
And hang-dog faces, dreading words of blame ;
They blush to hear the folk say : " We are dry !
Each year those fellows feed us with the same
Musty old comedies that stink of mould !
We will not be insulted, laughed at, sold ! "
    I swear by all the elements to you,   ·
Kind public, that to win your love once more,
They'd let their teeth be drawn, and eyeballs too !
They sent me to say this—nay, do not roar,

---

[1] The actors in Sacchi's company were : Antonio Sacchi, *Truffaldino ;*
Atanagio Zanoni, *Brighella ;* Agostino Fiorelli, *Tartaglia ;* Cesare Darbes,
Pantalone ; Adriana Sacchi Zanoni, *Smeraldina ;* Antonia Sacchi, *Beatrice ;*
together with Ignazio Casanova and Gaetano Casali.   How the parts of
Leandro, Clarice, Rè di Coppe, Celio, Morgana, Creonta, Ninetta were
distributed, we do not know.   Antonia Sacchi (the *Beatrice* of the
troupe) probably played Clarice.

Restrain your wrath, sweet gentle audience, do ;
Lend me your ears three minutes, I implore ;
When I have spoken what I'm sent to say,
Deal with me as you list, I won't cry nay !
    We've lost all sense and knowledge how to please
The public on our scenes, in this mad age.
The plays that took last year now seem to freeze ;
· And something quite brand-new is all the rage.
The wheel of taste and fashion, as one sees,
Moves with a wind no prophet can presage ;
We only know that when the world's agog,
Our throats are moist and stomachs filled with prog.
    Taste rules this year that all the modern plays
Should be crammed full with intrigue, strange events,
Fresh characters, adventures that amaze,
Wild, thrilling, unexpected incidents ;—
Dumbfounded by these laws, we stand at gaze,
Huddling together timorous in our tents ;
And yet because we must have bread to eat,
We've come with our old wares your wrath to meet.
    I know not, gentle listener, who it is
Hath rendered us unfit to charm your ear :
To us who once enjoyed your courtesies,
So many and so sweet, it seems most queer.
Is Poetry perchance to blame for this ?
Well, well ; all things are doomed to disappear ;
Mortals must learn to bear and bide their fate ;
Yet, ah ! your hatred is a scourge too great !
    For our part, we'll leave nothing new untried ;
We'll don the poet's singing-robes and bays,
If this may give us back your grace denied ;
Nay, we *are* poets in these latter days !
Our breeches shall be sold and ink supplied,
Our coats we'll change for paper to write plays ;
And if we've got no genius, well, what's that ?
So long as you are pleased, all's right, that's flat.
    Our purpose 'tis with new-pranked comedies,
Fine things, ne'er seen before, to fill our stage.
Don't ask when, where, and how we met with these,
Or who inscribed the pure Phœbean page ;
After fine weather when the deluges

Of rain descend, *Lo, new rain !* cries the sage ;
Yet though he thinks it new rain, 'tis quite plain
That rain is nought but water, water rain.
    Not all things keep one course through endless time.
What's up to-day, to-morrow shall be down.
Your great-great-grandsire's garment Mode, the mime,
Steals from his picture-frame to deck the town.
'Tis taste, opinion, gusto make sublime,
Make beautiful, what tickles prince and clown ;
And we can swear upon the book our plays
Have ne'er appeared in these or other days.
    We've plots and arguments to turn old folk
Back to their infancy and nurse's arms ;
Parents who kindly bear their children's yoke
Will bring the babes to listen to our charms ;
High solemn geniuses we daren't invoke,
Nor will their absence cause us great alarms ;
Why should we snuff at pence ?   Whether they scent
Of ignorance or learning, we're content.
    On strange and unexpected circumstance
You shall sup full to-night ; on wonders wild,
Whereof you may have heard or read perchance,
Yet never seen by woman, man, or child ;
Beasts, birds, and house-doors shall your ears entrance
With verses by crowned poet's labour filed ;
And if Martellian verses they shall prove,
These *must* compel your plaudits and your love !
    Your servants wait, impatient to begin ;
But first I'd like the story to rehearse ;
Ah me ! I quake and tremble in my skin—
You're sure to hiss me or do something worse !
The Love of the Three Oranges !—I'm in,
And don't repent the plunge, although you curse.
Imagine then, my darlings, heart's desires,
You're sitting with your granddams round your fires.

[The touch of satire in this prologue, directed against poets who were trying to trample down Sacchi's company of improvisatory players, is too obvious, and my intention of supporting the latter by introducing the series of my dramatised nursery-tales upon the theatre is too evident, to call for detailed commentary. In the choice of my first fable, which I took from the commonest among the stories told to children, and in the base alloy of the dialogues, the action, and the characters, which are obviously degraded of set purpose, I wanted to ridicule *Il Campiello, Le Massère, Le Baruffe Chiozzotte*, and many other plebeian and very trivial pieces by Signor Goldoni.]

FIRST ACT.

Silvio, King of Diamonds,[1] the monarch of an imaginary realm, whose habit exactly imitated that of his majesty upon the playing cards, confided to Pantalone the deep distress caused to his royal mind by the misfortune of his sole son and heir, Tartaglia. The Crown-Prince had been subject, for the last ten years, to an incurable malady. The first physicians diagnosed the case as hopeless hypochondria, and gave their patient up. The King wept bitterly. Pantalone, sending doctors to the devil with his sarcasms, suggested that the admirable secrets of certain charlatans, at that time famous, might be tried. The King protested that all such means had been employed with no result. Pantalone, letting his fancy

---

[1] In Italian, *Rè di Coppe*. The Italian suits are *Coppe* or cups, *Danari* or coins, *Spade* or swords (whence our Spades), *Bastoni* or clubs.

play upon the hidden causes of the malady, asked
his liege in secret, so as not to be overheard by the
royal bodyguard, whether his Majesty had perhaps
contracted something in his younger days, which,
being communicated to the constitution of the Prince,
might still be extirpated by the exhibition of mercury.
The King, assuming an air of stately seriousness,
replied that he had been invariably faithful to his
consort's bed. Pantalone then submitted that the
Prince might be concealing, out of a befitting sense
of shame, the consequence of boyish peccadilloes.
His Majesty assured him seriously that his own
paternal inspection of the patient excluded that hypo-
thesis; the young man's illness was solely due to
hypochondria of a grave and malignant nature; the
physicians declared that, unless he could be made to
laugh, he must sink slowly into his grave; a smile
upon his face would be the favourable sign of con-
valescence. That was too good to be expected. To
this he added that the prospect of his own decrepitude, the sight of his son and heir upon a death-bed,
the inevitable succession to the crown of his niece
Clarice, a young woman of strange temper, bizarre
fancies, and cruel passions, caused him the deepest
affliction. Thereupon he began to bewail the future
misery of his subjects, broke down into a flood of
tears, and quite forgot the dignity of his high station.
Pantalone consoled him, urged on his attention the
propriety of restoring the court to merriment and

gladness, if all depended on Prince Tartaglia's re-
covering the power of laughter. Let festivities,
games, masquerades, and spectacles be set on foot.
Let Truffaldino, well approved for making people
laugh and chasing the blue-devils from their brains,
be summoned to the Prince's service. The Prince
had shown some inclination for Truffaldino's society.
He might succeed in bringing smiles again upon
the royal features. The remedy could but be tried,
and possibly a cure might ensue. The King allowed
himself to be convinced, and began to plan arrange-
ments.

To these persons entered Leandro, Knave of Diamonds,[1] and first Minister of the realm. He too
was dressed like his figure on a pack of cards. Pantalone, aside, expressed his suspicion of some treachery
on the part of Leandro. The King commanded festivities, games, and Bacchic entertainments, adding
that whoever made the Prince laugh should receive
a noble prize. Leandro tried to dissuade his Majesty,
and urged that such remedies were likely to prejudice
the sick man's health. The King repeated his orders
and retired. Pantalone rejoiced. Aside, to the audience, he explained that Leandro was certainly plan-
ning the Prince's death. Then he followed the King.
Leandro remained stubborn, muttered that he detected
some opposition to his wishes, but from what quarter
he could not guess.

---

[1] In Italian, *Cavaliere di Coppe.*

To him appeared the Princess Clarice, niece of
the King. There was never seen upon the stage a
princess of so wild, irascible, and determined a character as this Clarice. [I have to thank Signor Chiari
for furnishing me with abundant models for such
caricatures in his dramatic works.] She had settled
with Leandro to marry him, and raise him to the
throne, upon the death of her cousin. Accordingly
she burst into reproaches against her lover for his
coldness. Were they to wait until Tartaglia died of
a disease so slow as hypochondria? Leandro excused
himself with circumspection. Fata Morgana, he said,
his powerful protectress, had given him certain charms
in Martellian verses, which were to be administered
to Tartaglia in wafers. These would certainly work
his destruction by sure if tardy means. [This was
introduced to criticise the plays of Chiari and Goldoni,
whose Martellian verses bored every one to death by
their monotony of rhyme.] Now Fata Morgana was
hostile to the King of Diamonds, having lost much
of her treasure on his card. She loved the Knave of
Diamonds, because he had brought her luck in play.
She dwelt in a lake, not far from the city. Smeraldina, a Moorish woman, who performed the *servetta*
in this scenic parody, acted as intermediary between
Leandro and Morgana. Clarice fumed with fury at
hearing the slow means appointed for Tartaglia's
death. Leandro confessed that he entertained some
doubts about the efficacy of Martellian verses to

secure a happy dispatch. He was uneasy, too, at the unexplained appearance of Truffaldino at court, a very facetious fellow ; and if Tartaglia laughed, his cure was certain. Clarice's rage boiled over ; she had seen Truffaldino, and the mere sight of him was certain to make anybody laugh. [In this dialogue my readers will detect a defence of the mirth-making comedy of the masks as against the melancholy drama in verse of the poets in vogue.] Meanwhile, Leandro had sent Brighella, his servant, to Smeraldina, to learn the explanation of Truffaldino's appearance, and to demand assistance from Morgana.

Brighella entered ; and with much show of secrecy related that Truffaldino had been sent to court by a certain wizard Celio, Morgana's enemy, and the King of Diamonds' friend, for reasons exactly opposite to those which had incensed Morgana against him. Truffaldino, he continued, was an antidote to the morbific influences of Martellian verses ; he had come to protect the King, the Prince, and all the people from the infection of those melancholic charms.

[It may be pointed out that the hostility between Fata Morgana and Celio the wizard symbolised the warfare carried on between Goldoni and Chiari. Fata Morgana was a caricature of Chiari, and Celio of Goldoni.]

Brighella's news threw Clarice and Leandro into consternation. They laid their heads together how to kill Truffaldino by some secret device. Clarice suggested arsenic or a blunderbuss. Leandro was for trying Martellian verses in wafers, or opium. Clarice objected that there was not much to choose between Martellian verses and opium, and that Truffaldino had the stomach to digest such trifles. Brighella added that Morgana, informed of the festivities designed for the Prince's recovery, meant to appear and neutralise the action of his salutiferous laughter by a curse which should quickly send him to the tomb. Clarice retired. Leandro and Brighella went to superintend the preparation of the shows.

The next scene disclosed the chamber of the sick Prince. He was attired in the most laughable caricature of an invalid's costume. Reclining in an ample lounging-chair, Tartaglia leaned against a table, piled with medicine-bottles, ointments, spittoons, and other furniture appropriate to his melancholy condition. With a weak and quavering voice he lamented his misfortunes, the various treatments he had tried with no success, and the extraordinary symptoms of his incurable malady. The eminent actor, who sustained this scene alone, kept the audience in one roar of laughter by his exquisite burlesque and natural drollery. Then Truffaldino entered, and tried to make the patient laugh. The extempore performance of this duet by two of the best comic players of our day afforded excellent mirth. The Prince looked on approvingly while Truffaldino exhibited his pranks. But nothing could bring a smile upon his lips. He insisted upon returning to his illness, and asking Truffaldino's advice. Truffaldino entered into a labyrinth of physiological and medical arguments, highly humorous and spiced with satire. He smelt the Prince's breath, and swore that it stank of a surfeit of undigested Martellian verses. The Prince coughed, and asked to spit. Truffaldino brought him the vessel, examined the expectoration, and found in it a mass of rancid rotten rhymes. This scene lasted above a quarter of an hour, to the continual amusement of the audience. Instruments of music were then heard, announcing the festivities in the great court of the palace. Truffaldino wanted to conduct the Prince to a balcony from which he could survey them. Tartaglia protested that this was impossible. Truffaldino, in a rage, threw all the medicines, cups, and ointments out of window, while the Prince squealed and wept like a baby. At last Truffaldino carried him off by main force, howling as though he was being massacred, and bore him on his shoulders to enjoy the show.

The third scene was laid in the courtyard of the palace. Leandro entered, and declared that he had carried out the King's commands; the people, plunged in grief, but eager to refresh their spirits, were all masked ; he had taken precautions to make many persons assume lugubrious disguises, in order to aug-

ment the Prince's melancholy ; the hour had sounded
for unbarring the court-gates to the populace.

Morgana then entered, in the travesty of a ridiculous old woman.   Leandro expressed his astonishment
that such an object should have obtained entrance
before the gates were opened.   Morgana discovered
herself, and said she had come in that disguise to
work the Prince's swift destruction.   Leandro thanked
her, and styled her the Queen of Hypochondria.
Morgana drew to one side, and the gates were thrown
wide.

On a terraced balcony, in front of the spectators,
sat the King, and Prince Tartaglia, muffled in furred
pelisse, Clarice, Pantalone, the guards, and afterwards Leandro.   The spectacles and games were precisely such as are related in the fairy story.   The
people flocked in.   There was a tournament, directed
by Truffaldino, who arranged burlesque encounters
for the knights.   At every turn, he addressed himself
to the balcony, inquiring of his majesty if the Prince
had laughed.   The Prince only shed tears, complaining that the air hurt him, and the noise made his
head ache.   He entreated his royal sire to send him
back to his warm bed.

There were two fountains, one of which ran with
oil, the other with wine.   Round these the rabble
hustled, disputing with vulgar and plebeian violence.
But nothing moved the Prince to laughter.   Then
Morgana hobbled out to fill her cruse with oil.

Truffaldino assailed the hag with a variety of insults, and finally sent her sprawling with her legs in air. [These trivialities, taken from the trivial story-book, amused the audience by their novelty quite as much as the *Massère, Campielli, Baruffe Chiozzotte*, and all the other trivial pieces of Goldoni.] On seeing the old woman's fall, Tartaglia burst into a long sonorous peal of laughter. Truffaldino gained the prize. The people, relieved of their anxiety about the Prince's health, laughed uncontrollably. All the court was glad. Only Leandro and Clarice showed wry faces.

Morgana, raising herself from the ground in a spasm of fury, abused the Prince, and hurled the following awful malediction in the true style of Chiari at his devoted head : [1]

" Open thine ears, barbarian ! let my voice assail thy heart !
Nor wall nor mountain stay the sound my words of doom impart.
As riving thunderbolts descend and split the solid rock,
So may my curses split thy breast with their tremendous shock.
As boats against a running tide the tug triumphant tows,
So let my malediction strong still lead thee by the nose.
Oh awful curse ! oh direful doom ! To hear it is to die,
Like quadrupeds within the sea, or fish on flowers that lie !
I call on Pluto, gloomy god, to Pindar winged I pray,
That thou with the Three Oranges may'st fall in love to-day.
Threats, tears, entreaties now are nought, leaves shaken by the breeze ;
Haste to the horrible acquist of the Three Oranges !"

---

[1] I have adopted the old English fourteen-syllable line for the translation of Gozzi's Martellian verses. It seemed to me that the lumbering effect of this metre lent itself to the spirit of his parody. What Martellian verses were has been explained at p. 97.

Morgana disappeared. The Prince suddenly conceived a firm and resolute enthusiasm for the love of
the Three Oranges. He was led away amid the confusion and consternation of the court.

What nonsense ! What a mortification for the
two poets ! The first act of the fable ended at this
point with a loud and universal clapping of hands.

ACT THE SECOND.

In one of the Prince's apartments, Pantalone,
beside himself with despair, describes the terrible
effect of the hag's malediction on Tartaglia. Nothing
could be done to calm him down. He had asked
his father for a pair of iron shoes, to walk the world
over, and discover the fatal Oranges. The King had
commanded Pantalone, under pain of the Prince's
displeasure, to find him such a pair. The matter
was one of the most pressing urgency. [This motive
suited the theatre, and conveyed a sprightly satire on
the dramatic motives then in vogue.]

Pantalone retired, and the Prince entered with
Truffaldino. Tartaglia expressed impatience at this
long delay in bringing him the iron shoes. Truffaldino asked a number of absurd questions. Tartaglia
declared his intention of going to find the Three
Oranges, which, as he heard from his grandmother,
were two thousand miles away, in the power of

Creonta, a gigantic witch. Then he called for his armour, and bade Truffaldino array himself in mail, for he meant him to be his squire. A scene of excellent buffoonery followed between these highly comical personages, both of them fitting on corslets, helmets, and huge long swords, with burlesque military ardour.

Enter the King, Pantalone, and guards. One of the latter carries a pair of iron shoes upon a salver. This scene was executed by the four principal performers with a gravity which made it doubly ridiculous. In a tone of high tragedy and theatrical majesty the father dissuaded his son from this perilous adventure. He entreated, threatened, relapsed into pathos. The Prince, like a man possessed, insisted. His hypochondria was sure to return, unless he was allowed to set forth. At last he burst into coarse threats against his father. The King stood rooted to the ground with amazement and grief. Then he reflected that this want of filial respect in Tartaglia arose from the bad example of the new comedies. [In one of Chiari's comedies a son had drawn his sword to kill his father. Instances of the same description abounded in the dramas of that day, which I wished to censure.] Nothing would silence the Prince, till Truffaldino shod him with the iron shoes. The scene ended with a quartet in dramatic verse, of blubberings, farewells, sighs and sobs. Tartaglia and Truffaldino took their leave. The

King fell fainting on a sofa, and Pantalone called aloud for aromatic vinegar.

Clarice, Leandro, and Brighella came hurrying upon the stage, rebuking Pantalone for the clamour he was raising. Pantalone replied that, with a King in a fainting fit, a Prince gone off on the dangerous adventure of the Oranges, it was only natural to kick up a row. Brighella answered that such matters were mere twaddle, like the new comedies, which turned everything topsy-turvy without reason. The King meanwhile recovered his senses, and fell to raving in true tragic style. He bewept his son for dead; ordered the whole court to wear mourning; and shut himself up in a little cabinet, to end his days under the weight of this crushing affliction. Pantalone, vowing that he would share the King's lamentations, collect their mingled tears in one pocket-handkerchief, and bequeath to coming bards the argument for interminable episodes in Martellian verse, withdrew in the train of his liege.

Clarice, Leandro, Brighella gave way to their gladness, and extolled Morgana to the skies. Whimsical Clarice then insisted on coming to conditions before she raised Leandro to the throne. In time of war she was to command the armies. Even if she suffered a defeat, she was sure to subdue the victor by her charms; when he was drowned in love, and lulled by her blandishments, she meant to stick a knife into his paunch. [This was a side hit at Chiari's *Attila*.]

Clarice further reserved to herself the right of distributing court-offices. Brighella, as the reward of his services, begged to be appointed Master of the King's Revels. The three personages now disputed upon the choice of different theatrical diversions. Clarice voted for tragic dramas, with personages who should throw themselves out of windows and off towers, without breaking their necks, and such-like miraculous accidents (*id est*, the plays of Chiari). Leandro preferred comedies of character (*id est*, Goldoni's plays). Brighella recommended the *Commedia dell' Arte*, as very fit to yield the public innocent amusement. Clarice and Leandro flew into a rage. What did they want with stupid buffooneries, rancid relics of antiquity, unseemly in this enlightened age? Brighella then began a pathetic speech, commiserating Sacchi's company, without mentioning it by name, but making his meaning plain enough. He deplored the misfortunes of an honourable troupe, who had done good service in their day, but were now downtrodden, and forced to behold the affections of the public they adored, and whom they had for many years amused, withdrawn from them. He retired with the applause of that public, who thoroughly understood the real drift of his discourse.

The next scene opened in a wilderness. Celio the wizard was discovered drawing circles. As the protector of Prince Tartaglia, he summoned Farfarello, a devil, to his aid. Farfarello appeared, and with a formidable voice uttered these Martellian lines :

> "Hullo ! who calls? who drags me forth from earth's drear centre dark?
> A wizard real art thou, or wizard of the stage, thou spark ?
> If only of the stage thou art, I need not tell thee then
> That devils, wizards, sprites, are out of fashion among men."

[Allusion was here made to the two poets, who wanted to abolish the masks, magicians, and fiends in writings for the stage.] Celio answered in prose that he was a real wizard. Farfarello continued :

> "Well, be thou what thou wilt ; yet if thou of the stage may be,
> At least thou might'st respond in verse Martellian to me."

Celio swore at the devil, and told him that he meant to go on talking prose. Then he inquired whether Truffaldino, whom he had sent to the court of the King of Diamonds, had done any good, and whether Tartaglia had been obliged to laugh, and had lost his hypochondria. The devil answered :

> "He laughed ; recovered health ; but then, Morgana, thy great foe,
> With malediction spoiled thy pains, and wrought a double woe.
> With fury winged and breathless he, both burning cheeks on fire,
> Is after the Three Oranges, inflamed with fierce desire.
> With Truffaldin the Prince is sped ; Morgana sends a sprite
> To wait upon the pair and blow them forward in their flight.
> A thousand miles the men have gone, and soon they will descend,
> Here by Creonta's fort, half-dead, at their long journey's end."

The devil disappeared. Celio monologised against his mortal foe Morgana, explaining the great perils of Tartaglia and Truffaldino when they should arrive at the castle of Creonta on the quest of the fatal

BRIGHELLA (1570)

Illustrating the Italian Commedia dell' Arte, or Impromptu Comedy

Oranges. Then he retired to make the necessary preparations for saving two persons of high merit and great social utility.

[Celio, who stood for Goldoni in this piece of nonsense, ought not to have protected Tartaglia and Truffaldino. I admit the error, which deserves to be condemned, if a mere dramatic sketch of such a trivial kind comes within the scope of criticism. At that time Chiari and Goldoni were enemies and rivals. I wanted Morgana and Celio to caricature their opposite dramatic styles; and I did not care to protect myself against censure by multiplying personages more than needful.]

Tartaglia and Truffaldino entered armed, and proceeding at a tremendous pace. They had a devil with a pair of bellows following behind, and blowing their backsides to make them skim along the ground. The devil ceased to blow and disappeared. They sprawled on the grass at the sudden cessation of the favouring gale.

[I am under infinite obligations to Signor Chiari for this burlesque conception, which produced a very excellent effect upon the stage. In his dramas, drawn from the Æneid, Chiari made the Trojans perform long journeys within the space of a single action, and without the assistance of my devil and his bellows. This writer, though he pedantically insulted everybody else who broke the rules, allowed himself singular privileges. In his tragedy of *Ezelino*, after

I

the tyrant's downfall, a captain is sent to beleaguer
Treviso, and reduce Ezelino's garrison. This takes
place in one scene. In the next scene the same
captain returns victorious, having ridden more than
thirty miles, captured the town, and butchered the
tyrant's troops. He delivers a rhetorical oration,
ascribing this miracle to the matchless spirit of his
horse! Tartaglia and Truffaldino had to perform a
journey of two thousand miles, and my device of the
devil with the bellows explained their exploit better
than Chiari's charger.]

The two comedians rose from the ground, half-
stunned and astonished at the mighty wind which
wafted them. Their geographical description of the
countries, mountains, rivers, and oceans they had
passed, was crammed with burlesque absurdities.
Tartaglia concluded that the Three Oranges must be
nigh at hand. Truffaldino, feeling tired and hungry,
asked the Prince whether he had brought a good
stock of cash or bills. Tartaglia spurned such low
considerations and idle questions. Spying a castle
on a hill, and judging it to be Creonta's, he set
manfully forward, while Truffaldino trudged behind
in the hope of finding food.

Meanwhile Celio entered, and sought in vain to
dissuade the Prince from his perilous adventure. He
described insuperable obstacles fraught with danger
on the way. They were exactly the same as are told
to children in the story-book; but Celio enlarged

upon them with wide rolling eyes, and magnified the molehills into mountains. There was an iron gate rusted with time, a famished dog, a well-rope rotten with damp, a baker's wife, who, having no broom, was forced to sweep the oven out with her own dugs. The Prince, unterrified by these appalling objects, determined to assail the castle. Celio, seeing his mind made up, gave him a magic ointment to smear the bolt of the gate, a loaf to throw the dog, and a bundle of brooms to give the baker's wife. The rope he bade them hang out in the sun to dry. Then he added that, if by lucky chance they should acquire the Oranges, they were to leave the castle at once, and be mindful to open none of the Oranges except in the immediate neighbourhood of some fountain. Finally, he promised, if they escaped the perils of their theft, to send the same devil with the bellows, to blow them home again. Then he recommended them to Heaven and left them. Tartaglia and Truffaldino, carrying the articles provided by Celio, went forward on their journey.

Here a tent was lowered, which represented the pavilion of the King of Diamonds.—What an irregularity !—Nay, what misapplied criticism !—Two short scenes followed, one between Smeraldina and Brighella, rejoicing over the loss of Tartaglia ; the other with Morgana, who bade Brighella inform Clarice and Leandro that Celio was assisting the Prince. This she had learned from the devil Draghinazzo.

Then she bade Smeraldina follow her to the lake, where Tartaglia and Truffaldino would certainly arrive if they escaped Creonta's clutches. Some new snare might then be devised to entrap them. The parley broke up in confusion.

The next scene disclosed a courtyard in Creonta's castle. [I was able to observe, upon the opening of this scene, with the grossly absurd objects it contained, what an immense power the marvellous exerts over the human mind. A gate constructed with an iron grating, a famished dog which howled and roamed around, a well with a coil of rope beside it, a baker's wife who swept her oven with two enormously long breasts, kept the whole theatre in silent wonder and attention quite as effectually as the most thrilling scenes in the works of our two poets.] Outside the grating appeared Tartaglia and Truffaldino, engaged in smearing the bolt; and lo! the portal swung upon its hinges. Great miracle! They passed in. The dog barked and leapt upon them. They threw him the bread and he was still. Great portent! Truffaldino, trembling with fright, then hung the cord up to dry, and gave the baker's wife her brooms, while the Prince entered the castle and came out again, capering for joy and holding the three enormous Oranges he had seized.

The moving accidents of this scene did not end so suddenly. The sky darkened, the earth quaked, and loud claps of thunder were heard. Tartaglia handed the Oranges to Truffaldino, who kept trembling like an aspen leaf. Then there issued from the castle an awful voice, which was Creonta's own. She spoke as the story-book dictates :

> "O baker's wife, O baker's wife, abide not my just ire !
> Take those two fellows by the feet, and cast them in the fire."

The baker's wife, following the fable with equal fidelity, replied thus :

> "Not I ! How many months have passed, how many months and years,
> While with my milk-white breasts I sweep, and waste my life in tears !
> Thou, cruel dame, a single broom ne'er gav'st me at my need ;
> These brought a bundle ; let them go in peace ; I will not heed."

Creonta cried :

> "O rope, O rope ! hang up the knaves !"

And the rope, still observing the text, answered :

> "Hard heart ! hast thou forgot
> Those many years, those many months, thou left'st me here to rot ?
> By thee was I abandoned long in damp to waste away ;
> These stretched me to the sun ; let them go forth in peace, I say."

Creonta howled aloud :

> "Dog, faithful watch-dog ! rend and tear those wretches limb from limb."

The dog retorted :

> "Nay, why, Creonta, should I rend poor fellows at thy whim ?
> So many years, so many months, I've served thee without food ;
> These filled my belly full : thy cries shall not control my mood."

Creonta, again :

"Portal of iron, close ! Grind yon base knaves and thieves to dust !"

And the gate :

"Cruel Creonta ! vainly now your threats on me are thrust !
So many years, so many months, in rust and woe to pine,
You left me here ; they oiled my bolts ; no ingrate's heart is mine."

It was very funny to see Tartaglia's and Truffaldino's mock astonishment at the fine flow of the
poet's eloquence. They stood dumbfounded to hear
bakers' wives, and ropes, and dogs, and gates talking
in Martellian verse. Then they thanked those courteous objects for the kindness shown them.

The audience were hugely delighted with these
puerilities, and I confess that I joined heartily in
their laughter, half-ashamed the while at being forced
to relish a pack of infantile absurdities, which took
me back to the days of my babyhood.

The giantess Creonta now appeared upon the stage.
She was of towering stature, and attired in a vast
sweeping *andrienne*. Tartaglia and Truffaldino fled
before her horrible aspect. Then she gave vent to
her despair in Martellian verses, not forgetting to
invoke Pindar, whom Signor Chiari treated compla-
cently as his own twin-brother :

"Woe to you, faithless servants ! Woe, false rope and dog and gate !
Base baker's wife, I curse thee too ! Ye traitors found too late !
Alas ! Sweet Oranges ! Ah me ! Who stole you unaware ?
Dear Oranges, my hope, my soul, my love, my life, my care !
Woe's me ! I burst with bitter rage ; there's boiling in my breast
Chaos, the Elements, the Sun, the Rainbow, and the rest !

I scarce can stand against it all : O Jove, the Thunderer, send
Thy lightnings on my pate, and me down to the slippers rend !
Help to me ! Ho ! Who helps me ? Fiends ! Who lifts me from
    this world ?—
A friendly thunderbolt descends ! I burn, I'm soothed, I'm hurled."

[These last verses were no bad parody of both Chiari's
sentiments and style of writing.] A thunderbolt
fell and reduced the giantess to ashes. Here ended
the second act, which had been followed with more
marked applause than the first. My bold experiment
began to seem less culpable than it had done at the
commencement.

ACT THE THIRD.

The first scene opened near Fata Morgana's lake.
There was a great tree visible and underneath it a
large stone seat. Several rocks and boulders were
strewn about the meadow. Smeraldina, who talked
the jargon of an Italianised Turk, was standing at the
brink of the lake impatiently awaiting the fairy's
orders, and calling out. Morgana rose from the sur-
face, and began to relate a journey she had made
to hell, where she learned that Tartaglia and Truffaldino, victorious in their achievement of the Three
Oranges, were coming by the help of Celio and the
devil with the bellows. Smeraldina soundly abused
the fairy for her want of skill in magic. Morgana
bade her spare her breath. Owing to precautions
she had taken, Truffaldino would reach the spot where

they were standing, separately from the Prince. Thirst
and hunger, sent by wizard's arts, should annoy him;
and since the Oranges were in his custody, great
catastrophes would take place. Then she consigned
two bedevilled pins to Smeraldina, adding that she
would see a fair girl sitting on the stone beneath
the tree. She was to contrive to fix one of these
needles in the girl's hair, whereupon the latter would
become a dove, and Smeraldina was to take her place
upon the stone. Tartaglia should marry her and
make her Queen. During the night, while sleeping
with her husband, she was to fix the other needle in
his hair, whereupon he would become a beast, and
the throne would be left vacant for Clarice and
Leandro. The Moorish woman raised some difficulties,
which Morgana easily disposed of. Then, observing
Truffaldino approaching with the infernal blast behind
him, they withdrew to mature their plans.

Truffaldino entered, carrying the Three Oranges in
a wallet. The devil with the bellows disappeared,
and Truffaldino related how the Prince had tripped
up a little while back, and that he must wait for him.
He seated himself. Intolerable thirst and hunger
tormented him. At last he resolved to eat one of
the Oranges. But conscience stung him; he declaimed in tragic style; then, driven mad by thirst,
made up his mind to risk the sacrifice. After all,
he reflected, the damage could be made good with
two farthings. So he proceeded to cut open an

Orange. Oh, what a surprise! There issued from its rind a girl clothed in white, who, following the text of the story-book, spoke immediately:

> "Give me to drink! I'm fainting! Ah! I'm dying! Quick, my dear! Of thirst I'm dying! Oh, poor me! Quick, cruel man! Death's here!"

She fell upon the earth oppressed with mortal languor. Truffaldino, who had forgotten Celio's directions about opening the Oranges within reach of water, being besides a fool by nature, and not noticing the lake in his distraction, thought he could not do better than to slice another of the Oranges and quench the dying girl's thirst with the juice of that. Accordingly, he went, like a donkey, and sliced another Orange, out of which there appeared a second lovely female, exclaiming:

> "Woe's me! Of thirst I'm dying! Ho! Give me to drink! I rave! Cruel! I die of thirst! Ah God! 'Twill kill me! Lord! oh save!"

She sank down exhausted like the other. Truffaldino flung himself about in fits of desperation. He roared, screamed, leapt like a maniac, while one of the girls spoke as follows, in an expiring voice:

> "Hard destiny! Of thirst to die! I'm dying! I am dead!"

Then she breathed her last, and the other continued:

> "I'm dying! Barbarous stars! Ah me! Who'll soothe my burning head?"

Then she too breathed her last. Truffaldino wept abundantly, and murmured over them words of im-

passioned tenderness. He decided to cut the third
Orange in the hope of saving both girls alive. While
he was upon the point of doing this, Tartaglia entered
in a rage and stopped him. Truffaldino took to his
heels and left the Orange lying on the grass.

The stupor of this grotesque Prince, the inimitable
reflections he poured forth over the rinds of the two
Oranges and the dead bodies of the girls, soar beyond
the powers of language. The masked actors of our
Commedia dell' Arte, in situations like this, invent
scenes so droll and yet of such exquisite grace, with
gestures, movements, and *lazzi* so delightful, that no
pen can reproduce their effect, and no poet could
surpass them.

After a long and ridiculous soliloquy, Tartaglia
caught sight of two country bumpkins passing by,
ordered the corpses to be decently buried, and bade
the fellows carry them away. Then the Prince turned
to gaze upon the third Orange. To his utter amazement it had swelled to a portentous size, and was as
large now as the biggest pumpkin. Seeing the lake
at hand, and bearing Celio's injunctions in mind, he
thought the place convenient for cutting the fruit
open. This he did with his long sword ; and there
stepped forth a tall and lovely damsel, attired in
robes of white, who fulfilled the conditions of her
part in the story-book by speaking as follows :

> " Who drew me from my living core ? Ah God ! Of thirst I die !
> Give me to drink at once, or else vain tears you'll shed for aye !"

The Prince understood upon the spot the meaning of Celio's precepts. But he was embarrassed to find any vessel capable of holding water. The case did not admit of ceremony. So he unbuckled one of his iron shoes, ran to the lake, filled it with water, and making a thousand excuses for the improvised cup, presented it to the fair damsel, who slaked her thirst, and stood up in full vigour, thanking him for his timely assistance.

She said that she was the daughter of Concul, king of the Antipodes; Creonta, by enchantment, had enclosed her, together with her two sisters, in the rinds of three Oranges, for reasons which were as probable as the circumstance itself. A scene of comical love-making followed, at the close of which Tartaglia promised to make her his wife. The capital was close at hand. The Princess had no decent clothes to wear. The Prince bade her take a seat upon the stone beneath the tree, while he went off to fetch costly raiment and summon the whole Court to attend her. That settled, they parted with sighs.

Smeraldina, astounded by what she had been witness to, now entered. She saw the form of the fair maid reflected in the lake. Of course she proceeded to do everything dictated for the Moorish woman in the story-tale. She dropped her Italianate Turkish. Morgana had put a Tuscan devil into her tongue. Thus armed, she defied all the poets to speak with more complete correctness. Advancing to the young

Princess, whose name was Ninetta, she began to coax
and flatter, offered to arrange her hair, came to close
quarters and betrayed her.   One of the magic pins
was promptly stuck in the girl's head.   Ninetta took
the form of a dove and flew away.   Smeraldina
seated herself upon the stone and waited for the
Court.

These miraculous occurrences, together with the
childish simplicity of the successive scenes, and the
burlesque humour of the action, kept the audience,
instructed as they had been by their grandmothers and
nurses in the days of babyhood, upon the tenter-hooks
of curiosity.   They followed the plot with serious
attention, and took the profoundest interest in watching each step in the development upon the stage of
such a trifle.

Then, to the music of a march, the King of
Diamonds entered, with the Prince, Leandro, Clarice,
Pantalone, Brighella, and the Court.   On beholding
Smeraldina in the place of the bride whom he had
come to fetch away, Tartaglia flew into the wildest
astonishment and fury.   Smeraldina, so altered by
Morgana's artifice that no one recognised her, swore
she was the Princess Ninetta.   Tartaglia continued to
make a burlesque exhibition of his misery.   Leandro,
Clarice, and Brighella, suspecting the real source of
the mystery, rejoiced among themselves.   The King
of Diamonds gravely and majestically enjoined upon
his son the duty of keeping his princely word and

marrying the Moor. The Prince submitted with a wry face and new demonstrations of comical grief. Then the band struck up, and the procession filed away to celebrate the marriage in the palace.

Truffaldino meanwhile remained behind in the royal kitchen, to the charge of which Tartaglia had appointed him, after condoning his mistakes about the Oranges. He was preparing the nuptial banquet, when a new scene opened, which is perhaps the boldest in this jocose parody.

[The rival partisans of Chiari and Goldoni, who were present in the theatre, and saw that a strong stroke of satire was about to fall, did their best to excite the indignation of the audience, and to stir up a commotion. They did not succeed, however. I have already said that Celio represented Goldoni, and Morgana Chiari. The former of these gentlemen had served his apprenticeship at the Venetian bar, and his style smacked of forensic idioms. Chiari plumed himself upon his sublime pindaric flights of poetry ; but I may submit, with all respect, that there never was a tumid and irrational author of the seventeenth century who surpassed him in extravagant conceits and bombast.

Well, Celio and Morgana, animated by mutual hostility, met together in this scene, which I will transcribe literally, just as the dialogue was spoken. I must first remind my readers that parodies miss their mark unless they are surcharged ; and, keeping this in view, I beg them to look with indulgence upon a caprice, which was begotten by jesting humour, without any animosity against two worthy individuals.]

CELIO (*entering with vehemence, to Morgana*). "Wicked enchantress! I have discovered all your base deceits. But Pluto will assist me. Infamous beldame, accursed witch!"

MORGANA. "What do you mean, you charlatan of a wizard? Do not provoke me. I will give you a rebuff in Martellian verses, which shall make you die foaming."

C. "To me, rash witch? You shall get tit for tat from me. I defy you in Martellian verse. Here's at you![1]

"It shall be always held a vain injurious assault,
   Fraudulent, without proper grounds, in justice real at fault;
   To wit these, and whatever else, malignant, fury-fraught
   Spells by Morgana cast, with all etceteras basely wrought:
   And as these premises declare, what bane may hence ensue
   Is cancelled, quashed, estopped, made void, condemned by order
     due."

M. "Oh, the bad verses! Come on, you twopenny-halfpenny magician!

"First shall the glorious rays of gold which beam from Phœbus' breast
   Be turned to lumps of vulgar lead, and East become the West;
   First shall the darkling moon on high, her silver beams so bright
   Change with the glimmering stars, and lose the empire of the night;
   The murmuring streams that purling roll along their crystal bed,
   With Pegasus aloft shall fly, and on the clouds be spread;
   But thou, base slave of Pluto's power, shalt never have the force
   To scorn the sails and rudder of my pinnace in her course."

C. "O fustian fairy, blown out like a bladder!

"On the main paragraph I'll win the verdict in this suit,
   Which by the first preamble shall be made to bear its fruit:
   Princess Ninetta, changed by you into a dove, shall be
   Reconstituted in her rights and due estate by me:

---

[1] I cannot pretend to give a literal translation of these gross parodies of Goldoni's forensic verbiage. The most I can do is to stuff the verse with more or less of legal phraseology.

And through the second paragraph, which follows from the first,
Clarice and Leandro shall sink into want accursed ;
While Smeraldina, who can claim no hearing from the court,
By mere endorsement shall be burned, to give the people sport."

M. "Oh, the stupid, stupid versifier ! Listen to me, now. See if I
don't terrify you.

"On flying plumes soars Icarus, and climbs the heaven with pride,
Treads on the clouds, then stoops, rash youth, and skims along the
tide.
O'er Pelion piled, see Ossa frown, Olympus on her back ;
This wrought the Titans, impious brood, to work high heaven
wrack.
But Icarus erelong must sink, and drown in salt sea-spume ;
Jove's bolt will hurl the Titans bold in ashes to their tomb.
Clarice shall ascend the throne, false Mage, in thy despite ;
Tartaglia, like Actæon, mock the antlered deer in flight."

C. (aside). "She is trying to beat me down with poetical bombast.
If she thinks to shut me up in that way she is quite mistaken.

" I will not leave one plea unturned without demurrers sound,
And 'gainst your swelling lies will file a protest firm and round."

M. "The realm of Diamonds avoid ! Let lawful monarchs reign !"
(Taking her departure.)

C. (crying after her). "And I'll claim costs, stay execution, file my
bills again." (Here Celio went in.)

The last scene was laid in the royal kitchen.
Never did mortal eyes behold a more miserable king's
kitchen than this. The remainder of the performance
followed the old story-book precisely ; nevertheless,
the spectators watched it with sustained attention.
The parody turned upon some trivialities of detail
and some basenesses of character in dramas written
by the two poets. Excessive poverty, dramatic impropriety, and meanness gave the satire point.

Truffaldino appeared spitting a joint. He related how, there being no turnjack in the kitchen, he was obliged to watch the revolutions of the spit himself. While thus engaged, a dove alighted on the window-sill, and a conversation took place between him and the bird. The dove had said: "Good morning, cook of the kitchen." He had replied: "Good morning, white dove." She continued: "I pray to Heaven that you may fall asleep, that the roast may burn, so that the Moor, that ugly mug, may not be able to eat." A mighty slumber overcame him; he fell asleep, and the roast was burned to cinders. This accident happened twice. In a precious hurry he set the third joint before the fire. Then the dove reappeared, and the conversation was repeated. Again the mighty slumber overcame his senses. Truffaldino, honest fellow, did all he could to keep awake. His *lazzi* were in the highest degree facetious. But he could not resist the spell, began to nod, and the flames reduced the third roast to ashes.

You must ask the audience why and wherefore this scene afforded exquisite amusement.

Pantalone entered scolding, woke up Truffaldino; said that the King was in a fury; soup, boiled meat, and liver had been eaten, but the roast had not appeared at table. [All honour to a poet's daring! This outdid the lowness of Goldoni's squabbles about a brace of pumpkins in his *Chiozzotte*.] Truffaldino told the strange occurrence with the dove. Pantalone dismissed it as an idle story. But the dove at this point reappeared and repeated her ominous speech. Truffaldino was on the point of going off into a doze when Pantalone roused him, and they both gave chase to the dove, which flew fluttering about the kitchen.

The attempts to catch the dove, made by these facetious personages, amused the audience above measure. At last they caught it, placed it on a table, and began to stroke its feathers. Then they detected the enchanted pin stuck into a knot upon its head. Truffaldino drew the pin forth, and behold the bird was transformed into the Princess Ninetta!

A scene of stupors and astonishments. His Majesty the King of Diamonds arrived; pompously, with sceptre in hand, he rebuked Truffaldino for the non-appearance of the roast-meat at his royal table, whereby he had been put to shame before illustrious guests. The Prince followed, and recognised his lost Ninetta. Joy bereft him of his wits. Ninetta related what had befallen her; the King remained lost in amazement. Then the Moor and the rest of the Court came crowding into the kitchen, to find their monarch. He, with an air of haughty dignity, bade the princely couple retire into the scullery. He chose the hearth for his throne, and took his seat there with majestic sternness. The courtiers assembled round him; and as it happens in the story-book, the King now performed his part of ultimate adjudicator. What, he inquired, would be proper punishments for

the several parties incriminated in these occurrences?
Various opinions were offered. Then the King in
his fury condemned Smeraldina to the flames. Celio
appeared. He unmasked the hidden culpability of
Clarice, Leandro, and Brighella. They were sentenced
to cruel banishment. The two Princes were finally
summoned from the scullery, and universal gladness
crowned the termination of this high act of justice.

Celio warned Truffaldino that it was his most
solemn duty to keep Martellian verses, those inventions of the devil, out of all dishes served up at the
royal table. His function was to make his sovereigns
laugh.

The play wound up with that marriage festival
which all children know by heart—the banquet of
preserved radishes, skinned mice, stewed cats, and
so forth. And inasmuch as the journalists were
wont in those days to blow their trumpets of applause over every new work which appeared from
Signor Goldoni's pen, we concluded with an epilogue,
in which the spectators were besought to use all
their influence with these journalists, in order that
a crumb of eulogy might be bestowed upon our rigmarole of mystical absurdities.

It was not my fault that a courteous public called
for the repetition of this fantastic parody on many
successive evenings. The theatre was crowded, and
Sacchi's company began to breathe again after their
long discouragement.

VI.

Such is Gozzi's own account of his first acted fable.

The public had been invited to sit as umpires in the controversy between him and their two favourite playwrights. They had been requested to suspend their judgment before finally pronouncing sentence against the *Commedia dell' Arte*. The result of the experiment was a decided triumph for the author of the *Three Oranges*, for Sacchi's company, and for the Granelleschi. But, what was more important, Gozzi, at the commencement of his forty-first year, now discovered himself to be possessed of dramatic ability in no common degree, and of a peculiar kind. The success of the *Three Oranges* suggested the notion that use might be made of fairy tales, not only for maintaining the impromptu style of Italian Comedy, and amusing the public with piquant novelties, but also for conveying moral lessons under the form of allegory, and mingling tragic pathos with the humours of the masks. Accordingly Gozzi composed a succession of similar pieces, gradually suppressing the burlesque elements, enlarging the sphere of didactic satire, pathos, and dramatic action, relying less upon the mechanical attractions of transformation scenes and *lazzi*, writing the principal parts in full, and versifying a considerable portion of the dialogue.

Il Corvo was produced at Milan in the summer of 1761, and at Venice in October 1761. *Il Rè Cervo* appeared in January 1762; *Turandot* perhaps in the same month; *La Donna Serpente* in October 1762; *Zobeide* in November 1763; *I Pitocchi Fortunati* in November 1764; *Il Mostro Turchino* in December of the same year; *L'Augellino Belverde* in January 1765; *Zeim, Rè de' Geni* in November 1765. These, with *L'Amore delle Tre Melarancie*, form the ten *Fiabe*. After the production of *Zeim*, Gozzi judged that the vein had been worked out, and turned his attention to adaptations of Spanish dramas for the stage.

The occasional origin of the *Fiabe*, on which I have already insisted, accounts for their want of plastic unity, their jumble of oddly contrasted ingredients. They were not the spontaneous outgrowth of artistic genius seeking to fuse the real and the fantastic in an ideal world of the imagination; but monsters begotten by an accident, which the creative originality of a highly-gifted intellect turned to excellent account. Gozzi's predilection for burlesque, his satirical propensity and fondness for moralising on the foibles of his age, found easy vent in the peculiar form he had discovered by a lucky chance. But these motives were not subordinated to the higher coherence of imaginative poetry. IIis fancy, command of dramatic situations, intuition into character, rhetorical eloquence, and inexhaustible inventiveness expatiated in the region of caprice and wonder. Yet we do not feel that he has succeeded in harmonising these divers elements with the spiritual instinct of an Aristophanes or a Shakespeare. Probably he did not seek to do so. The numerous reflections on the *Fiabe*, which are scattered up and down his works, prove that art for art's sake was far from being the leading consideration in their production. They remained with him pastimes, which had partly a practical, partly a didactic purpose—convenient vehicles for indulging his literary bias and airing his ethical opinions — serviceable ammunition in the battle against men whom he regarded as impostors and pretenders—excellent means of putting money into the purses of his protegés, the actors, and of keeping himself in favour with his friends, the actresses. To the last they retained something of the *punctilio*, which, as he says, inspired him at the outset.

VII.

In all his *Fiabe* Gozzi employed the four Masks and the Servetta, Smeraldina.[1] He not unfrequently wrote the whole part of a mask, so that nothing re-

---

[1] See above, p. 112, for the names of the five actors who sustained these parts in Sacchi's company.

mained for impromptu acting but "gag" and *lazzi*.
Truffaldino's rôle, however, was invariably left to
improvisation ; perhaps in compliment to Sacchi's
talents and his prominent position. The other masks
were dealt with as Gozzi thought best. When the
dialogue acquired dramatic or satirical importance,
he wrote it out for them. On ordinary occasions he
intrusted the whole or a considerable portion of each
scene to their extempore ability, only indicating the
movement of the plot in a *scenario*. The parts of the
masks were treated in dialect and prose. The serious
actors, who had to sustain the scheme of the fable,
as lovers, magicians, queens, fairies, good and evil
spirits, spoke in Tuscan blank verse, occasionally
heightened by the use of Martellian rhymed couplets
at thrilling moments of the action. Thus it will be
seen that the text of Gozzi's plays offers every condition of dramatic utterance, from mere stage-direc-
tions, through carefully dictated prose, up to rhetorical
soliloquies and dialogues in verse of several descriptions. His dexterity as a playwright is shown in
the tact with which he employed these various resources.

The handling of the five fixed characters is masterly
throughout. Whether Gozzi writes their lines or
only indicates a theme for their impromptu declamation, he shows himself in perfect sympathy with an
intelligent and practised group of actors. The humour
of the man comes out to best advantage in this de-

partment. IIis language is most idiomatic and spontaneous here. IIere too we find his raciest characters. Powerfully conceived and boldly projected,
each comic personage breathes and moves with
vivid realism. Study of the Masks, as Gozzi treated
them, makes us feel what a wonderful thing of
plastic beauty the *Commedia dell' Arte* must have
been. IIere, in a work of carefully considered literary art, we have its long tradition and its manifold
capacities preserved for us. Reading a *Fiaba* is like
opening a bottle of rare old wine. The bouquet of
the fragrant vintage exhales into the chamber, and
we taste the bloom of bygone summers. But the
very conditions under which Gozzi exhibited this side
of his dramatic mastery render translation impossible.
In a translation the colours of the dialects are lost.
The gradations of style, passing from a laconically
worded *scenario* through half-dialogue into elaborated
scenes, are bound to disappear. Tuned to a foreign
language, our inward eye and ear fail to reconstruct
the *lazzi*, which rendered this part of the drama
humorous. That is why Schiller's *Turandot* is
inferior to Gozzi's; and yet, when Schiller selected
this piece for the German stage, he showed a right
artistic instinct. It is the one in which the fable
predominates, and can best be separated from the
humours of the Masks.

I dare not enlarge here upon the variety of shades
and complexions given to the five fixed types of

character, according as the plot demanded more or less of serious action from the several personages. This inquiry would be interesting, since it reveals their singular elasticity beneath a master's touch. It must, however, be left to amateurs of curiosities in art. The development of the subject in detail implies previous acquaintance with the ten *Fiabe*, and would involve a lengthy dissertation. Some general points may, nevertheless, be indicated.

Pantalone retains marked psychological outlines under all his transformations. He is the good-humoured, honourable, simple-hearted Venetian of the middle class, advanced in years, Polonius-like, with stores of worldly wisdom, strong natural affections, and healthy moral impulses. Gozzi has drawn the character in a favourable light, purging away those baser associations which gathered round it during two centuries of the *Commedia dell' Arte*. His Pantalone recalls the Cortesani, described in a chapter of the Memoirs ; but a touch of senility has been added, which lends comic weakness to the type.

Tartaglia stammers, and preserves something of the knave in his composition, burnished with Neapolitan abandonment to appetite and brazen disregard for moral rectitude. This general conception of the character explains the transformation of Tartaglia, in the *Three Oranges*, into the Tartaglia of the *Augellino Belverde*.

Brighella is an intriguing, self-interested individu-

ality, trying to turn the world round his fingers, and
not succceding, or succeeding only by some lucky
accident. He frequently assumes the form of a
simpleton befooled by his short-sighted cunning.

Truffaldino blossoms before us as an ubiquitous
and chameleon-like creature of caprice and humour;
the liberal, carnal, careless boon-companion; the
genial rogue and witty fool; bred in the kitchen;
uttering words of wisdom from his belly rather than
his brains; pliable, fit for all occasions; a prodigious coward; trusty in his own degree; taking the
mould of fate and circumstance, adapting himself to
external conditions; understanding nothing of the
higher sentiments and awful destinies which rule the
drama; but turning up at its conclusion with a rogue's
own luck in the place he started from, and on which
his heart is set, the larder. He runs like an inex-
pressibly comic thread of staring scarlet through the
warp and woof of Gozzi's many-coloured loom. The
most serious use made of him is when, in the *Augellino Belverde*, for purposes of pungent parody, Gozzi
invests him with the vizard of a Machiavellian egotist.
At the close of that supremely caustic scene, Truffaldino drops his disguise, and willingly assumes the
rôle of a domestic buffoon. Our author's trenchant
irony, that "smile on the lips with venom in the
heart," of which Goldoni wrote so lucidly, that touch
of bitterness which renders him akin to Swift, was
displayed by a stroke of genius here. Truffaldino,

the whelp whose antics dispelled melancholy, becomes for once in Gozzi's hands a stick wherewith to beat the dog of modern science.

Smeraldina, under her numerous manifestations, maintains the lineaments of vulgar womanhood. Sometimes a good mother or nurse, sometimes a shifty waiting-woman, sometimes a blustering amazon, sometimes a bad wife or would-be virgin, she never soars into the regions of ideality, and mates eventually with Truffaldino, if she escapes from being burned for blundering atrocities upon the road to commonplace felicity.

With these fixed characters, which form the most delightful ingredients of the *Fiabe*, Gozzi interweaves a fairy-tale, abounding in magic, flights of capricious fancy, marvels, transformations, perilous adventures. There is always a conflict of beneficent and malignant supernatural powers, ending in the triumph of good over evil, the reward of innocence, and the punishment of crime. There is a fate to which the heroes and heroines are subject, and which can only be overcome by protracted trials, by patience through dark years, by sustained endurance, terrible struggles, and faith in supernatural protectors. Thus the texture of the *Fiabe* is similar to that of our pantomimes, except that in the former the fairy-tale and the harlequinade are interwoven instead of being disconnected.

The fairy-tale is always treated in a serious spirit.

The didactic allegory, on which the author set such store, and which he regarded as the main purpose of his art, finds expression here. The fairy-tale is romantic, pathetic, heroic, sometimes acutely tragic. Gozzi interests himself in the creatures of fantastic fiction, and forces them to utter tones which vibrate in our entrails. Some scenes, written under the high pressure of dramatic œstrum, stir tears by their poignancy, by the accents of grief and anguish on the lips of *fantoccini*. It is a singular species of art, soaring by spasms and short gasps to dramatic sublimity, casting flashes of electric light on human nature in the garb of puppets, then passing away by abrupt transitions into mechanical improbabilities and burlesque absurdities—an art for marionettes rather than living actors, yet withal so vivid that able representation on the stage might translate it to our senses as an allegory of the masquerade world in which man lives :—

> " We are such stuff
> As dreams are made of, and our little life
> Is rounded with a sleep."

The Masks take part in the action, generally as subordinate personages, sometimes as persons of the first rank, never as mere accessories to move laughter, nor as a stationary chorus. In this way the comic element is ingeniously connected with the tragic and didactic. This sounds like a contradiction of what I have said above, about the want of plastic unity in

Gozzi's work.   Yet the two apparently contradictory
statements are true together.   Gozzi interweaves the
wires of humour and romance with remarkable skill.
But he does not fuse them into one poetic substance.
He fails to create an ideal world in which both tragedy
and comedy are necessary to the spiritual order, as are
the systole and diastole of the heart to an organised
being.   Though interlaced, they stand apart, each
upon its own clearly defined basis.   You pass from
the one sphere to the other, and have sudden shocks
communicated to your sensibility.   There is a lack of
atmosphere in the wonderfully brilliant and exciting
picture, an absence of spontaneous transition from
this mood to that, a suggestion that the playwright's
sympathies have been touched to diverse issues by
divers portions of his task.   Very probably, the
atmosphere, which I have indicated as wanting in
the *Fiabe*, may have been communicated by the
interaction of the members of Sacchi's troupe upon
the stage at Venice.   But this is only tantamount
to admitting that Gozzi understood the theatre.   It
does not prove that he was a dramatic poet in the
highest sense of that term.   Had he been this, we
should have submitted to his magic wand while reading him.   That is precisely what we wish to do, and
cannot always actually do.   His *Fiabe* remain stupendous sketches in a style of audacious and suggestive
originality.   They are not the inevitable products of
creative genius, fusing and informing—the children

of imagination, "dead things with inbreathed sense
able to pierce."

Had Gozzi been a great spontaneous poet, or a
consummate artist, this invention of the dramatised
Fiaba might have become one of the rarest triumphs
of artistic fancy.   It is difficult to state precisely what
his work misses for the achievement of complete
success.   Perhaps we shall arrive at a conclusion
best by inquiry into points of style and details of
execution.

VIII.

By singular irony of accident, the author of the
Fiabe, though he dealt so much in the fantastic, the
marvellous, and the pathetic, was far more a humo-
rist and satirist than a poet in the truer sense.   Of
sublime imagery, lyrical sweetness or intensity, ver-
bal melody and felicity of phrase, there is next to
nothing in his plays.   The style, except in the parts
written for the Masks, is coarse and slovenly, the
versification hasty, the language diffuse, commonplace, and often incorrect.   Yet we everywhere discern a lively sense of poetical situations and the
power of rendering them dramatically.   The resources
of Gozzi's inventive faculty seem inexhaustible; and
our imagination is excited by the energy with which
he forces the creations of his capricious fancy on our
intelligence.. The passionate volcanic talent of the

man almost compensates for his lack of the finer
qualities of genius.

What he wants is not the power of poetical conception, but the power of poetical projection; and
the defects of his work seem due to the partly
contemptuous, partly didactic, mood in which he
undertook them. It would be difficult to surpass
the pathos of Jennaro's devotion to his brother in *Il
Corvo*, or the dramatic intensity of Armilla's self-
sacrifice at the conclusion of that play. *Turandot*
is conceived throughout poetically. The melancholy
high-strung passion of Prince Calaf passes through
it like a thread of silver. In the *Rè Cervo*, Angela
has equal beauty. Her love of the man in the king,
and her discernment of her real husband under his
transformation into the person of a decrepit beggar,
are humanly and allegorically touching. Cherestani,
the Persian fairy, who loves a mortal in spite of the
doom attending her devotion, is admirably presented
at the opening of *La Donna Serpente*. The subter-
ranean labyrinth of lost women, degraded to monstrous shapes by their tyrannical seducer, in *Zobeide*,
merits comparison with one of the *bolge* in Dante's
Hell. Its horror is almost appalling. The love of
Barbarina for her brother in *L'Augellino Belverde*,
which melts the stony hardness of the girl's heart,
and changes her from a vain worldling to a woman
capable of facing any danger, is no less romantic
than Jennaro's love in *Il Corvo*. The picture of

Pantalone and his daughter Sarchè, in *Zeim Rè de'*
Genj, passing their quiet life aloof from cities on the
borders of an enchanted forest, touches our imagination with something of the charm we find in *Cymbe-*
line.   *Il Mostro Turchino* is romantically passionate
and highly-wrought.   It seems to call for music,
such music as Mozart invented for the *Zauberflöte*.
Or, since Gozzi had little in common with the gra-
cious spirit of Mozart, we might wish that this wild
fable had fallen into the hands of Verdi.   The composer of *Aïda* would have given it the wings of immortality.   Gulindì, by the way, in this last fable,
is a terrible portrait of the Messalina-Potiphar's-
wife.

    In selecting these passages for emphatic praise, I
wish to call attention to the power and beauty of
Gozzi's conception.   Not as finished literature, but
as the raw material of dramatic presentation, are they
admirable.   They need the life of action, the adjuncts
of scenery, the illusion of the stage.   And for this
reason it seems to me that, by means of prudent
adaptation, the *Fiabe* might furnish excellent *libretti*
to composers of opera.   This is a hint to musicians
of the school of Wagner—to that rare dramatic
genius, Boito!   Could the Masks be revived, and
their burlesque parts be spoken on the stage, while
orchestra and song were reserved for the serious
elements of the fable, I feel convinced that a new
and fascinating work of art might still be evolved

from such pieces as *La Donna Serpente* and *Il Mostro Turchino*.[1]

But this is a digression, which has for its object to indicate the region in which Gozzi's chief merit as a playwright seems to me to lie. The satire, which forms so prominent a feature in the *Fiabe*, impairs their artistic harmony. So far as this is literary (in the *Tre Melarancie, Il Corvo*, and elsewhere), it has lost its interest at the present day. So far as it is philosophical and didactic (as in *L'Augellino Belverde* and *Zeim*), it tends to break the unity of effect by the author's over-earnestness. So far as it is purely ethical, as in *Zobeide*, Gozzi loads his palette with colours too sinister and sombre. Perhaps, the political touches of satire in *I Pitocchi Fortunati* are the lightest and most genially used. Gozzi, as we have seen already, was a confirmed conservative. An optimist as regarded the institutions, religion, and social manners of the past, he was a bitter pessimist in all that concerned the changes going on around him. The new literature, the new philosophy, the new luxury, the new libertinism, which seemed to be flooding Italy from France, were the objects of his hatred and abhorrence. Calmon, in the *Augellino Belverde*, expresses Gozzi's personal convictions and beliefs in their fullest extent. But

---

[1] I wrote this in the spring of 1888, before I was aware that Wagner had set the *Donna Serpente* to music. His early piece, *The Fairies*, was composed in 1833, and first performed this year in June at Munich.

IL DOTTORE (1653)

Illustrating the Italian Commedia dell' Arte, or Impromptu Comedy

the following speech may be extracted from *Zeim Ré de Genj* as a fair summary of his social stoicism.[1] A Princess of Balsora, who has been brought up by one of the capricious tricks of fortune as a slave, is speaking :

> "Who am I ? That I know not. An old man,
> With snows upon his beard, in snow-white robes
> Attired, of serious and austere aspect,
> Reared me beneath a humble cottage roof.
> He told me that one day upon the bank
> Of foaming Tigris, wrapped in swaddling-clothes,
> He found me ; peradventure by my kin
> Abandoned, the cast fruit of shame and scorn.
> This good man taught me I was born to serve,
> To suffer, to endure ; and that I ought
> To bow beneath the will of supreme Heaven.
> ' Providence, holy, in her ways unknown,'
> He said, 'rules all things : in the scale ordained
> Of human beings great folk have their seat ;
> And so, by steps descending through all ranks,
> Down to the lowest folk, men live and work
> Subordinate. Ah ! do not be seduced,
> (He often warned me) by sophistic sages,
> Who bent on malice paint of liberty
> False lures for mortals, your own place to quit,
> The order due designed by Heaven for man !
> These sophists breed confusion, anarchy,
> Duty neglected at the cost of peace ;
> They stir up murders, thefts, impieties,
> And glut with blood the shambles of the state.
> Daughter, respect the great, love them, endure
> What in thy lot seems bitter, woo content,

---

[1] Act ii. sc. 5. In Masi's edition, vol. ii. p. 458. Readers who care for further diatribes *à la* Gozzi on these topics, may be referred to the *Astrazione* which serves as introduction to his translation of Boileau, Op., vol. vii. p. 53.

And stifle that snake envy in thy breast !
In the just eyes of Heaven a great man's acts,
Rightly performed, have no superior merit
To those of servants rightly done ; the road
Toward immortality lies open unto kings
And children of the people ; 'tis all one.
Only the soul that suffers and is strong,
Finds happiness.' So spake the firm old man ;
And firmly, in his strength of soul unshaken,
He sold me slave ; so I account me blessed,
As you shall trust me for a faithful slave."

IX.

Gozzi drew the subjects of his *Fiabe* from divers
sources. The chief of these was a book of Neapolitan
fairy-tales called *Il Pentamerone del Cavalier Giovan
Battista Basile, ovvero lo Cunto de li Cunti*. This
collection enjoyed great vogue in Italy during the
seventeenth and eighteenth centuries, and is still
worthy of attentive study by lovers of comparative
folklore. Some of the motives of the *Fiabe* have
been traced to the *Posilipeata di Massillo Repone*,
the *Biblioteca dei Genj*, the *Gabinetto delle Fate*,
the *Arabian Nights*, and those Persian and Chinese
stories which were fashionable a hundred and fifty
years ago. It was Gozzi's habit to interweave several
tales in one action ; and this renders researches into
the texture of his dramatic fables difficult. But the
inquiry is not one of great importance, and may well
be dismissed until the star of Gozzi shall reascend

the heavens, if time's whirligig should ever bring about this revenge.

L'Amore delle Tre Melarancie is both the simplest in construction and also the most artistically perfect of the ten *Fiabe*. In it alone the fairy-tale and the Masks are brought into complete harmony. No serious note breaks the burlesque style of the piece, while a sustained parody of Chiari's and Goldoni's mannerisms lends it the interest of satire. As he advanced, Gozzi gradually changed the form of his original invention. That fusion of fairy-tale and impromptu comedy in subordination to literary satire, which distinguishes the *Tre Melarancie*, was never repeated in his subsequent performances. The fable, with its romance, pathos, passion, adventure, magic marvels, and fantastic transformations, began to detach itself against the comedy. Both formed essential factors in Gozzi's later work; but the links between them became more and more mechanical. Satire, in like manner, did not disappear; but this was either used occasionally and by accident, or else it absorbed the whole allegory. The three ingredients, which had been so genially combined in the first piece, were now disengaged and treated separately. The sunny light of sportive humour, which bathed that wonderworld of fabulous absurdity, darkened as the clouds of didactic purpose gathered. The fairy-tale acquired an inappropriate gravity. Becoming aware of his dramatic talent, Gozzi assumed the tone of tragedy.

He treated the loves and hatreds, the trials and triumphs, the vices and virtues, the heroism and the baseness, of his puppets seriously. Nevertheless, he preserved the preposterous accidents of the fable. On those enchantments, whimsical oracles of fate, metamorphoses, talking statues, monsters, good and wicked genii, he was of course unable to bestow the same reality as on his human characters. Yet, having carried the latter out of the sphere of burlesque, he had to maintain a tone of realism with the former. But he could not wield the Prospero's wand of imaginative insight which brings the supernatural and the incredible within the range of actualities. Thus the marvellous elements of the fable remained stiff and artificial beside the natural pathos and passion of humanity.

Having recapitulated the chief features of the *Fiabe* in their later form, I will now analyse *L'Augellino Belverde*.

X.

Many years have elasped since Tartaglia married Ninetta. His father is dead, and he has fallen under the malignant influence of the Queen-Mother, Tartagliona. She persuades him that Ninetta has given birth to a pair of puppies, male and female, whereas the twins are really a fine boy and girl, called Renzo and Barbarina. Ninetta is condemned to be buried alive ; and Pantalone, Tartaglia's minister, receives commission to drown the supposed puppies. Instead of executing these orders, Pantalone sews the children up in oil-cloth, and sets them floating down a river. They are found and rescued by Smeraldina, a woman of good heart, who is married to the dissolute and worthless Truffaldino, a pork-butcher. When the play opens, eighteen years are supposed to have elapsed since the burial of Ninetta. All this while she has been kept alive by the Beautiful Green Bird, who is the King of Terradombra, condemned to take this form by magic arts. The Green Bird also has become the lover of Barbarina. Meanwhile Tartagliona is being courted by Brighella, who now appears in the character of a burlesque poet and seer. His pindaric prophecies and exaggerated flights of passion, alternating with the lowest language of the proletariate, afford excellent opportunities for caricature.

Renzo and Barbarina, growing up in the house of the pork-butcher, have improved their minds by assiduous reading of French philosophical treatises sold for waste paper. This education has persuaded them that all human actions and affections proceed from self-love, and that it is the duty of rational beings to preserve a cold impartiality, indifferent to emotions, regardless of comfort and vain pleasures, governed only by the dictates of the reason. Accident reveals to them that Smeraldina is not their mother, and that they are nameless foundlings. They determine to go forth alone, and seek their fortunes in the world. The scene in which they take leave of their kindly warm-hearted foster-mother is excellent. Gozzi has painted a pair of consummate prigs, whose natural instincts have been perverted by a false theory of life, and who have learned to call that reason which is really inhumanity. They tell Smeraldina that her unselfish charity to the foundling infants was a form of self-love, and that her continued attention to them for the last eighteen years had no higher motive.

Having quitted Smeraldina, with the loftiest airs of condescension, they set forth upon their travels. Getting lost in the wilderness, it begins to dawn upon them that self-love is one of the cardinal facts of human nature, to which even the most philosophical characters, when threatened with death by cold and famine, are subject. In the midst of these reflections, they are terrified with an earthquake and sudden darkness. A statue appears walking toward them, who informs them that he too was once a miserable philosopher, who petrified his own humanity and that of others by perverse principles analogous to those which have infected them. Consequently, he was doomed to be a statue, lying lifeless and inert among the rubbish of neglected things, until one of Renzo's and Barbarina's ancestors rescued him from filth and set him up in a garden of the city. This benefit he now means to repay by watching over the twins. First of all, he ardently desires to save them from the petrifaction which awaits all souls made frigid by a false philosophy. Next, he tells them that, though he knows the secret of their parentage, he may not reveal it. They have a dreadful doom impending over them ; and their eventual happiness can only be secured by the assistance of the Green Bird. His own name in the world was Calmon ; and he has now become the King of Images :[1]—

> " Molti viventi
> Sono forse più statue, ch'io non sono.
> Tu proverai qual forza abbia una statua,
> E come simulacro un uom diventi."

Then Calmon gives the twins a stone. They are to return to the city, and Barbarina is to throw the stone down before the royal palace. They will immediately become rich. In any great disaster, let them call on Calmon.

In this way Gozzi allegorises his own prejudice against the cold and shallow theories of society, which were infiltrating Italy from France.

The second act reveals Tartaglia. He is the victim of remorse, haunted by the memory of Ninetta, whom he buried alive in a hole beneath the scullery-sink. There is the floor on which she

---

[1] " Many are now alive,
Who haply are more statues than I am.
Thou shalt experience what power hath a statue,
And how a live man may ecome an image."

used to walk. There is the kitchen where she fluttered in the form of a dove. "O spirit of Ninetta, where art thou?" Tartaglia preserves the burlesque note of his Mask. Only one friend remains to him, his old henchman Truffaldino; but Truffaldino has become a pork-butcher, and forgotten him. Truffaldino at this juncture appears. He too gives himself philosophical airs, without concealing his gross appetites and greedy love of self. Tartaglia kicks him out of doors, and then passes to a scene of vituperation against his wicked mother, Tartagliona, the Queen of Tarocchi,[1] who has been the cause of all his misery. Tartagliona shows the worst side of her coarse malignant nature in the ensuing altercation, and departs vowing vengeance.

Her only consolation is that she is beloved by Brighella, the most famous poet of the age :[2]—

> " Non mancano
> In me vezzi, e lusinghe, ond' al mio fianco
> Fedel sia sempre. Ah, non vorrei, che alfine
> Le mie finezze a lui, negli altri amanti
> Destasser gelosia."

---

[1] *Tarocchi* is the name for the cards, seventy-eight in number, used in a now well-nigh forgotten game. Fifty-six cards of the whole series consist of the four Italian suits: Coppe, Spade, Bastoni, and Danari. The remaining twenty-two are properly called *Tarocchi*, and in the game of Taroc take precedence of any cards of the four ordinary suits.

> [2] " I too have charms,
> Sweet flatteries, dulcet wiles ; and to my side
> He shall be faithful ever. Yet I would not
> That, loving him, my kindness should arouse
> In hearts of others jealousy."

A new scene introduces Renzo and Barbarina. They have returned to the city, and are standing in front of the palace. Renzo begs his sister to throw the magic stone. Barbarina reminds him that if they become rich, all will be over with their philosophy. At last he persuades her to throw it, and she does so, bidding herself be mindful that a wretched pebble is the source of her future magnificence. In a moment a gorgeous palace rises, fronting the royal dwelling. Renzo's and Barbarina's rags are exchanged for splendid raiment. Moorish servants issue from the great gates with torches, and welcome their princely masters.

No sooner have the twins taken up their abode in this magic palace, than they begin to act like *parvenus* and *nouveaux riches*. Every folly, vanity, and false desire enters their heads. Their philosophy is forgotten. Brighella, in his character of seer, divines, meanwhile, that their presence threatens danger to the person of Tartagliona. He therefore endeavours to persuade the Queen to make her will in his favour. She very sensibly refuses, and bids him do all in his power to prolong the life of one whom he adores. He is obliged to meet her wishes, and divulges a plan whereby the twins shall be destroyed. The fairy Serpentina, he reminds her, owns apples which sing, and golden water which plays and dances. The adventure of stealing these magical objects involves the greatest peril. Certainly Barbarina will be

ruined if she longs to have them.   Accordingly,
when she appears at the window of her palace, Tartagliona from the opposite balcony is to repeat these
rhymes : [1]—

> " Voi siete bella assai ; ma più bella sareste,
>   S'un de' pomi, che cantano, in una mano areste.
>
> .   .   .   .
>
> Figlia voi siete bella ; ma più bella sareste,
>   S'acqua, che suona e balla, nell' altra mano areste."

The scene now changes to the interior of the
palace of the twins.   Barbarina is contemplating her
charms in the looking-glass, when Smeraldina suddenly enters, full of affection.   She has heard of the
good fortune of her foundlings, and forgetting their
recent ill-treatment of her, has come to congratulate
them.   Barbarina exclaims against her rudeness,
calls the servants, throws a purse of gold at her
foster-mother, and bids her depart.   Smeraldina, who
cannot stifle her affection for the ungrateful girl,
changes tone, and humbly asks to be allowed to
stay and serve her.   Barbarina, much to her own
surprise, feels touched by this display of feeling, and
magnanimously allows the good woman to remain
as a menial.   Smeraldina's soliloquy at the end of

---

[1] " Fair, yea, most fair thou art in sooth ; yet still more fair wouldst be
    Didst thou an apple hold which sings, plucked from the magic tree.

.   .   .   .

Daughter, I trow that thou art fair ; yet still more fair wouldst be
Didst thou that water hold which plays and dances merrily."

the scene reveals her sound sense no less than her warm heart:[1]

> " Questa è quella filosofa, che andava
> Ieri per legna al bosco, ed oggi ! . . . basta . . .
> Seco volea restar, perchè l'adoro,
> E seco resto alfin ; del tacer poi
> Ci proveremo ; ma non sarà nulla.
> Non la conosco più.   Quanta superbia !
> Che diavol l'ha arrichita in questa forma ?
> Io non vorrei, che questa frasconcella . . .
> Forse qualche milord . . . ma saprò tutto."
>
> *[Entra.*

Next we have Renzo.   He has fallen desperately in love with a beautiful statue which he found in the garden of the palace.   Truffaldino enters, frankly confesses that he has come to live at ease with his quondam foster-child, professes himself a true sage, and expounds the cynical philosophy of interested motives.   Renzo cannot resist laughing at the knave's candour, but is not yet disposed to bear his insolence.   Truffaldino sees that he must alter his tone.   So he begins to whine and flatter.   Renzo is softened, and consents to keep him as a buffoon.

---

[1] " So ! this is my philosopher, who went
  Yesterday picking sticks, and now ! . . . But patience ! . . .
  I wished to stay with her, for I adore her ;
  And stay with her I shall.   We must contrive
  To hold our tongue ; and yet this may not be.
  I vow I scarcely knew her !   What grand airs !
  Some devil must have daubed her o'er with gold.
  'Twould vex me sorely if the little hussy . . .
  Some rich milord perhaps. . . . Well, I'll know all."

  [Exit.

His cynicism and his hyperbolical adulation will
serve to make the hours pass pleasantly.

Tartaglia and Pantalone appear upon the royal
balcony. Barbarina enters on the other side, and
Tartaglia falls head over ears in love with her at first
sight. The scene is carried out with much burlesque
humour, until Tartagliona and Brighella join the
group below. Tartagliona utters the magic verses,
and Barbarina becomes madly bent upon the apples
which sing and the water which plays and dances.
Renzo, touched by his sister's despair, agrees to
attempt the adventure ; but before he goes, he gives
her a dagger. So long as this is bright, he will be
alive. If it drops blood, that is a sign that her
brother has died in the attempt.

A scene between Ninetta in her living tomb and
the Green Bird who brings her food, is here interpolated, in order to prepare the audience for what
ensues.

Renzo and Truffaldino arrive at Serpentina's garden, and fail in their adventure. Then Renzo calls
on Calmon, who appears, and summons a band of
statues—the female figure on the fountain at Treviso
and the Moors of the Campo de' Mori at Venice [1]—to
his aid. By their assistance a singing apple is pro-

---

[1] There are five of these old statues, painted, in Moorish costumes.
One of them has the name Rioba carved above his head. Everybody
in Venice, of course, knew them ; and their appearance on the stage
must have been mirth-promoting.

cured, and some of the dancing water is bottled in a phial. But Calmon and his band of statues remind Renzo that he is in duty bound to be grateful. Calmon lacks his nose; the fountain of Treviso's breasts are injured; the Moors have, each of them, some broken limb. Renzo must undertake to restore them properly, and all will go well with him.

Renzo promises; but he very soon forgets the shattered statues. Lost in admiration before the image of beautiful Pompea, he spends his days in wooing her. At length Pompea finds her voice, and confides to him her previous experience. She was the daughter of a great Italian prince, the prince of a corrupt but mighty city; and she has now become an idol through her self-idolatry.

At this juncture enters Truffaldino with exciting news. Tartaglia has made a declaration of his love through Pantalone to Barbarina. She wavers between the splendid prospects of a royal match and the affection which she feels for the Green Bird, her lover and consoler in their days of poverty. Meanwhile Tartagliona breaks negotiations off by declaring that Barbarina must bring the Green Bird as dower; else she can never be Tartaglia's bride. At this announcement Barbarina falls into hysterics, kicking Pantalone downstairs, and screaming out that nothing but the Green Bird will satisfy her. Truffaldino, partly out of compassion for Barbarina's state, partly from a sense of modesty, leaves her presence.

He arrives to rouse his master to a sense of the situation. This is no time to make platonic love to statues, &c.

Renzo replies that he is quite ready to attempt the adventure of the Green Bird. He knows from Calmon that the bird alone is capable of solving the problem of his own parentage, and also of evoking Pompea from her marble immobility. Consequently he has a strong personal interest in the capture of the bird ; and his sister's troubles are an additional reason why he should no longer delay. With Truffaldino for his squire, he will ride forth into the forest of the Goblin, who holds the bird in meshes of diabolical enchantments. Let Smeraldina remind his sister that the dagger which he gave her will assure her of his good or evil fortune in the perilous essay.

While Renzo is on his journey, Barbarina keeps continually gazing on the dagger. It does not cease to shine. But Smeraldina and the speaking statue of Pompea work upon her feelings by suggesting the perils her brother is undergoing, to which her own vanity has exposed him. Moved at last by simple human sympathy, she finds the situation intolerable, and resolves to follow Renzo to the place of danger. It is this return to nature which saves her, and brings about a happy catastrophe. Barbarina renounces her wish to wed Tartaglia, and thinks only of arresting Renzo in his dangerous course. She sets

off with Smeraldina; and the magic palace is left
desolate, in mourning, all its splendour gone.

Renzo and Truffaldino have now reached the
Goblin's hill, where the Green Bird is seen upon a
perch, chained by the leg. Trying to capture him,
Renzo turns into a statue; and there is a whole
gathering of similar statues in the place—men who
essayed the same adventure, and failed.

Barbarina and Smeraldina arrive at the scene of
action. The dagger drops blood. Barbarina's mask
of false philosophy and selfish vanity drops off. She
becomes a simple woman, filled with repentance and
anguish for her brother who is dead. She flings herself upon the bosom of poor Smeraldina, whom she
had so villainously treated. At this juncture, when
all seems lost, Calmon appears, and reads her a
sound moral lecture. Then he points to a scroll
before her feet, and instructs her what she has to do.
She must walk up to within a hair's-breadth—no
more and no less—of the bird, and take good heed
that he does not utter a sound before she has read
aloud the words inscribed upon the scroll. If she
succeeds in this feat, all may yet come right. There
is a breathless moment, during which Barbarina
executes what Calmon told her. The bird is captured,
and begins to talk. Let her take a feather from his
tail. That will restore the statues to life.

The drama is quickly wound up. By means of
the bird's tail-feather, Renzo and Pompea are made

happy lovers. Ninetta returns from her hole. Tartagliona is changed into a tortoise, and Brighella into
a donkey. The Green Bird resumes his form as
King of Terradombra and plights his faith to Barbarina. Tartaglia recognises his lost son and daughter,
and is fain to be contented with the resuscitated wife
whom he had so wantonly condemned to a lingering
death.

.   .   .   .

This analysis, if any one takes the trouble to read
it, will suffice to show the sprightliness of Gozzi's invention, and also the essential weakness of his artistic
method. The magic and the transformations at the
close are mechanical. The fate of the Green Bird is
connected by no proper motive with the fate of Tartaglia and the twins. Calmon and the statues, allegorically useful, are in like manner independent of
the main dramatic action. Ninetta's doom is atro-
cious. Tartaglia is only saved from being disgusting
by his burlesque absurdity.

XI.

In the spring of 1762, having exhibited *Le Tre
Melarancie, Il Corvo, Il Rè Cervo,* and *Turandot,*
Gozzi proved that he had won the game against
Chiari and Goldoni. Sacchi's company removed
from the theatre at S. Samuele to a more commodi-

ous house at S. Angelo. Chiari retired to his native city, Brescia, and left off writing for the stage. Goldoni departed for Paris. None of Goldoni's biographers deny that he took this step in consequence of Gozzi's triumph. In his own Memoirs he omitted all references to the literary quarrels of the years 1756–62 ; and he gives excellent reasons, quite independent of Gozzi, for his setting off to seek fortune in the French capital. Certainly, the last piece he presented to the Venetian public, *Una delle ultime sere di Carnovale*, was received with enthusiasm. "It closed the theatrical year of 1761," he says ;[1] "and the evening of Shrove Tuesday brought me an ovation. The theatre rang with thunders of applause, among which could be distinguished these farewells: *A happy journey ! Come back to us ! Be sure you do not fail to do so !* I confess that I was touched to tears." Yet the simultaneous retirement of both Chiari and Goldoni at this critical moment justifies our believing that the latter judged it expedient to leave Venice after the revolution effected by Gozzi. He did so without ill-will on either side. Count Gasparo Gozzi, Carlo's brother, and a distinguished member of the Granelleschi, undertook the charge of seeing a new edition of Goldoni's plays through the press in his absence.

For some years after this event, Carlo Gozzi and Sacchi's company had the theatres of Venice pretty

---

[1] *Mémoires*, part ii. cap. 45.

much at their own disposal. But the success of the
Fiabe was ephemeral. Before their author's death,
he saw his own dramatic novelties cast into the shade
and Goldoni's realistic comedies restored to favour.
A poet of such eminence as Goethe, surveying all
things Italian with curiosity in 1786, paid a well-
considered tribute to Gozzi's sympathy with the
Venetian public, praised the energy and nature of
the *Commedia dell' Arte*, but reserved his highest
panegyric for a representation of Goldoni's *Baruffe
Chiozzote* at the theatre of S. Luca.[1] "At last I am
able to say that I have seen a comedy," are the
emphatic words with which Goethe opens a detailed
description of this piece.

In the course of the last hundred years, Goldoni
has secured a signal and irreversible victory over his
rival. One of the best theatres at Venice is called
by his name. His house is pointed out by gondoliers to tourists. His statue stands almost within
sight of the Rialto on the Campo S. Bartolommeo,
where people most do congregate. His comedies
are repeatedly given by companies of celebrated
actors. Gozzi's *Fiabe* have been relegated to the
marionette stages, where some of their *scenari* in a
mutilated form may still be seen. There exist no
memorials to his fame in Venice. Not even a tablet
with the words *Qui nacque Carlo Gozzi* is to be

---

[1] Letters from Italy, dated October 4, October 6, and October 10, 1786.

found upon the ancient palace at S. Cassiano. The
sacristan of the church, where his dust is gathered
to his fathers, cannot point to the Gozzi vault.

The vicissitudes of Gozzi's reputation turn upon
the different views which have been taken of his
merits in relation to Goldoni.   In Italy the balance of
opinion tends to sink against him.   Baretti, that fiery
member of Sam Johnson's club, the fierce opponent
of Goldoni, pronounced at first in Gozzi's favour,
lamented that he could not bring Garrick to one
of his plays, proposed to translate the *Fiabe* into
English, and swore that Gozzi stood next to Shakespeare in dramatic genius.   But when Baretti read
the *Fiabe* in print, he declaimed against the buffooneries of the Masks, and dropped his enthusiasm.
Tommasei found no words too strong to express
his contempt for a writer whose genius he denied,
and whose character inspired him with repugnance.
Tommasei was a champion of Goldoni.   Omitting
further details, it is enough to say that Italy has
elected to ignore Gozzi and to deify Goldoni.   The
causes are not far to seek.   Gozzi's vogue depended
partly upon controversy and satire.   It was confined
to the locality of Venice.   His plays required the co-
operation of the Masks ; and these expired in his own
lifetime.   Moreover, they appealed to a rare combina-
tion of sensibilities, romantic and humorous, which
is not common in Italy.   Lastly, for their proper
mounting on the stage, they demanded an expendi-

ture of ingenuity and money, which their fading popularity prohibited. Goldoni, on the other hand, suited the temper of the growing age by his simplicity, his truth to nature, his realism, and the freshness of eternal youth which lends charm to the facile productions of his amiable genius. His comedies can be put upon the stage without the least difficulty; and they afford scope for the display of varied talents in actors of several descriptions.

In Germany Gozzi enjoyed wide posthumous reputation, not as a playwright with the public, but as a poet among men of letters. He was early chosen, during the *Sturm und Drang* period, to perform the part of champion of Romantic against Classical forms of art. How mistaken this view of Gozzi really is, I have attempted to prove. Yet if critics ignore what Gozzi wrote about the origin of his *Fiabe*, and keep out of sight his intentions while composing them—if they only regard the printed plays—it is not difficult to make him assume this false position. Franz A. C. Werthes translated the *Fiabe* into German so early as 1777–79, and published them at Bern. No less than twelve separate versions of selected plays have since appeared, up to the date 1877.[1] Among these may be mentioned Schiller's *Turandot*, which was executed from the translation of Werthes, and a reproduction of *I Pitocchi Fortunati* by Paul Heyse. Schlegel introduced the *Fiabe*

---

[1] See Masi's Essay, p. cxxxii.

to public notice, emphasising their value as specimens of the Romantic style, and connecting them with
the indigenous art of Italy.   Hoffmann declared his
enthusiasm for Gozzi; and if he did not borrow
motives from the *Fiabe* and the *Memoirs* for his
own fantastic productions, he undoubtedly regarded
their author as a genius of the same species as himself.   Wagner, I may parenthetically observe, based
one of his earliest operatic productions on *La Donna
Serpente*.   It was composed in 1833, and was first
exhibited at Munich in 1888.   To follow the several
steps by which Gozzi came to be regarded in Germany
as a Romanticist, snuffed out by the Revolution, would
lead me beyond the limits of this introduction.   I
suspect that he was known there mainly in the translation of Werthes, and that his works were quarried
as a mine of motives by writers of romantic tendencies,
who lacked invention.   There is a pocket edition of the
Fiabe in Italian, 3 vols., published by Hitzig, 1808.

The German conception of Gozzi as a Romantic
poet of the purest water spread to France.   It took
the French imagination just when the Romantic
movement was at its height.   Philarete Chasles
treated his works from the point of view of Spanish
dramatic literature.   Paul de Musset pounced upon
the Memoirs, condensed them into a small volume
with considerable literary ability, and so ingeniously
manipulated their text in the process as to create the
illusion that Gozzi had pronounced himself to be

iu fact what his German admirers found in him.
This clever travesty of Gozzi's autobiography presented him to the world as the victim of sprites,
the creature of his own inventions, the plaything of
superstition, instead of the caustic, practical, sometimes dissembling, and often sinister, man of thwarted
passion, violent caprice, hard head, and conservative
heart, who will presently be revealed in my version
of the Memoirs. I do not blame Paul de Musset
for his literary escapade. I understand his motive,
and appreciate the joke. He wanted, at one and the
same time, to place Gozzi, as the Germans had already
placed him, among the fathers of Romanticism, and
also to construct a telling novel of adventure out
of the copious materials furnished by the Memoirs.
But, by so doing, Paul de Musset misled writers who
had no access to the sole edition of Gozzi's *Memorie*,
or who were perhaps too careless to seek this document
out.   Among these I may mention M. Paul Royer,
the translator of five of Gozzi's *Fiabe* into French,[1]
and Vernon Lee, the talented authoress of a deserv-
edly popular book entitled *Studies of the Eighteenth
Century in Italy*.[2] . Both of these distinguished
writers have fallen into the trap laid for them by
Paul de Musset, and have accepted a false conception
of the man who forms the subject of these volumes.

[1] *Carlo Gozzi, Théatre Fiabesque, Alphonse Royer.* Paris, Michel Levy,
1865.
[2] London, W. Satchell & Co. 1880.

Gozzi, who plumed himself upon his Democritean philosophy of laughter, his Stoic-Epicurean acceptance of every wayward stroke of fortune, would have been the first to smile sardonically, yet not without a touch of benignant humour, upon the mask he has been made to wear by Germans and by Frenchmen. English critics, with the exception of Vernon Lee, have had little or nothing to do with him up to this date.[1] Let the man speak for himself in the account of his own life, which I now for the first time present to the multitude of English readers.

August 8, 1888.

---

[1] Through the courtesy of Mr. John P. Anderson of the British Museum I am able to state that, besides a short article in the *Encyclopædia Britannica*, he can only discover an essay in *Lippincott's Magazine* (vol. xx. p. 347, &c.), entitled "A Venetian of the Eighteenth Century," which deals with Carlo Gozzi.

CARLO GOZZI.

I.

My Pedigree and Birth.

THERE are people foolish enough to make every family history the object of their ridicule and satire. For the sake of wits of this sort I shall give a short but truthful account of my ancestry, in order that they may have something to quiz.

Our stock springs in the fourteenth century from a certain Pezòlo de' Gozzi. This is proved by an authentic genealogy, which we possess; the authority of which has never been disputed, and which has been accepted as evidence in law-courts, although it is but a dusty document, worm-eaten and be-cob-webbed, not framed in gold or hung against the wall. Since I am no Spaniard, I never applied to any genealogist to discover a more ancient origin for our race. There are historical works, however, which derive us from the family de' Gozze, extant at the present epoch in Ragusa, and original settlers of that

venerable republic. The chronicles of Bergamo relate that the aforesaid Pezòlo de' Gozzi was a man
of weight and substance in the district of Alzano,
and that he won the gratitude of the most serene
Republic of Venice for having imperilled his property
and person against the Milanese in order to preserve
that district for her invincible and clement rule.
His descendants held office as ambassadors and
podestàs for the city of Bergamo, which proves that
they were members of its Council; while two privileges of the sixteenth century show that two separate
branches of the family obtained admission to the
citizenship of Venice.[1]   They erected houses for the

---

[1] The Gozzi family were thus *Cittadini Originari* of Venice. These
Cittadini had to prove legitimate birth in the city ; three generations
during which the family had exercised no mechanical arts ; freedom from
any criminal stain, debts to the state, or factious behaviour. Citizenship, as in the case of the Gozzi, was also granted by privilege. The
Cittadini formed a class of burgher aristocracy, ranking below the
patricians and taking no part in the actual government of the State,
since they did not vote in the Consiglio Grande. Their names, pedi-
grees, and arms were enrolled in a book, of which many copies exist,
and which was commonly called the *Libro d'Argento*, to distinguish it
from the *Libro d'Oro* of the patricians. In a MS. of the seventeenth
century, which belonged to Cicogna, now at the Museo Civico, entitled
Le Due Corone della Nobiltà Veneziana, Corona Seconda, the Gozzi arms
are blazoned thus : "Or, on the topmost branches of an olive-tree vert
a dove ppr., and round the stem of the tree a scroll argent inscribed
Signum Pacis." The family is described as wealthy ; but no pedigree
is given : *Non vi è albero*. Carlo Gozzi, in his *Lettera Confutatoria,
Memorie*, vol. iii. p. 31, asserts that the privilege of citizenship was
given to his ancestors by the Doge Cicogna (1585-95). It is neither
impossible nor improbable that the Gozzi of Bergamo were derived from
the same stock as the Gozze or Gozzi of Ragusa. These latter drew

living and provided tombs for their dead in the quarter
and the Church of San Cassiano, as may be seen at
the present day.[1] One of these branches was honoured
with adoption into the patrician families of Venice
in the seventeenth century,[2] and afterwards expired.
The branch from which I am descended remained
in the class of Cittadini Originari, on which they
certainly brought no discredit whatsoever.

None of my ancestors aspired to the honourable
and lucrative posts which are open to Venetian
citizens.[3] They were for the most part men of peaceful unambitious temper, contented with their lot in
life, or perhaps averse from the disturbances of competition. Had they entered upon a political career,
I am quite sure that they would have served their
Prince faithfully, without pride and without vain
ostentation.

---

their pedigree from Herzegovina, and were therefore Slavs. We know
that the patrician families of Polo and Sagredo came originally from
Sebenico.

[1] Their palace is still inhabited by a Conte Gozzi. The *arca*, or family
sepulture, can no longer be traced in the church. It was at the foot of
the altar in the Chapel of the Madonna. Here Carlo Gozzi was buried.

[2] In a voluminous MS. written by Cicogna, embodying all he could
collect about the *Famiglie Cittadine* (now at the Museo Civico), we find
that *Alberto Gozi detto delle Sede* was inscribed among the patricians in
1646. I may mention that Cicogna tricks the arms of Gozzi without
the dove.

[3] The Grand Chancellor, the Ducal Notaries, and the Secretaries of
many Magistracies, were chosen from the *Cittadini*, who were also sent,
after holding such posts, as ambassadors of the second class, or Residents,
to foreign Courts.

About two centuries ago, my great-great-grand-father purchased some six hundred acres of land,[1] together with buildings, in Friuli, at the distance of five miles from Pordenone. A large portion of these estates consists of meadow-land, and is held by feudal tenure. All the heirs-male are bound to renew the investiture, which costs some ducats. Upon this point the officials of the Camera de' Feudi at Udine are extremely vigilant. If the fine is not paid immediately after the death of the last feudatory, they confiscate the crops derived from the meadows subject to this tenure. That happened to me after my father's decease. A few months' negligence cost me a considerable sum in excess of the customary fine. It is probably by right of some old parchment that we own the title of Count, con-ceded to our family in public acts and in the ad-dresses of letters.[2] I should feel no resentment, if this title were refused me ; but it would anger me extremely, if my hay were withheld.

My father was Jacopo Antonio Gozzi ; a man of fine and penetrative intellect, of sensitive and delicate honour, of susceptible temper, resolute, and some-

---

[1] The word, which I have translated acre, is *campo*. Now the *campo* differed in different provinces of Lombardy. But the *Campo Padovano* corresponded pretty nearly to an English acre ; and from another passage in Gozzi (*Memorie*, vol. iii. p. 226) it appears that he was in the habit of using the Paduan standard.

[2] The Gozzi were what are called in Venice *Conti di Terra Ferma*, and their title seems to have been dependent upon these feudal tenures.

times even formidable. His father Gasparo died while he was yet a child, leaving this only son to the guardianship of his mother, the Contessa Emilia Grampo, a noble woman of Padua. The estate was sufficient to sustain his dignity with credit; but he indulged dreams of magnificence. Sole heir, and educated by a tender mother, who humoured every fancy of her son, he early acquired the habit of following his own inclinations. These led him into lordly extravagances—stables full of horses; kennels of hounds; hunting-parties; splendid banquets—nor did he reflect upon the consequences of a marriage, which he made without deliberation in his early manhood, to indulge a whim of the heart. My mother was Angela Tiepolo, the daughter of one branch of that patrician house, which expired in her brother Almorò Cesare.[1] He died, a Senator of the Republic, about the year 1749.

---

[1] At the time when Gozzi wrote, this was the eldest branch, called Di San Fantin. Two remote branches, of S. Apollinare and San Polo, survived. They descended from a collateral ancestor, Girolamo Tiepolo, who died in 1516. The branch of S. Polo expired in 1820. See Litta, *Famiglie Celebri.* The Tiepolo family was one of the oldest and most illustrious among the patrician houses. It ranked with the *Case vecchie,* as distinguished from the *Case nuove.* These *Case vecchie* were also called *tribunizie,* from having exercised the highest offices of State at the time when Venice was still governed by tribunes, and before the foundation of the Dogeship. Of these oldest and purest noble houses there were twenty-four. The closing of the Grand Council in 1297, which determined the oligarchical character of the Venetian government, led to an attempted revolution in the State by Baiamonte Tiepolo. Tiepolo's conspiracy was really an effort in the interests of the old aristocracy to

I shall perhaps have wearied my readers with these facts about my pedigree and birth. Satirists will not, however, find in them anything to excite ambition in myself or to wing their pen with ridicule. Social ranks have always been regarded by me as accidental, though necessary for the proper subordination on which our institutions depend. As for my birth, I think less of whence I came than of whither I am going. Conduct unworthy of a decent origin might cause sorrow to my deceased parents, whose memory I hold in honour, and might cover myself and all my posterity with shame.

My name is Carlo. I was the sixth child born by my mother into the light, or shall I say the shadows of this world. I am writing on the last day of April in the year 1780. I have passed fifty, and not yet reached the age of sixty.[1] I shall not put the sacristan to trouble in order to view the register of my baptism, being quite sure that I was christened, and not

throw off the yoke which *novi homines* were fixing on the commonwealth. An excellent essay on Baiamonte Tiepolo will be found in H. F. Brown's *Venetian Studies*. I may add to this note that the Gozzi had previously intermarried with the Corner, Zuccato, Donà, and Morosini, patrician houses of high respectability.

[1] Carlo Gozzi was born December 13, 1720. He probably knew that he was in his sixtieth year; and this passage enables us to measure the exact amount of duplicity which he thought venial in composing his Memoirs. It was Gozzi's object to extenuate the fact that his *liaison* with Teodora Ricci had been carried on when he was past the age of fifty. When he asserts that he had "not yet reached the age of sixty," he was just within the bounds of veracity; for he wanted more than seven months to complete his sixtieth year.

having the stupid vanity to pass for a curled dandy.
That is obvious, and has been always obvious, from
the fashion of my clothes and the way I dress my
hair. ' Besides, I set no value on the age of men.
Human beings die at all ages ; and I have seen boys
who are adult, while grown-up men or grey-beards
are often nothing better than peevish and ridiculous
children.

II.

My Education and Circumstances down to the Age of Sixteen—
Concerning the Art of Improvisation, and my Literary
Studies.

Our family consisted of eleven children, male and
female.   I could record nothing but what is credit-
able of my brothers and sisters, had I proposed to write
their memoirs.   But this is not my thought ; and they
are capable of writing their own, if the whim should
take them ; for the epidemic of literature was always
chronic in our household.

A succession of priests with little learning were
our domestic pedagogues up to a certain age.   I say
a succession advisedly ; each in turn having earned
his dismissal by impertinent behaviour and intrigues
with the serving-maids.

From early childhood I was always a silent observer
of men and things, by no means insolent, of imper-

turbable serenity, and extremely attentive to my lessons.   My brothers used my taciturn and peaceable
temper to their own advantage.   They accused me to
our common tutor of all the naughtinesses of which
they had been guilty.   I did not condescend to excuse
myself or to accuse them, but bore my unjust punishments with stoicism.   I venture to affirm that no boy
was ever more supremely indifferent than I was to the
terrible penalty of being sent away from table just as
we were sitting down to dinner.   Smiling obedience
was my only self-defence.   Enemies may conclude from
these traits of character that I was a stupid lout, and
friends that I was a philosopher in embryo.   Nothing
is rarer than the eye of equal justice.   Yet any one
who takes the trouble to inquire of my acquaintances
and servants, will learn that my taciturnity, my toler-
ance, my stoical endurance, have not changed with
years—that I continue to view the events of this life
with a smile, and that only those have nettled me
which touched my honour.

The growing disorder in our family affairs did not
at first deprive us boys of a sound education.   My
two elder brothers, Gasparo and Francesco, went to
public schools,[1] and were in time to drink at all the
fountains of the regular curriculum.   Extravagant
expenditure, however, combined with the needs of
a numerous progeny, soon rendered anything like

---

[1] *Collegi.*   Gasparo was educated in the Somaschan establishment at
S. Cipriano on the island of Murano.

an adequate course of studies impossible for the younger children. I was intrusted for some years to a learned country-parson, and then to a priest in Venice, of decent acquirements and excellent morality. After this I entered the academy of two Genoese priests, who supplied instruction to some youths of noble birth, and to some of no nobility whatever. There were about twenty-five pupils in this academy. We pursued the same studies, with some difference according to our classes. Here I had the opportunity of observing that teachers are very valuable guides to youths who love learning, and mere images of ineffectual deities to such as hate it. For my part, being fond of books and eager for information, I imbibed my fill of such instruction as a boy can acquire before the age of fourteen. But sloth and vicious habits extirpate the seeds of learning planted by preceptors in the minds of ill-conditioned lads. Therefore I saw, and still see, more than two-thirds of my fellow-pupils sunk in a slough of baseness. Grammar, the classics, and rhetoric only taught them to get drunk in taverns, to carry sacks for hire upon their shoulders, and to cry "*Baked apples, plums, and chestnuts!*" about the streets, with a basket on their heads and a pair of scales slung round their waists. Wretched fate to be a father!

When I became aware that our domestic difficulties would prove an obstacle to my remaining

long at school, I determined to utilise the little I
had already learned, and to carry on my education
by myself. My elder brother Gasparo's example,
whose passion for study had won public recognition,
and my own good-will, kept me nailed to books of
all sorts; nor could I imagine any pleasure worth a
thought, beyond reading, meditating, and writing.

Poetry, choice Italian, and correct style were then
in vogue. The young men of Venice met to discuss
these three topics, which have now been utterly
forgotten—possibly for the greater advantage and
convenience of our citizens. I see crowds of young
people, hair-brained, conceited, idle, frivolous, presumptuous, and harmful to society. Heaven knows
what their studies are! Not poetry, not the nice-
ties of the Italian language, not correction of style.
And then, forsooth, I am to admire a hurly-burly
of well-born persons, who claim in their foolhardiness to be omniscient, who produce nothing whatsoever, who cannot write three lines of a letter which
shall express their sentiments, and which shall not
swarm with revolting faults of grammar and of
spelling!

I will omit to observe that respect for nobles in a
state is necessary; but that the respect shown simply
for their birth and wealth is not respect but false
feigned adulation. I will refrain from asserting that
a daily correspondence, maintained with a large
variety of persons—people who may not perhaps be

scientific, but who understand whether a letter is well written or ridiculous—may be capable of securing a large part of the regard, or of occasioning a large part of the contempt, bestowed on nobles. I make no mention of the rich man in Signor Mercier's comedy of Indigence, who found it impossible to write a letter of the utmost importance because his secretary was away from home. I will say nothing to those scientific tutors of the scions of our aristocracy, who instil derision and disdain for polite literature and the art of elegance in diction into the brains of their pupils, moulding them into geometricians, mathematicians, philosophers, physicists, astronomers, algebraical professors, naturalists, a whole deluge of sciences, but who cannot after all their labour express in writing what they have taught or what the common business of life requires.

All these things, and everything which imposture has presented to my senses and impressed upon my mind, must remain unwritten in my pen. I have no wish to make enemies.

Yet we cannot prevent drops of ink from falling sometimes from the pen and making blots upon our papers. Just so, while I am dictating these memoirs of my life, I shall not be able to avoid splutterings, however out of place and inconvenient.

I am almost ashamed to confess the intense assiduity with which I applied myself to those frivolous literary studies of which I have been speak-

ing. They brought on a hæmorrhage from the
nostrils, so violent and so frequent, that I was more
than once or twice given up for dead in the manner
of Seneca.[1] In their anxiety about my health, my
friends hid away all my books, and deprived me of
paper and inkstand; but I was the cleverest of thieves
in searching for them, and went on doggedly reading and writing by stealth in the uninhabited attics
of our mansion. After relating this fact about my
boyhood, malicious people may think that I am
claiming to be considered worthy of a panegyric.
They are quite mistaken. I fix them with my eye-
glass, and assure them that it is rather my intention
to provide them with another good reason for quizzing
me. The famous Doctor Tissot angrily rebukes excessive application to those studies which are universally esteemed as useless. He reserves his praise
for folk who ruin their health in pursuits considered
beneficial to humanity; and such, I do not doubt,
are the studies affected by himself and his admirers.

The Abbé Giovan Antonio Verdani, keeper of
the select and extensive library of the patrician
family Soranzo, was a man of vast literary erudition.
He felt compassion for my weakness, which coincided
with his own, and directed my reading by lending me
the rarest books, masterpieces of pure Italian diction in prose and poetry. To estimate the quantities

---

[1] Casanova, in the first chapter of his Memoirs, says that he suffered
during his boyhood from the same violent hæmorrhages.

of paper which I covered with my thoughts in verse and prose, would be beyond my powers. I tried to imitate the style of all the early Tuscan writers who are most admired. Assuredly I never approached the perfection of their language ; but I am none the less sure that the diligent and attentive perusal of a mass of the best works, treating of a vast variety of subjects, cannot fail to furnish a better head than mine with instruction and ideas, with the power of making just reflections and probable conjectures, and with the principles of sound morality. I am also convinced that the imitation of style in writing, pursued methodically, enables a man to express his own thoughts with facility, propriety of colouring, exactitude of phrase and term, according to the variety of images, grave or gay, familiar or dignified, which we desire to develop and to communicate under their true aspect in prose or poetry.

Without attaining to the mastery of style at which I aimed, I acquired the miserable satisfaction of finding myself in the very select group of persons who know this truth. I also earned the wretchedness of being forced to read with insuperable aversion and disgust the works of many modern Italian authors, which are full of false fancies and sophisms, the rhetoric and diction of which never vary however the subject-matter changes, which are defiled by all manner of gibberish, bombast, nonsense, with periods involved in unintelligible vortices, and with preposterous phraseology. The sciences, the discoveries, the branches of new knowledge which are now so loudly vaunted, ought to be accepted as useful, and are worthy of respect. For this reason it is wrong to profane them and to render them contemptible by barbarous impurity and impropriety of diction. Francesco Redi, that great man, great philosopher, great physician, great naturalist, confirms my doctrine by his written works.[1] As regards the literature of art and wit and fancy, it is obvious that without correction of style this is absolutely worthless and condemned to merited oblivion. No one could count the fine and ample sentiments which perish, smothered in the mire of inartistic writing. Not less numerous, on the other hand, are the small but brilliant thoughts, duly coloured with appropriate terms, and placed at the right point of view by a master-hand, which sparkle before the eyes of every reader, be he learned or simple.

There is no disputing about tastes. Yet I think it could be easily maintained that our century has lapsed into a shameful torpor with regard to these things. I have written and printed quite enough upon the subject; without effect, however; and now I see no reason why I should not utter a last funeral lament over the mastery of art I longed to possess.

---

[1] Gozzi might have cited Galileo, whose style, formed by the study of the "divine" Ariosto, is a model of exquisite and urbane Italian diction.

That mastery, which nowadays is reckoned among the inutilities of existence, has been freely conceded to me by the verdict of contemporaries—blind judges, governed not by intelligence but by ignorant assumption—so that their opinion does not sustain me with the sure conviction of having attained my purpose. Nevertheless I am grateful even to the blind and deaf, who see and hear what gives them pleasure in my writings.

My pursuit of culture advanced on the lines I have described, whether for my happiness or my misfortune it is worthless to inquire. I read continually, and wasted enormous quantities of ink; paid close attention to men and manners; profited by the encouragement of the Abbé Verdani and Antonio Federigo Seghezzi; walked in the steps of my brother Gasparo; and frequented a literary society which met daily at our house. From a Piedmontese, who knew how to read and nothing more, I learned the first rudiments of French; not that I wished to talk French in Italy, an affectation which I loathed; but because it was my desire, by the help of grammar and dictionary, to study the books, most excellent in part, in part injurious to society, which issue daily from the French press. It was thus that I formed those literary tastes, to which I have always clung for innocent and disinterested amusement, and which, now that my hairs are grey, will be my solace till the hour of death. The giants of science, to whom I

dare not raise my quizzing-glass for fear of committing an unpardonable sin, will perceive that in describing the scanty sources of my education, I am only
painting the portrait of a literary pigmy in all humility.

As regards my moral training, it is only necessary
to observe that the family of which I was a member
has always cherished a deep and fervent reverence
for the august image of religion, and that my father,
careless as he was in matters of economy, never
neglected religious duties or the good ensample of
honourable conduct.   He was a bitter enemy of
falsehood.   His delicate susceptibility detected a lie
by the inflection of the voice, and he punished it
upon the spot with sounding boxes on the ears of
his offspring.

Being a bold rider and passionately fond of horses,
he taught us to ride, and liked to see us every day on
horseback during our summer visits to the country.
It was useless to plead timidity, or to shrink from
the snortings and jibbings of some half-broken beast
he wanted us to back.   Up we went; a cut or two
of the switch across our legs set us off at a gallop;
and there we were in full career, without a thought
for broken shins or necks.   Some jockeys, who came
to break in vicious colts, put me up to tricks for
mastering a hard-mouthed bolting animal.   One of
these tricks stood me in good stead upon an occasion
I shall afterwards relate.   Indeed, I may say that I
owe my life to a jockey.

We had a little theatre of no great architectural
pretensions in our country-house; and here we
children used to act.[1] Brothers and sisters alike
were gifted with some talent for comedy; and all of
us, before a crowd of rustic spectators, passed for
players of the first quality. Beside tragic and comic
pieces learned by heart, we frequently improvised farces
with a slight plot upon some laughable motive. My
sister Marina and I had the knack of imitating certain
married couples notorious in the village for their
burlesque humours. We used to interpolate our
farces with scenes and dialogues in which the famous
quarrels of these women with their drunken husbands
were reproduced to the life. Our clothes were copied
from the originals; and the imitation was so exact
that our bucolic audience hailed it with Homeric
peals of laughter, measuring their applause by the
delight it afforded their coarse natures. My father and
mother took a fancy to see themselves represented
in this way. My sister and I were shy at first, but we
had to obey our parents. Finally, we regaled them
with a perfect reproduction of their costume, their
gestures, their way of talking, and some of their

---

[1] Compare what Goldoni says about the marionette theatre at his
grandfather's country-seat. In some of the great villas of the Venetian
nobility these private stages were built on an enormous scale. The
account of Marco Contarini's theatre at Piazzola near Padua, and of the
sumptuous dramatic performances which took place there, reads like a
passage from the *Arabian Nights*. See Romanin's *Storia di Venezia*,
vol. vii. p. 550.

familiar household bickerings. Their astonishment was great, and their laughter was the only punishment of our dutiful temerity.

I learned to twang the guitar with a certain amount of skill, and vied with my brother Gasparo in improvising rhymed verses, which I sang to music in our hours of recreation. This was done with all the foolhardiness inseparable from a display which the vulgar are only too apt to regard as miraculous. Since I have touched upon the point, I will digress a little on this so-called miracle. In my opinion, the immense crowds of people hanging with open mouths upon the lips of an *improvisatore* only prove that, in spite of the contempt into which poetry has fallen, it still possesses that power over the minds and the brains of men which their tongues deny it. Cristoforo Altissimo, a poet of the fifteenth century, is said to have publicly improvised his epic in octave stanzas on the Reali di Francia; the words were taken down from his lips, just as he composed them at the moment. The book was published; and though it is extremely rare, I have read it through the kindness of the Abbé Verdani. Only a few stanzas, out of all that ocean of verse, are worthy of the name of poetry; and yet we may believe that before the work was given to the press, some pains had been bestowed upon it. I have listened to many extempore versifiers, male and female, the most famous of our century. It has always struck me that if the

deluges of verses which they spout forth with face
on fire, to the applause of frantic multitudes, were
written down, they would have very little poetical
value, and that nobody would have the patience to
read the twentieth part of them. Padre Zucchi, of
the Olivetan Order, whom I heard in my youth,
surpassed his rivals; now and then he produced
sensible stanzas; but he improvised so slowly that
reflection may have had some part in the result. I
do not deny that these extempore rhymesters may be
people of culture and learning, qualified to discourse
well upon the themes proposed to them. Yet they
would not be listened to, if they spoke ever so
divinely in prose. In order to draw a crowd, they
are forced to express their thoughts and images, just
as they come, with voluble rapidity, in bad rhymed
verses, which often are no better than a gabble of
words without sense. This throws their audience
into a trance of astonishment. Humanity has
always quested after the marvellous like a hound. If
a painter sought to depict foolhardiness or imposture
wearing the mask of poetry, I could recommend
nothing better than the portrait of an improvisatore,
with goggle-eyes and arms in air, and a multitude
staring up at him in stupid dumb amazement. These
being my sentiments, I am willing, out of mere politeness and good manners, to approve the coronation of
a Cavaliere Perfetto or a Corilla on the Capitol. But
I can only accept with cordial and serious enthu-

siasm the honours of that sort paid to a Virgil, a Petrarch, and a Tasso.

The Arcadians will laugh when I proceed to speak about an improvisatore, whom I knew and whom I have listened to a hundred times. Yet I should be committing an injustice if I did not mention him, and declare my opinion that he was the single really wonder-worthy artist in this kind, with whom I ever came in contact. He used to pour forth anacreontics, octave stanzas, any and every metre, extempore, to the music of a well-touched guitar. His verses rhymed, but had no *Clio, Euterpe, Plettro, Parnaso, Aganippe, Ruscelletto, Zefiretto,* and such stuff, in them. They composed a well-developed discourse, flowing evenly, not soaring, but with abundance of well-connected images, and natural, lively, graceful thoughts. He invariably used either the Venetian or the Paduan dialect; which will augment the derisive laughter of Arcadia, and make the Campidoglio ring. On one occasion, while he was improvising on the theme: *diligite inimicos vestros,* it happened that two enemies were present. At another time, he dilated on his own grief for a cavaliere [1] who had been kind to him, and who was then dying, given over by the doctors. Not only did the audience hang upon his lips with rapt attention;

---

[1] I may here say that the title of cavaliere, or knight, was commonly given to members of patrician families at Venice, irrespective of their being laymen or in orders.

but in the former case, the enemies were reconciled, while in the latter tears were freely shed for the poet's expiring benefactor. Such influence over the passions of the heart reveals a true poet; for such a man I reserve the laurel crown upon my Campi-doglio. His name was Giovanni Sibiliato, brother of the celebrated professor of literature in the University of Padua.

Returning from this digression, I will resume the narrative of my boyhood. I learned to fence and to dance; but books and composition were my chief pastime. Before a numerous audience in our literary assemblies I felt no shyness. In private visits, among people new to me, the reserve of my demea-nour often passed for savagery. My first sonnet of passable quality was written at the age of nine. Beside the applause it won me, I was rewarded with a box of comfits; and for this reason I have never forgotten it. The occasion of its composition was as follows. A certain Signora Angela Armano, midwife by trade, had a friend at Padua whose pet dog died and left her inconsolable. Signora Angela wished to comfort her friend; indulged in condolements for her loss; and sent a little spaniel of her own, called Delina, to replace the defunct pet. Delina was to be given as a present, and a sonnet was to accom-pany the gift, expressing all the sentiments which a lady of Signora Angela's profession might entertain in a circumstance of such importance. Though our

family was a veritable lunatic asylum of poets, no
one cared to translate the good creature's gossipping
garrulity into verse. Moved by her entreaties, I
undertook the task; and the following Bernesque
sonnet was the result :—

> " Madama io vi vorrei pur confortare
>   Con qualche graziosa diceria,
>   Ma la sciagura vuole, e vostra, e mia,
>   Che in un sonetto la non vi può stare.
> Non vi state, mia cara, a disperare,
>   Che la sarebbe una poltroneria,
>   L'entrar per un can morto in frenesia ;
>   Chi nasce muor, convien moralizzare.
> Vi sovvenite, ch' egli avrà pisciato
>   Alcuna volta in camera, o in cucina,
>   Che in quell' istante lo avreste ammazzato.
> Io vi spedisco intanto la Delina
>   Che più d'un cane ha d'essa innamorato,
>   E può farvi di cani una dezina.
>   È bella, e picciolina ;
>   Di lei non voglio più nuova, o risposta,
>   Servitevi per razza, o di supposta."

Two years later, a new edition of the poems of
Gaspara Stampa appeared in Venice, at the expense
of Count Antonio Ramboldo di Collalto of Vienna,
a prince distinguished for his birth and writings.
Scholars know that this sixteenth-century Sappho
sighed her soul forth in love-laments to a certain
Count Collaltino di Collalto, doughty warrior and
polished versifier, and that she was reputed to
have died of hopeless passion in her youth.[1] The

---

[1] Gaspara Stampa was born at Padua, but was a gentlewoman of
Milan by descent. She died about 1554, at the age of thirty. If this

ladies of our century will hardly believe her story; for Cupid has changed temper since those days, and kills his victims with far different and less honourable weapons. Some verses by contemporary writers in praise of our literary heroine were to be appended to this edition of her works. I dared to enter the lists, and wrote a sonnet in the style of the earliest Tuscan poets. Such as it is, the sonnet may be found printed in the book which I have indicated. It appears from this juvenile production that I already acknowledged a mistress of my heart; compliance with fashion was alone responsible for my precocity.

This trifling composition was read by the famous Apostolo Zeno. He deigned to inquire for the author, who had reproduced the antique simplicity of Cino da Pistoja, Guittone d'Arezzo, and Guido Cavalcanti. On my presenting myself, Signor Zeno politely expressed surprise at discovering a mere boy in the learned writer of the sonnet, treated me with kind attention, and placed his choice library at my disposal.[1] The encouragement of this distinguished

---

edition of Gaspara Stampa's *Rime* is the one prepared for publication by Luisa Bergalli (Gozzi's sister-in-law), there is the same confusion of dates here as I have noticed above. It was published when Gozzi had reached his seventeenth year.

[1] A tablet over the entrance to the restaurant at the Calcina on the Zattere, records that Apostolo Zeno dwelt there. It was, perhaps, to this house that young Gozzi paid his visit. Zeno (b. 1668, d. 1750) exercised considerable influence over the Italian drama. He wrote plays for music and oratorios. For some years he held the post of Cesarean poet at Vienna, which he resigned to the more celebrated Metastasio.

poet, true lover of pure style, and foe to seventeenth-century conceits, added fuel to the fire of my literary passion. From that day forward not one of those collections of verses appeared, in which marriages, the entrance of young ladies into convents, the election of noblemen to offices of state, the deaths of people, cats, dogs, parrots, and such events, are celebrated in Venice and other towns of Italy, but that it contained some specimen of my Muse in grave or playful verse.

Books, paper, pens and ink formed the staple of my existence. I was always pregnant, always in labour, giving birth to monsters in remote corners of our mansion. I scribbled furiously, God knows how, up to my seventeenth year. Besides innumerable essays in prose and multitudes of fugitive verses, I wrote four long poems, entitled *Berlinghieri*, *Don Quixote*, *Moral Philosophy* (based upon the talking animals of Firenzuola), and *Gonella* in twelve cantos. The Abbé Verdani took a fancy to this last, and wished to see it printed. Signor Giulio Cesare Beccelli, however, had published a poem at Verona on the same subject, which robbed my work of novelty; and though mine was richer in facts drawn from good old sources, I did not venture to enter into competition with him. The three years' absence from home, which I shall presently relate, and the revolution in our domestic affairs which surprised me on my return, exposed these boyish literary labours to ruin and dispersion. It is probable that pork-butchers and fruit-vendors exercised condign justice on the children of my Muse.

III.

The Situation of my Family, and my Reasons for Leaving Home.

In the course of these years, the early deaths of a brother and a sister had reduced our numbers from eleven to nine. Meanwhile, our annual expenditure exceeded the resources at our command, and left but little for the needs of a numerous offspring, too old to be contented with a toy or plaything. Some law-suits, which we lost, diminished the estate. Clouds of doubt and care began to obscure the horizon, and in a few years the family was plunged in pecuniary embarrassment.

My brother Gasparo had taken a wife in a fit of genial poetical abstraction. Even poetry has its dangers. This man, who was really singular in his absolute self-dedication to books, in his indefatigable labours as an author, and in a certain philosophical temper or indolence, which made him indifferent to everything which was not literary, learned to fall in love from Petrarch. A young lady, ten years older

than himself, named Luigia Bergalli,[1] better known
among the shepherdesses of Arcady as Irmenia Par-
tenide, a poetess of romantic fancy, as her published
works evince, was my brother's Laura.   Not being a
canon, like Petrarch, he married her in Petrarch's
spirit, but with due legal formalities.   This woman,
of fervent and soaring imagination, which fitted her
for high poetic flights, undertook to regulate the
disorder in our affairs.   Impelled by the instincts of
a good nature, with something of ambition and a
flattering belief in her own practical ability, she did
the best that in her lay.   Yet all her projects and
administrative measures revolved within a circle of
romantic raptures and Pindaric ecstasies.   Thirsting
with soul-passion after an ideal realm, she found
herself the sovereign of a state in decadence.   It
was the desire of her heart to make us all happy,
in the most disinterested way.   Yet she accomplished nothing beyond involving every one, and her-

---

[1] Luisa Pisana Bergalli was born at Venice in 1703, of humble
parentage, being descended from a Piedmontese shoemaker.   Luigi
Mocenigo and Pisana Cornaro held her at the font, and gave her their
two Christian names.   She showed distinguished talents in early youth,
and was educated by the painter Rosalba Carriera, afterwards by Cate-
rino and Apostolo Zeno.   At twenty-three she published a tragedy and
an anthology of Italian poems by female writers ; at twenty-five another
tragedy ; at thirty a translation of Terence, and a comedy dedicated to
Count Jacopo Antonio Gozzi.   It appears from this dedication to *Le
avventure del poeta* that she was the protégée of both Count Gozzi and his
wife, and on the best of terms with their children.   She was thirty-
five and Gasparo was twenty-five when they married.   See Tommasei,
Storia Civile nella Letteraria, pp. 185–188.

self to boot, in the meshes of still greater misfortune. Her husband, poring perpetually upon his books, could only oppose her at the sacrifice of ease and quiet. This he was incapable of doing.—In order to judge people equitably, it is necessary that character, temperament, and circumstances should be thoroughly explained.

I know how unphilosophical it is to ascribe the discords of a family to malignant planetary influences. Our domestic circle consisted of a father, a mother, four brothers, and five sisters, all of them good-hearted, honourable, mutually well-inclined ; and yet it became the very mirror of infelicity at every moment and in each of the persons who composed it. Minute investigation into the causes of this painful fact would probably reveal them. But it is better to adopt the language of the vulgar, and to say that a bad star pursued our family. Otherwise, analysis might lead one into acts of unkindness, and involve one in hatred.

The confusion in which we lived at that period, and the bitter discomforts we had to bear, were augmented by expenses due to my brother's increasing progeny. Our worst disaster, however (and this wound I carry in my heart even to the present day), was a cruel stroke of apoplexy which laid my beloved father low. He continued to exist, an invalid, for about seven years after the sad event; dumb and paralytic, but in possession of all his mental faculties—a circumstance which rendered his deplorable condition almost unbearable to a man of my father's extreme sensibility.

The tears of five sisters, the births of nephews and nieces, a house swarming with female go-betweens, brokers, and the Hebrew ministers of our decaying realm—all this whirlpool of economical extravagance and folly, to utter one word against which was reckoned mutiny or treason, drove my second brother, Francesco, into exile. He went into the Levant with the Provveditore Generale di Mare,[1] his Excellency the Cavaliere Antonio Loredano, of happy memory. At that period I was about thirteen.

Letters written from Corfu by this brother describing the kindness shown him by his Provveditore, and the rank of ensign to which he soon attained, awoke in me a burning desire to escape like him from those domestic turmoils, the gravity of which I felt in experience and measured by

---

[1] The title *Provveditore Generale di Mare* was given to the supreme head of the Venetian naval and military forces in the Levant. He resided at Corfu, where he maintained a princely court, and ruled like a sovereign, being only responsible for his actions to the Senate. Next in importance to this functionary was the *Provveditore Generale di Dalmazia*, of whose Court we shall hear much in Gozzi's Memoirs. Casanova, who went to Corfu in the train of the Prov. Gen. Dolfino, called Il Bucentoro because of his grand manner, and the father of the famous Caterina Dolfin Tron, gives an excellent account of the Court there, its military, naval, and civil establishment. Chapters xiii.–xvi. of the first volume of his Memoirs deserve to be compared with the corresponding part of Gozzi's.

anticipation, but which my state of boyhood rendered me unable to remedy. Our uncle on the mother's side, Almorò Cesare Tiepolo, recommended me to his Excellency Girolamo Quirini, Provveditore Generale elect for Dalmatia and Albania. Furnished with a modest outfit, in which my book-box and guitar were not forgotten, I bade farewell to my parents at the age of seventeen,[1] and went across seas as volunteer into those provinces, to study the ways and manners of my fellow-soldiers, and of the peoples among whom we were quartered.

IV.

I Embark upon a Galley, and Cross the Seas to Zara.

I was not slow to perceive that I had adopted a career by no means suited to my character, the proper motto for which was always the following verse from Berni :

"Voleva far da se, non commandato."

My natural dislike of changeableness kept me, however, from showing by outward signs of any sort that I repented of my choice ; and I reflected that abundant opportunities were now at least offered for observations on the men of a world new to me.

---

[1] Not at seventeen, but at twenty. Gozzi was born in 1720, and Quirini took the government of Dalmatia in 1740.

This thought sufficed to keep me in good spirits and a cheerful humour through all the vicissitudes of my three years' sojourn in Illyria.

According to orders received from his Excellency, the Provveditore Generale Quirini, I embarked before him on a galley called *Generalizia*, which was riding at the port of Malamocco. There I was to wait for his arrival. A band of military officers received me with glances of courtesy and some curiosity. In a Court where all the members are seeking fortune, each newcomer is regarded with suspicion. Whether he has to be reckoned with or may be disregarded on occasions of promotion, concerns the whole crew of officials, who, like him, are dependent on the will of the Provveditore. It was perhaps insensibility which made me indifferent to these preoccupations; this the sequel of my narrative will show; and yet such thoughts are very wood-worms in the hearts of courtiers.

I had to swallow a great quantity of questions, to which I replied with the laconic brevity of an inexperienced lad upon his guard. Some of those gentlemen had known my brother Francesco at Corfu. When they discovered who I was, they seemed to be relieved of all anxiety on my account, and welcomed me with noisy demonstrations of soldierly comradeship. I expressed my thanks in modest, almost monosyllabic phrases. They set me down for an awkward young fellow, unobliging, and proud. This was a mistake, as they freely confessed a few months later on. I had retired into myself, with the view of studying their characters and sketching my line of action. The quick and penetrative intuition with which I was endowed at birth by God, together with the faculty of imperturbable reserve, enabled me in the course of a few hours to recognise in that little group some men of noble birth and liberal culture, some nobles ruined by the worst of educations, and some plebeians who owed their position to powerful protection.

Gaming, intemperance, and unbridled sensuality were deeply rooted in the whole company. I laid my plans of conduct, and found them useful in the future. My intimacies were few, but durable. The vices I have named, clung like ineradicable cancers to the men with whom I associated. Sound principles engrafted on me in my early years, regard for health, and the slenderness of my purse helped me to avoid their seductions. At the same time, I saw no reason why I should proclaim a crusade against them. Holding a middle course, I succeeded in winning the affection of my comrades. They invited me to take part in their orgies. I did not play the prude. Without yielding myself to the transports of brutal appetite, I proved the gayest reveller at all those lawless meetings. Some of my seniors, on whom a career of facile pleasure had left its inevitable stigma, used to twit me with being a reserved young simple-

ton.   I did not heed their raillery, but laughed at
the inebriation of my comrades, studied the bent of
divers characters, observed the animal brutality of
men, and used our uproarious debauches as a school
for fathoming the depths of human frailty.

Now I will return to the point of my embarkation
on the galley *Generalizia* in the port of Malamocco.
While awaiting the arrival of the Provveditore, I had
two whole days and nights to spend in sad reflections
on humanity.   These were suggested by the spectacle
of some three hundred scoundrels, loaded with chains,
condemned to drag their life out in a sea of miseries
and torments, each of which was sufficient by itself
to kill a man.   An epidemic of malignant fever raged
among these men, carrying away its victims daily
from the bread and water, the irons, and the whips
of the slavemasters.   Attended in their last passage
by a gaunt black Franciscan friar, with thundering
voice and jovial mien, these wretches took their flight
—I hope and think—for Paradise.

The Provveditore's arrival amid the din of instruments and roar of cannon roused me from my dismal
reveries.   I had visited this gentleman ten times at
least in his own palace, and had always been received
with that playful welcome and confidential sweetness
which distinguish the patricians of Venice.   He made
his appearance now in crimson—crimson mantle, cap,
and shoes—with an air of haughtiness unknown to
me, and fierceness stamped upon his features.   The

THE FRANCISCAN FRIAR ON THE GALLEY

Original Etching by Ad. Lalauze

other officers informed me that when he donned this
uniform of state, he had to be addressed with profound and silent salaams, different indeed from the
reverence one pays at Venice to a patrician in his
civil gown.[1]   He boarded the galley, and seemed to
take no notice whatever of the crowd around him,
bowing till their noses rubbed their toes.   The
affability with which he touched our hands in Venice
had disappeared; he looked at none of us; and
sentenced the young captain of the guard, called
Combat, to arrest in chains, because he had omitted
some trifle of the military salute.   My comrades
stood dumbfounded, staring at one another with
open eyes.   This singular change from friendliness
to severity set my brains at work.   By the light of
my boyish philosophy I seemed to comprehend why
the noble of a great republic, elected general of an
armament[2] and governor of two wide provinces, on
his first appearance in that office, felt bound to
assume a totally different aspect from what was
natural to him in his private capacity.   He had to
inspire fear and a spirit of submission into his subordinates.   Otherwise they might have taken liberties
upon the strength of former courtesy displayed by him,

---

[1] *Togato.* The State dignitaries of Venice wore robes of various
colours and forms, according to their office.   A simple nobleman was
bound to go abroad in a flowing robe of silk, or toga, ample enough to
conceal whatever costume he may have worn beneath it.

[2] *Armata,* composed of naval and military forces, to act equally on
sea and shore.

being for the most part presumptuous young fellows, apt to boast about their favour with the general. For my own part, since I was firmly bent on doing my duty without ambitious plans or dreams of fortune, this formidable attitude and the harsh commands of the great man made a less disheartening impression on me than on my companions. I whispered to myself: "He certainly inspires me with a kind of dread; but he has taken immense trouble to transform his nature in order to produce this effect; I am sure the irksomeness which he is suffering now must be greater than any discomfort he can cause me."

The general retired to his cabin in the bowels of our floating hell, and sent Lieutenant-Colonel Micheli, his major in the province, to make out a list of all the officers and volunteers on board, together with the names of their protectors. Nobody expected this; for we had been personally presented to the general at Venice, and had explained our affairs in frequent conversations. Once more I reflected that this was his way of damping the expectations which might have been bred in scheming brains before he exchanged the politenesses of private life for the austerities of office. The Maggiore della Provincia Micheli—a most excellent person and very fat— bustled about his business, sweating, and scribbling with a pencil on a sheet of paper, as though the matter was one of life or death. Everybody began to shy and grumble and chafe with indignation at passing under review in this way. When my turn came, I answered frankly that I was called Carlo Gozzi, and that I had been recommended by the patrician Almorò Cesare Tiepolo. I withheld his title of senator and the fact that he was my maternal uncle, deeming it prudent not to seem ambitious.

The *Generalizia*, convoyed by another galley named *Conserva* and a few light vessels of war, got under way for the Adriatic;[1] and the night fell very dark upon the waters. I shall not easily forget that night, because of a little incident which happened to me, and which shows what a curious place of refuge a galley is for young men leaving their homes for the first time. A natural necessity made me seek some corner for retirement. I was directed to the bowsprit; on approaching it, an Illyrian sentinel, with scowling visage, bushy whiskers, and levelled musket, howled his " *Who goes there?* " in a tremendous voice. When he understood my business, he let me pass. My next step lighted on a soft and yielding mass, which gave forth a kind of gurgling sound, like the stifled breath of an asthmatic patient, into the dark silent night. Retracing my path, I asked the

---

[1] It seems from the names of these larger galleys that they were the official ships of the Provveditore, his own flag-ship and her attendant convoy. Romanin (vol. viii. p. 372) says that at this epoch Venice kept fifteen heavy galleys, ten lighter, nine sailing ships of the frigate build, and twenty-four armed craft of other descriptions. The galleys and sailing ships were commanded only by patricians. This was her peace establishment.

sentinel what the thing was, which responded with
its inarticulate gurgling voice to the pressure of my
feet. He answered with the coldest indifference that
it was the corpse of a galley-slave, who had succumbed
to the fever, and had been flung there till he could
be buried on the sea-shore sands in Istria. The hair
on my head bristled with horror. But my happy
disposition for seeing the ludicrous side of things
soon came to my assistance.

After twelve days of much discomfort, and twelve
noisome nights, passed in broken slumbers under the
decks of that galley, which only too well deserved its
name, our little fleet entered the port of Zara. We
went on shore at first privately and quietly; and
after a few days the public ceremonies of official
disembarkation were gone through. The Provveditore
Generale Jacopo Cavalli handed his baton of command over to the Provveditore Generale Girolamo
Quirini with all the formalities proper to the occasion.
This solemnity, which is performed upon the open
sea, to the sound of military music, the thunder of
artillery, and the crackling of musket-shots, deserves
to be witnessed by all who take an interest in imposing spectacles. An old man, fat and short of
stature, with a pair of moustachios bristling up
beneath his nostrils, a merry and most honest fellow
to boot, who bore the name of Captain Girolamo
Visinoni, was appointed master of these ceremonies,
on account of his intimate acquaintance with

their details. I had no other duty that day but to wear my best clothes, which did not cost much trouble.

V.

I Fall Dangerously Ill ; Recover ; Form the only Intimate Acquaintance I made in Dalmatia.

When the new Regency had been established and the Court settled, I had but eight days to learn my duties as volunteer or adjutant[1] to his Excellency, as it is called there, before I fell ill of a fever which was declared to be malignant. Alone among people whom I hardly knew, at the commencement of my career, poorly provided with money, and lying in a wretched room, the windows of which were closed with torn and rotten paper instead of glass, I could not but compare my present destitution with the comforts of our home. Here I was battling with a mortal disease in solitude. There, at the least touch of illness, I enjoyed the tender solicitude of a sister or a servant at my pillow, to brush away the flies which settled on my forehead. Fortunately, I was not so strongly attached to life as to be rendered miserable by unavailing recollections and gloomy forebodings.

---

[1] Gozzi says *adjutante* alone. *Adjutante di campo* is aide-de-camp.

It happened one day, as I lay there burning, that a convict presented himself at the door of my miserable den, and asked me if I wanted anything which he could fetch me. He was one of those men who prowl around the officers' quarters, wrapped in an old blanket with a bit of rope about the waist, ready to do any dirty business and to pilfer if they find the opportunity. I gave him a few farthings and told him to send me a confessor—an errand very different from what he had expected. Before long a good Dominican appeared, who prepared me to die with the courage of an ancient Roman. Our modern sages may laugh at this plebeian wish of mine to make my peace with Heaven; but I have never been able to dissociate philosophy from religion. Satisfied to remain a little child before the mysteries of faith, I do not envy wise men in their disengagement from spiritual terrors.

The chief physician, Danieli, a man of prodigious corpulence and blackness, who had been sent to my assistance by the Governor, spared no attentions and no remedies. As usual, they proved unavailing; and he bade me prepare myself for death by receiving the holy sacrament. I summoned what remained to me of vital force, and went through this ceremony with devotion. There seemed to be so little difference between a sepulchre and the room in which my body lay, that I felt no disgust at relinquishing my corpse to the grave-diggers. I was now ready for the

last unction, when an attack of hemorrhage from the
nostrils, like those which had already nearly brought
me to death's door, recalled me for the nonce to
life. All the ordinary remedies—ligatures, powders,
herbs, astringent plasters, sympathetic stones, muttered charms, old wives' talismans—were exhibited
in vain. After filling two basons with blood, I lapsed
into a profound swoon, which the doctor styled a
syncope. To all appearances I was dead; but the
blood stopped; in a quarter of an hour I revived; and
three days afterwards I found myself, weak indeed,
but wholly free from fever and on the road to recovery. My ignorance could not reconcile this
salutary crisis with Danieli's absolute prohibition of
blood-letting in my malady. But I suppose that
a score of learned physicians, each of them upon
a different system of hypotheses, conjectures, well-
based calculations, and trains of lucid argument,
would be able to demonstrate the phenomenon to
their own satisfaction and to the illumination or
confusion of my stupid brain. Stupendous indeed
are the mental powers which Almighty God has
bestowed on men!

The readers of these Memoirs will hardly need to
be informed that my slender purse had nothing in
it at the termination of this illness. Under these
painful circumstances I found a cordial and open-
hearted friend in Signor Innocenzio Massimo, nobleman of Padua, and captain of halbardiers at the

Dalmatian Court. This excellent gentleman, of rare
distinction for his mental parts, the quickness of his
spirit, his courage, energy, and honour, was the only
intimate friend whom I possessed during my three
years' absence from home. When they were over,
our friendship continued undiminished by lapse of
time, distance, and the various vicissitudes of life.
I have enjoyed it through thirty-five years, and am
sure that it will never fail me. Some qualities of his
character have exposed him to enmity; among these
I may mention a particular sensitiveness to affronts,
an intolerance of attempts to deceive him, and a
quick perception of fraud, together with a firm resolve
to stem the tide of extravagance and fashionable
waste in his own family. His many virtues, the
decent comfort of his household, his hospitality to
friends and acquaintances, his careful provision for
the well-being of his posterity, his benevolence to
the poor and afflicted, his successful efforts as a
peacemaker among discordant fellow-citizens, his expenditure of time and trouble upon all who come to
him for advice or assistance, have not sufficed to dis-
arm the malignity of a vulgar crowd, corrupted by
the false philosophy of our century, which goes from
bad to worse in dissolution and ill manners.

VI.

Short Studies in the Science of Fortification and Military Exercises.—Some Reflections which will pass for Foolishness.

On the restoration of my health, his Excellency placed me under Cavaliere Marchiori, Lieutenant-Colonel of Engineers, to learn mathematics as applied to fortification. This gentleman sent for me, and said that he had heard from my uncle of my aptitude for study, adding that the subject he proposed to teach me was of the greatest consequence to a soldier. I perceived at once that I was being treated on a different footing from the other volunteers, and that the studied forgetfulness of the Provveditore had been, as I suspected, a politic device to humble ambitious schemers. I thanked Signor Marchiori, and followed his instructions with pleasure, without however abandoning my own interest in literature.

He questioned me regarding my knowledge of arithmetic, which was only elementary; and when I saw that I must master it, in order to pursue the higher branch of study, I gave my whole head to the business. In the space of a month, I could cipher like a money-lender, and was ready to receive my master's teaching. My friend Massimo possessed a good collection of instruments for engineering draughtsmanship, and a library of French works on geometry, mathematics, and fortification, both of which he placed at my disposal. Signor Marchiori's lectures, long discussions with Signor Massimo, perusal of Euclid, Archimedes, and the French books, soon plunged me in the lore of points and lines and calculations. I burned with the enthusiasm, droll enough to my way of looking at the world, which inspires all students of this science. Yet I did not, like them, regard moral philosophy and humane literature as insignificant frivolities. I bore in mind for what good reasons the Emperor Vespasian dismissed the mathematicians who offered their assistance in the building of his Roman edifices. I knew that innumerable vessels, fabricated on the principles of science, have perished miserably in the tempests ; that hundreds of fortresses, built by science, have been destroyed and captured by the same science ; that inundations are continually sweeping away the dykes erected by science, to the ruin of thousands of families, and that the inundations themselves are attributable to the admired masterpieces of science bequeathed to us by former generations ; that, in spite of science and her creative energy, the buildings she erects are not secured from earthquakes, conflagrations, and the thunderbolt. It remains to be seen whether Professor Toaldo's lightning-conductors will prove effectual against the last of these disasters. Then I reckoned up the blessings and curses which this vaunted science has conferred on humanity, arriving at the conclusion that the harm which she has done infinitely exceeds the good. I shuddered at the hundreds of thousands of human beings ingeniously massacred in war or drowned at sea by her devices ; and took more pleasure in consulting my watch, her wise invention, for the dinner-hour than at the hour of keeping an appointment with my lawyer. Without denying the utility of sciences, I stuck resolutely to the opinion that moral philosophy is of more importance to the human race than mechanical inventions, and deplored the pernicious influence of modern Lyceums and Polytechnic schools upon the mind of Europe.

Signor Massimo and I kept house together in a little dwelling on the city walls, facing the sea. The sun, in his daily revolutions, struck this habitation on every side ; and there was not an open space of wall or window-sill without its dial, fabricated by my skill, and adorned with appropriate but useless mottoes on the flight of time. A lieutenant named Giovanni Apergi, upright and pious, especially when the gout he had acquired in the world's pleasures made him turn his thoughts to Heaven, gave me friendly lessons in military drill. I soon learned to handle my musket, pike, and ensign ; and sweated a shirt daily, fencing with Massimo, who was ferociously expert in that fiendish but gentlemanly art. We also spent some hours together over a great chessboard of his, covered with wooden soldiers, which we moved from square to square, forming squadrons, and studying the combinations which enable armies to kill with prodigality and to be killed with parsimony, —fitting ourselves, in short, for manuring cemeteries in the most approved style.

I was already half a soldier, and meant to make myself perfect in my profession; not, however, without a firm resolve to quit the army[1] at the expiration of my three years' service. Twelve months spent in studying my comrades convinced me that, though some worthy fellows might be found among them, their society as a whole was uncongenial to my tastes. I had neither the ambition nor the greed of gain which might have sapped this resolution; and my persistence during the appointed time was mainly due to a dislike of seeming fickle. I wanted to gain the respect of my relatives, whom I hoped to help one day with my counsel, my credit, and the example of my perseverance.

After eight months spent in the study of fortification, I lost my poor master. He died suddenly of a fit of spleen a few days after winning his company in a regiment called Lagarde. This promotion he

---

[1] This word is in the Italian *armata*. The *armata*, to which Gozzi belonged, was properly an armament of mixed naval and military forces, and *armata* would naturally be translated "navy." He was attached to it, however, in the quality of soldier, and was eligible (as we shall afterwards see) for transfer into the land forces of the State in Lombardy. Thus he belonged to the Venetian army.

obtained by competition ; and some insulting words
dropped upon the occasion, which he was unable to
resent, caused his mortal illness. Every one deplored
the death of Marchiori ; but no one more than I
did. His goodness, sweetness, affability, and friendly
patience left a powerful impression on my memory.
Gradually my interest in geometry declined, and I
resumed my former studies with fresh ardour, attending meanwhile to my military duties, and waiting
philosophically till the three years should be over.

VII.

*This Chapter proves that Poetry is not as useless as people
commonly imagine.*

I am bound to confess that my weakness for poetry
and Italian literature was great. In the Venetian
service, and particularly in Dalmatia, there were very
few indeed who shared these tastes. I wrote and
read my compositions to myself, without seeking the
applause of an audience or boring my neighbours
with things they do not care for, as is the wont of
most scribblers.

The secretary of the Generalate, Signor Giovanni
Colombo, took some interest in literature. I may
mention, by the way, that he afterwards rose to high
dignity, which involved a calamity for him, sweetened,

however, by a splendid funeral; in other words, he died Grand Chancellor of our most serene Republic.[1] This man, of gentle spirit and jovial temper, knowing the epidemic of poetry which possessed the Gozzi family, encouraged me to read him some of my trifles, and seemed to take pleasure in listening to them. He owned a small but well-chosen library, which he courteously allowed me to use. My verses, satirical for the most part and descriptive of characters—without scurrility indeed, though based on accurate observation of both sexes—were communicated to him and Massimo alone.

The town of Zara was bent on testifying its respect for our Provveditore Generale Quirini by a grand public display. A large hall of wood was accordingly erected on the open space before the fort, and hung with fine damask. Tickets of invitation were then distributed to various persons, who were to compose an Academy upon the day of the solemnity. Every academician had to recite two compositions in prose or verse, as he thought fit. The subjects were set forth on the tickets, and were as follows:—First, Is a prince who preserves, defends, and improves his dominions in peace, more praiseworthy than one

---

[1] This was the highest office in the State to which a *cittadino* could aspire. It conferred the rank of cavaliere. The Grand Chancellor could open public despatches; he attended the sittings of the Grand Council and the Senate, but without a vote, and was the official chief of all the civil servants.

who seeks to extend them by force of arms? The
second was to be a panegyric of the Provveditore
Generale. An old nobleman of Zara, named Giovanni
Pellegrini, was chosen to preside in the Academy
and to dispense the invitations. He wore a black
velvet suit and a huge blonde wig, done up into
knotted curls, and possessed a fund of eloquence in
the style of Father Casimir Frescot.[1]

I did not receive an invitation, which proves either
that I was an amateur of poetry unknown to fame, or
that Signor Pellegrini, in his gravity and wisdom,
judged me a mere boy, unworthy of consideration in
an enterprise which he treated with true Illyrico-
Italian seriousness. Signor Colombo and my friend
Massimo urged me to prepare two compositions on
the published themes; but I reminded them that I
had no right to appear uninvited. Nevertheless, I
amused myself by scribbling a couple of sonnets,
which I consigned to the bottom of my pocket.
As may be imagined, I defended peace in the one,
and did my best to belaud his Excellency in the
other.

The Provveditore Generale, attended by his officers
and by the magnates of the city, entered the temporary hall, and took his seat upon a rich fauteuil
raised many steps above the ground. A covey of
literary celebrities, collected Heaven knows where,

---

[1] Probably Freschot, the author of several works on Venice, a French-
man by birth.

ranged their learned backs along a row of chairs, which formed a semicircle round him.

Strolling outside the damasked tabernacle, I saw some servants who were preparing beverages and refreshments with a mighty bustle. I was thirsty, and thought I should not be committing a crime if I asked one of them for a lemonade. He replied that express orders had been given not to quench the thirst of anybody who was not a member of the Academy. This discourteous rebuff, repeated to the *sitio* of several officers, raised a spirit of silent revolt among us. I resolved to put a bold face on the matter, and to proclaim myself an academician, thinking that the title of poet might win for me the lemonade which was denied to the dignity and the weapons of an officer.

This little incident confirmed my opinion of the usefulness of poetry against the universal judgment which regards it as an inutility. Poetry stood me in good stead by procuring me a lemonade and saving me from dying of thirst. Having swallowed the beverage, I proceeded to one of the seats in the assembly, exciting some surprise among its members, who were, however, kind enough to tolerate my presence. For three whole hours the air resounded with long inflated erudite orations and poems not remarkable for sweetness. A yawn from the General now and then did honour to the Academy and the academicians. I must in justice say that some tolerable compositions, superior to what I had expected, struck my ears. A young abbé in holy orders gushed with poetic eloquence. I have heard that he is now become a bishop. Who knows whether poetry was not as serviceable to him in the matter of his mitre, as she was to me in the matter of my lemonade !

I declaimed my sonnets in their turn ; the second of which, by Apollo's blessing, pleased his Excellency, and consequently was received with general approval. It established my reputation among the folk of Zara, and led to a comic scene two days later. The Provveditore Generale was in the habit of riding in the cool some four or five miles outside the city ; a troop of officers galloped at his heels, and I galloped with them. While we were amusing ourselves in this way, his Excellency took a fancy to hear my sonnet over again ; for it had now become famous, as often happens with trifles, which go the round of society upon the strength of adventitious circumstances. He called me loudly. I put spurs to my horse, while he, still galloping, ordered me to recite. I do not think a sonnet was ever declaimed in like manner since the creation of the world. Galloping after the great man, and almost bursting my lungs in the effort to make myself heard, with all the trills, gasps, cadences, semitones, clippings of words, and dissonances, which the movement of a horse at full speed could occasion, I recited the sonnet in a storm of sobs

and sighs, and blessed my stars when I had pumped
out the fourteenth line.   Knowing the temper of the
General, who was haughty and formidable in matters
of importance, but sometimes whimsical in his diversions, I thought at the time that he must have been
seeking a motive for laughter.   And indeed, I believe
this was the case.   Anyhow, he can only have been
deceived if he hoped to laugh more at the affair than
I did.   Yet I was rather afraid of becoming a laughing-
stock to my riding-companions also.   Foolish fear!
These honest fellows, like true courtiers, vied with
each other in congratulating me upon the partiality
of his Excellency and the honour he had done me.
They were even jealous of a burlesque scene in
which I played the buffoon, and sorry that they had
not enjoyed the luck of performing it themselves.

VIII.

Confirmation of a hint I gave in the Second Chapter of these
Memoirs relating to a great danger which I ran.

I related in the second chapter of this book that
I once owed my life to a trick taught me by a jockey.
The incident happened during one of our cavalcades
with the Provveditore Generale.

At the hour appointed for riding out, all the officers
of the Court sent their saddles and bridles to the

General's stables, and each of us mounted the animal which happened to be harnessed with his own gear. Now the Bashaw of Bosnia had presented the governor with a certain Turkish stallion, finely made, but so vicious that no one liked to back the brute. One day I noticed that the grooms had saddled this untamable Turk for me. Who knows what motives determine the acts of stable-boys? I am not accustomed to be easily dismayed; besides, I had ridden many dangerous horses in my time, and this was not the minute to show the white feather before a crowd of soldiers. I leapt upon the animal like an antique paladin, without looking to see whether the bit and trappings were in order. Our troops started; but my Bucephalus reared, whirled round in the air, and bolted toward his stable, which lay below the ramparts. Pulling and working at the reins had no effect upon the brute; and when I bent down to discover the cause, I found that the bit had not been fastened, either through the negligence or the malice of the grooms.

Rushing at the mercy of this demon through the narrow streets and low doors of the city, I began to reflect that I was not likely to reach the stables with my head upon my shoulders. Then I remembered the jockey's advice, and rising in my stirrups, leaned forwards, and stuck my fingers into the two eyes of the stallion. Suddenly deprived of sight, and not knowing whither he was going, he dashed furiously

up against a wall, and fell all of a heap beneath me.
I leapt to earth with the agility of a practised rider,
and made the Turk get up; he was trembling like
a leaf, while I with shaky fingers fastened the bit
firmly; then I mounted again, and rejoined my
company among the shouts of applause which always
greet dare-devil escapades of this kind. The middle
finger of my left hand had been flayed by striking
against the wall. I still bear the scar of this glorious wound.

IX.

Little incidents, trifling observations, moral reflections of no
value, gossip which is sure to make the reader yawn.

Our forces had little to occupy them in those provinces, so that my sonnet in praise of peace exactly
fitted. Some interesting incidents, and several journeys which I undertook, furnished me, however, with
abundant matter for reflection. I shall here indulge
myself by setting down a few observations which
occur to my memory.

The regular troops which garrison the fortresses of
Dalmatia had been recalled to Italy, in order to defend
the neutrality of Venice during the wars which then
prevailed among her neighbours. In these circumstances the Senate commissioned our Provveditore
Generale to levy new forces from the subject tribes,

not only for maintaining the military establishment
of Dalmatia, but also for drafting a large number of
Morlacchi[1] into Italy. It was a matter of no difficulty to enrol garrisons for the Illyrian fortresses ; but
the exportation of the Morlacchi cost his Excellency
the greatest trouble. These ruffianly wild beasts,
wholly destitute of education, are aware that they
are subjects of Venice ; yet their firm resolve is to
indulge lawless instincts for robbery and murder as
they list, refusing obedience in all things which do
not suit their inclinations. To reason with them is
the same as talking in a whisper to the deaf. They
simply resisted the command to form themselves
into a troop and leave their lairs for Italy.

Their chiefs, who were educated men, brave and
loyal to their prince, strained every nerve to carry
out these orders. It was found needful to recall the
bandits, who swarm throughout those regions, out-
lawed for every sort of crime—robberies, homicides,
arson, and such-like acts of heroism. Bribes too
were offered of bounties and advanced pay, in order
to induce the wild and stubborn peasants to cross
the seas. I was present at the review of these Anthro-
pophagi ; for indeed they hardly merited a more civi-
lised title. It took place on the beach of Zara under
the eyes of the Provveditore, with ships under sail,
ready for the embarkation of the conscripts. Pair

---

[1] The native Dalmatians of Slav origin, inhabiting the inland villages
and country districts, were called by this name.

by pair, they came up and received their stipend; upon which they expressed their joy by howling out some barbarous chant, and dancing off together with uncouth gambols to the transport ships. I revered God's handiwork in these savages while deploring their bad education, and felt a passing wish to explore the Eden of eternal beatitude in which the Morlacchi dwell.

It is certain that the Italian cities under our benign government were more disturbed than guarded by these brutal creatures. At Verona, in particular, they indulged their appetite for thieving, murdering, brawling, and defying discipline, without the least regard for orders. At the close of a few months, they had to be sent back to their caves, in order to deliver the Veneto from an unbearable incubus. Even at the outset, their spirit of insubordination let itself be felt. Scarcely had the transports sailed, when the sight of the Illyrian mountains made them burn to leap on shore. The seamen did their best to restrain the unruly crew; but finding that they ran a risk of being cut in pieces, they finally unbarred the pens before this indomitable flock of rams.

What I am now writing may seem to have little to do with the narrative of my own life, and may look as though I wished to calumniate the natives of Dalmatia. The rulers of those territories will, however, bear me out in the following remarks. I

have visited all the fortresses, many districts, and
many villages of the two provinces. In some
of the cities I found well-educated people, trust-
worthy, cordial, and liberal in sentiment. In places
far removed from the Provveditore Generale's Court
the manners of the population are incredibly rough.
All the peasants may be described as cruel, supersti-
tious, and irrational wild beasts. In their marriages,
their funerals, their games, they preserve the customs of pagan antiquity. Reading Homer and Virgil
gives a perfect conception of the Morlacchi. They
hire a troop of women to lament over their dead.
These professional mourners shriek by turns, reliev-
ing one another when voice and throat have been
exhausted by dismal wailings tuned to a music which
inspires terror. One of their pastimes is to balance
a heavy piece of marble on the lifted palm of the
right hand, and hurl it after taking a running jump.
The fellow who projects this missile in a straight
line to the greatest distance, wins. One is reminded
of the enormous boulders hurled by Diomede and
Turnus.

In their mountain homes the Morlacchi are fine
fellows, useful to the State of Venice on occasions
of war with the Turks, their neighbours, whom they
cordially detest. The inhabitants of the coast make
bold seamen, apt for fighting on the waters. Toward
Montenegro the tribes become even more like
savages. Families, who have been accustomed for

some generations to die peaceably in their beds or
kennels, and cannot boast of a fair number of murdered ancestors, are looked down upon by the rest.
On the beach outside the city walls of Budua, for
which these men and brothers leave their hills in
summer-time to taste the coolness of sea-breezes, I
have witnessed their exploits with the musket and
have seen three corpses stretched upon the sands. A
member of one of the pacific families I have described, being taunted by some comrade, burned to
wipe out the shame of his kindred, and opened a
glorious chapter in their annals by slaughtering and
being slaughtered. Fierce battles and armed encounters between village and village are frequent
enough in those parts. The men of one village who
kill a man of the next village, have no peace unless
they pay a hundred sequins or discharge their debt
by the death of one of their own folk. Such is the
current tariff, fixed without consulting their sovereign, among these people, who regard brutality as
justice. I learned much about these traits of human
nature from a village priest of Montenegro, who
conversed with me nearly every day upon the beach
at Budua. He talked a strange Italian jargon,
narrated the homicides of his flock with compla-
cency, and let it be understood that a gun was
better suited to his handling than the vessels of
the sanctuary.

The thirst for vengeance is never slaked there.

It passes from heir to heir like an estate in tail. Among the Morlacchi, who are less bloodthirsty than the Montenegrins, I once saw a woman of some fifty years fling herself at the feet of the Provveditore Generale, extract a mummied head from a game-bag, and cast it on the ground before him, weeping as though her heart would burst, and calling aloud for pity and justice. For thirty years she had preserved this skull, the skull of her mother, who had been murdered. The assassins had long ago been brought to justice, but their punishment was insufficient to lay the demon of ferocity in this affectionate daughter. Accordingly, she . presented herself indefatigably through a course of thirty years before each of the successive Provveditori Generali, with the same maternal skull in her game-bag, with the same shrieks and tears and cries for justice.

I liked seeing the Montenegrin women. They clothe themselves in black woollen stuffs after a fashion which was certainly not invented by coquetry. Their hair is parted, and falls over their cheeks on either shoulder, thickly plastered with butter, so as to form a kind of large shiny bonnet. They bear the burden of the hard work of the field and household. The wives are little better than slaves of the men. They kneel and kiss the men's hands whenever they meet ; and yet they seem to be contented with their lot. Perhaps it would not be amiss if some Montenegrins came to Italy and changed our

fashions with regard to women ; for ours are somewhat too marked in the contrary direction.

Climate renders both the men and women of
those provinces extremely prone to sensuality. Legis-
lators, recognising the impossibility of controlling
lawless lust here, have fixed the fine for seduction of
a girl with violence at a trifle above the sum which
a libertine in Venice bestows on the purveyor of his
venal pleasures., At the period of my residence in
Dalmatia, the cities retained something of antique
austerity. This did not, however, prevent the fair
sex from conducting intrigues by stealth. It is
possible that, since those days, enlightened and
philosophical Italians, composing the courts of successive Provveditori Generali, may have removed
the last obstacles of prejudice which gave a spice of
danger to love-making.

In Dalmatia the women are handsome, inclining
for the most part toward a masculine robustness ;
among the Morlacchi of the villages, a Pygmalion
who chose to expend some bushels of sand in polish-
ing the fair sex up, would obtain fine breathing
statues for his pains. These women of Illyria are
less constant in their love than those of Italy ; but
merit less blame for their infidelity than the latter.
The Illyrian is blinded and constrained by her fervent temperament, by the climate, by poverty and
credulity ; the Italian errs through ambition, avarice,
and caprice. I consider myself qualified for speaking

with decision on these points, as will appear from the chapter I intend to write upon the love-adventures of my youth.

The land of those provinces is in great measure mountainous, stony, and barren. There are, however, large districts of plain which might be extremely fertile. Neither the sterile nor the fertile regions are under cultivation, but remain for the most part fallow and unfruitful. Onions and garlic constitute the favourite delicacies of the Morlacchi. The annual consumption of these vegetables is enormous; and it would not be difficult to raise a large supply of both at home. They insist, however, on importing them from Romagna; and when one takes the peasants to task for this sluggish indifference to their own interests, they reply that their ancestors never planted onions, and that they have no mind to change their customs. I often questioned educated inhabitants of those regions upon the indolence and sloth which prevail in rural Dalmatia. The answer I received was that nobody, without exposing his life to peril, could make the Morlacchi do more than they chose to do, or introduce the least reform into their agriculture. I observed that the proprietors might always import Italian labour and turn those fertile plains into a second Apulia. This remark was met with bursts of laughter; and when I asked the reason, my informants told me that many Dalmatian gentlemen had brought Italian peasants over, but that a few days after their arrival, they were found murdered in the fields, without the assassins having ever been detected. I perceived that my project was impracticable. Yet I wondered at my friends laughing rather than shedding tears, when they gave me these convincing answers.

It is a pity that Illyria and Dalmatia cannot be rendered fertile and profitable to the State. As it is, they cost our treasury more than they yield, through the expenses incidental to their forming our frontier against Turkey. But I never made it my business to meddle in affairs of public policy; and perhaps there are good reasons why these provinces should be left to their sterility. The opinion I have continually maintained and published, that we ought to begin by cultivating heads and hearts, has raised a swarm of hostile projectors against me. Such men take the truths of the gospel for biting satires, if they detect the least shadow of opposition to their views regarding personal interest, personal ambition, or particular prejudice. Yet the real miseries which I noticed in Dalmatia, the wretched pittance which proprietors draw from their estates, and the dishonesty of the peasants, suffice to demonstrate my principles of moral education beyond the possibility of contradiction.

During my three years in Dalmatia I used to eat superb game and magnificent fish for a mere nothing; often against my inclination, and only because the opportunity could not be neglected. When you are in want of something, you rarely find it there. The fishermen, who live upon the rocky islands,[1] ply their trade when it pleases them. They take no thought for fasts, and sell fish for the most part on days when flesh is eaten. The fish too is brought to market stuffed into sacks. I could multiply these observations; but let what I have already said suffice. It is my firm opinion that the economists of our century are at fault when they propose material improvements and indulge in visions of opulence and gain, without considering moral education. Wealth is now regarded by the indigent with eyes of envy and the passions of a pirate; rich people act as though they knew not what it was to possess wealth, and make a shameless abuse of it in practice. The one class need to learn temperance, moderation, and obedience to duty; the other ought to be trained to reason and subordination. The sages of the present day entertain very different views from these. In their eyes nothing but material interest has any value; and instead of deploring bad morals and manners, they seem to glory in them.

---

[1] *Scogli.* A long low island opposite the harbour of Zara is so called.

X.

I am enrolled in the Cavalry of the Republic.—What my
military services amounted to.

Some fifteen months of my three years' service had
elapsed, when the recall of our regular troops and
the enrolment of fresh forces in Dalmatia, which
have been described by me above, took place. I
have now to mention that the Provveditore Generale
chose this moment for placing me upon the roll of
the Venetian service.

He had me inscribed as a cadet noble[1] of cavalry.
Accordingly I blossomed out into a proper soldier at
the age of about eighteen. Signor Giorgio Barbarigo,
the paymaster,[2] a short, fat, honest fellow, informed
me that my commission was registered, and that I
was qualified to draw the salary of thirty-eight *lire*
in good Venetian coin monthly at his office. The
news surprised me, and I went at once to pay my
acknowledgments to his Excellency.

He told me that, nearly all the regular troops
having been recalled to Italy, he saw no prospect of
awarding me a higher rank during the term of his

---

[1] This and other French terms show to what extent the military system
of Venice had been modernised.

[2] Razionato.

administration, a considerable part of which had already elapsed. To this he added some ironical remarks to the following effect—"Although, indeed, I do not think you mean to follow a military career, having observed from many points in your behaviour that you are rather inclined to assume the clerical habit." I chose to interpret the irony of my chief to my advantage, and answered cheerfully that although I felt little inclination for the military profession, nothing would ever induce me to become an ecclesiastic; meanwhile I was glad to have studied human nature as one finds it in an army and in those provinces; above all things, I recognised the advantage of having been allowed to serve his Excellency during the three years of his office. I perceived that this reply had not been unacceptable, and retired after making the regulation bow.

I discharged my military duties with punctuality; and if my courage had been put to the test, I feel sure that I should have faced death with romantic enthusiasm. Yet I cannot boast of having earned my monthly pay by any particular services. In addition to the daily and nightly routine of discipline, I attended his Excellency upon visits of inspection by sea and land to the various fortified places of the territory. When the plague broke out, I spoiled my shirts and ruffles in fumigating the mass of correspondence which used to reach the Provveditore Generale from infected villages. I delivered sentences of arrest by word of mouth to Venetian patricians, noblemen, and officers—always much against the grain. I lay, together with several of my comrades, under arrest on a false charge of malpractice, and owed my liberation after a few hours to the intercession of a gentle lady of the Veniero family. While enumerating these martial deserts, I ought not perhaps to include the sufferings endured upon my journeys, whether riding the worst of nags under a fierce sun and sleeping in jackboots upon the open fields, or rocking at sea all night aboard some galley on a coil of cable, half devoured by myriads of bugs. Great as these sufferings were, I must admit that I endured greater in the disorderly garrison amusements which I joined of my own accord. Some account of these I intend to give in another chapter.

It will be observed that my services to the State were but slender. Yet many men have gained promotion or a pension on the strength of nothing better. And now I think upon it, I will mention one notable achievement, which, though it be not martial, might have put some other soldier laddie in the way of rising to his colonelcy. I hardly expect to be believed, but I am telling the truth, when I affirm that I acquired renown throughout Dalmatia as a *soubrette* in improvised comedy upon the boards of a theatre.

XI.

*My theatrical talents; athletic exercises; imprudences of all
kinds; dangers to which I exposed myself; with reflections which are always frivolous.*

All through the carnival, tragedies, dramas and
comedies used to be performed by amateurs in the
Court-theatre, for the amusement of his Excellency,
the patricians on the civil staff, officers of the garrison,
and the good folk of Zara.[1]

Our troop was composed exclusively of male
actors, as is the case in general with unprofessional
theatres; and young men, dressed like women, played
the female parts. I was selected to represent the
soubrette.

On weighing the tastes of my audience, and
taking into account the nation for whom I was to
act, I invented a wholly new kind of character. I
had myself dressed like a Dalmatian servant-girl,
with hair divided at the temples, and done up with
rose-coloured ribbands. My costume corresponded
at all points to that of a coquettish housemaid of

---

[1] This chapter will be read with interest by students of the *Commedia
dell' Arte*. It throws light upon the way in which an actor of originality could adapt one of the fixed characters of that comedy, in this
case the *servetta*, to his own talents and to local circumstances.

Sebenico.   I discarded the Tuscan dialect, which is spoken by the *soubrettes* of our theatres in Italy, and having learned Illyrian pretty well by this time, I devised for my particular use a jargon of Venetian, altering the pronunciation and interspersing various Illyrian phrases.   This produced a very humorous effect, and lent itself both in dialogue and improvised soliloquies to the expression of sentiments in keeping with my part.   Courage and loquacity were always at my service ; after studying the plot of a comedy, which had to be performed extempore, I never found my readiness of wit at fault.   Accordingly, the new and unexpected type of the *soubrette* which I invented was welcomed with enthusiasm alike by Italians and natives.   It created a *furore* in my audience, and won for me universal sympathy.

My sketches of Dalmatian manners studied from the life, my satirical repartees to the mistresses I served, my piquant sallies upon incidents which formed the talk of town and garrison, my ostentatious modesty, my snubs to impertinent admirers, my reflections and my lamentations, made the Provveditore Generale and the whole audience declare with tears of laughter running down their cheeks that I was the wittiest and most humourous *soubrette* who ever trod the boards of a theatre.   They often bespoke improvised comedies, in order to enjoy the amusing chatter and Illyrico-Italian jargon of Luce ; for I ought to add that I adopted this name, which is the same as

our Lucia, instead of Smeraldina, Corallina, or
Colombina.

Ladies in plenty were eager to know the young
man who played Luce with such diablerie and ready
wit upon the stage.   But when they met him face
to face in society, his reserve and taciturnity were so
unlike the sprightliness of his assumed character, that
they fairly lost their temper.   Now that I am well
stricken in years, I recognise that their disappoint-
ment was anything but a misfortune for me.   The
conduct of those few who concealed their feelings
and pretended that my self-control and seriousness
had charms to win their heart, justifies this moral
reflection.   Meanwhile my talent for comedy relieved
me of all military duties so long as carnival lasted.
Each year, at the commencement of this season, the
Provveditore Generale sent for me, and affably requested me to devote my time and energy to his
amusement in the Court-theatre.

During summer he set the fashion of pallone-
playing, which had hitherto been unknown at Zara.[1]
I had made myself an adept in this game at our Friulian country-seat.   Accordingly his Excellency urged
me to display my accomplishments for the entertain-

---

[1] *Pallone* is a game played with a large leather ball, filled with air,
and something like our football.   In Italy it is struck with the hand,
which is armed for the purpose with gloves or a flat short bat fixed on
the palm.   Sides are chosen, and the game roughly resembles tennis on
a large scale.   Pallone is the original of our balloon.

ment of the public. In a short time my seductive
costume of fine white linen, with a waistband of
black satin and fluttering ribands, cut a prominent
figure among the competitors in this noble sport. My
turn for study, literary talent, grave demeanour, and
seriousness of character made far less impression on
the fair sex than my successes on the stage and the
pallone-ground. It was these and these alone which
put my chastity to the test and conquered it, as will
appear in the chapter on my love-adventures. I
might here indulge in a digression hardly flattering
to women. But I prefer to congratulate them on
their emancipation from the ideality of Petrarch's
age. Now they are at liberty to float voluptuously
on the tide of tender and electrical emotions, in
company with youths congenial to their instincts,
who have abandoned tedious studies for occupations
hardly more exacting than a game at ball or the impersonation of a waiting-maid.

The truth of history compels me to touch upon
some incidents which put my boyish courage to the
proof; yet I must confess that my deeds of daring in
Dalmatia were nothing better than mad and brainless
acts of folly. While recording them, I dare hardly
hope—although I should sincerely like to do so—
that they will prove useful to parents by exposing
the kind of life which young men lead on foreign
service, or to sons by pointing out the errors of
my ways.

We had no war on hand, and our valour was obliged
to find a vent for itself. I should have passed for a pol-·
troon if I had not joined the amusements and adventures of my comrades. These consisted for the most
part in frantic gambling, serenading houses which
returned our serenades with gunshots, ·entertaining
women of the town at balls and supper-parties,
brawling in the streets at night, disguising ourselves
to frighten people, and breaking the slumbers of the
good folk of the towns and fortresses where the
Court happened to be fixed. I remember that one
summer night in the city of Spalato, eight or ten of
us dressed up for the latter purpose. Each man put
on a couple of shirts, thrusting his legs through the
sleeves of one and his arms through the other, with a
big white bonnet on his head and a pole in his hand.
Thus attired, we scoured the town like spectres from
the other world, knocking at doors, uttering horrid
shrieks to rouse the population, and striking terror
into the breasts of women and children. Now it is
the custom there to leave the stable-doors open,
because of the great heat at night. Accordingly we
undid the halters of some fifty horses, and drove
them before us, clattering our staves upon the pavement. The din was infernal. Folk leaped from
their beds, thinking that the Turks had made a raid
upon the town, and crying from their windows:
" Who the devil are you? Who goes there? Who
goes there?" They screamed to the deaf, while we

went clattering and driving on.   In the morning the whole city was in an uproar, discussing last night's prodigy and skurrying about to catch the frightened animals.

My guitar-playing accomplishments made me indispensable in these dare-devil escapades of hair-brained boys, which by some miracle never seemed to reach the Provveditore Generale's ears.   Had they done so, I suppose they would have been punished, as they deserved ; for he was a man who knew how to maintain discipline.   The Italians and Illyrians do not dwell together without a certain half-concealed antipathy. This leads to frequent trials of strength and valour, in which the Italians are most to blame.   They insult the natives and pick quarrels with a people famous for their daring and ferocity.   The courage displayed in maintaining these quarrels and facing their attendant dangers deserves the name of folly rather than of bravery.   After stating this truth, to which indeed I was never blind, I dare affirm that no one met musket-shots and menaces with a bolder front than I did.   Physicians versed in the anatomy of the human frame may be able to explain my constitutional imperturbability under all circumstances of peril.   I am content to account for it as sheer stupidity.

We were at Budua, toward Montenegro, my friend Massimo and I.   In this city women are guarded with a watchful jealousy of which Italians

have no notion; while homicides occur with facility
and frequency. Massimo began a gallant correspondence from the window of our lodging with a
girl who was our neighbour. She belonged to one
of the noblest families of the place, and was engaged
to a gentleman of the city. Nevertheless, she returned my friend's advances with the eagerness of
one who has been kept in slavery. I must add that
the future bridegroom obtained some inkling of this
aërial intrigue. He was a rough Illyrian of no breeding. One morning this fellow opened conversation
with us officers in a little square, where we were
seated together on stone benches. With much
circumlocution and a kind of awkward sprightliness,
addressing himself to Massimo, and smiling half-
sourly and half-sillily, he expressed his own stupid
contempt for Italian customs with regard to women.
The long and the short of this involved discourse was
simply that all the men in Italy were cuckolds, and
all the women no better than they should be. Massimo took care not to emphasise the meaning of the
fellow's innuendoes, which would have called for blood
and vengeance; but contented himself with bluntly
defending our social institutions. In the course of his
argument he proved that the barbarity and tyranny
of men toward women, who are always sharp of wit
and full of cleverness in every climate, caused more
of immorality and intrigue in Illyria than freedom of
intercourse between the sexes caused in Italy. To

my mind, he spoke what was partly true and partly
false; for it cannot be maintained that the facilita-
tion and toleration of licentiousness remove it from
our midst. The Illyrian, however, lacked eloquence,
and felt ill at ease in carrying on a wordy warfare.
So he did not attempt to confute Massimo; but
rolled his head and knit his brows, and told him that
he might soon be taught at his own cost how badly
the Italians conduct themselves in this respect.

Nothing more was wanted in the way of challenge
to set us Italians on our mettle. A trifle of this sort
turned us at once into knights-errant, championing
our nation's cause among half-savages, who murder
men with the same indifference as they kill quails
or fig-peckers. Massimo turned to me and said
that, when night fell, I must take my guitar and
follow him. Obeying the rash romantic impulse of
my heart, I replied that nothing should prevent me
from attending on him. The other Italians who
were present at this interview, with more prudence
than ourselves, affected to hear nothing.

It happened that a young Florentine named Stef-
fano Torri was at this time clerk in the secretary's
office of the Generalato. He played female parts in
our comedies and tragedies with much ability, and
sang like a nightingale. In order to give our noc-
turnal enterprise the character of a serenade—a thing
quite alien to the customs of that district—Massimo
invited this poor lad to warble, without informing

IL CAPITANO (1668)

Illustrating the Italian Commedia dell' Arte, or Impromptu Comedy

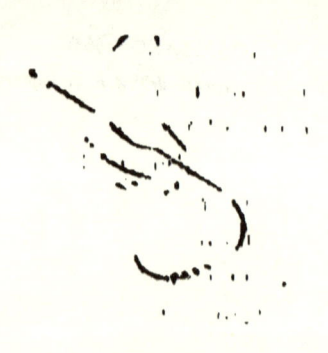

him of what had happened. He was only too glad
to let his fine voice be heard ; and being besides an
obliging creature, he gave his promise on the spot.

Night came. It was September ; the season warm,
and the moon shining brightly. We girt our swords,
stuck a brace of pistols in our belts, and took up our
station in the principal street, which was long and
straight, beneath the windows of Massimo's Dulcinea.
Torri sent melody after melody forth into the silent air,
while I twanged my guitar-strings for a good hour's
space. Suddenly a window, belonging to the mansion
we were honouring with our duet, flew violently open.
A great black head appeared, from which there issued
a hoarse voice like that of Charon in Dante's Inferno.
"What insolence !" it uttered with a bad Italian
accent. We knew that the huge skull was consecrate,
and belonged to a certain Canon, uncle of the girl.
But something more was needed than the big bovine
voice of an ecclesiastic to disturb our tranquillity.
Torri, however, being a civilian and no soldier, began
to be aware that his melodious airs were out of place.
The prudence which is born of fear made him reflect
upon the situation, and he asked leave to retire. We
persuaded him to stay awhile, pointing out that the
street was public, that our amusement was lawful
and innocuous, and that it conferred an honour on
our nation. He resumed his singing; but from this
moment the melodies had a certain quaver in them,
which the composer had not calculated. The first

assault by the Canon was sustained and repulsed; for after roaring out "What insolence!" three or four times, he shut the window in our faces with a crash.

The second attack upon our obstinacy was something very different and far more formidable than a priest's voice, however horrible. It effectually shut the mouth up of our young musician. By the light of the moon we could discern six men at a distance entering the street with six lowered and gleaming muskets; the cowls of their cloaks concealed their faces, and they advanced at a slow pace toward us. At this apparition our musician took to his heels, and did not stop running till he reached his lodging. Massimo and I stood our ground like Orlando and Rodomonte. I went on playing; my friend, to keep the singing up, howled out some rustic ditties in a bold voice, which was however, I am bound to say, even less agreeable than the Canon's. His discords were enough to cast eternal shame upon Italian music; and if the young lady heard them, they must have frightened her out of her wits instead of giving her the pleasure of a serenade.

Observing our determination to stand firm, the six cowled men advanced to within twenty paces. We heard the click of their six gunlocks, as they cocked them, ready to give fire. At this point our intrepidity deserved no other name than madness; it called for the lancet, hellebore, strait-jackets, a good drubbing. Without budging an inch, we raised our pistols at the muffled band. They looked at us, we looked at them, for good two minutes. Then they made their minds up to defile past, leaving us at a little distance, but always keeping their eyes fixed with a haughty defiance on our faces. We, on our part, made our minds up to let them pass, returning no less haughty glances. Perhaps they wished to give us time for repentance, or for wholesome reflections, which should make us quit our post. Anyhow, they moved onward till they reached the end of the street, when once again they turned and faced us.

Little did those cowled and mantled fellows know the length and breadth of our stupidity! We recommenced our duet with a more hideous din than ever. They retraced their steps, and advanced steadily toward us. But when they found the pair of little fighting-cocks still standing with raised pistols on the watch, they judged it wiser to pursue their course and disappear. The removal of the Court from Budua, which took place one day after this memorable exploit, probably saved us from being shot down by an ambuscade. I also imagine that the men only wished to frighten us away. Possibly our expected departure from the city, or else respect for our staff-uniform, restrained their fingers on the trigger. Such considerations had certainly more weight with those fierce natives than the insane bravado of two insects armed with pistols. Anyhow, I have always regarded our courage in this danger as fool-hardiness rather than magnanimity.

I could relate an infinity of such adventures, in all of which we risked our lives on some puerile point of honour, or in pursuit of some impertinence which called for castigation. One night at Spalato our serenading party was welcomed with a storm of heavy stones, which made us skip like kids, but could not drive us from our post. We were paying this compliment to a handsome girl of Ragusa, the mistress of one of the chief nobles of the city, and we maintained our station for the honour of Italy, with skulls unbroken, till the day rose.

In the society of unemployed and lazy officers, a young man may be said to have worked miracles who preserves the good principles implanted in him at home. Unless he conforms to the tone and fashion of his comrades, he is sure to be derided and despised. If he does conform, he is likely to lose substance, health and reputation at cards, with women, or by drinking. Besides this, he constantly risks life and limb in the so-called pastimes I have just described.

I am able to boast without exaggeration that I never played for high stakes, that I never surrendered myself to debauchery, that I preserved the sound principles of my home education, and yet that I was popular with all my comrades, owing to the clubbable and fraternal attitude which I assumed at some risk, it is true, yet always with the firm determination to leave a good character behind me when my term of service ended.

XII.

Shows how a young Cadet of Cavalry is capable of executing a military stratagem.

Having described the dangers to which my system of conduct in the army exposed me, I ought in justice to myself to show that I was able on occasion to reconcile our absurd code of honour with prudence and diplomacy. With this object I will relate an incident, which is neither more nor less insignificant than the other events of my life.

The city of Zara is traversed by a main street of considerable length, extending from the piazza of San Simeone to the gate called Porta Marina. Several lanes and alleys, leading downwards from the ramparts on the side toward the sea, debouch into this principal artery. It so happened that some of the officers, wishing to traverse one of these lanes on their way to the promenade upon the ramparts, had been intercepted by a man muffled in a mantle, who levelled an eloquent enormous blunderbuss at their persons, and forced them to change their route. This act of violence ought to have been reported to

the Provveditore Generale, and he would have speedily
restored order and freedom of passage.   Our military
code of honour, however, forbade recourse to justice
as an act of cowardice ; albeit some of my comrades
found it not derogatory to their courage to recoil
before a blunderbuss.

My readers ought to be informed that a girl of
the people, called Tonina, one of the loveliest women
whom eyes of man have ever seen, lived in this lane.
She had multitudes of admirers ; and the cozening
tricks she used to wheedle and entice a pack of
simpletons, made her no better than any other cheap
and venal beauty.   Yet she contrived to sell her
favours by the sequin.   A gentleman, whom I shall
mention lower down, was madly in love with this
little baggage.   Wishing to keep the treasure to himself, he adopted a truly Dalmatian mode of testifying
his devotion, and stood sentinel in her alley.   On
two consecutive evenings the passage was barred ;
we talked of nothing else in the ante-chamber of the
General, and laid plans how to reassert our honour.
A number of officers agreed to face the blunderbuss ;
I received an invitation to join the band ; and acting
on my system of good-fellowship, I readily consented.

Our discussion took place in the ante-chamber ;
silence was enjoined ; we settled that each of the
conspirators should wear a white ribband on his
hat, and that three hours after nightfall we should
assemble under arms at our accustomed mustering-

place. This was a billiard-saloon, whence we were to sally forth to the assault of Buda.

An Illyrian nobleman, Signor Simeone C——, of handsome person, honourable carriage, and a resolute temper, which inspired even soldiers with respect, although he held no military grade, was sitting in a corner of the ante-chamber, half-asleep, and apparently inattentive to our project. I knew him to be frank and genial, and he had often professed sentiments of sincere friendship for myself. After our scheme had been concerted, I passed into the reception-room of the palace. He followed, and opened a conversation on indifferent topics, in the course of which he drew me aside, changed his tone, and began to speak as follows :—

"The moment has arrived for me to testify the cordial friendship which I entertain for you. I regret that you have promised to join those fire-eaters this evening. On your honour and secrecy I know that I can count. I am sure that you will not reveal what I am about to disclose ; else the higher powers, whom we are bound to regard, might be involved, and cowardice might be suspected in those whose courage is indisputable. This preamble will enable you to judge what I think of you, and to measure the extent of my friendship. I am the man in the mask. To-night there will be four blunderbusses in the alley. I shall lose my life ; but several will lose theirs before the lane is forced. I am sorry that you

are in the affair. Contrive to get out of your engagement. Let the rest come, and enjoy their fill of pastime at the cost of life or limb."

This blunderbuss of an oration took me by surprise.
But I did not lose my senses or my tongue, and
answered to the following effect:—

"I am amazed that you should have begun by
professing friendship and preaching caution. You
do not seem to understand the first elements of the
one or the simple meaning of the other. I am
obliged to you for one thing only, your belief that I
am incapable of divulging what you have just told
me. Upon this point alone your discernment is not
at fault. I would rather die than expose you. Yet
you want me, under threats, to break my word, and
to render myself contemptible in the eyes of all my
comrades. This you call a proof of friendship. It
is as clear as day, too, that you have yielded to a
hussy's importunities, risking your own life and the
lives of your friends upon a silly point of honour in a
shameful quarrel. This is the proof of your prudence.
If you withdraw from the engagement, no harm will .
be done, and cowardice will only be imputed to a
nameless mask. But if I break my word, you cannot
free me from the imputation of having proved myself
a renegade and a dastard. I shall become an object
of scorn and abhorrence to the whole army. If I act
as you desire, my oath of secrecy to you will violate
the laws of friendship, prudence, everything which

men hold sacred. Your promise of secrecy again puts
my honour in peril. How can you be sure that one of
your accomplices will not privily inform his Excellency
of your name and your mad enterprise? Where shall
I then be? No: it is clearly your duty to obey the
counsels dictated by my loyal friendship and my
sound prudence. Leave the alley open; and then
you will in truth oblige me. Make love to your
Tonina with something more to the purpose than
a blunderbuss. Her physical shape excuses your
weakness for her; her mind deserves your scorn;
but I. am not going to preach sermons on objects
worthy or unworthy of love; I feel compassion for
human frailty."

It was obvious that Signor Simeone C—— felt
the force of these arguments. But he writhed with
rage under them, and showed no sign of consenting.
In his fierce Dalmatian way he burst into bare protestations, swore that he would never quit the field,
and wound up with a vow to sell his life as dearly
as man ever did.

At this point I judged it needful to administer
a dose of histrionic artifice. After gazing at him
for some seconds with eyes which spoke volumes,
I assumed the declamatory tone of a tragedian, and
exclaimed: "Well then, I promise to be the first to
enter the lane this evening, and, without attacking
you, I shall offer my breast to your fire. I have only
this way left of proving to you that you are in no

real sense of the word my friend." Then I turned my back with a show of passion, taking care, however, to retire at a slow pace. Except for the ferocity instilled by education, he was at bottom an excellent good-hearted fellow. Seizing me by the arm, he begged me wait a moment. I saw that he was touched, and maintaining the tragic tone, I persuaded him to leave the access to the alley free, without resigning his exclusive right to the Tonina. For my part, I undertook never to reveal our secret. This promise I have kept for thirty-five years. Lapse of time and the probability of his decease—for he was much older than I—excuse me for now breaking it.

On three following nights I joined the allied forces at the billiard-room, armed to the teeth, and with a white ribbon flying from my hat-band. I was always the first to brave the blunderbusses, being sure that no resistance would be offered. Indeed, the victory, on which we piqued ourselves, had been won beforehand in my battle of words. The culpable conduct of Tonina, a girl of the people, who had exposed so many gentlemen to serious danger, remained fixed in my mind. I shall relate the sequel to this incident, which took a comic turn, in the next chapter. For the present, it is enough to add that Signor Simeone C——'s infatuation for this corsair of Venus rapidly declined, as is the wont of passions begotten by masculine appetite and feminine avarice. Tonina,

however, did not lack lovers, and the badness of her
nature continued to spread discord and foment disorder in our circle.

XIII.

*The fair Tonina is rudely rebuked by me upon an accidental
occasion in the theatre. — My reconciliation with the
young woman.—Reflections on my life in Dalmatia.*

One evening during the last carnival of my three
years' service, the Provveditore Generale bespoke an
improvised comedy at the Court-theatre. The officers
arranged a supper-party and a ball in private rooms,
intending to pass the night gaily when the farce was
over. I had to play the part of Luce, married to
Pantalone, a vicious old man, broken in health and
fortune. I was reduced to extreme poverty, with
a daughter in the cradle, the fruit of my unhappy
marriage.

There was a night-scene, in which I had to solilo-
quise, while rocking my child and singing it to sleep
with some old ditty. This lullaby I interrupted from
time to time with the narrative of my misfortunes and
with sallies which made the audience die of laughter.
Bursts of applause brought the house down as I told
my story, enlarged upon my reasons for marrying an
old man, related the incidents of my life, alluded in

modest monosyllables to what I had to bear, described what a fine figure of a woman I had been, and
what a scarecrow matrimony had made me. I complained of cold, hunger, evil treatment. I did not
make milk enough to suckle my baby; and what I
made was sour, nay, venomous from fits of rage and
all the sufferings I had to go through. This bad
milk gave my darling, the fruit of my womb, the
stomach-ache. It kept bleating all night like a lamb,
and would not let me close an eye. The night was
far advanced. I was waiting for my old fool of a
husband. What could be keeping him abroad? He
must surely be in the Calle del Pozzetto, notorious
at Zara for its evil fame. I had a presentiment of
coming troubles, moralised upon the woes of life,
and burst into a flood of tears, which made everybody laugh. The truth was that one of our officers,
Signor Antonio Zeno, who played the part of Pantalone excellently, had not turned up at the proper
time to enter into dialogue with me. Until he
arrived, I was forced to continue my soliloquy,
which had already occupied the attention of the
audience full fifteen minutes. A good extempore
actor ought never to lose presence of mind, or to
be at a loss for material. In order to prolong
the scene, I pretended that my baby was crying,
and that it would not go to sleep for all my
lullabies and cradle-rocking. In a fit of impatience
I took it up, unlaced my dress, and laid it with en-

dearing caresses to my breasts to quiet it. This fresh
absurdity, together with my lamentations over the
non-existent teats I said the greedy little thing was
biting, kept my audience in good-humour. From
time to time I turned my eyes to the sides, being
really disturbed at Signor Zeno-Pantalone's non-
appearance, and racking my brains in vain for some
new matter to sustain the soliloquy.

Just then I happened to catch sight of Tonina
seated in one of the front boxes of the theatre,
resplendent with beauty, and attired in a gala dress
which cast a glaring light upon her dubious career.
She was laughing with more assurance and sense
of fun than anybody at my jokes. The catastrophe
which she had nearly caused flashed suddenly
across my mind. I felt that I had discovered a
treasure ; and plunged like lightning into a new
subject. What I proceeded to do was bold, I admit,
yet quite within the limits of good taste upon our
amateur stage, where personal allusions were allowed
perhaps a little too liberally. I called my doll-baby
by the name of Tonina, and addressed my speech to
it. I caressed it, admired its features, flattered my
maternal heart with the hope that Tonina would
grow up a lovely girl. So far as I was concerned,
I vowed to give her a good education, by example,
precepts, chastisement, and watchful care. Then,
taking a tone of gravity, I warned her that if, in
spite of all my trouble, she fell into such and such

faults, such and such acts of imprudence, such and such immoral ways, and caused such and such dis- turbances, she would be the worst Tonina in the world, and I prayed God to cut her days short rather in the cradle. All the evil things I mentioned were faithfully copied from anecdotes about Tonina in the front box, with which my audience were only too well acquainted.

Never in my whole life have I known an improvised soliloquy to be so tumultuously applauded as this of mine was. The spectators at one point of the speech turned their faces with a simultaneous movement towards Tonina in her gala dress, clapping their hands and laughing till the theatre rang again. His Excellency, who had some inkling of the siren's ways, honoured my unexpected satire with explosions of unconcealed merriment. Tonina backed out of her box in a fit of fury, and escaped from the theatre, cursing my soliloquy and the man who made it. Pantalone finally arrived, and the comedy ended without any episode more mirthful than the scene between me and my baby.

Do not imagine that I have related this incident to brag about it. Although the young woman in question was a girl of the people, whose dissolute behaviour and ill-nature had been the cause of many misadventures, and though the Provveditore Generale applauded my performance, I blamed myself, when it was over, for yielding to a mere impulse of vanity, and exhibiting my power as a comedian at the cost of committing an act of imprudence and indiscretion. Much has to be condoned to youth which is never conceded to maturity.

I have mentioned that a ball and supper-party had been arranged by us officers after the play, and that I was a member of the company. I went in my costume of Luce, partly to save time, and partly to carry on the joke. Tonina was among the guests. She did not expect me, and was sitting in a corner, angry and out of spirits. When she saw me, one would have thought she had set eyes on the fiend ; she looked as though she meant to leave the room. I took her hand, and protested I would rather go than that the company should lose its loveliest orna-ment. I vowed that she was adorably beautiful, and that it was a pity she was not equally good. I begged her in gentle terms to take the accident of the even-ing into account, to reflect upon the universal verdict given by the audience on her ways of life, and to guard against the private flatterers who blinded her to the truth. I told her that God had meant to send in her an angel, and not a devil into this world. I interwove so many praises with so many insolences, and with such complete frankness, that she could not but laugh. Everybody laughed, down to her very lovers. She expressed a wish to dance with me. I accepted the invitation. This looked like a token of peace ; but it was only treachery. While dancing, she exerted all the charms, enticements, captivating humours, pressures of the hand, and so forth, which her bad vindictive and seductive nature could suggest to enslave me.

A woman's coquetries directed to some purpose of revenge are always blind, and give the best advantage to a clever roué. The reason is that the woman, piqued to the point of seeking a victory at any price, lowers herself to the utmost, without being aware of what she is conceding. I was not a roué; and woe to me if I had let myself be snared by the wiles and artifices of that viper smarting under the sense of recent insult!

Our pleasure party was resumed soon after supper, during which my fair foe kept me at her side. We broke up about sunrise; and Tonina never ceased to call me her accursed little devil; that was the sweet Dalmatian term of endearment which she used. Compelled by these compliments, I promised to pay her a visit, but I did not keep my word.

I have now given some general notion of my ways of thinking and acting, my character and conduct, up to the age of eighteen on to .twenty. Nothing but the truth has dictated these reminiscences, from which I have undoubtedly omitted many things of similar importance. I am sure that if I had been guilty of anything really wrong during this period, it would not have escaped either my memory or my pen. I have never hardened my heart against the

stings of remorse, and I would far rather frankly
record facts to my discredit than bear the stings of
conscience by suppressing what is true. Reviewing
the veracious picture of myself which I have painted,
friends will see in me a somewhat eccentric young
man, but of harmless disposition ; enemies will take
me for a worthless scapegrace ; the indifferent, who
know me superficially by sight, will discover some
one very different from their conception based on my
external qualities. At the proper place and time I
shall account for this not unreasonable and yet fal-
lacious conception formed of me by strangers. The
reasons will appear clearly in the detailed portrait I
intend to execute of myself, and which will surpass
the best work of any painter.

XIV.

*The end of my three years' service.—I cast up my accounts,
and reckon debts; calculate upon the future, with a
sad prevision of the truth.—My arrival in my home
at Venice.*

The three years of my military service were nearly
at an end, when I contracted a slow fever, not dangerous to life, but tedious. The time had come
for settling accounts, and seeing how I stood. My
family, since I left home, had furnished me with only

two bills of exchange, one for fourteen, the other for six sequins. My useless duties to the State had brought me thirty-eight lire per month. Against these receipts I balanced my expenses: so much for my daily food; so much for my lodging, clothing, and washing; so much for a servant, indispensable in my position; so much for two illnesses, together with the small sums spent on unavoidable pleasures of society. The result was that I found myself in debt to my friend Massimo for exactly the sum of fifty-six sequins and sixteen lire, or 200 ducats.[1]

If the necessities of life are not to be considered vices, this debt was certainly a modest one. Still it weighed upon my mind. I consoled myself by re-calling my friend's nobleness of nature, and felt sure that I should be able to repay him on reaching home. I computed that the gross sum I had received during those three years amounted to 480 ducats; and I did not think I had been a spendthrift in consuming about 150 ducats a year on my total expenditure. I could indeed have saved something by attending the table which the Provveditore Generale kept daily for the officers of his Court and guard, but which his sublime Excellency never honoured with his presence.

---

[1] The sequin at this time was worth twenty-two *lire Venete*. The worth of the *lira* was about half a franc, says Romanin (vol. viii. p. 302). Romanin in the same place fixes the ducat at eight *lire*. Gozzi's debt amounted to 1248 *lire*. This would make only 156 ducats at the above rate. But the relation of the ducat to the sequin and the *lira* is very obscure, and seems to have varied according to the kind of ducat.

Little did he know what a gang of ruffians, with the exception of a few patient souls constrained by urgent need, defiled his table, or what low tricks were perpetrated at it. Since the day of my arrival I had heard the infamous and compromising talk which went on there, had watched the squabbles between guest and guest, and guests and serving-men, had seen the cups and platters flying through the air—and, like a naughty boy perhaps, I preferred to contract a debt of 200 ducats rather than accept a hospitality so prostituted to vile uses. I attended this table of Thyestes, as it seemed to me, only when I could not help it, on the days when I had to mount guard.

The financial statement I have just made will appear to many of my readers a mere trifle, unworthy of recording here. They are mistaken. When they have learned in what a state of desolation I found my father's house, and how I strove to stem the tide of prodigality and waste which was bringing our family to ruin, they will understand my reasons for insisting on these trifles. Heads heated by anger and resentment are only too ready to invent false accusations; and I shall soon be made to appear a prodigal, a reckless gambler, a consumer of the substance of my family during the three years I spent abroad. This is why I am so scrupulous in telling the plain truth about my cost of living in Dalmatia. I have never been ashamed of letting the whole world know how modest are my fortunes.   I should think it a greater shame to pretend to possess more than I really own.   Riches have always seemed to me to be a name, and to reside in the imagination. If I cast my eyes on a carpenter, then raise them to a duke, and finally lift them to a king, I obtain convincing demonstration of the fact that he alone is rich who has the mental wealth—to be contented with his lot.   Alas! that only I and many millions upon their deathbed recognise this truth.

My three years were over.   The new Provveditore Generale, Jacopo Boldù, arrived in Dalmatia, and received the staff of office with the usual formalities from his Excellency Quirini.   In my moments of leisure I had composed several poems in honour of the latter, and had procured others from Venice. These I copied out in the beautiful handwriting which I then possessed, sewed them together, added a respectful dedication, and had them bound in a fine velvet cover.   Then I paid my respects to his Excellency in company with my friend Massimo, and laid my literary tribute at his feet.   I was no Virgil, nor was I born in the golden age of Augustus.   Only my fanaticism for the art of poetry made me imagine that verses could be anything worth offering as a gift.

The Cavaliere accepted my donation with affability. He said: "I thank you.   At least I have the wherewithal to show that, while a member of my Court, you have remained at school."

Afterwards I learned that he made a present of this book to the Very Eminent Cardinal, his uncle, Bishop of Brescia. His Excellency inquired whether I preferred to return to Venice or to stay in Dalmatia, occupying the post of cadet noble of cavalry on my promotion. I begged him to take me in his train to Venice, and he graciously accepted.

Some one else than I would have looked around for testimonials little to be trusted, which might have kept me fraudulently drawing pay upon the muster-roll of Venice from a too indulgent Government. But I had renounced the military career, and had no mind to spunge upon the public treasury. Our Prince I regarded as a common father, but did not think it just to saddle him with thievish sons, each one of whom by coaxed protections, adulations, hypocrisies, and the vilest offices, eats into the common patrimony of the nation, which ought to be reserved for urgent needs. I was a poor lad, with a debt of 200 ducats ; but I knew that the services rendered to the State by me constituted no claim upon the public purse. If I was poor, this came from our being too many in our family and from the maladministration of our property.

My wants were moderate. I flattered myself that I could satisfy them by attending to the management of the estate ; and I felt sure that my father, paralysed and speechless as he was, would never refuse to pay the trifling debt I had contracted. Meanwhile it is not improbable that my name remained upon the muster-roll long after I left Dalmatia. Somebody may have pocketed my pay and pilfered from the treasury to this extent. I was not responsible for this, and had no right to inquire into the matter, since I never asked to be cashiered in form. Poor I was, poor I am, and poor I expect to die. At any rate, I am sure that I should die in desperation if I felt on my deathbed that I had earned a fortune by deceit, injustice, and intrigue.

It was in the month of October when at last I embarked for Venice on the galley of his Excellency. Wind and weather were against us. After a painful voyage of twenty-two days, we came in sight of home, and I drew breath again. After paying my respects and returning thanks to the Cavaliere who had brought me back, I set off for our ancestral mansion at San Cassiano, accompanied by Signor Massimo, whom I had invited to stay with me upon his way to Padua. There I hoped to be able to pay my friend some attention by giving him good quarters during his sojourn in Venice.

XV.

Disagreeable discoveries relating to our family affairs, which
dissipate all illusions I may have formed.

Leaving the horrors of the galley for the ancient
home of my ancestors, I palpitated between pleasure
at escaping into freedom, hope of being able to make
my friend comfortable, and uneasiness lest this hope
might prove ill-founded.

We reached the entrance, and my companion
gazed with wonder at the stately structure of the
mansion, which has really all the appearance of a
palace. As a connoisseur of architecture, he compli-
mented me upon its fine design. I answered, what
indeed he was about to discover by experience, that
attractive exteriors sometimes mask discomfort and
annoyance. He had plenty of time to admire the
façade, while I kept knocking loudly at the house-
door. I might as well have knocked at the portal
of a sepulchre. At last a woman, named Eugenia,
the guardian-angel of this wilderness, ran to open.
To my inquiries she answered, yawning, that the
family were in Friuli, but that my brother Gasparo
was momently expected. Our luggage had now been
brought from the boat, and we began to ascend a handsome marble staircase. No one could have expected

that this fine flight of steps would lead to squalor and the haunts of indigence. Yet on surmounting the last stair this was what revealed itself. The stone floors were worn into holes and fissures, which spread in all directions like a cancer. The broken window panes let blasts from every point of the compass play freely to and fro within the draughty chambers. The hangings on the walls were ragged, smirched with smoke and dust, fluttering in tatters. Not a piece remained of that fine gallery of pictures which my grandfather had bequeathed as heirlooms to the family. I only saw some portraits of my ancestors by Titian and Tintoretto still staring from their ancient frames. I gazed at them; they gazed at me; they wore a look of sadness and amazement, as though inquiring how the wealth which they had gathered for their offspring had been dissipated.

I have hitherto omitted to mention that our family archives contain an old worm-eaten manuscript, in which are registered the tenths[1] paid to the public treasury. From this document it appears that the father of my great-grandfather was taxed on upwards of ten thousand ducats of income. It is perhaps a folly to moralise on such things; yet the recollection of those mournful portraits gazing down upon me in the squalor of our ancient habitation prompts me to tell an idle truth. Nobody will be the wiser for it;

---

[1] *Decime.* Taxes annually raised upon the whole property of a Venetian.

certainly none of our posterity in this prodigal age.
My grandfather left an only son and a good estate
settled in tail on heirs-male in perpetuity. Four
excellent residences, all of them well-furnished, one
in Venice, another in Padua, another in Pordenone,
another in the Friulian country-town of Vicinate,
were included in this entail, as appears from his last
will and testament. Little did he think that the
solemn appointments of the dead would be so lightly
binding on the living.

I had informed my friend Massimo of the exact
state of our affairs at home, so far as these were
known to me. I could not acquaint him with the
grave disasters which had happened in my three years'
absence, being myself in blessed ignorance as yet.
The news that my two elder sisters had been married
inclined me to expect that our domestic circumstances
were improving. Cruel deception wrapped me round,
and a hundred speechless but eloquent mouths were
now proclaiming, from the walls and chambers of my
home, how utterly deceived I had been.

Before long I broke, as usual, into laughter, and
gaily begged my comrade's pardon for bringing him
to such a wretched hostelry. I assured him that my
heart, at any rate, was not so ruined as my dwelling,
and engaged him in conversation, while we roamed
around its chambers, every nook of which increased
my mirth by some new aspect of dilapidation. Then I
bade him refresh his spirits with a survey of the noble

façade ; till at last we settled down as well as circumstances permitted.   Two days afterwards, my brother
Gasparo arrived.   I presented the stranger I had
brought to share our hospitality, frankly expressing
my sense of his worth and my obligations to him as
a friend.   Upon this we established ourselves in a
little society of three, enlivened by the conversation
of my brother, who, even with a fever on him, never
failed to be witty.

Gasparo and I were anxiously awaiting an opportunity to talk alone like brothers after my long
absence.   When the moment came, I inquired after
my poor father, our mother, and the circumstances
of the family.   What I had already seen on my
arrival prepared me for the disagreeable news I had
to hear.   With his usual philosophy, but not without
an occasional sign of painful emotion, he gave me
the following details.   The family was reduced to
really tragic straits.   Our father lived on, but speechless and paralytic, in the same state as when I left
him.   My two elder sisters, Marina and Giulia, were
married respectively to the Conte Michele di Prata
and the Conte Giovan-Daniele di Montereale.   About
ten thousand ducats had been promised for their
dowries.   To raise this sum, such and such portions
of the estate had been sold, and a debt of more
than two thousand ducats had been contracted.   A
lawsuit was pending between the family and the
Conte Montereale concerning part of the dowry still

due to him.   Our other three sisters, Laura, Girolama, and Chiara, were growing into womanhood, and
gave much to think of for their future.

I saw, to my great annoyance, that it would be
impossible to liquidate my debt upon the spot.   But
all these terrifying details did not make me regret
my resignation of the post of cadet noble in the
cavalry.   A few days later, Signor Massimo left for
Padua, with the assurance that his two hundred
ducats would be paid in course of time by me.
Upon this matter he only expressed the sentiments
of cordial friendship.

It was not too late in the season for a visit to the
country.   I felt a strong desire to reach Friuli, and
to kiss the hands of my unhappy father.   Thither
then I went, together with my brother, armed with
a giant's fortitude, which was not long in being put
to proof.

XVI.

Fresh discoveries regarding the condition of our family.—
Vain hopes and wasted will to be of use.—I abandon
myself to my old literary studies.

Our country-house had been originally constructed
on an old-fashioned, roomy, and convenient scale,
with numbers of out-buildings.   It was now reduced
to one of those dilapidated farms, which I have de-

scribed in my burlesque poem *La Marfisa Bizzarra,*
canto xii., stanza 126.[1] Two-thirds of the edifice
had been demolished, and the materials sold. The
remaining fragments were inhabited, but bore written
on their front : " Here once was Troy."

Prepared as I was by the misery of our town-house
for the desolation of this rural mansion, I hardly
cared to cast a glance upon it. What I noticed on
arriving was a certain air of jollity and gladness,
breathing health, betokening contentment, which
all the faces of the village people wore. Amid the
jubilations of relatives, guests, serving-folk and lads
about the farm, not omitting a pack of barking dogs,
I descended from the calèche with my brother.
A whole crowd of people, whom I did not know and
could not number, fell upon my neck to bid me
welcome. Something of a military carriage, which I
had picked up abroad, but which had no relation to

---

[1] Opere, vol. vii. p. 393.   This is the stanza—

> Gli antichi di provincia tuoi fedeli
> Son quasi tutti fuggiti alle ville,
> In castellacci discoperti a' cieli,
> Con figli e figlie e nipoti e pupille,
> Ripieni di pensieri acri e crudeli,
> Allor che suonan mezzodì le squille.
> Educazion non han, mangiar, nè bere ;
> Pensa se daran nerbo alle tue schiere !

This is said to the burlesque Carlo Magno of the poem.   The passage
in the text confirms the theory that Gozzi intended his Carlo Magno
to represent the decrepit majesty of Venice.

my real self, made our farm-folk stare upon me like
a comet.

Then I raised my eyes, and saw my poor father at
a window in the upper storey, with trembling limbs,
dragging himself forward on his stick to catch a
glimpse of me. All the blood turned suddenly and
galloped through my veins. I rushed up the stairs,
burst into the room where he was standing, seized
one of his hands, and kissed it in a transport of filial
affection. He fell upon my shoulder, more paralytic
than he had been when I last embraced him, and, in
his inability to speak, broke into a piteous fit of
weeping. The effort I made to restrain my own tears,
lest they should add to his unhappiness, made me
feel as though my lungs would burst. Leaning on
my arm, he slowly tottered after me, and little by
little we reached another room which he frequented.
October was nearly over, and the cold in that Friulian
climate was very sensible. A good fire burned on
the hearth, near which stood the arm-chair of my
father, who for seven years had dragged his life out
in this wretched state. All the resources of medical
science had been tried in vain. Physicians sometimes agreed and sometimes differed about his treatment. But their concord and their discord were
equally impotent to effect a cure; and he had not
yet reached the age of fifty-five.

I found my mother in the same apartment. She
uttered sentiments which were not inappropriate to

her maternal character, but in a frigid tone and with an air of stately self-control. I always loved and respected her, not merely from a sense of duty, but with a true filial instinct. She, on her side, used frequently to protest when there was no need for protestation, that she loved all her nine children with exactly the same amount of affection. She often repeated the following words with gravity, raising her eyebrows as she spoke: "Cut off one of my fingers and I suffer pain; cut off a second and I suffer;" and so on through nine fingers, amputated by the same figure of speech, with equal agony in each case. Notwithstanding this, I believe that the loss of eight fingers would not have given her the same pain as that of the first-born finger, in other words, of my brother Gasparo. He is still alive, a man of honour, and a sage if ever sage existed; and I feel sure that he would admit the truth of this statement, if called on to confirm it.

In my long and anxious study of human nature, I have seen so many mothers with the weakness of my own, that I never dreamed of blaming her. It seemed right to me that my brother's mental gifts and noble qualities should earn for him more of her love than she bestowed on all her other eight children. Mothers, however, who are so devoted to a son generally spoil him, notably by extolling what is good in his character, but also by defending his natural frailties. Acting thus, my mother favoured

Gasparo's marriage, which subjected her beloved son
to a real martyrdom. Her lifelong devotion to him,
and the prejudice displayed in his favour by her will,
only served to increase the unhappiness of a man
whom I always loved, loved still, and shall love as
friend and brother till the end of my days on earth.
This digression was rendered necessary by what will
follow in my Memoirs.

The room was soon full of relatives and intimate
friends, all curious about me. My father strove to
ply me with questions, but his tongue refused its
office, and he relapsed into weeping. Sad at heart
as I was for him, I contrived to relate the most
amusing anecdotes I could remember concerning my
life in Dalmatia and my travels. In this way I kept
him laughing, together with the whole company,
through the rest of that day.

The perfect country air; a table abundantly served
with rural dainties, though somewhat deficient in
elegance; the joviality, wit, and pleasant sallies which
never failed in our domestic circle,—all this prevented me from attending to the defects of our establishment. Next day I began to discover that the real
cause of trouble was not in the building, but in the
minds of its inhabitants. I could not have explained
why, but I seemed to be a person of importance in
the eyes of everybody. My three sisters confided to
me in secret that my brother Gasparo's wife, in close
alliance with my mother, who doted on her as the

consort of her favoured first-born, ruled all the affairs of the family, which were rapidly going from bad to worse. My father's authority as head of the house had ceased to be more than a mere instrument for carrying out what my sister-in-law advised and my mother sanctioned. Unless I managed to stem the tide of extravagance, we should all be plunged into an abyss of ruin. One of my sisters, Girolama, a girl devoted to reading, writing, and translating from the French—for she too was bitten with our family cacoethes—spoke like a sibyl, gravely and eloquently, on these painful topics. At the same time, my brother's wife contrived secret interviews, in which she explained to me that her husband was indolent, torpid, drowned in fruitless studies, devoted to the company of a certain clever person, and wholly averse from thoughts or cares about domestic matters. She had done everything in her power—God knew she had. She would go on doing her best—God should see she would. Then she described her plans and projects, which, to tell the truth, were pure poetical stupidities. She vowed that she was not in any sense the mistress of the establishment, the administrator of the estate, or the disposer of its revenues; she merely gave advice, made suggestions, and exerted herself for the common benefit and to supply the needs of the family in general. She exhorted me to speak seriously to her husband; I was to make him abandon his unprofitable studies, make him, above all things, give up those visits of taste and soul, which did so much harm ; in fine, I was to force him to sustain his wife in her stupendous labours, and to concentrate his thoughts upon his children, who were five in number.

When I came to analyse the curious compound of truths, lies, and fancies which issued from the fevered brains of this poor lady—always hard at work, always embarrassed in a labyrinth of business—I seemed to perceive that what moved her most was the fear of being made herself responsible for our financial failure. It was also clear that her original ambition of acting the part of prime minister in a realm which only existed in her own imagination, kept her always on the stretch; while a certain little devil of feminine jealousy against her husband added to her disquietude. He, good fellow, had forgotten the long collection of Petrarchan poems written by him for her honour in the past, and which she had repaid with the gift of five children. Not the least little sonnet issued from his pen to celebrate her now. His lyrics were addressed to another idol of the moment.

Meanwhile she set great store upon her personal importance. Every member of our family, who wanted a ducat, a pair of shoes, or something of the sort, came to her with humble supplications, imploring her good offices at head-quarters—and Heaven knew where head-quarters were. This honour and glory made up to her for all her heroic labours in

the little realm, which she administered with real
authority, though her right to do so was contested,
and her schemes were pindarically unpractical.

My younger brother, Almorò,[1] was also at our villa,
on a holiday from school—the non-existent school
he never went to. His education seemed to have
been of the slightest, and his wardrobe left even more
to be desired. A boy of good heart and parts, however; gay-spirited and innocent; he was not old
enough and had not time to reflect upon our troubles;
setting snares for little birds was all his pastime, and
when he talked to me, I heard only of the number
and the kinds of birds he caught, and the important
adventures he had met with in his fowling expeditions.

My father did not converse with me, because he
could not; my mother, because she would not. Gasparo's five children with their quarrels and their
games broke in upon the only solace which I had,
that of reading and writing.

To all the complaints I heard, to all the exhorta-
tions which were daily heaped upon me, I gave one
only answer: we will see and think it over.

One thing emerged with distinctness from this
hurlyburly of our family. If I attempted any salutary innovation in the wasp's nest of my relatives, I
should find no difficulty in gaining supporters to

---

[1] Almorò is the Venetian form of the name Ermolao.

assist me in my opposition to the government; but the government was in the hands of women, under the shadow of my father's authority; I should therefore be misrepresented to him, prejudiced as he was by education, susceptible and hot-blooded by temperament, enfeebled by chronic illness; and he was still the master, still my father, loved and respected by me. I doubted whether anything which I could do would not prove ineffectual or worse. I was afraid of becoming the object of everybody's hatred; for I observed that personal considerations, rather than wise reflection and moderate ambitions, were the motive principles of all the folk I had to deal with. Finally I dreaded giving such a shock to my father's declining frame as would cut short the few days of life which still remained to him. The sequel will show that these anticipations were not ill-founded.

In these circumstances I determined to exercise the strictest self-control, and to bear with everything during my father's lifetime. Literature and my favourite studies of the world meanwhile would suffice to entertain me. Knowing that my uncle Almorò Cesare Tiepolo was in the country on an estate of his not far from where we lived, I went to pay him my respects. He inquired how I had been treated in Dalmatia by his Excellency Quirini. I answered that he had treated me very well indeed, but that he could not give me any permanent com-

mission, because our troops had been drafted into
Italy.   He then proposed to recommend me to his
Excellency the Provveditore Generale at Verona.   I
replied that I was grateful for his interest on my
behalf, but that Mars had not inspired me with a
vocation for military service.   I foresaw that I should
have to employ all my energies upon the affairs of
my family, which were calling loudly for my assistance.   Shaking his head and pursing up his lips, he
answered that what I said was only too true.

XVII.

*Return from Friuli to Venice with my family.—I pursue my
    chosen path in life, and open new veins of experience.—
    Yet further painful discoveries as to our circumstances.—
    The beginnings of domestic discord.*

The month of November was wearing away when
our family began to think of Venice.   It amused me
to watch the preparations for our journey and our
luggage, which in no wise resembled that of the
General's suite I had been used to.   My father, an
invalid ; my mother, serious and diplomatical ; my
sister-in-law, the woman of business ; my brother
Gasparo, wool-gathering ; our little sisters, intent
upon the custody of their old-fashioned bonnets ;
Almorò, plunged in grief at leaving his birds and

cages, which he consigned by something like a last will and testament to the bailiff; I, giving myself military airs, quite out of season; some serving-maids and men in worn-out livery; a few cats and dogs; these composed our travelling party, which might have been compared to a troupe of comedians upon the march.

I shall perhaps be told that there was no reason to enumerate these humiliating circumstances. But I have never had to blush for unworthy actions in my family; and it seems to me a poor philosophy that feels ashamed where no shame is. Such as it was, our caravan arrived in Venice, joking and laughing all the way, There we installed ourselves with as much disorder and as little comfort as was proper to a fine large mansion with nothing to fill its empty spaces.

For my own use I chose out a little room at the top of the house, where I set up a rickety table, provided myself with a huge inkstand and plenty of pens and paper, and spent at least six hours a day in reading and scribbling poetic nonsense. This was my best amusement; but I ought to add that I devoted some of my time to the cafés, studying types of character and listening to conversation; nor did I neglect our theatres, where I saw the various tragedies and comedies which appeared. My brother Gasparo had already given several serious pieces to the stage. They pleased the public then; and though they may be out of fashion now, they would not fail to please me still. I know the instability of taste too well to change my old opinions.

I had mixed with all sorts of men and learned to know their characters—generals, admirals, noblemen, great lords, officers, soldiers, the people of Illyrian cities, the Morlacchi of the villages, Mainotti, Pastrovicchi, convicts, galley-slaves. It was time, I thought, to become acquainted with my own Venetians. I began by cultivating a set of men who go in Venice by the name of Cortigiani.[1] My companions of this kind were chiefly shopkeepers and handicraftsmen, with a priest or two among the number; clever fellows, respectable, and versed in all the ways of our Venetian world. Their courage and readiness to take part in quarrels won them the respect of the common people, and they carried the art of getting the maximum of pleasure at a minimum of outlay to perfection. On certain holidays I joined their boating-parties, and went to shoot birds on the marshes with them. Or else we lunched together on the Giudecca, at Campalto, Malcontenta, Murano, Burano, and other neighbouring islands. My share

---

[1] Gozzi's description of the Venetian *Cortesan* may serve as illustration to a popular play of Goldoni's, *Momolo Cortesan*. This was the first comedy of character Goldoni composed. Its title-rôle was written for a celebrated Pantalone, Golinetti (see Goldoni's *Memoirs*, part i. ch. 40). When he printed it, he translated the title into *L'Uomo di Mondo*, finding no exact equivalent for the Venetian phrase *Cortesan.* Goldoni's account of the character tallies with Gozzi's.

of the expense on these occasions was not much
above sixpence, and I gained the hearty good-will
of my companions by contributing some slices of
excellent Friulian ham to our common table. The
characters and manners of these men delighted me ;
I took pleasure in listening to the stories of their
quarrels, reconciliations, love-adventures, misfortunes,
accidents of all kinds, told in racy Venetian dialect,
with the liveliness which is natural to our folk.
What is more, I learned much from them.   Alas !
the race of Cortigiani has degenerated, like everything else in this corrupt age.   When I chance to
meet a survivor of the honest jolly crew, he strikes
his forehead, and confesses that the good days of his
youth are irrecoverable, and that the Cortigiano is an
extinct species.

Meanwhile I took good care to interfere with
nobody and nothing in the household.   This I did
for my poor father's sake.   But I kept my eyes open
to observe the intrigues, schemes, and movements of
the government.   Some Jews, some brokers, and a
crowd of women were always coming and going on
secret conferences with my sister-in-law.   These
attracted my attention, and formed the subject of my
earnest cogitations.   It grieved me to see my brother
Gasparo immersed in his philosophy and poetry,
never for one moment giving the least thought to
domestic economy.   It grieved me ; but I grieved
in silence.   There was one circumstance, however,

which fairly put me out of patience.   We had three
sisters in the house ; and a swarm of drones, hulking
young fellows of the freest manners, kept buzzing
round them.   When I came home and found these
visitors at their accustomed chatter, I used to scowl
at them, lift my hat and put it on again, turn my
back, and climb the stairs to my own den, with
the fixed intention of making the gentlemen perceive how little their company attracted me.   This
manœuvre had its effect.   My sister-in-law took it
upon her to read me a matronly lecture on the impropriety of insulting friends of the family by my
rough ways.   I replied that I knew very well what
friendship was, but that I could distinguish the false
from the true ; I was not conscious of having been
rude to anybody ; my father was the master, and if
he did not mind some things which seemed to my
inexperience imprudent and irregular, a mere lad's
opinions were not worthy of consideration.   This
hint of my displeasure made all the women of the
house regard me like a serpent.   Even my three
sisters, who loved me sincerely, and were excellent
creatures, imbued with the soundest religious principles, could not help harbouring a trifle of suspicion
in their feminine brains.   For the rest, I said what I
thought when I was consulted upon affairs of no importance.   My advice in such matters pleased nobody.
I ran on little errands if these were intrusted to me ;
and above all, I devoted some hours of every evening

to my father, who always received me with tenderness and tears.

From conversation with my sisters I learned that the five thousand ducats raised by sale of lands in Friuli, ostensibly to make up portions for my married sisters, had either not been paid by the purchasers or had only reached the hands of the husbands in part. The same had happened with the drapery, linen, and jewels, for which a large debt had been contracted with a company of merchants. These and similar confidences made it clear to my mind that the marriages of my two sisters had not been arranged for their settlement in life so much as with the view of raising money under colourable pretexts, and of alienating entailed property with some show of legality. In fact, I scented disastrous dealings of the sort which are known at Venice by the name of *stocchi*.[1] As natural consequences of this crooked

---

[1] In these and several passages which follow, Gozzi ascribes the pecuniary embarrassments of his family to the maladministration of his mother, aided by his sister-in-law. It is only fair to say, that Gasparo Gozzi's correspondence confirms his veracity. That favourite and favoured eldest son complains bitterly that, even to the last days of her life, his mother insisted on managing the property, and that she made underhand contracts to the prejudice of himself and his children. It was, in fact, a misfortune for the Gozzi that their father, Jacopo Antonio, married into a patrician family of higher rank and pretensions than his own. Angela Tiepolo, knowing herself to be one of the last representatives of a very noble house, with considerable expectations from her childless brother, drove her easy-going husband into ruinous expenditure, and domineered over her kindred by right of a marriage which savoured of a mésalliance. See the article upon her in Litta's *Famiglie Celebri*, sub tit. "Tiepolo."

policy, urgent needs for ready money and embarrassments of all sorts had ensued, which led to fresh
expedients and ever-growing financial distress.

Without attributing malice to any one, I merely
blamed the bad luck of our family, owing to which
my grandfather's fine estate had passed into the
hands of women under two administrations, and had
been wasted by a course of insane irregularities. I
took care to send an accurate report of our domestic
circumstances to my brother Francesco at Corfu.
And now I must embark upon the sea of my worst
troubles.

XVIII.

I become, without fault of my own, quite unjustly, the object
of hatred to all members of my household.—Resolve to
return to Dalmatia.—My father's death.

It had not escaped my notice that my mother
and sister-in-law were in the habit of going abroad
together in the mornings. During the five winter
months they wore masks, and their proceedings had
all the appearance of some secret business.[1] Now
Carnival was over. We had reached the month of
March 1745, a date which will be always painful

---

[1] The *bautta* and the mask were permitted at Venice from the first
Sunday in October until Ash Wednesday.

to my recollection. Every morning the two ladies left the house together, no longer masked, but wearing the *zendado*.[1] I asked my sisters if they knew the object of these daily expeditions. They answered to the following effect: all they knew for certain was that my father's invalid condition made a residence in Venice irksome to him; now that the spring was advancing, he wished to go into Friuli with my mother, leaving our sister-in-law at the head of affairs in Venice; meanwhile the treasury was empty, the barns and cellars of our country-house had nothing left in them. I shrugged my shoulders, and kept silence.

A few days afterwards, while I was attempting to drive away care by study in my little upper chamber, my three sisters entered. They were weeping, and my first fear was lest my father should have died. Reassuring me upon this point, they passionately besought me to interpose between the family and shameful ruin. I alone was capable of doing this. The secret expeditions of my mother and sister-in-law had resulted in a contract with a certain Signor Francesco Zini, cloth merchant. He undertook to pay down six hundred ducats in exchange for our ancestral mansion, agreeing, moreover, to hand over

---

[1] This was a very long scarf of black silk, which, draped above the head, and falling over the shoulders, was tied in a knot, and allowed to hang on both sides of the wearer's skirts. The mask or *bautta* was only permitted during the prolonged Venetian Carnival.

a little dwelling of his own in the distant quarter of San Jacopo dall' Orio. They added that my father was ready to give his assent to this bargain, and my brothers Gasparo and Almorò would offer no opposition. I felt deeply moved by the distress of these poor girls as well as by my own keen sense of humiliation; and when they concluded by enjoining the strictest secrecy upon myself in the transaction, a gulf of dissensions, disagreeableness, and misery of all kinds seemed to yawn before my feet. Our pressing want of money, the contract verbally completed by my mother and sister-in-law, my father's consent, the adhesion of my brothers to the scheme, the obligation to secrecy laid upon me by my sisters, my own bad reputation in the household as a disturber of domestic quiet, my lack of friends and supporters in Venice, all filled me with terror. Yet I resolved to try what I could do to gratify my father's desire for the country, and to put a stop to this humiliating contract. With that object in view I also undertook a secret mission and went to visit Signor Francesco Zini.

I laid myself open to him in terms of flattering politeness, appealing to his excellent disposition, and pointing out that he was about to enter on a business which would expose him to risk and us to notable humiliation. I told him that my father had been an invalid for many years, that our ancestral mansion was subject to a strict entail, that on my

father's death he would lose his money and the
house, that all the sons of the family were not prepared to sanction the contract, that one of them was
in the Levant, that I had not the least intention
of assenting, and that the utmost I could do would
be to abandon the house at my father's express command. Then I passed to the pathetic. I described a
numerous family departing with their scanty bundles
from the loved paternal nest, bowed down with grief
and shame before the eyes of all their neighbours,
who would be exclaiming: "See those gentlefolk upon
the move, because their home has been sold over their
heads!" I proved to him that if he gained a fine
house to live in, he would also gain an odious and
ugly reputation. Finally, I besought him, as a man
of worth, to seize some plausible pretext for breaking
a bargain which, happily for his advantage and our
own, had not been ratified.

Over the fat, red, small-pox-pitted features of
Signor Zini spread amazement and perplexity. He
did not understand my rigmarole, he said; he was
an honest man, pouring out his blood, not water,
to obtain the house; my mother and sister-in-law,
together with the broker of this honourable bargain,
had assured him that my father wished to conclude
it, and that all his sons were prepared to emancipate
themselves from the paternal authority, in order to be
able to sign the contract, thus giving it validity, and
securing the rightful interest of the innocent pur-

chaser. The affair had been settled, the necessary deeds were waiting on the bureau of Marchese Suarez, his advocate. Most assuredly, unless my father's male heirs procured their emancipation, in order to give validity to the contract in perpetuity, he would not unbutton his pockets to disburse a penny; he was not a fool, to be imposed upon with fibs and fables.

I commended the fat gentleman's perspicacity and caution; repeated that I had no intention of procuring my emancipation, and that nothing on earth would force me to consent; once more I begged him to find some excuse for breaking off the bargain; and wound up by imploring him to keep silence upon my interference in the matter. I made it clear that only a brute, devoid of Christian charity, would reject a son's entreaties, and render him odious to mother and father without any advantage to himself. He promised to respect my secrecy, wagging his huge scarlet jowl and lifting his night-cap, with so many protestations of being touched to the heart, that I ought to have been put upon my guard. I did not yet know human nature, and retired as happy as if I had taken Gibraltar by assault, feeling confident that my prudence and discretion had averted a lamentable catastrophe.

Nothing was said by me about the course which I had followed, even to my three sisters. I reflected that they were women, and awaited a quiet termination of the affair, trusting to Signor Zini's humanity.

Meanwhile I ruminated how to procure my father's removal to the country, and how to help the family without waiting for the harvest, which would be finished in three months. I computed the value of my clothes, my watch, my snuff-box; prepared as I was then, to sell everything I possessed. But these calculations only reduced me to despair. My one real friend was Signor Massimo, then at Padua. I remembered that I already owed him two hundred ducats, and that he was living on an allowance from his father. Yet I knew that both father and son, as well as a brother of my comrade, were no less generous toward persons on whose character for loyalty and friendship they relied, than they were suspicious of intriguers and impostors. I was also aware that they were in a position to render me substantial services. How often, during the tempestuous vicissitudes of my existence, have I not had the opportunity to verify this fact!

While thus engaged in studying ways and means, Signor Zini broke rudely in upon my meditations. Possessed with the desire to obtain our dwelling for his own, he divulged the secret of my visit, and exposed what I had said to him in terms of his own choosing. My belief is that his communication amounted to this :—unless the hot-headed impetuous young fellow, who had come to treat with him, were brought to reason, and compelled to sign the contract, he refused to disburse two shillings.

I was in my upper chamber, studying as usual, and talking with my brother Almorò about his wretched schooling, when my mother appeared one day. Something of philosophical severity in her toilette, something imposing in her manner, which concealed, however, an internal irritation, proclaimed the gravity of her mission. She addressed herself pointedly to me, with the features of a judge rather than a mother, and began a long narration of the straits to which we were reduced. She said that, God be blessed, she had been inspired and assisted to discover six hundred ducats in the hands of a benevolent merchant, which would be placed immediately at her disposal upon such and such conditions. The notary was ready to engross the necessary deeds; and she begged me to declare what I thought about this special providence.

At the bottom of her heart I read Signor Zini's act of treason, and saw that I was lost. However, I answered respectfully that a contract of this kind struck me as anything but providential; still my father had full power to do what he thought fit, without rendering an account of his actions to his sons. She flamed up, and cried with a threatening air that my consent was also needed; she could not believe that I should be so rash and headstrong as to prevent a plan which would relieve my father and the family in our present painful circumstances. I could have uttered several truths without a wish to wound;

but certain truths, once spoken, wound incurably. Therefore, I contented myself with observing that I was ready to shed my blood for my father, but that I could not assent to a contract so humiliating and ruinous, the last of a whole series dictated by suicidal policy. People who understood economy were in the habit of calculating and making provision for the future, not of selling or mortgaging their property to meet embarrassments created by their own extravagance. The latter course was rapidly bringing our whole family to the workhouse. Under a disastrous financial system our income had been reduced to three thousand ducats; yet I could not comprehend how we were in such straits as she had described. When people were unable to maintain a decent state in the capital, they could live at ease in the country at one-third of the same cost. Houses ought to be let, and not sold. Still my father had the power to make any contract he thought right; only I did not believe him capable of forcing me to give consent against my will and judgment.

The gestures of submission, respect, and supplication with which I accompanied this speech had no power to mollify the pungency of its significance. My mother rose, with her arms akimbo, and inquired who it was I meant to blame for our misfortunes. Instead of telling the bitter and irrefutable truth, I said that I only blamed fate and the misfortunes themselves. "I reckon," she replied with a smile of

fury, " that you will give in your adhesion." " Indeed
I shall not," was my answer ; and the profound bow
with which I spoke these words had the appearance
of impertinent irony, although God knows I did not
mean it. This was enough to fan the smothered
flames into a Vesuvius in eruption. My mother bent
her stormy brows upon me—upon the sixth finger of
her maternal hands—and broke into the following
declamation. " From the moment of my return she
had prophesied, like Cassandra, that I should turn
the household upside. down. She did not know me
for one of her own children. The intimacy of a
certain friend to whom I had attached myself was
ruining the family, as it had ruined me. (Poor innocent generous Signor Massimo !) If I had behaved
well during my three years' service, his Excellency
Quirini would certainly have rewarded me with some
good military situation. As it was, my excursion
into Dalmatia had been a source of burdensome expense. I had led a vicious life there . . . she knew
. . . she did not mean to speak . . . but . . . enough
. . . and my debt of two hundred ducats to Massimo
was merely a sum lost by me at basset."

Now this debt had not yet been paid, and had
therefore been of no inconvenience to my family.
Such extravagant accusations took me by surprise ;
and the reader will now perceive the reason of the accounts which I rendered in a former passage of these
Memoirs. I should perhaps have flown into a fury

alien to my real nature, if these reproofs had been
based on truth. The wounding allusion to Signor
Massimo nearly roused me, but I preserved my self-
control. It was clear that my mother had been
deeply prejudiced and cruelly instigated against
me. The consciousness of my innocence and a
sense of duty made me stand before her rigid and
mute as a statue. With an impulse of affection,
maternal as it seemed, my mother took my brother
Almorò by the arm, and gazing at me with contempt,
which strove to be compassionate, she addressed
these words to him : " Come away, my dear boy;
let us leave that madman to the error of his ways ! "
Then she turned her back and led him from the
room, as though she were saving an innocent creature from some fearful danger.

Convinced by this tragi-comedy that I was the
victim of a family cabal, I saw no other course open
but to resume my commission as a cadet of cavalry.
I left my room, went downstairs, and found all the
family (except my father) assembled in commotion,
listening to the commiserations of their usual friends
enraged against me. It had been proclaimed aloud
that I had called them all thieves, retorted against
my mother with scandalous and impious audacity, and
betrayed my determination to make myself the tyrant
of the household. Even my three sisters, who had
urged me into opposition, showed themselves sulkily
scornful ; and though I might have exposed them

before the whole company, I did not deign to do so.
Confirmed in my resolve to leave Venice for Dalmatia,
I buckled on my sword, wasted no words about my
intention, and repaired to the Riva dei Schiavoni, to
see if I could find a ship for Zara. There I discovered that a *trabacolo* would set sail in four or
five days. The captain was a certain Bernetich.
I took down his name, and, wrapped up in my own
dark thoughts, spent all that day in exile, wandering
far from home.

On my return, I noticed that, though everybody
wore a crabbed face against me, something had happened to their satisfaction. Signor Zini, it appeared,
was willing to execute the contract without requiring my consent. I did not know that my brother
Francesco had left a power of attorney to act for him
in Gasparo's hands. With voices of triumph they
all exclaimed together that the great sacrifice was to
be solemnly and legally performed next day. I did
not care to inquire how things had been brought to
this conclusion; but putting on as cheerful a face as
possible, I went to keep my poor father company as
usual for a few hours in the evening.

It will be as well at this point to describe the
topography of our house. It was originally built for
two separate residences, with double entrances upon
the street and water-side, two staircases and two
cisterns. At the time when it was planned, the
Gozzis formed two families, which were afterwards

reduced to one. We occupied the lower floor and some apartments in the highest storey. The second floor was let for 150 ducats a year to an honest iron-monger called Uccelli ; but this portion of the mansion had also been sold upon my father's life, by one of those contracts which were only too frequent in our family, for the sum of 1200 ducats to his Excellency the Procuratore Sagredo.

I did all in my power to avoid the least allusion to the painful scenes of the preceding day ; but my dear father kept gazing earnestly at me, and shedding tears from time to time. In vain I tried to inspire him with happier thoughts. Would that I could banish all recollection of that night, which was one of the most sombre, the most painful, in the whole course of my existence. Paralysed and dumb for seven long years, he yet retained his mental faculties in their full vigour. Summoning all his force, by signs and stammerings and tears, he made it only too clear how much he suffered from the miserable straits to which the family had been reduced. He also con-tinued to express his sympathy with me for my dis-like to sign the projected contract. To my surprise and grief, he intimated that I had only a brief time to wait ; his swift approaching death would restore to us the upper dwelling, which had been sold upon his life, and which was much better than the one we occu-pied. This inarticulate but eloquent discourse ended in a flood of tears. Deeply moved to the bottom of

my heart, I strove to tranquillise his mind, and direct
his thoughts from such afflicting topics.   I perceived
that no pains had been spared to make me odious in
my father's eyes, and that this had been done without the least regard for his infirmity.   Yet I did not
attempt to justify my conduct, and said nothing
about my firm resolve to leave home.   His departure
for Friuli had been fixed on the third day after this
fatal evening, and I mentally decided to set out for
Dalmatia two days later on.   My assumed cheerful-
ness, and the merry turn I gave to all those dismal
subjects of reflection, seemed to tranquillise him.
Then he tried to lift himself from his arm-chair, as
though to get to bed.   I helped to raise him, but he
tottered more than usual, and sank with his knees
toward the ground.   I took him in my arms to keep
him from falling.   Agonising moment !   It was clear
that a last stroke of apoplexy was carrying away my
father from my arms.   In a loud voice and with perfect articulation he pronounced the words : " I am
dying ! "   They fell like lead upon my heart, with
such cruel force that I nearly dropped.   My mother,
who was present, fled from the room.   I called aloud
for aid.   Servants hurried in ; one of these I dis-
patched for medical assistance, while the others helped
me to place my poor dear father, now quite incapable
of any movement, on his bed.   A physician, Doctor
Bonariva by name, had him bled at once.   But
nothing could be done to save his life.   Assisted

by Don Pietro Pighetti, now Canon of S. Marco, in the last religious duties of our creed, he displayed all the signs of Christian resignation and intelligence; and after eight hours of oppression, toilsome suffering, and the pangs of death, my unhappy parent closed his eyes upon the vast obscurity in which his family was plunged.

XIX.

My attempts at pacification defeated.—Useless philosophical reflections.—A terrible domestic storm begins to brew.

No sooner had my father breathed his last than my lady sister-in-law, all activity and bustle, issued from the room of mourning, and took upon her to console his sorrowing children with the convincing statement that he was the most lovely corpse which eyes of men had ever seen.   This wholly unexpected statement, which had nothing of humanity, morality, or philosophy in it, and which she kept repeating and affirming upon oath for our relief, filled me then, and fills me now, with such fury, that I should be angry to think that any of my readers could laugh at it.

One disastrous thought kept breaking in upon our sorrow at this tragic moment.   Am I to record it? We had neither the wherewithal to provide a decent interment for my father, nor the credit to obtain it. The habitués of. the. house. gave words in abundance, but no pecuniary aid.. I had. only one friend, Massimo,. my creditor, the object of my relatives' calumnies. Grief inspired me with the thought of writing to lay our difficulties before his generous mind. The special messenger by whom I sent this letter returned with a sum of money more than sufficient to defray the expenses of a becoming funeral. On receiving it, I took my brother Gasparo apart, placed the money in his hands, and told him who had given it. Then I begged him not to misinterpret what I was about to say. He was my elder, and I willingly acknowledged him to be the head of our family. He could not be blind to the deplorable condition into which we had declined. Duty required that: he should. take the reins with manly resolution, and should withdraw the. management of our affairs from the hands of those who had brought us to utter shipwreck. My brother accepted the money and my speech as well as might have been expected from a man of his excellent disposition and superior intelligence. He admitted that he saw the necessity of a thorough economical reform, carried through with virile firmness. Some increase of income, owing to the expiration of contracts made upon my father's life, would facilitate the undertaking. He was willing to relinquish literary occupations, which were neither appreciated nor remunerated in Italy, for the

sake of being able to devote his energy and time to
the administration of our common property.

I did not flatter myself that anything so much to
be desired would come to pass. I knew how impossible it is for people to change their character and
nature. I knew his wife's meddlesome, restless, imperious thirst for ruling—his own peaceable temperament, averse from opposition, addicted to the habits
of a student. Yet I saw the necessity of taking the
step I did, if only to correct the bad impression of
myself, which had grown up under malevolent influences in the family.

I had no heart to follow my father to the grave,
but shut myself up in my little chamber, where I
gave way through three days and three nights to
grief, not unmingled with remorse for having inno-
cently helped to hasten his death. Nothing less
than this tragedy was needed to cancel Signor Francesco Zini's contract.

I feel some repugnance at sitting down to write
what happened at this epoch in my family. I wish
that I could tell the tale without appearing to censure
any of my relatives and without seeming to draw
a vain-glorious picture of myself. The truth at any
cost has to be reported; but I protest with emphasis,
and this is also true, that I always experienced real
pain when I beheld the disastrous consequences
which the faults of others brought upon themselves,
and that I neither took pleasure in revenge, nor

cherished sentiments of ambition in doing good to my family—if indeed I did do good. The reader will be able to judge of that from the sequel of these Memoirs.

When a group of closely related persons in one household fall to quarrelling, all the causes which perpetuate faults of character and conduct begin to operate. Each member of the company is perfectly acquainted with the weak side of his neighbour, and knows exactly how to sting him to the quick. Exacerbated tempers and prejudiced minds judge everything awry, while partisans and flatterers add fuel to the fire. Zeal is misconstrued into craft and tyranny; no protestations and no arguments suffice to remove such false impressions. The torment of the hell in which one has to live blinds reason and enslaves the freedom of volition; years of unhappiness pass by before the weapons of vindictive rage are blunted by constant acts of toleration and dis-interested deeds of kindness, and the innocent are seen in their true light. To blame the doings of a family divided against itself is much the same as blaming the actions of somnambulists.

We had never used the outward demonstrations of affection, kisses and caresses, in our domestic circle. Yet we were bound together by real senti-ments of friendliness and love on all sides. Un-luckily the seeds of discord had already begun to germinate in our brains. Besides my mother, three brothers and three sisters, my sister-in-law was there, with her hot, headstrong, vindictive temperament, her aptitude for colouring everything to suit her own purpose, and her established dominion over the minds of my relations. During my father's long illness there had been no real head in the household. Everybody passed for master. No one learned the virtues of submission and filial obedience. Each member of the family had his own engagements, his own separate obligations, together with the passions proper to himself as a human being. There was no defect of intelligence or mental energy. But lacking a central authority which might have brought man's egotistic passions into wholesome subjection, self-love and caprice turned the individuals of the group into so many political agents, bent on achieving their own ends, without regard for the common interest. I must not omit the chronic malady under which we suffered—that predilection for poetry, which tinged all we thought and planned with romanticism. During a period of many years no records had been kept either of the income derived from our estate, or of the sales which had been made. With perfect justice each in turn denied that he had directed our affairs. In such circumstances the death of the father leaves a family exposed to direst intestine warfare ; and I should be both indiscreet and inhuman if I were to lay the whole blame of what ensued upon any of the six relatives whom I have mentioned.

A young man like myself, of little more than twenty years, prone to thinking rather than to speaking, with a military air acquired abroad, when he found himself in the middle of so many working brains, and attempted to effect a total revolution, could not but raise irascibilities of all sorts and expose himself to odious suspicions. The portrait which I mean to paint of my own physical and other qualities will perhaps reveal defects which rendered such suspicions, unjust as they are, at any rate excusable.

My mother was not so overwhelmed by the recent loss of her husband as to be unable to think of business. She demanded the repayment of her dowry, small as it was, like one who feels the coming shipwreck and seeks a skiff for his salvation. My sister-in-law, bent as usual on displaying her talent for affairs, called the brokers, Jews, and female go-betweens around her. My sisters were always conferring in secret among themselves, or with my sister-in-law, who kept promising them husbands and marriage-portions. My brother Gasparo, at the very moment when he solemnly promised to assume the reins of government, handed over the money I had got from Padua to his wife, to do as she thought best with, reserving only a few coins for his own purse. Then he relapsed into his ordinary ways of life, his literary studies, his society of wit and genius, and gave no signs of any firm intention to make himself the master.

About twenty days had passed since my father died, when I was summoned to a serious conference with my elder brother, my mother, and my sister-in-law. We seated ourselves upon four straw-bottomed rickety chairs, and my sister-in-law, with an air betokening the gravity of the occasion, moved the following resolution. Signor Massimo ought to be repaid (this, mark well, was meant to gain me over). With a view to discharging the debts we owed him, and for other urgent necessities, it would be advisable to sell the upper dwelling in our town-house for the sum of 1200 ducats on the lives of us four brothers. A purchaser was ready (possibly Signor Francesco Zini). The capital left over would enable us to put our affairs in order, and to go forward swimmingly upon a new and proper method of administration. My mother blinked approval of this fine idea. My brother declared that it was the only course left open to us. They all looked at me and waited for my assent. I did not comprehend by what right my mother and sister-in-law took part in the conference, or how my brother was not ashamed of cutting the figure he did there, and of following his wife's suggestions with such docility. A hell of squabbling yawned before me, and I answered as coldly as I could that, so far as Signor Massimo was concerned, I could trust his generous indulgence towards a friend in difficulties, and that I did not approve of selling property upon our joint lives.

Such a step seemed to me mere progress on the former road to ruin. I should prefer to let our mansion, removing the whole family to the country, where we could live for one-third of the expense, until our debts were paid and the estate was nursed into comparative prosperity.

This scandalous ultimatum, which wounded the inclinations and the self-interest of every member in the family, won me the reputation of a very Dionysius of Syracuse. Day by day, in secret conclaves, the storm against me grew and gathered strength. My brother Francesco, however, had written from Corfu that he was coming home, and I judged it prudent to await his arrival. Until I gained his support, I stood alone, hated and dreaded like a fatal comet by my kindred. To distract my mind from painful thoughts, I summoned all my mental forces, and poured forth torrents of verse and prose and bizarre fancies upon paper. All through my long and troubled life I have drawn relief from two main sources. One is my own robust and democratic[1] bent of mind. The other is my aptitude for studying human nature and for writing. I may truly say that

---

[1] The Italian is *democraziano*. Perhaps Gozzi wrote *democriziano*, from Democritus, the sage who laughed at all things. In either case the adjective is wrongly formed. It ought to be either *democratico* or *democritico*. But *democrazia* may have led him to *democraziano*. He not infrequently employs this phrase, which always puzzles me, because nobody was really less democratic than Carlo Gozzi, and as yet, in 1780, he had no reason, under the pressure of the Revolution, to dissemble.

the exercise of fancy and the art of composition have been to my mental pains what opiates are to physical torments.

XX.

We plunge from bad to worse, deeper and deeper into the mire.

When my brother Francesco arrived from the Levant, I explained to him the state of our affairs, and my own wishes with regard to their administration. We both decided that he should repair to Friuli, and undertake the management of our estates there. Gasparo was to remain titular head of the family, while Francesco received rents, kept strict accounts, and provided for the common household. Meanwhile we begged our mother to charge herself with certain domestic duties, and our sister-in-law with certain others, hoping by this apportionment of officers to introduce harmony and order into the establishment. My sister-in-law displayed a really exemplary resignation, merely expressing her desire that, at this juncture, the account-book of expenditure which she had kept for some years past should be signed by her husband and his three brothers, in token of approval and in discharge to her of all pecuniary obligations.

I strove to make her understand that there was no need for such a receipt in form ; nobody would dream of calling her to account, and we were all very grateful for her services. She would not listen to my arguments, but insisted on our signing a certain notebook scrawled with cabalistic characters and numbers. Francesco observed that we might safely sign, for the sake of peace and quiet. Having entered our family without a farthing, accompanied by her father and mother, whom we had supported for many years and buried at our own charges, she was incapable of making claims on the estate. To this he added that he had consulted lawyers, and that he was quite convinced of the propriety of yielding to her wishes.

The sequel of this history will show that his reasoning, though plausible enough, was faulty, and that the policy he recommended led to further complications. Gasparo and Almorò had already signed; Francesco was prepared to follow suit; I did not care to take the odium of standing out alone. Accordingly, four signatures were generously appended to the mass of undecipherable hieroglyphics, without any attempt on our part to examine the accounts, which by this act we formally accepted.

Francesco set off for Friuli, after promising to maintain a detailed correspondence with Gasparo on the state and management of our farms there, and not to let himself be wheedled out of money or produce at the demand of every one and anybody. I did not then know what a worthless coadjutor I had summoned to support my policy. Without the least intention to defraud, he was governed by an insect's blind instinct for his own particular advantage. Under a compliant exterior, he concealed the subtlety of a diplomatist. His sole aim was to temporise and make concessions, with the view of bringing matters to a rupture and of obtaining his own share in the division of our common patrimony. This end he pursued in secrecy and silence, without reflecting on his duties to the family, or the position of our three unmarried sisters, and the discords which his pursuit of self-interest was bound to foment.

What followed after his departure for Friuli seemed conclusively to prove that a plan had been laid to drive him to the Levant and me to Dalmatia by involving us in embarrassments of all sorts. I accuse nobody; the heated passions which raged round us, and the injuries from which I suffered, deserve compassion more than blame.

Scarcely a day passed without letters being sent from Venice, begging my brother to dispatch provisions or money on various pretences. He complied with every application, whether it bore the name of Gasparo or of my mother or my sister-in-law. In the course of some seven months he had exhausted the whole harvest of that year, without asking for accounts or disputing the claims made upon the property he managed. In like manner the profits of certain houses in Venice, and of some farms at Bergamo and Vicenza, amounting to 800 ducats, had been dissipated. When letters still kept coming, demanding supplies and setting forth our urgent needs, my brother could only answer that there was nothing left to send. It was vain to inquire how the casks of wine and sacks of corn and bags of cash had vanished. Everybody had taken something to defray his own particular expenses. One said, " I got only so much ; " another, " I got so much ; I did this, and I did that." Gasparo knew less than anybody how matters had been managed, and had kept no account of the least article. The conclusion arrived at was that we must all die of hunger unless we sold some piece of the estate upon our joint lives.

> " Ora incomencian le dolenti note."
> " And now begins the Iliad of our woes."

XXI.

My attitude of patient calm is useless.—Volcanic eruptions, machinations, tragi-comic civil wars within our household.

At this point I resolved to step forth boldly and to take the whole weight of our affairs upon my shoulders, without troubling my head about being called a tyrant and disturber of domestic peace. I proclaimed aloud that the family must retire for some time into the country and economise. Nothing would induce me to consent to sales or mortgages. Then I began to contract debts on my own account, and to part with my personal trifles for the support of the household. I soon saw that it was impossible in this way to keep fifteen people, servants included, at Venice. Whenever I insisted upon the necessity of leaving for the country, all the women rose in revolt, and turned their backs without a word of answer. Our dining-table became the scene of daily quarrels, sullen faces, surly glances, biting speeches. I was deeply grieved to observe that a final division of the estate was drawing nearer and nearer. To avert this catastrophe seemed impracticable, and I reflected gloomily upon the condition to which my brother Gasparo would be reduced, with a wife and five children to support upon the fourth part of our encumbered property. Meanwhile I could not blame him except for his incurable indolence and absolute immersion in studies for which I shared his weakness.

Among the habitués of the house, none of them friends of mine, were certain lawyers. I noticed that these gentlemen had frequent conferences with the ladies of the family who ruled my brother. They were clearly plotting against me, and seeking means to set the machinery of the law in movement in order to hamper my free action. There was also a lady to whom the female members of my family paid visits

every evening. She was the Countess Elisabetta
Ghellini of Vicenza, widow of the patrician Barbarigo
Balbi, who died some years before this epoch, leaving
her the mother of an only son. It is exceedingly
rare to find a lady endowed with the excellent
qualities of heart and head which she possessed in
a supreme degree. About forty years of age, infirm
of health, and exposed to constant litigation through
various claims advanced against her moderate estates,
she bore the trials of life with steady courage and
constant trust in Heaven. Her chief interest was
the education of her son, a boy of eight or nine, for
whom she had provided masters, while she herself
instilled into his mind the principles of sound
religion and morality. Gifted with a lively intellect,
and fond of literature, she spent a large part of the
day in reading poetry, and opened her house to
a society composed mainly of persons who had
suffered in the battles of life. Her extreme sympathy for the afflicted led her to despoil herself with
admirable intrepidity, and to bestow on others what
was needed for her own support. This compassionate
and pious lady had for her adviser and advocate
in the numerous lawsuits to which she was condemned, the celebrated Conte Francesco Santorini.

It will appear from the sequel that this digression
upon the Countess Ghellini was needed to explain
an important passage in my life. Amid the din and
squabbles of our home, I used at times to catch frag-

ments of the panegyrics poured forth by my female relatives and Gasparo upon this lady, and heard them rehearse the sonnets which they intended to recite in her honour, or to offer for her recreation.   Such was the common custom at that period, observed by poets in the houses they frequented.   I speedily divined that a plot was in process of formation to secure the assistance of a very famous advocate against me. Trusting this intuition, I resolved to introduce myself, although I had received no invitation, to the lady whom my enemies so warmly praised.

She received me, and asked who I might be.   On giving my name, the noble and yet kindly distance of her manner changed suddenly to sternness.   A few phrases which I thought it right to utter about her interest in my relatives increased this expression of reserve ; and she began to speak as follows, with the happy choice of words which was peculiar to her : " Sir, I am a poor woman as regards the wealth of this life, but by the grace of God I am rich in the possession of good sentiments and a sound education. Your family is cultivated, and deserves to meet with kindly feeling and esteem from all the world.   It is a pity that such a family should be annoyed and brought to sorrow by a certain individual bound to it by ties of blood, duty, and respect.   A mother of very noble birth treated with contempt, sisters domineered over, persons of merit regarded with hatred—all kinds of extravagances and injustice—such things dishonour the individual of whom I speak." This preamble made me feel inclined to bow myself out of the room in silence, since I am by nature far from prone to justify my innocence; but politeness and a fear that a certain famous advocate, if prejudiced against me, might upset my plans, kept me where I was. I suffered, however, keenly from the barbarous picture which had been presented to me, and began to plead in self-defence. She interrupted me by saying that she did not believe me to be entirely bad-hearted, and that if I ceased to follow the counsels of a certain friend of mine, I might become a rational and right-feeling young man. So then, here was Signor Massimo once more made a scape-goat—the friend who had assisted me in Dalmatia, succoured my family in our distress, and who still remained our uncomplaining creditor. The impropriety of this attack stung me so sharply that I could not hold my tongue. I had been treated as a knave and fool without losing patience; but never in my life have I heard my friends insulted without resenting the injustice.

I told the lady, knitting my brows and speaking seriously, that she was bound to listen to me: unless, as I thought not, she was indifferent to equity. Prejudice, I said, is a very unjust judge, and I did not wish her to fall into that category. Then I entered into a candid narration of our family affairs. I described the ill results of reckless mal-administration. I related what had already happened and was sure to happen, what I wanted, how I was opposed, my honourable intentions, the plots and schemes to thwart me, the services rendered by my friend and his guiltlessness of any machinations. I could see that she was both surprised and penetrated by my reasoning. Just at this point Conte Francesco Santorini entered the apartment, tired and drowsy. We exchanged greetings, and the lady spoke to him in this way: "Count, you were quite right to doubt about the Gozzi. This gentleman has put a very different face upon the matter, and I know not what to think." The Count sank sleepily into a chair, murmuring: "Did I not tell you that you ought to hear both sides? The chatter of women, heated brains" . . . And having said these words, he subsided into slumber.

I begged this noble lady to continue her protection to our family, and to receive the visits which I hoped to pay her; if she sought to help us, she could do so by allaying the fever which was burning in so many irritated bosoms. For my part, I cultivated her friendship through many long years, until death forced me to deplore the loss of one whom I esteemed and reverenced. My relatives, on the other hand, gradually relaxed in their attentions, ceased to visit her, and changed their eulogistic sonnets into petty satires.

XXII.

The dogs of the law are let loose on me by my family.—It is impossible to avoid a separation.

As time went on, my steady intention to remove our family into the country, and my other plans of reform, roused my domestic antagonists to various pettifogging stratagems. The black-robed seedy myrmidons of the courts began to haunt our dwelling, taking inventories of every nail on the pretext of my mother's dowry, delivering demands in form from my three sisters for maintenance and marriage portions, presenting bills for drapery and jewels furnished by a company of merchants to the tune of 1500 ducats, and suing on the part of my two brothers-in-law for some 4000 ducats owed to them. Little creditors of all descriptions rose in swarms around us; and what was still more astounding, my sister-in-law advanced a claim of 900 ducats, due to her, she said, upon the statement of accounts which we had signed so negligently. One would have thought the myrmidons and ban-dogs of the law had been unleashed by hunters bent on driving a wild beast from his lair; while the satisfaction and triumph depicted on the faces of my relatives showed too clearly who were the real authors of this legal persecution.

I bore the brunt of these attacks with my habitual philosophy of laughter, drew closer to my brother Almorò, and informed Francesco by letter of what was being conspired against us. Count Francesco Santorini helped me at this pinch with excellent advice. Under his direction I took the following measures. Francesco received instructions to hold fast by every rood of our Friulian property, and to send me copies of any writs which might be served upon him there. I recognised my mother's dowry, and offered annual payments to the merchants and my brothers-in-law. To my sisters I replied in writing that their maintenance should be duly attended to, but that it was impossible to create marriage portions for them under the conditions of entail to which the estate was subjected. With regard to the monstrous claims advanced by my sister-in-law, I flatly denied their validity until they had been submitted to a court of justice. Then I proceeded to meet the current expenditure of our establishment as well as I was able, while waiting for the time of harvest; and all this I did without mooting the question of Gasparo's separation from our brotherhood, in the hope that little by little things would settle down in peace and quietness. Vain and idle expectation! My reforms, by cutting at the root of vested interests, and checking the arbitrary sway of Heaven knows whom, merely fanned the flames of rage which burned against me. In a private memorial, addressed to my

mother, brother, sister-in-law, and sisters, I finally
explained the impossibility of supporting the family
any longer at Venice, exposed as I was to annoying
and expensive litigation with the very persons who
ate and drank at the same table. I might just as well
have talked to images. Writs issued by my mother,
my sister-in-law, my sisters, fell in showers. Slights
and insults thickened daily. Our common table had
become a pit of hell, worthy to be sung by Dante.
To such a state of misery had irrational dissensions
brought a set of relatives who really loved each
other.

In order to shelter Almorò and myself from the
wordy missiles which fell like hail all dinner-time,
I had a little table laid for us two in a separate
apartment. The covers were removed with rudeness,
on the pretext that the linen, plates, dishes, &c.,
belonged to my mother's dowry, and that if I wanted
such furniture I must buy it. Pushed in this way to
extremities, I decided to leave a house which had
become for me a hell on earth. Perhaps it was im-
politic to take this step. But I could not stand
these petty persecutions longer. Before quitting the
infernal regions, I begged permission from my mother
to take away the beds in which my brother Almorò
and I enjoyed our troubled slumbers, offering to pay
their price to the credit of her dowry. She replied with a sardonic smile of discontent that she
could not grant my request, since the beds were

needed by the family. I accepted this refusal with hilarity.

"E quindi uscimmo a riveder le stelle."
"And thence we issued to review the stars."

XXIII.

Calumnious reports, negotiations, a legal partition of our family estate, tranquillity sought in vain.

I had hardly settled down with my brother Almorò in the remote quarter of S. Caterina, where lodgings are cheap in proportion to their inconvenience and discomfort, before the whole town began to talk about our doings. Three of the brothers Gozzi, it was rumoured, had laid violent hands upon the family estate; their eldest brother with his wife and five children, their three unmarried sisters, and their mother, a Venetian noblewoman worthy of all respect, had been plunged in tears and indigence by the barbarous inhumanity of these unnatural monsters. The hovel I had hired, and where I suffocated with Almorò in the smoke of a miserable kitchen, ill-furnished and waited on by an old beldame called Jacopa, was besieged by the myrmidons of the law. Everything was done to dislodge me from the city, and to make me abandon the line of action on which I had resolved. Democritus and my innocence came to

my aid ; and I determined to stand firm with silent
and passive resistance.

In these painful circumstances I heard to my great
sorrow that my brother's wife had persuaded him to
become the lessee of the theatre of S. Angelo at
Venice.[1]   Her romantic turn of fancy, together with
her love of domination, made her conceive wild
hopes of profit from this scheme. A company of
actors were engaged at fixed salaries ; and she was
to play the part of controller, purse-holder, and stage-
manager for the troupe at Venice and on the main-
land.   Moved by pity for my brother and his innocent children, I did everything I could, without
appearing personally in the matter, to dissuade this
hot-headed woman from so perilous an enterprise.
She repelled all such attempts with scorn, being
firmly convinced that she would gain a fortune and
make her brothers-in-law bite their nails with envy.

I saw that the division of our patrimony could no
longer be postponed, and civilly intimated to Gasparo
that the time was come for taking this supreme step.
Articles were accordingly drawn up, whereby the
several parcels of our estate in Friuli, Venice, Bergamo, and Vicenza were partitioned into four lots.
Provision was made for the repayment of my mother's
dowry and for the proper maintenance of my three

---

[1] The theatres of Venice were called by the names of the parishes in
which they stood, or of non-parochial churches to which they were con-
tiguous. S. Angelo was one of the smaller.

sisters, all of whom elected to reside with Gasparo.
A fund was formed for the liquidation of debts, the
charge of which devolved on me. I undertook to
render an annual report of this operation, showing
how I had bestowed the monies in my hands as
trustee for the family. Nothing was fixed about my
sister-in-law's claims for reimbursement; but it will
be seen that when her theatrical speculation proved
a ruinous failure, I had to take these also into
account. Gasparo expressed a wish to obtain the
upper dwelling in our mansion as part of his share.
The lower dwelling was conceded to Francesco,
Almorò and myself. To my mother and sisters we
offered the hospitality of sons and brothers, in case
at any time they should repent of their decision to
abide with Gasparo.

It might be imagined that, while these negotiations were in progress, I had no time to spend on
literary occupations. Nothing could be further from
the fact. I found in them my solace and distraction,
pouring forth multitudes of compositions, for the
most part humorous and alien to the cares which
weighed upon my mind. The course of my Memoirs
will bring to light many curious incidents which
these literary pastimes occasioned, and the narration
of which will prove, I hope, far from saddening to
my readers.

XXIV.

I enter on a period of toilsome litigation, and become acquainted with Venetian lawyers.

I should have been an arrant fool had I flattered myself with the hope that this partition would introduce the olive-branch of peace into our midst. On the contrary, I looked forward, and with justice, to all kinds of coming troubles. Two-thirds of the estate were saved from extravagant administration by the process; but the minds of Gasparo's family had been almost incurably embittered by the same cause. When I wanted to lay my hands upon our documents, in order to study the nature of various entails and trusts under which the estates were settled, I found that all these papers had been sold out of spite. Who had done this I did not learn, but I was informed in great secrecy by a servant-maid that they had been sold to a certain pork-butcher. I repaired immediately to his shop, and was only just in time to repurchase some abstracts and wills, which had not yet been used to wrap up sausages. Then I set to work in the cabinets of notaries and advocates and in the public archives, following the scent afforded by my recovered papers. More than eighty bulky suits in my own handwriting remain to show how patiently I studied the rights and claims of our estate, and now I prepared myself for the task of laying these before the courts.

At this epoch I made acquaintance with the celebrated pleader, Antonio Testa, under whose direction and advice I embarked upon a series of litigations which kept me fully occupied for eighteen years, and in the course of which I became acquainted with the men who haunt our palace of justice, and learned the chicaneries of legal warfare. Inveterate abuses, introduced in the remote past, and complicated by the ingenuity of lawyers through successive generations (most of them men of subtle brains, some of them devoid of moral rectitude), have been built up into a system of pleading as false as it is firmly grounded and imbued with ineradicable insincerity. This system consists, for the most part, of quibbling upon side-issues, throwing dust in the eyes of judges, cavilling, misrepresenting, taking advantage of technical errors, doing everything in short to gain a cause by indirect means. And from this false system neither honourable nor dishonest advocates are able to depart.

In justice to the legal profession, I must, however, say that I found many practicians who combined the gifts of eloquence and intellectual fervour with urbanity, cordiality, prudence, and disinterested zeal. Outside the vicious circle of their system they were men of loyalty and honour. Among these I ought

to pay a particular tribute to my friendly counsel
and defender, Signor Testa. Knowing my circumstances and my upright motives, he refused to take
the fees which were his due, and not unfrequently
opened his purse to me at a pinch in my necessities.
I have never met with a lawyer more quick at
seizing the strong and weak points of a case, more
rapid in his analysis of piles of documents, more
sagacious in divining the probable issue of a suit, or
more acute in calculating the mental powers, the
bias, and the equity of judges. Time and the circumstances of our several lives have drawn us somewhat apart. But nothing can diminish the feeling of
deep gratitude which I shall always cherish for one
who helped to heal the distractions and to improve
the fallen fortunes of my family.

The final result of eight or nine tedious lawsuits,
carried through with the assistance of Signor Testa,
was that I received several parcels of our estates
in Friuli, Vicenza, Bergamo, and Venice, which had
been alienated by fraudulent evasions of entail.[1]
Meanwhile I found time to visit my mother and

---

[1] I have condensed in this sentence the details of a long and tiresome
chapter (chap. xxix.). It is worth adding here that the law of Venice
with regard to entail was very strict; time gave no title to a purchaser
who had obtained possession of an estate subject to *fidei commissa*.
One of Goethe's most interesting letters from Venice (October 5, 1786)
contains the full description of a cause he heard pleaded in the Ducal
palace for the recovery of illegally alienated real property. Goethe
remarks upon the extraordinary permanence of trusts in Venice.

Gasparo's family. The latter were busily engaged in concocting and translating plays for my brother's theatre. These visits, paid with cordiality and frankness on my side, were usually the occasions of requests for money on my mother's. She begged with maternal dignity for little loans. I complied to the best of my ability, and forgot to remind her of her debts. My sister-in-law forced herself to treat me with an affectation of flattery. My sisters looked upon me with real affection, checked in its expression by I know not what untoward influence. My brother accepted me with philosophical indifference.

XXV.

A collision with my brother's family, due to old grudges and to present needs.—They make me a married man without my having taken a wife.

My brother Gasparo's income, derived from his portion of the family estates, from the interest on my mother's dowry and the annual allowance for my sisters' maintenance, together with the profits of his writing and of certain literary services rendered to his Excellency Marco Foscarini,[1] late Doge of glorious memory, amounted to about 1500 ducats, free

---

[1] The author of an unfinished work on Venetian literature.

of all debts and obligations. This was certainly
nothing very splendid ; but neither would the wealth
of Crœsus have been anything to boast of . in the
hands of an extravagant family, ruled only by the
caprice of its component members.

I have mentioned above that Gasparo obtained the
upper dwelling in our house at Venice, which was let
for 150 ducats, while we three brothers received the
lower dwelling, at that time inhabited by him. Some
few months were allowed him to remove from the
one apartment to the other. But no sooner had he
entered into legal possession of his new habitation
than he, or perhaps I ought to say his wife, let it
again to the noble lady Ginevra Loredan Zeno. She
paid the rent of several years in advance, and installed herself in Gasparo's part of the mansion, while
he, with all his family, continued to inhabit our
part with the utmost sang-froid, taking no further
heed of the engagement he was under to us three
brothers. Now we had resolved to put this tenement
into good repair and to let it for some years, until the
debts of the estate had been discharged and we could
go to live in it at peace. With this view we had
already found a tenant, who was no other than the
Contessa Ghellini Balbi. She, on her side, had given
up her old apartment, which was already let in advance
to other tenants by her landlord. Time went on, and
I saw no sign of our house being abandoned to our
use, according to the family agreement. It appeared

only too clearly that the partition I had demanded,
my resolve to pay the family debts out of income
without resorting to sale or mortgage, and my application to the courts for annulment of contracts made
during my father's lifetime, were all of them unpardonable offences in the eyes of those who had
made the debts, the mortgages, the contracts.

I began by gently asking for the house which was
our portion, seeing that we had resigned the upper
dwelling to our brother at his particular request.
No answer reached me ; but rumours ran around
the city that I was now attempting to turn my old
mother, my three marriageable sisters, my brother,
his wife, and five innocent children into the streets.
At this point I expected that one of those interminable lawsuits, which are the dishonour of the legal
profession, but which never lack advocates to keep
them going, would be commenced against me. In
order to lend colour and substance to their false
report, my relatives determined to give me a wife
without consulting me. It was impossible to fix
definite calumnies upon Mme. Ghellini Balbi, because
of her exemplary life and conspicuous piety. But my
daily visits to her house offered a pretext for injurious insinuations ; and I soon heard it announced that
I was secretly married to this lady, and that all my
plots had only this one end in view. Such gossip
did me honour in some respects. Yet I was grieved
that a lady of excellent conduct, devoted to her only

son, and old enough to be my mother, should be
made the butt of malignant animosity.[1]

Without wasting time or breath in contradicting
these unjust and lying vociferations of my private
enemies, I made my mind up to obtain possession of
my house by all the straightforward means in my
power. Accordingly I managed to meet my brother
apart from the din of women, and laid a clear statement before him of my obligations to Mme. Ghellini Balbi (who ran the risk of remaining without a
roof to shelter her) and of my well-founded rights
which were being iniquitously set at nought. The
poor fellow seemed on the point of weeping. His
gestures reminded me of patient Job, while he protested that he had nothing whatever to do with a state
of affairs the injustice of which he frankly admitted.
He added that he had to put up with infernal
clamourings—that he was called a chicken-hearted
poltroon, a father without entrails for his offspring—
in short, that he was neither obeyed nor listened
to at home. Then, to convince me that it was not
he who opposed my entrance into our part of the
house, he took a pen and wrote and signed a declaration to the effect that he fully acknowledged the
title of his brothers Francesco, Carlo, and Almorò,
and that he would never interfere to prevent our
taking possession of our lawful property.

---

[1] It seems probable that Gozzi was really at one time on the point of
marrying this lady.

All these steps proved fruitless. Time pressed, and I found myself obliged to bring my cause before a judge, who chanced to be his Excellency Count Galean Angarano, at that time Avvogador del Comune.[1] What was my astonishment when I saw my sister-in-law, like an advocate in petticoats, at the head of my mother and my sisters, with my henpecked brother to bring up the rear, come marching into court. I will not dwell upon this too too comic scene—

" For my Thalia takes no thought to sing."

The judge recognised that my claims were indisputable. But before pronouncing sentence in my favour he strove to settle matters by mediation. Conferences took place ; first between the bench and his Excellency the Senator Daniele Reniero, who acted for Mme. Ghellini Balbi ; then between the Senator and my sister-in-law, who was the rock and stone of our vexation. I was curious to know the upshot of these whispered confabulations. At length Senator Reniero came up and told me that if I was willing to disburse sixty ducats, which my sister-in-law had pressing need of, I might enter at once into posses-

---

[1] The Avvogadori del Comune, or *Advocatores Comunis*, corresponded in a certain sense to the modern Procuratori di Stato, and had some resemblance to the Roman tribunes. They formed a High Court of Justice for the guardianship of property accruing to the Exchequer, for the protection of private rights in property, rights of minors and widows, the superintendence of registers of births and marriages, &c. Three patricians formed the board.

sion of the house without a verdict from the bench. Such a verdict would be appealed against and would certainly lead to indescribable delays. I thanked his Excellency for suggesting this arrangement. My sister-in-law received her ducats, and we obtained our dwelling. I had it straightway put into repair, for it looked as though it had sustained a siege. Mme. Balbi went at once to live there with a lease of five years only, while I retired with my brothers into a cheap house, which I had taken at S. Ubaldo and furnished with strict regard to economy. Here I arranged for Almorò's tuition by an excellent ecclesiastic. For my own part, I went on paying off debts, rebuilding such of our houses as needed it, prosecuting my lawsuits, and amusing myself in leisure hours with literature.

XXVI.

A serious event, depicting the character of my uncle, the Senator Almorò Cesare Tiepolo.

A very long time had elapsed since I visited my maternal uncle, the Senator Almorò Cesare Tiepolo. I imagined that my mother and the persons about her, who were assiduous in paying court to him from motives wholly alien to my nature, might have prejudiced the good old man against me. Still I did not choose to undergo the mortification of defending myself, especially as I could only do so by accusing those for whom at the bottom of my heart I felt both love and reverence. I knew, moreover, that our Venetian patricians, though just and dispassionate upon the bench in their capacity of judges, were singularly liable to be influenced by what they heard in private at their own homes from suitors or clients, and that it was extremely difficult to remove impressions which had once been made upon their minds. This weakness I have always ascribed to their amiability, and have regarded the nobles of our Republic as really adorable for qualities of the heart, in spite of the sentimental bias I have mentioned.

My habitual taciturnity and solitary ways of life, my neglect of petty social duties, my habit of asking and desiring nothing from fortune, together with the freedom of my pen, might have won me formidable enemies, if any such had deigned to look down upon a person of so little consequence as I am.

My wise and good uncle, who was suffering from a dropsy in the chest, and not far from death's door, let me know that he should like to see me. I went at once to his house ; and was bidden to take a seat at his bedside. He began to complain gently that I had so long neglected to visit him. I answered frankly that I had stayed away through fear of his having been wrongfully prejudiced against me, and also because I heard that he was angry with me, perhaps on account of my prolonged absence. "If I complained," he said, "that my sister and your mother was being exposed to ill-treatment and affronts, this was no reason why you should suspend your visits." "I see," I replied, "that my suspicions and my fears are not without foundation. But this is not the proper time to trouble you with lengthy narratives in self-defence. Your health is a matter of concern to me for your sake and for my own. I have tried everything in my power to avert discords and divisions, even to the point of doing violence to my naturally pacific temper. I feel sure, when you recover, as I hope you will with all my heart, that I shall make it clear to you that I have hurt nobody and attacked nobody, and that I am only doing all I can to benefit our family, without the least regard for my mere private interest; nay, that I am bearing the burden of enormous cares and weighty business, not to speak of exposing myself to risks and dangers, for the common good."

He was just, prudent, a philosopher, and ill. Therefore he made no immediate answer. I renewed my daily visits, and had the satisfaction of hearing afterwards that the venerable old man expressed himself in these words to my mother: "Believe me, your son Carlo is a good young fellow."

His illness kept increasing, and I perceived, by the persons whom he urged to visit him, that he was anxious to be reconciled with all of his acquaintances who might be under the impression that he bore a grudge against them. A certain Frate Bernardo of the Gesuati, who then passed for a learned ecclesiastic, acted as his spiritual director, and used to read at his request portions of the Holy Scriptures aloud to him. Observing his indifference upon the point of death, this excellent friar was moved to say : "I do not want you to prepare yourself for death too much like a philosopher."

Though he had filled important posts in the Government, and had frequently sat as member of the sublime Council of Ten, he was never heard, throughout his last illness, to utter the least word regarding the tribunals of justice or the state.

During his whole lifetime he had taken delight in gathering company around his hospitable board, and seeing the table furnished with good cheer, especially with the choicest kinds of fish. Now that he was sick unto death, and could only take some spoonfuls of such broth as are administered to dying persons, he still would have the table served as formerly for guests. Every morning he used to send for one of his gondoliers, and inquire what sorts of fine fish were that day in the market. On receiving the man's report, he commented in praise or blame, as this might be, upon the season and the quality of the fishes for sale, and the various waters in which they had been caught. After settling these affairs of the household, he proceeded to religious exer-

cises, grave discourses with his spiritual director, and
prayers of fervent piety. I ought further to testify
that he breathed his last in the spirit of a great man,
philosophically Christian, and that his example inspired me with the desire to imitate his end.

He possessed the virtue of patience in the highest
degree. No one ever saw his temper stirred by any
untoward accident which happened to him. In order
to give a single instance of his intrepid constancy,
I will relate an event which happened some years
before his death. One evening, while alighting from
his gondola, he caught his foot in the long and
ample robes of the patrician mantle, and was upon the
point of falling into the canal. The gondolier, in
his anxiety to catch and keep him up, let the oar
go which he was holding in his hands. The oar fell
with violence upon the right arm of his master, and
broke it. The gondolier was not aware of what had
happened; and my uncle, though he knew very well,
uttered no complaint. He ascended the stairs, and
when he reached his apartment, the valet came forward to help him off, as usual, with his cloak. Then
at last he remarked with imperturbable long-suffering:
"Pull gently, for my right arm is in two pieces."
The uproar among the servants, who were greatly
attached to him, was tremendous. The gondolier
ran up, weeping bitterly and begging to be pardoned.
He bade them all be calm, and said to the man:
"You did me harm when you were meaning to do

me good. What fault have you committed, which
requires my pardon ?" After this he had to lie forty
days in bed without altering his position, at the
surgeon's orders ; yet he never uttered a syllable
that betrayed any impatience. I could relate a
number of such traits of character, but they have
nothing to do with the Memoirs of my life.

After his death, which I felt very deeply, as every
one could see, a certain Signor Giovannantonio Guseò
came to call on me. This man practised as notary,
land-surveyor, advocate, registrar, and judge in certain courts of Friuli. He was known to be more
wily than the old Greek Sinon, and had assisted my
brother's wife in procuring the alienation of certain
portions of our entailed estates. Now he suggested
that it would do me great honour, as a sign of affectionate remembrance, if I were to contribute ten
sacks of flour and two casks of wine annually to my
mother, in addition to her dowry. I saw at once
from whom this proposal emanated, and admired the
address with which the proper moment had been
chosen for working on my feelings. Such artifices,
however, were repugnant to my nature ; and chang-
ing my tone from sadness to cold reserve, I replied to
the following effect. " I thought my mother's prefer-
ence for my brother Gasparo's family unfortunate ;
my own house was always open to her, and here she
would be revered and loved by three respectful sons.
Here she would enjoy her yearly maintenance, and

the income of her dowry.   By refusing our offer, she
only affronted us.   By accepting it, she would confer
a benefit on Gasparo, the number of whose family
would be diminished.   Meanwhile, the obligation I
was under of reducing debts, repairing buildings on
the property, and reclaiming parts of the entailed
estates, rendered it impossible that I should weaken
the insufficient resources at my command by any
such donation as Signor Guseò had proposed."   This
answer set tongues wagging again, and revived the
opinion that I was a downright Phalaris.

The estate of my uncle Tiepolo had gained nothing
by his regency of Zante and by other lucrative appointments.   The probity of his character did not
suffer him to enrich himself at the expense of the
State.   Accordingly, he provided by will that all his
debts should be paid off, appending a schedule of his
creditors.   The residue he bequeathed to his sister
Girolama for her lifetime, with reversion to my
mother.   On the same sad occasion my mother
inherited a portion of some landed property in
Friuli, which had belonged to an old aunt Tiepolo,
who died intestate.   This, united to her dowry,
formed a sufficient fund for her establishment.

My mother continued to regard me as her sixth
finger, amputated without any suffering on her part.
Of course she had the right to dispose of her affections as she felt inclined, and to keep her tender heart
open for the persons who possessed her favour.   It was

my misfortune not to possess it, but I did not envy those who had that privilege ; and I can assure my readers that what caused me the greatest annoyance with regard to my mother, was seeing her always without a ducat to spend according to her fancy. This state of things continued when the whole property of that branch of the Tiepolos passed into her hands upon the death of her sister Girolama, who left furniture and a considerable amount of money to my mother, jointly with my brother Gasparo and his children.

XXVII.

It is decided that I was a husband, though I had no wife.—
Some anecdotes of a serious character.

An event happened which clenched the gossip of my imaginary marriage to the Contessa Ghellini Balbi. The patrician Benedetto Balbi, Canon of Padua and Abbot of Lonigo, a gentleman abundantly endowed with gifts of nature and of fortune, who was this lady's brother-in-law, had caused himself to be legally appointed sole guardian of his nephew Paolo, the widow's only son. The lad may have been about ten years old at this epoch ; and his uncle resolved to separate him from his mother, and to place him in a school kept by the Somascan fathers, at San Cipriano

on the island of Murano.[1] His mother, who was ten-
derly devoted to her son, did not oppose his entrance
into this college, but resented his being torn from
the arms which had nursed and fostered him till now,
as though she were a peril to his youth and had no
claim to supervise his education in the school. Sharp
and angry words passed ; and Mme. Balbi applied
to the courts, demanding to be nominated guardian
together with her brother-in-law. The conflagration
spread, and I, innocent as I was, found myself involved in it. With the object of strengthening his
case, the Cavaliere went about the town, loudly
protesting that his sister-in-law had contracted a
second alliance with Count Carlo Gozzi ; that she
had ceased thereby to be a Balbi, and had lost all
rights over the boy, who belonged to his family. I
laughed, as usual, with the lady over the pertina-
city of folk in thinking we were married. But my
laughter was turned to seriousness, when the Cavaliere finally declared his intention to be free of legal
quarrels, and to abandon all the schemes which he

---

[1] The Somascan Order was founded about 1540 by Girolamo Miani,
a Venetian senator, upon the model of the Theatines. Its object was
education, principally of the poor. With regard to the school at S.
Cipriano, it is worth mentioning that the famous adventurer, Casanova,
was placed there by his guardian the Abbé Grimani in the year 1740
or thereabouts. He gives a full account of the institution in his
Memoirs (vol. i. ch. vi.), from which it appears that at this epoch about
150 youths were educated by the Somascan monks. Readers of Casanova
need hardly be reminded that he was expelled from the seminary after
a few weeks' residence. Gasparo Gozzi was also educated here.

had formed for his nephew's advantage, leaving him entirely to his mother's authority.

Assuming a Catonian gravity, I pointed out to Mme. Balbi that she ought to waive her just claims and to stomach her natural resentment for the sake of her son. I firmly believed in my own soul that an ounce of sincere love was worth more than a hundred pounds of gold. Yet I reminded her that she was not in the position to make up to her boy for the loss of his uncle's property. This reasoning, which I regard as mere sophistry, but which the world accepts as irrefutable, made the lady burst into a flood of tears and then exclaim : " You are right ! I am a poor woman, and should be condemned by everybody, perhaps even in the future by my own son. I am ready to sacrifice my rights ; I will bury in my breast the stirrings of maternal love, the sense of insult and of injury, all that may prove prejudicial to the interests of my adored son, on whom I am unable to confer those benefits which lie within his uncle's power. Pray do me the further kindness of undertaking to explain the unalterable decision at which I have arrived."

I praised her virtuous resolution, and reported to the noble gentleman, her brother-in-law, from whom I have always received distinguished marks of politeness, the decision she had come to. In doing so, I attempted to draw a picture of her merits, and to maintain that her feelings were not merely excusable, but worthy of the highest commendation. The Cavaliere replied with some emotion: "You must not take me for a wild beast! I mean that the boy shall be visited by his mother, and looked after in all his wants, the charge of supplying which I take for the future on myself. I am quite willing to let her bring him back from time to time to dine with her, and only stipulate that her demonstrations of tenderness shall not interfere with his education and discipline." These solemn words of covenant having been exchanged, I was the instrument of separating the boy from his mother's embraces, and of conducting him to his appointed school. His behaviour on this occasion, in which firmness blent with filial emotion, made me feel sure that he was destined to reward his mother's virtues and his uncle's benevolence with conduct worthy of the highest honours of his country. Only death, which spared neither of his relatives, and which prevented them from reaping the fruits of their respective love and kindness, defeated these prognostications. The mother died twelve, and the uncle fifteen years after the events I have narrated. Young Balbi grew up to be an ornament, by his intellectual and moral qualities, by his probity and purity of manners, by his sympathy for the oppressed, and by his thoroughly national temper, to the Venetian Republic, in the administration of which his birth opened for him a career of usefulness and honour.

XXVIII.

I should not have believed what is narrated in this chapter, if I had not seen it with my own eyes.

Family jars and discords have this effect upon embittered minds that each member, wherever the wrong may really lie, is apt to think, not only that he is in the right, but that the right is absolutely and wholly on his side. For my part, I am not altogether sure that I was justified in doing what I did, and what I have described above with perfect candour.

I was aware that the theatrical speculation into which my brother had been induced to enter had taken a bad turn, and that worse might be expected in the future. A malignant and vindictive spirit would have found some satisfaction in these circumstances. As it was, I felt sincerely sorry, and flattered myself on being therefore free from malice. In proportion as things went from bad to worse, the rancour against myself increased, as though I had been responsible for an enterprise which I had always solemnly condemned by act and word.

I kept up relations with my brother's family, wishing to maintain the links of relationship unbroken, and to explain from time to time what I was doing

for the common good.   In spite of these demonstrations of a kindly feeling, which I admit were never
very gushing, I saw to my deep regret that the
wounds caused by the partition of our patrimony
had not ceased to bleed.

The youngest of my sisters, Chiara by name, induced perhaps by some presentiment of coming
trouble, asked me one day to take her under the
protection of us three brothers.   I cordially acceded
to her request, and would have done the like by my
mother and our two other sisters, had they not
spurned the acceptance of what they had hitherto
rejected as a great misfortune.

I told this youngest of my sisters that, our mother
not being under my roof, my brother Francesco
occupied with the estates in Friuli, Almorò a mere
boy engaged in studies, and I absorbed in legal
affairs for the common interests of the family, she
could not with any propriety be left to the custody
of a rough and stupid serving-woman.   I therefore
begged her to enter a convent for a while, until we
should have changed our mode of living, and should be
in a position to receive her more suitably and to take
thought for her proper establishment.   My sisters
are neither foolish nor ill-natured.   Chiara accepted
my proposal, and was placed in the convent of S.
Maria degli Angeli at Pordenone, as a young lady in
charge of the Superior.

Any one exposed, as I was, to the rage of angry

tongues, blackening me with the epithets of unjust,
inhumane, tyrannical, marrying me against my will,
and capable of insinuating the worst of charges
against me for my guardianship of a sister, would
act rightly if he took the precautions I did. Yet the
precautions of the most prudent man on earth do
not always bear the good results expected of them.
I speak with experience derived from long study of
ill-inclined men and worse-inclined women, who have
invariably taken my unalterable good faith for venomous maliciousness.

I was excessively pained to observe that the
bitterness created in my brother Gasparo's family by
the events I have narrated remained unconquerable.
It is true that they concealed, as far as possible, their
grudge against me, whenever I paid them visits and
treated them with brotherly good-will. This grudge,
however, could not help showing itself in public ;
and it did so in a monstrous fashion, which I should
not have credited unless I had been an eye-witness
of the scandal.

My brothers and I were in the habit, during car-
nival-time, of frequently attending the theatre of
S. Angelo, which was under the direction of my sister-
in-law far rather than her husband. Amusement
was less our object than the wish to support, so far
as in us lay, a speculation to which we feared our
brother had been sacrificed. We persuaded Mme.
Ghellini Balbi to accompany us ; and she entered

into our designs by applauding as heartily as any of
the audience.

They had given at this theatre a translation of the
French comedy called *Esop at the Court*, which
succeeded partly by the elegance of my brother's
Italian version, and partly by its novelty. Rumour
told us that the sequel, by the same French author,
entitled *Esop in the Town*, was being translated and
would soon appear. We were eager to be present
at the first night, to back the piece with our approval,
and to witness its triumph.

A worthy fellow, who aired his eloquence at Gasparo's house and also in our own, took me apart one
day, and spoke with an air of secrecy and consternation to the following effect: "You must know that
the forthcoming play of *Esop in the Town* will
contain a scene, interpolated, not translated from the
original, in which you, your brothers Francesco and
Almorò, and Mme. Ghellini Balbi, are held up in
a cruel satire to the public scorn. Do not let my
name transpire; but take means to prevent this
scandal; the comedy will be represented in five days
from now." I was far from disbelieving that what
my friend said was the truth; yet I took care to
let no sign of my belief escape me. I thanked him
for the friendly interest which had prompted him to
warn me, but laughed the matter off as something
beyond the range of possibility. He strained every
nerve to convince me, but got nothing for his pains

beyond smiles and ironical protestations of gratitude. I left him there fuming with anger at my obstinate hilarity.

I kept guard over my tongue in the presence of my brothers and the lady, and made a show of great anxiety to see the new play produced upon the boards. At last the first night came, and we all provided ourselves with a convenient box for the occasion. We were disappointed to find the theatre ill-attended, and to notice that the comedy dragged. *Esop at the Court* had caught the public by something piquant in its chief character, by his grotesque, crook-backed figure, and by the appropriate fables which had been written with real dramatic skill for the part. *Esop in the Town* was no less worthy of attention, but the novelty had evaporated; it seemed a plagiarism of the former piece, and wearied the audience like a composition which has lost its salt. At length the interpolated scene, of which my friend had warned me, came on.[1]

An ancient dame, attired in black, made her entrance, and unfolded the tale of her self-styled calamities to Esop. Pouring forth an interminable catalogue of woes, she enumerated all the lies which

---

[1] This scene has actually been preserved and printed in Gasparo Gozzi's works. Opere, Minerva, Padova, vol. vii. It forms the 6th scene of the 3rd act of *Esopo in Città*, and is very much as Carlo Gozzi describes it. The ancient lady throws the principal blame for her domestic sufferings upon a certain "Sicofante, Dottor legista di questa città," whom I take to be Carlo's lawyer, Testa.

had been circulated against myself and Mme. Balbi
at the period of our family dissensions.   The ancient
dame summed up by saying that she had been turned
out of house and home, together with a loving
son, three daughters, a daughter-in-law, and five
grandchildren, by three of her own male children,
the barbarous perverted offspring of her womb.
Then she appealed with tears for counsel and advice
to Esop, who expressed his sympathy in a frigidly
elaborated fable.   The ancient dame, attired in
black, was an exact image of our poor mother, who
had been blinded by a touch of spite against me and
by the mud-honey of her favouritism into allowing
herself to be exposed in this way on a public stage
for the mirth of the populace.

The scene was very long; it had nothing to do
with the action of the piece, having been foisted in to
gratify a private animosity.   The audience, ignorant
of what it meant, began to yawn; and it contributed
in no small measure to the failure of the play.

While this indecent and malignant episode was
dragging its slow length along, I saw Mme. Ghellini
Balbi becoming momently more taciturn and out of
humour, my two brothers flaming into anger and
preparing for some act of violence.   The shouts of
laughter with which I greeted this abortion of a
satire added fuel to their fire, and Francesco, spurred
by martial ardour, was on the point of defying the
players.   He only made me laugh the louder; but I

had some difficulty in persuading my companions to quench their indignation in a cup of water, and to wrap themselves around with imperturbable indifference. They obeyed me. If we had made a disturbance, we should have put the cap on our own heads. As it was, our cold behaviour snuffed out the whole episode, without awaking anybody's interest. And such will, peradventure, be the fate of these Memoirs I am writing of my life.

In after days I was glad to have laughed at this indecent exhibition. The perusal of an anecdote in Ælian confirmed my self-congratulation. It was to the following effect. "When," says he, "a firm courageous spirit is attacked before the public in quizzical caricatures and gibing insults, these trifles vanish like mist before the wind; but if they meet with a nature which is base and proud and abject all at one and the same time, they fill it with melancholy and madness, which often lead it to the grave.[1] Take the proof of these remarks. Socrates, when he was ridiculed upon the public stage by Aristophanes, enjoyed the fun and laughed at it. Poliagros, under the same circumstances, went mad and hanged himself."

In concluding this episode, which I leave my readers to characterise with stronger epithets than I

---

[1] Gozzi can hardly not have been thinking of poor Gratarol, when he penned these lines. Mentally he contrasts his own conduct under the inconvenience of a stage-satire with Gratarol's.

shall use, I wish to affirm that I never have believed, or can believe, that my brother Gasparo lent his pen or his assent to the production of the scene in question.

XXIX.

A disagreeable action at law brought against me.

While busily engaged in prosecuting my many lawsuits, I was unpleasantly surprised by the revival of my sister-in-law's old claim for reimbursement of monies expended by her in the management of our affairs during my father's lifetime.[1] This preposterous claim had long been lying dormant, and the better terms on which we were gradually coming to live together made me forget it as a chimera of the past.

My brother Gasparo's direction of the theatre of which he was the sole lessee bore such fruits as every one predicted. Instead of the pecuniary profits he had been encouraged to expect, the poor fellow was worried with vexatious and aggressive opposition, peculiarly trying to one of his gifts and temperament, but only too usual in enterprises of this kind.

Wounded pride and thirst for vengeance, together with the hideous necessity of meeting debts con-

---

[1] See above, p. 319.

tracted in this unsuccessful speculation, were the causes which roused his wife to bring her alleged claims upon the family into a law-court. The defendants in this suit were myself and my two brothers Francesco and Almorò. It will be remembered that she had induced us to sign her cabalistic book of magic numbers with the sole object of freeing her from any possible pretensions upon our side. My elder brother, who had been the first to sign, in order to give a good example to his juniors, was not prosecuted by his wife.

Our legal advisers maintained, with some show of reason, that Gasparo was the real mover in this matter. For my part, knowing as I did his peaceful character, I felt certain, that though he was capable of countenancing irregularities through indolence and the desire to live a quiet life, he was incapable of stirring up litigious strife on such foundations. I was not ignorant that he had stooped to the theatrical speculation in order merely to escape from a vortex of domestic intrigues. I knew, moreover, that, after the partition of our patrimony, his wife and family had changed their residence at least six times, through restlessness, without informing him; so that he had gone to knock at empty house-doors, and had casually learned from neighbours in what quarter of the town his flighty brood had nested last. It also reached my ears that his wife was selling property upon his life, and that he had finally been driven by the tempest of his home to take a distant lodging of two rooms,[1] where he installed himself with his little heap of books and abandoned himself to study, seeking the peace he could not find. After all, the father of a family who flies domestic cares, only brings upon himself more carping cares than those which he has fled from. All these considerations put together enabled me to convince my counsel that Gasparo had no share in the proceedings of his wife.

In the pleadings which set forth my sister-in-law's cause, Signor Guseò, already named by me above, deposed on obviously false oath that he had been commissioned by us three brothers to examine her accounts, and that he had found her claim for reimbursement in the sum demanded to be just. To cut a long story short, our arguments upon the other side were useless. It was in vain that we expounded the inability of a woman who had entered our family without dowry, and had got the management of affairs into her hands through the indolence of its real head, to constitute herself its creditor ; in vain that we denounced the collusion of one brother with his wife against the interests of three innocent brothers, who had been absent many years without burdening the estate ; in vain that we showed how the father and the mother of the plaintiff had been received into our house and maintained for full

---

[1] On the Fondamenta Nuove, looking across Murano to the mountains of the Dolomites. See Tommasei, *op. cit.*, p. 258.

fifteen years until their death, and how her relatives had been more the masters there than its legitimate owners; in vain that we brought forward the chaotic account-book, signed by us in compliance with our elder brother for the sole sake of calming troubled tempers; in vain that we pointed out figures, garbled, cancelled, altered in these precious documents; in vain that we offered to discharge sums due to creditors for money or goods rendered to the plaintiff in her administration of the family affairs. All these solid pleas were like words thrown to the winds before the impudence of two scoundrelly pettifoggers, the very scum of the Venetian law-courts, who managed to convince our sapient judges that men ought to open their eyes wide before they signed papers. From that moment until now, I have always read my letters through ten times before appending my signature.

As usual, I consoled myself by laughing over the inevitable. Nor did I dream of complaining to Francesco, who had drawn me into the affair by his desire to settle matters. He, good fellow, met my laughter with a sorry countenance, protesting that he could never have anticipated such an abominable trick of fortune.

Seven hundred ducats were passed to my sister-in-law's credit on the termination of this suit. They did my brother's family no good. Debts to comedians had eaten up the capital beforehand; and I was obliged to pay a set of hungry fellows with the consent of him and his wife. The annoyance, however, did not stop here. In order to bolster up her claim, my sister-in-law had raked together a multitude of soi-disant creditors, who pretended to have supplied money or goods to our family; and declarations signed by them, recognising her as their sole debtor, were put into court as evidence. When they found their expectations frustrated, the wasp's nest swarmed out against us three brothers, and sequestrated our house-property for payment of their alleged debts. Before I succeeded in finally shaking them off, I had to transact much tiresome business and to fight several lawsuits.

XXX.

A long and serious illness.—My recovery.—The doctors differ.—One of my sisters takes the veil.—Beginnings of literary squabbles, and other trifles.

In the midst of these annoyances, I found the time and strength to pursue my literary studies, especially in the now neglected art of poetry, and enjoyed excellent health ; when suddenly, one night, a violent hemorrhage from the lungs warned me that the life of mortals hangs upon the frailest thread.

Bleeding, vegetable diet, and a frugality in food, which few, I think, are capable of continuing for as

long a space of time as I can, together with my
philosophical indifference to death, restored me to
something like a tolerable state of health.

It seemed to me at this period that my two brothers
and I, who always kept together, were in a position
to settle down again into our paternal home. Mme.
Ghellini Balbi, who had rented the house for more
than five years, politely retired at my request, and
found another habitation at S. Agostino. I furnished
our ancestral nest as decently as I was able; and
we were soon installed there. It was then that I
invited my youngest sister to leave her convent
and join us, travelling myself to Pordenone for this
purpose.

Whether through weakness, or human influence,
or Divine inspiration, I know not; but I found the
good girl obstinate against my prayers, my anger, and
my threats. She entreated with a holy stubbornness
to be left in prison, to be indulged in her desire
to pass her lifetime in that blessed aviary of virgins.
I commanded her to come home for at least three
or four months. At the end of that time, if she still
persisted in her pious fanaticism, I promised to play
the part of executioner at her request. She replied
with a serious enthusiasm, which made me laugh, that
she knew enough of the world to be experienced in
its wickedness; and when I insisted, she met me
with rather less than heavenly doggedness by remark-
ing that nothing short of cutting her in pieces would

make her quit the convent-gratings. Though I did
not believe that this ultimatum was dictated by the
angels, I bent my head in order to avoid a scandal.
On taking the veil, she received those appointments
and allowances which are usually bestowed upon the
brides of Christ.

Were I to fix my thoughts upon the troubles which
my four married sisters have had to suffer and still
suffer—and I am only too well informed about them—
I should be obliged to admit that the youngest chose
the better part in life. They were always in straits,
always weeping, with their gentle natures and their
illimitable powers of endurance. One of them died
before my eyes, to my deep sorrow, only because she
was a wife. Meanwhile, the nun, beloved by her
sisters, placidly smiled at things which we, refined
in pleasures, finding nowhere solid pleasure for our
satisfaction, would call barbarous tortures, and took
delight in little treats, which we philosophers, past-
masters in the arts of greed, are wont to scorn and
turn our backs upon. In due course she attained
the highest rank of Abbess in her convent; and I
believe she was more gratified with this honour than
Louis XVI. with his titles of King of France and of
Navarre.[1]

Time had at length allayed the discords of our
family. My two remaining sisters found husbands.

---

[1] This was written in 1780, but when it was printed in 1797, Louis
XVI. had little reason to be proud of his titles.

My brother Gasparo obtained a post at the University of Padua, which brought him six hundred ducats a year, besides pecuniary gratifications for extraordinary services.[1] This proves that literature is not wholly unremunerated in Venice. In addition to these emoluments, he found another way, legitimate indeed, but one which seems incredible, for accumulating the sequins so much needed after his theatrical disaster. There was not a marriage, a taking of the veil among our noble families, an election of a Doge, or procurator, or grand chancellor, without my brother being engaged to produce the panegyrics or poems which are usual on such occasions—more sought perhaps by fashion than by studious readers. The patricians made it their custom to reward him with a hundred sequins, which contributed to the splendour of their families, but did him little good, for in his hands money found wings and flew away.

These details have little to do with my Memoirs; yet they are honourable to my nation, and are not without a certain bearing on my subject. Poetical trifles, published by me in collections, found favour by some aspect of novelty and by genial satire on contemporary fashions. Unluckily, they got me the reputation of a good poet and good writer. Accordingly, many of our lords tried to press me into the ranks of the *Raccoglitori*—collectors and compilers

---

[1] He was made secretary to the Riformatori dello Studio.

of occasional verse-books. They did not know that
I had adopted for my motto that line of Berni :—

"Voleva far da se, non comandato."
"His master he would be, and no man's man."

Whenever they did me the honour to force this
function on me, I civilly declined, and sent their mes-
sengers on to my brother, without, however, refusing
compositions of my own, which swelled the collections, to their gain or loss as chance might have it.

I never abandoned the scheme I had formed of
moving at law against the Marchese Terzi of Bergamo in a suit for the recovery of lands and rights
belonging to us.[1] But while I was engaged on the
preliminary business, a fresh attack of pulmonary
hemorrhage cooled my ardour. Many learned physicians whom I consulted, looked upon me as a victim
of consumption, at the point of death. Beggars in
the street, when they saw me pass, promised to pray
for my life if I would fling them a copper. The
cleverest professors of medicine at Padua prescribed
ass's milk, which was tantamount to saying : "Phthi-
sical creature, go and make your peace with Heaven !"
My own doctor in ordinary, Arcadio Cappello by
name, now dead—an old man, experienced, well

---

[1] Gozzi here resumes a portion of the 29th chapter of his Memoirs,
which I have condensed in Chapter XXIV. above (see note to p. 336). It
seemed unnecessary to burden the translation of his autobiography with
more of legal details than was absolutely necessary for understanding
the tenor of his life-experience.

acquainted with my constitution, and a philosopher to boot—forbade me milk as though it had been poison. "You," he said, "are suffering from a nasty malady. Yet it has not the origin, nor has it made the progress, which these eminent physicians fancy. If you let your illness prey upon your mind, you will die. If you have the strength and heart to throw aside all thoughts about it, you will recover. It has in you no other basis than a hypochondriacal habit, which you have contracted by a sedentary life of worry, business, and excessive study. Raw milk of any kind is a pure poison in your case. Live regularly, cast aside reflections on your symptoms, take horse-exercise two or three hours a day. These are your best medicines."

Marchese Terzi owes no thanks to my malady. Bloodless as I was, through what I lost by hemorrhage and venesection, my intellect enjoyed the highest qualities of penetration and acumen. Stretched out upon my bed, I had the necessary papers for my lawsuit brought to me—abstracts and wills recovered from the pork-butcher—a whole paraphernalia of documents forbidden by my doctors—and set up a scheme of proofs and arguments, so clear and so convincing that they subsequently drove my enemy to desperate measures.

These annoying relapses of my malady continued for two years and a half to fall upon me when I least expected them. They were enough to dishearten

any man less stupid than myself, and make him
despair of living. Contrary to the advice of several
physicians, who protested with wide-open horror-
stricken eyes that riding would inflame my blood and
burst the arteries of my lungs, I followed the pre-
scription of Doctor Arcadio Cappello, half-suffocated
as I was with hemorrhage. He proved to be right.
Regular diet, contempt for my symptoms, and horse-
exercise completed my cure. It is now twenty years
and more since I have been reminded that I was
ever subject to this indisposition.

As I have often had occasion to remark, no business, no quarrels, no lawsuits, and no illnesses prevented me from devoting some hours every day to
poetry. This being the case, when controversies
arose in Venice on philology and the higher Italian
literature—controversies of which I mean to render
some account in the following chapters—I went on
vomiting blood from my veins, and scribbling sonnets,
satires, essays in defence of our great writers, treatises
on style, polemics against Chiari and Goldoni and
their followers. All these trifles, when I read them
aloud, made my friends laugh, as well as my doctor
and the surgeon who attended on me.

Before engaging in the circumstances which led
to my becoming a writer for the theatre, I will wind
up the history of our private affairs. First of all, I
let the lawsuit with Marchese Terzi drop. My reasons were as follows:—With the best intentions

in the world, and the strongest desire to reunite the scattered members of our family under one roof, I found this task impossible. My sisters married. My brothers Francesco and Almorò in course of time took wives and begat children. My mother's inheritance of the Tiepolo property (though strictly speaking it ought to have been treated as entailed upon her sons) ran to waste in the hands of Gasparo and his wife. I had the old debts of our estate still weighing on my shoulders. It seemed to me, in this condition of affairs, best to remain a bachelor, and to devote myself to the duties I had undertaken, without ambitious projects and without assuming heavier obligations. Freed from further responsibilities to my family, whom I had loyally served in their material interests, and against none of whom I harboured any rancour, I was master of my time and could devote myself to the literary exercises which were so congenial to my temper.

END OF VOL. I.

PRINTED BY BALLANTYNE, HANSON AND CO.
EDINBURGH AND LONDON.

www.ingramcontent.com/pod-product-compliance
Lightning Source LLC
Chambersburg PA
CBHW021340110726
47900CB00005B/1544